THE ASSASSINS OF CONSEQUENCE

THE THORN OF MARADAINE
BOOK FOUR

MARSHALL RYAN MARESCA

PRAISE FOR MARSHALL RYAN MARESCA AND THE MARADAINE SAGA

"Maresca offers something beyond the usual high fantasy fare, with a wealth of unique and well-rounded characters, a vivid setting, and complicatedly intertwined social issues that feel especially timely."

— PUBLISHERS WEEKLY

"Marshall Ryan Maresca is one of the most ambitious fantasy authors to burst on the scene in the last decade."

— BLACK GATE MAGAZINE

"In one fast-paced, funny, highly readable novel after another, Maresca continues to build out every nook and alleyway of Maradaine, which is fast becoming one of the most richly detailed settings in fantasy."

— BARNES & NOBLE FANTASY BLOG

"This epic adventure is hard to put down, leaving readers curious about the future progression of these characters while smoothly setting up the next adventure."

— BOOKLIST

"Maresca has achieved something truly magnificent here."

— CASS MORRIS, AUTHOR OF *FROM UNSEEN FIRE*

"It's a story about morality, about sacrifice, about what people want from life. It's a fun story–there's quips, swordfights, chases through the streets. It's a compelling, convincing work of fantasy, and a worthy addition to the rich tapestry that is the works of Maradaine."

— SCI-FI AND FANTASY REVIEWS

"Highly recommend this series to anyone who loves high fantasy, political intrigue, magic, fantastic world building, and characters who you can root for."

— GIZMO'S REVIEWS

"Veranix is Batman, if Batman were a teenager and magically talented.... Action, adventure, and magic in a school setting will appeal to those who love *Harry Potter* and Patrick Rothfuss' *The Name of the Wind*."

— *LIBRARY JOURNAL* (STARRED)

"*The Thorn of Dentonhill* was a fast-paced read with action from start to finish. I loved every minute of it."

— SHORT AND SWEET REVIEWS

"Maresca brings the whole package, complete and well-constructed. If you're looking for something fun and adventurous for your next fantasy read, look no further than *The Thorn of Dentonhill*, an incredible start to a new series, from an author who is clearly on his way to great things."

— BIBLIOSANCTUM

Also by
Marshall Ryan Maresca

Maradaine Saga Phase One

The Thorn of Dentonhill
The Alchemy of Chaos
The Imposters of Aventil

A Murder of Mages
An Import of Intrigue
A Parliament of Bodies

The Holver Alley Crew
Lady Henterman's Wardrobe
The Fenmere Job

Way of the Shield
Shield of the People
People of the City

The Ziaparr Cycle
The Velocity of Revolution

The Displaced Daughters
An Unintended Voyage

Maradaine Saga Phase Two

The Assassins of Consequence
The New King of Rose Street*

An Unkindness of Uncircled Mages*
A Pride of Partners*

The Quarrygate Gambit
The Andrendon Plan*

City of the Truth*
Truth of the Crown*

Maradaine Saga Shorts
The Mystical Murders of Yin Mara
Hultichia
The Withered Boy
The Royal First Irregulars*
A Proper Lady of Society*

*- Forthcoming

THE ASSASSINS OF CONSEQUENCE

BOOK FOUR OF
THE THORN OF MARADAINE

MARSHALL RYAN MARESCA

PREVIOUSLY IN MARADAINE

THE THORN OF DENTONHILL
(Maritan 7th–14th—mid-spring)

Veranix Calbert, magic student at the University of Maradaine and circus-trained acrobat and archer, waged a vigilante war against Willem Fenmere's drug empire, assisted by his friend **Kaiana Nell**, his roommate **Delmin Sarren**, and his cousin **Colin Tyson**, a captain in the Aventil street gang The Rose Street Princes. Veranix stole two magically empowering items, a rope and a cloak, which he used in his fight against Fenmere, including two low-level dealers named **Lemt** and **Jendle**. Veranix earned the sobriquet, "the Thorn," from Fenmere's men and the Aventil street gangs.

THE ALCHEMY OF CHAOS
(Joram 18th–22nd—late spring)

Veranix dealt with an alchemical prankster seeking revenge on campus, multiple assassins, and final exams, and shattered the fragile alliance between Fenmere, the Red Rabbits, and the alchemist **Cuse Jensett**. Veranix was attacked by three assassins: Bluejay, Blackbird, and Magpie. Veranix also found a savior and ally in Reverend Pemmick of Saint Julian's Church. Jensett was captured by Kaiana and sent to

Quarrygate. **Magpie** was also arrested and sent to Quarrygate, as was Jutie, one of the Rose Street Princes under Colin's command.

THE IMPOSTERS OF AVENTIL
(Soran 11th–19th—late summer)

At the Grand Collegiate Tournament, Veranix struggled to keep drugs off the U of M campus, but two imposter Thorns created trouble for him, including attacking the local Constabulary. Minox and Satrine came to Aventil to investigate, and became intertwined with the Thorn. One of the imposters was **Enzin Hence**, who was involved in the sale of the drug The Soldier Fist, and he was hunting the Deadly Bird assassins who had killed his family, which included Blackbird and Bluejay. After many mistakenly thought the Thorn had killed Blackbird and Bluejay, Enzin was apprehended after an overdose of a magically-affected dose of the Fist, which altered his body. Enzin's actions also drew the attentions of various other Deadly Birds, and Veranix and Minox had to work together to subdue them, including one named **Jackdaw.** The other imposter was **Erno Don**, a musician and mercenary who was hired to pretend to be the Thorn, injuring **Lieutenant Benvin** and killing one of his officers. Erno was stopped by Colin, who turned him over to the police, and then attacked the members of Fenmere's crew who hired Don. Colin's actions enraged **Vessrin**, the leader of the Rose Street Princes, and Colin resigned from the Princes after burning Vessrin's face, declaring himself kin to The Thorn.

Minox learned Veranix's identity as the Thorn, but decided to help him by providing files about Fenmere's operation. Fenmere's Poasian smuggling connections brought him a new drug, the more potent *efhân*. Satrine learned of the Altarn Initiatives, somehow tied to changes in the magic curriculum at the U of M.

THE FENMERE JOB
(Oscan 13th–17th—early autumn)

Veranix went out to West Maradaine upon learning that Fenmere was trying to expand his operation there. His initial actions lead to a misunderstanding with the Rynax Brothers, and their protégé **Mila Kendish**, but soon they were working to stop Fenmere's plans and the

Firewings Mage Circle. In working together, Veranix and Mila quickly grew close, especially as he learned she was going to be attending U of M shortly.   Veranix was instrumental in stopping the Firewings, including beating the mage **Pria Mandicall**. Verci built a special new bow and arrows for Veranix as thanks.

PEOPLE OF THE CITY

(Oscan 25th–28th—early autumn)

Veranix started the new semester at U of M, where his classes were starting to take a militaristic bent after the launching of the Altarn Initiatives, while also still working against Fenmere with the help of Delmin, Kaiana and now Mila as well.   Circumstances—partially directed by the mysterious Sister Myriem-- led Veranix to team with the Rynaxes, Minox and Satrine and others—to a massive battle in St. Bridget's Square, where Veranix helped defeat Crenaxin, the High Dragon of the Brotherhood of the Nine, after he had transformed himself into a giant flying creature.

THE ASSASSINS OF CONSEQUENCE
Nalithan 1215
Mid-Autumn

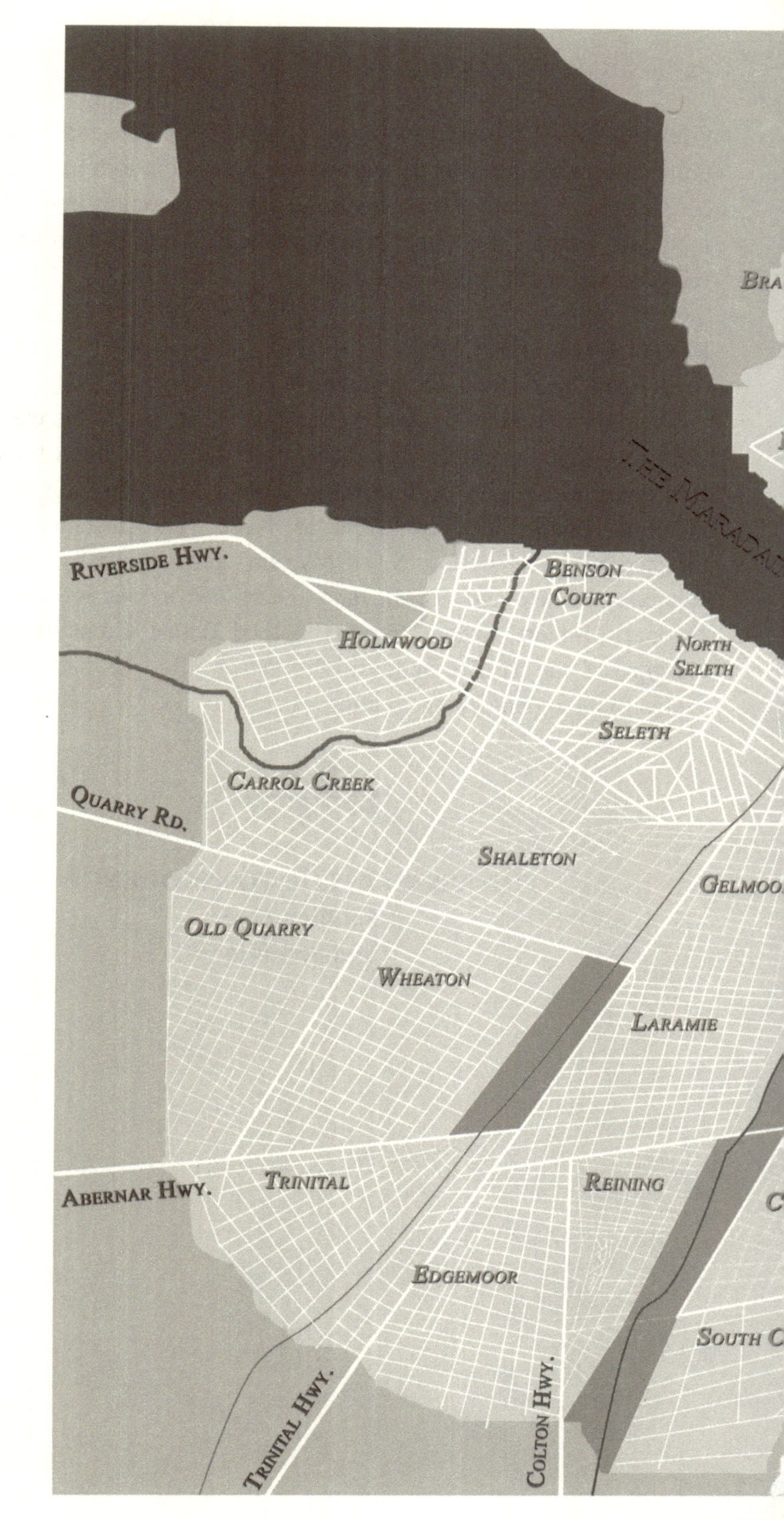

BRA
THE MARADA
RIVERSIDE HWY.
BENSON COURT
HOLMWOOD
NORTH SELETH
SELETH
CARROL CREEK
QUARRY RD.
SHALETON
GELMOO
OLD QUARRY
WHEATON
LARAMIE
ABERNAR HWY.
TRINITAL
REINING
C
EDGEMOOR
SOUTH C
TRINITAL HWY.
COLTON HWY.

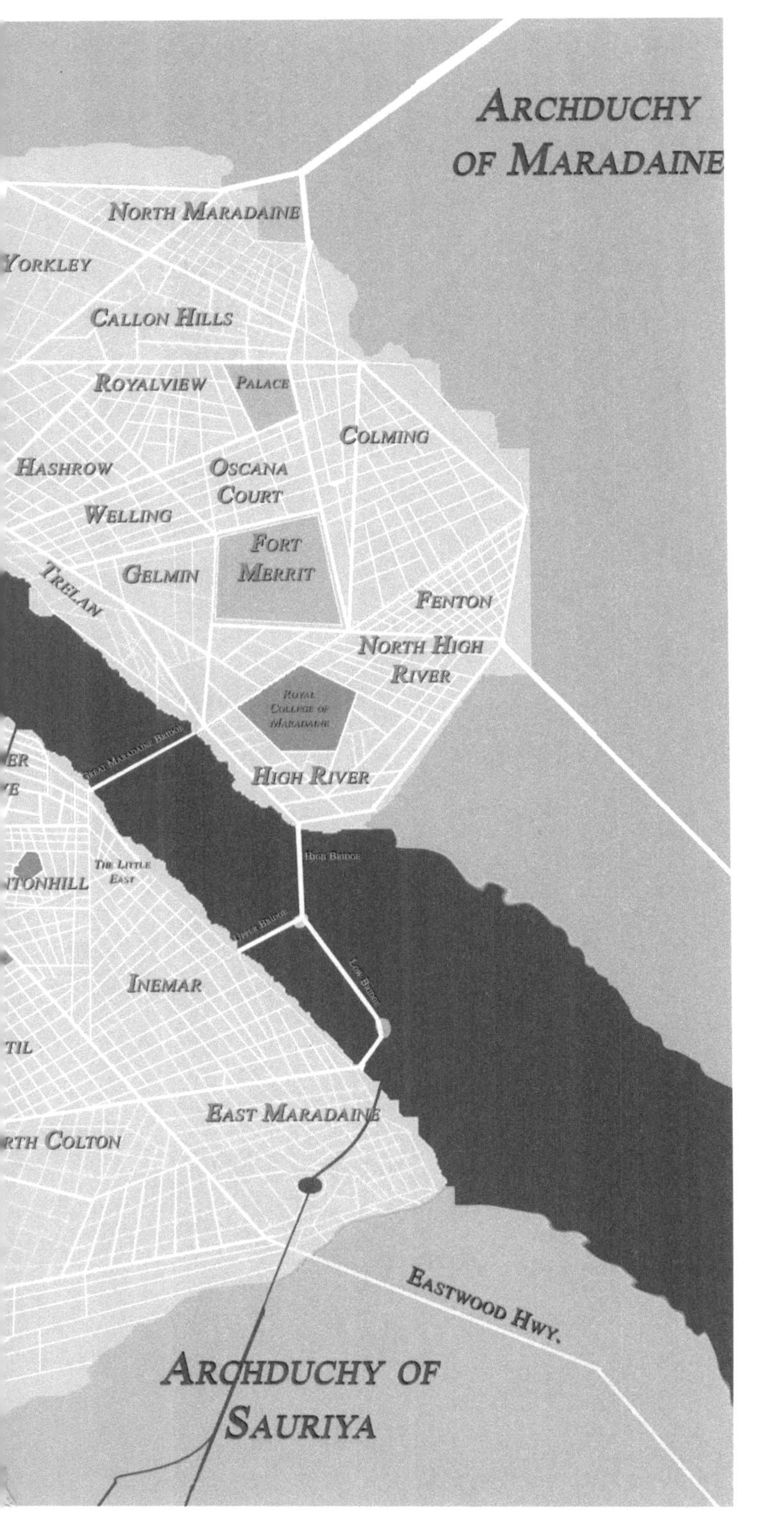

ARCHDUCHY OF MARADAINE
NORTH MARADAINE
YORKLEY
CALLON HILLS
ROYALVIEW
PALACE
COLMING
HASHROW
OSCANA COURT
WELLING
FORT MERRIT
GELMIN
TRELAN
FENTON
NORTH HIGH RIVER
ROYAL COLLEGE OF MARADAINE
GREAT MARADAINE BRIDGE
HIGH RIVER
HIGH BRIDGE
ER
'E
THE LITTLE EAST
TONHILL
UPPER BRIDGE
LOW BRIDGE
INEMAR
TIL
EAST MARADAINE
RTH COLTON
EASTWOOD HWY.
ARCHDUCHY OF SAURIYA

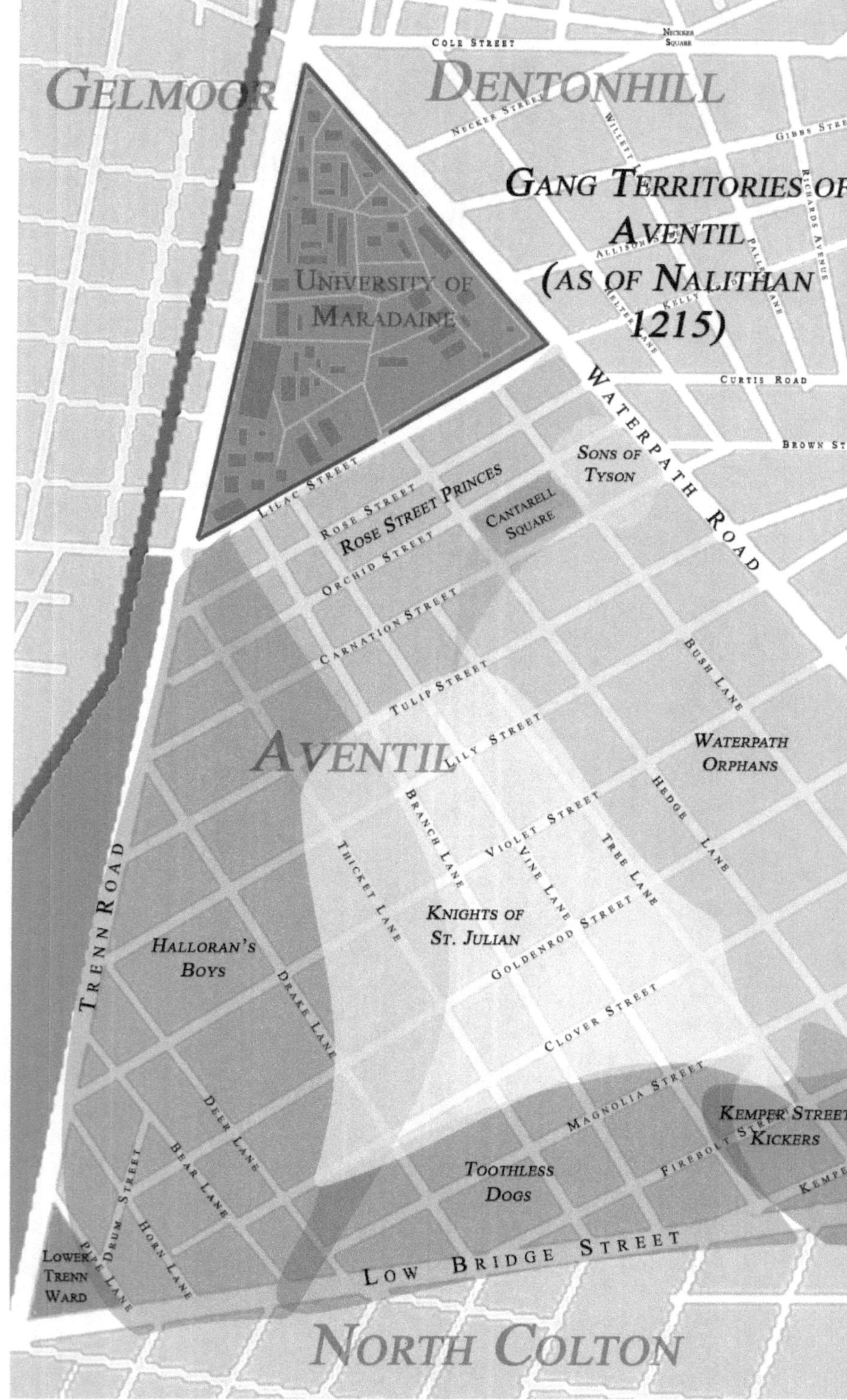

GELMOOR
DENTONHILL
GANG TERRITORIES OF AVENTIL (AS OF NALITHAN 1215)
COLE STREET
NECKER SQUARE
NECKER STREET
WILLETT STREET
GIBBS STREET
RICHARDS AVENUE
PALLANA LANE
KELLY
ALLISON STREET
SHELTER LANE
CURTIS ROAD
BROWN STREET
WATERPATH ROAD
UNIVERSITY OF MARADAINE
SONS OF TYSON
CANTARELL SQUARE
ROSE STREET
ROSE STREET PRINCES
ORCHID STREET
LILAC STREET
CARNATION STREET
BUSH LANE
TULIP STREET
WATERPATH ORPHANS
LILY STREET
AVENTIL
VIOLET STREET
HEDGE LANE
BRANCH LANE
VINE LANE
TREE LANE
TRENN ROAD
THICKET LANE
KNIGHTS OF ST. JULIAN
GOLDENROD STREET
CLOVER STREET
HALLORAN'S BOYS
DRAKE LANE
MAGNOLIA STREET
KEMPER STREET KICKERS
DEER LANE
FIREBOLT STREET
KEMPER
BEAR LANE
TOOTHLESS DOGS
DRUM STREET
HORN LANE
PIPE LANE
LOWER TRENN WARD
LOW BRIDGE STREET
NORTH COLTON

CHAPTER ONE

EVERY JOB IN DENTONHILL WAS sewage, so one might as well make a decent coin for doing the sewage, which was what Holder told himself about working for Fenmere.

Not that Holder ever saw Fenmere. He probably wouldn't even know the man if he walked straight up and popped Holder in the face. The most important man in Fenmere's organization Holder ever saw was Jullick, and that was only when something went really wrong in their count room. Usually he only saw Avi or Bobba, who dropped off product, picked up money, and checked Holder's books.

Holder made damn sure his books were square. The last time he saw Mister Jullick, was when he had lost his most of his crew, and even though he hated breaking in new blood, it was what he had to do for this sewage job.

Tonight, it was bringing in the new seller—a twitchy fellow who just went by Nix. Not that Holder needed or wanted full names. The less he knew about these folks, and the less they knew about him, the better.

"This da new blood?" Nags, the black-skinned girl whose real name Holder never was able to pronounce, asked as she looked at Nix. He couldn't ever place her accent, and when he had first thought she was chomie, she spat in his face and said, "Ain't no *tuk* that I'm a *kakla* Ch'omik, *sasa*." He had no rutting clue what half that meant, but he never called her that again. Nags was a solid seller, she knew how to make *effitte* move, and now that they were selling *efhân,* she was cleaning up. He was happy to have her on his crew, so he put up with her insolence.

"Yeah, well, gotta make the coin," Nix said. "You know how it runs."

"We know," Burt said from the corner. Burt was usually Holder's man for moving crates of *effitte*—arms like tree trunks, he had—but the *efhân* took up a lot less space in the den now. Weighed a lot less. But he kept Burt around, because Burt was exactly the fellow you wanted around when things went bad. Two words at a time was his usual mode of conversation.

"Yeah, so . . ." Nix said, rubbing his face. "Where's the stuff to sell?"

"Ease it down, saddle," Kam said, a wide, dangerous smile across his face. Kam was from out east, ranchland in Monim somewhere. Holder had no idea why someone would come across half the country— or half the world, in Nags's case—to end up in a rutting hole like Dentonhill, working for bastards like Jullick and Fenmere slugging drugs to the burnheads out here. Holder knew this job was sewage, but at least he was born here and didn't have any excuse.

"Sorry, sorry," Nix said. "I'm just, you know . . . I'm really ready to get to work. Glad the window opened for me."

"Yeah, you *sakka* why?" Nags asked. "You tell him, Kam?"

"Did I tell him about the guy?" Kam shot back. "Should I tell him?"

"Yeah," Burt said.

"Who . . . who is the guy?" Nix asked.

"Pay them no rutting mind," Holder said.

"No way, Holder," Nags said. "We gots to tell him about the Thorn."

"The who?"

"It's . . ." Holder swore under his breath. "It's just there's a guy out there who'll slap around dealers. Be aware of him."

"Aware how?"

"Eyes up, you know. Be safe out there. Burt will have your back."

"Not 'gainst the Thorn," Burt said.

"Burt's heard the stories," Kam said.

"Yeah," Burt said, taking a pipe out of his coat pocket. "I heard."

"What stories?" Nix asked. He looked around nervously. "What is this guy?"

"He's magic," Nags said. "Got a rope like steel, they say."

"Heard he tied up Miss Jads and left her in a water tower all night." Kam chuckled drily. "You hear about that, hoss?"

"Enough," Holder said. "Let's just—"

Nags's smile went as wide as the Maradaine River itself. "Oh, you know whatta I hear? I hear, couple moon back, dere was a whole row over in Seleth like? But not like just bar blokes having a tussle, no. A real ruckus, with monsters coming out of the ground."

"What?" Nix asked. He looked incredulous at this.

"Monsters, *sasa*. Skin like leather, ten feet tall, hands like a bear's claw. Tearing through the joint, except the Thorn, hesa fightin' them. Knocking the monsters back down."

"No."

"I heard," Burt said real quiet, "that in that fight, there was a guy who magicked himself into a giant winged snake, breathing fire. And this here Thorn, he jumped on top of it, wrapped his rope around its neck, and dragged it down to the ground." That was the most words Holder had ever heard out of Burt in one go.

"He kill it?" Nix asked.

Burt shrugged. "I just hear things."

"And this guy, he knocks down dealers like us?"

"Boy already saying like us," Kam said.

"Listen," Holder said, going over to one of the crates. "You just do your job, and you'll get paid. Try to keep a low profile, and you'll be fine."

"Right," Nix said. "So, where's the stuff to sell?"

"Burt?" Holder said. "Give him a bit to start."

Burt opened up a panel in the wall, and dragged out the trunk. He opened it up and got out a couple vials of *efhân* and brought it over to Nix.

"You sell that, you come back with eight crowns, and you get to walk out of here with half a crown in your pocket."

"And if I don't?" Nix asked.

"Then you don't walk," Burt said, looming over the kid.

"Huh," Nix said, looking at the vials in his hand. "You know, I think I heard a story about this Thorn fellow you're on about."

"Oh?" Holder asked.

"I hear," Nix said, a slight grin appearing on his face, "that he is really good at disguising himself."

"You—" Holder realized a moment too late. Nix's whole body blurred as he threw the vials in Burt's face, and suddenly he was wearing a flowing red cloak and hood, his face hidden in shadow, and he was holding a quarterstaff. Holder grabbed a crossbow off his desk. "Get him!"

But the Thorn—rutting blazes, it was the Thorn right rutting here— was already a whirlwind with that staff, knocking Burt two, three, four times. Burt stumbled backward as Holder raised up his crossbow and shot. But by the time he had pulled the trigger, the Thorn had already jumped onto Kam, and Holden's shot went into Burt's body.

The big guy dropped down.

"I am so glad the stories are out there," the Thorn said as he sent Kam to the floor like a sack of potatoes. "Because it really warms my heart to hear them."

Holder scrambled to reload his crossbow, his finger trembling. The Thorn's attention was on Nags. With a flick of his wrist, his great rope whipped off from his belt and wrapped around her. He lifted her off the ground with ease.

"It all true?" Nags asked.

"Monsters, dragon, trash like you," the Thorn said. "All in a day's work."

He casually tossed her across the room, crashing onto Holder. The two of them went tumbling into the wall. Holder cracked his head against the stone, sending his mind whirling into darkness.

"And I appreciate you all making it so easy," Holder heard the Thorn say as his awareness turned fuzzy and gray. "I am a very busy man."

EVERY PUB IN AVENTIL WAS TERRIBLE, BUT EACH ONE WAS AT LEAST terrible in its own special way. Colin Tyson hadn't come to terms with the Old Canal's brand of terrible, but the Old Canal was his pub now, so he had to accept that.

But the folks in this place couldn't make a decent striker to save their lives. Colin had considered threatening to stab the cook just to test that theory, but he decided that would be bad for morale.

And since the Old Canal, and the block on Orchid around it, was about all the street that his pathetic scrap of a gang, The Sons of Tyson, had control over, morale was about the only thing he had to hold on to.

"You gonna eat that?" Sella asked him. He had to admit, of all the Princes he thought might walk with him, stand by him as part of his new gang, he never would have guessed Sella. When she was part of his crew here on Orchid—that whole crew was never loyal to him in the first place—Sella was about as useful as loose button. All she cared about was scoring *doph* off of the sew-up below their flop. But here she was, next to him all the same.

Sella hadn't been the first to burn a scar on her arm, declaring herself one of the Sons of Tyson, but she had done it pretty early on. Same with Cober, Relly, and Cainey. None of them were the types Colin would have marked for street captains when they had all been Princes, but since stepping over with him, becoming Sons, they'd shown their mettle. He wasn't going to turn any of them down.

"Nah," Colin said, sliding the greasy striker over to her. "Have at it."

"Thanks, chief," she said, tucking into it eagerly. Her hand trembled as she ate. He had been paying attention, she hadn't gotten into the *doph* for a few weeks. Looked like holding off was getting to her.

Two new kids came crashing into the place. "Boss, we got a donny."

Colin didn't remember their names—they were a pair who had been Kemper Street Kickers until the sticks had all but busted that gang up. Colin had collected a motley bunch of scrappers from all seven of the Aventil gangs since he had broken off—mostly the cast-offs and forgottens who hadn't ever fit in with their crews—and most of his muscle had been Kickers. He was all right with that. Back in the day, Kickers and Princes, almost on opposite sides of Aventil, they had barely ever cracked skulls. No bad blood there.

"Who's on?" Colin asked, getting up.

"Couple of Orphans running a dice roll where the Trusted Friend was. Les and Rik tried to push them out, and it got to shoving. We need some numbers to hike them off."

Colin gave a whistle to the other Sons in the Canal. "Step up, friends."

The others all got up, knives and knucklestuffers out. Sella took a last bite of the striker and was first out the door, howling as she went. Probably too eager for a brawl. Too eager to get hurt. Colin followed the new boys behind while his other scrappers closed in with him.

"Our friend gonna be a part of this?" Terker asked. A former Orphan who had gotten outs with his captain, and Colin could see why. Ornery, contrary bastard he was. Colin would normally want nothing to do with the tosser, but he had a solid haymaker with his left. And Colin wasn't in a position to turn anyone away.

That was what the Sons of Tyson were, after all. The wayward fallbehinds of Aventil, gathered together under Colin's eye for mostly one reason.

"If he's around, he's around," Colin said. "Can't exactly whistle call him."

"Yeah, but I ain't ever seen him around," Terker said. "Word was, Thorn stood with the Sons of Tyson. Word was, he's your blood."

"That is the word," Colin said. "And it's the word for good cause."

"That's not you saying it's true, boss."

"I did notice that."

Terker grabbed Colin's arm, which was the sort thing that would have normally gotten a fellow a knife in the gut, but Colin knew he couldn't be doing that with his folks over any slight right now. His leadership here, the folks he had, all of that balanced on the edge of a blade.

"Why are you playing with us, Tyson? Is the Thorn a Son? Is he your kin?"

"He ain't gonna walk into the Canal and have a beer with us, that what you're asking," Colin said. "But he's always in the air."

Terker looked up at the roof. "You want me to believe he's watching all the time?"

"No," Colin said. "But you never know when he might be."

"You really know him?" Terker asked. "Because I can tell you, only reason Yessa hasn't roused up the Orphans and smashed through Orchid is because she's afraid of him being on your side."

"She should be," Colin said. "You checking for her? You gonna run back and squeal to your old crew about us? That what it is?"

"Naw, boss," Terker said. "But I need to know I ain't gonna die for nothing when the hard hammer comes down on us. And Orphans are looking to bring it before the Princes do."

Blazes. Probably why the Orphans were trying to stake a claim at the Trusted Friend right now, just to see if they could. See what the Sons would do.

I hope you are watching tonight, Vee.

He rounded the corner to the rubble of what had been the Friend, hearing the sound of laughing and hooting.

"You better run!" one of his boys was yelling. There were about six of them, plus the six who had come over with him from the Canal. All told, about a third of all the Sons right now. "You know what's good for you! The Thorn is our guy, you hear!"

"What happened?" Colin asked as he came over. "Boys said there'd be a brawl."

"Started to be one," Cainey said. Colin wasn't sure if he was anything remotely close to street captain material, but he had him flop down here by the Friend, keeping an eye on what was what by Cantarell Square. Cainey held a rag over his nose, blood trickling down his face. "We held ground, knowing you boys were coming, but there was nearly a dozen of those tossers."

"Testing us," Terker said. "Seeing where we yield."

"Yeah, I heard," Colin said.

"They were knocking us pretty good, boss," Cainey said. "And then like lightning—*thap thap thap*—arrows came down on the three in the front. One of them yelled to hold fast, keep on it, and that one suddenly got yanked up off the ground, screaming. And the rest ran."

"Did you see him?" Terker asked. "The Thorn?"

"Almost never see him," Sella said. She cracked her neck, rolling on the balls of her feet. "If you do, it's probably bad news for you."

"But he's our guy?"

"You saw those Orphans run off, hmm?" Colin asked. "He's our guy. You won't find him walking our blocks, or see him with a scald on his arm, but he's here when he can be."

"What's the word, chief?" Sella asked. She was clearly looking for someone to hurt, or looking to get hurt. Better give her something to do."

"Grab a few folks and do a sweep of the block to make sure it's clear. Cainey, get somebody to look at your face. Rest of you all, scatter. Ain't good us all standing about."

They all went off separate ways, but Colin looked up at the roof, hoping he could see something in the moonlight. But if there had been sign of his cousin up there, he couldn't see it now. Lucky that Veranix had happened by on his patrol.

But some night he won't be here, Colin thought. *What are you going to do then?*

Every day in Quarrygate Prison was just as bad as any other, but Jutie had a feeling that today was going to be especially bad.

Jutie had managed fine in his months at Quarrygate. Head down, stuck close to other Princes. The food was terrible, but not much more terrible than the food living with Colin and the crew, or with his mother, and at least they got it every day, twice a day. They were stacked up four bunks to a cell, cell no wider than the spread of your arm, but they could walk about the yard in the day. And there was a sew-up who had tended to Jutie's arm while he had been here. It had healed as well as he could have hoped, given how brutal a break it had been.

People found their own in the Gate, and for Jutie, that tended to be the other Princes, but he found the rest of the Aventil gangs were friendly enough to him. It took a bit before he realized that, in here, the difference between the Aventil gangs didn't mean much—they stood together against the rest of the folks in here. Especially the few Red Rabbits in here. That gang was pretty much dead, but there were a few alive in here, and they had turned out to be decent enough. He was bunking with one of them, a scrapper a bit older than Jutie, a fellow called Gank. Gank was a decent sort, having already been in the Gate for a few months when Jutie got hauled in. He had showed Jutie the ropes, let him know which guards to get in good with, and helped Jutie get a spot working in the kitchens with him.

One of the other folks working in the kitchens was a fellow who Gank was humble toward. Fawning, even. This fellow—Cuse, he was called—he didn't seem the type who any Red Rabbit would give a toss over. More the Uni type you'd safe walk to the Rose & Bush. He was very good in the kitchen, though, if exceptionally fussy about measuring ingredients perfectly.

"He ain't a Rabbit," Jutie said to Gank one day when they were working the kitchen.

"He ain't, but he kind of is," Gank said. "Kin to old bosses."

Jutie accepted that. A little odd, but it made a queer sort of sense. Still, Jutie steered clear once he heard from some of the others why Cuse was even in Quarrygate. He had been the Trickster, the one who caused that horse stampede, the one who had filled the square with smoke. The one the Thorn fought. In a real way, Jutie was here in the Gate because of this Cuse fellow.

And Cuse would mutter about the Thorn when they worked. That muttering had drawn attention.

That first attention came from Enzin. Jutie had felt bad for Enzin when he had shown up. The boy was a bit twisted up—one arm bigger than the other, same with his legs, and his skin had an almost greenish tint. He had come into the kitchen to talk to Cuse, and soon the two of them were often talking in low whispers to each other.

Then Erno showed up. Jutie didn't like Erno one bit. Too pretty, too charming. Too eager to throw out a line or two of a song in the middle of a conversation. Rubbed Jutie the wrong way.

When Erno first arrived, rumor was that he was the Thorn. But Jutie knew that was damn well not true, right from the start. It wasn't too long before everyone in the Gate knew he was just a mercenary with a smart mouth, was just as likely to sing a song as start a fight. Sometimes in the yard, he did both at the same time.

When Jutie worked in the kitchen, sometimes those three would be huddled in a corner, whispering and planning. Then a couple of the ladies from the south side of the Gate—the only place ladies and men in the Gate saw each other was in the kitchen and mess hall—came over and joined those three in their plotting.

One of those ladies—the blonde one called Magpie—was the slan who had broken Jutie's arm. He rutting well remembered her. The other —Jackdaw—was a Ch'omik lady who looked like she could lift Jutie over her head and throw him across the yard.

The five of them whispered plenty in the kitchen while Jutie worked. Head down, keeping quiet. Ears open. The phrase "the damned Thorn" was said a lot. All five of them had a grudge against him.

And then today, as Cuse, Enzin, and Erno worked in the back of the kitchen, he heard a few things that got his attention.

"You got what you need?"

"It's brewing. We'll be ready tonight."

And then a bit later.

"Don't worry, the Thorn will get his. We'll see to it."

Jutie grabbed a mop and bucket, got to work on the kitchen floor as he moved a bit closer.

"Let the Birds know, nine bells." That was from Cuse to Erno. Enzin grumbled something—Jutie had noticed that Enzin was not too friendly with the Birds, even with this strange alliance. Erno sauntered off and chatted up the two ladies until a guard chased him away from them.

All five of them looked far too smug for people in Quarrygate.

They all hated the Thorn. They were planning something, and they were coming for him.

Jutie had to do something about that.

Everyone was supposed to be in bunks by eight bells, though. So Jutie needed a plan.

"Hey, Dockers," he said right before bunk-in. Dockers was one of the better guards, from what Jutie had seen. "Something' s wrong with my arm. I need to see the sew-up."

"Wrong how?"

"Don't know. Been hurting like blazes all day, and it keeps getting worse. I don't want to make a thing, but ain't no way I can sleep like this. And I don't want to be wailing or nothing, keeping anyone else from their sleep, you know?"

Dockers frowned, but nodded, and took Jutie over to the sew-up ward. The doc poked at Jutie's arm, and Jutie put up a good show of pain, and the sew-up shrugged and put Jutie in a bunk in the ward and gave him a belt of *doph* for the pain. Jutie palmed it—it would have knocked him clean out—and then lay down, pretending to fall asleep.

The doc had been in his office, with a bottle of Fuergan whiskey and a "patient" from the ladies' side—his usual habit most nights—so Jutie waited until they were fully distracted and then slipped out of the ward, crept silent as he could to the kitchen.

"Can we just do this?" he heard Enzin growl. "What's the hold up? You said it would be ready!"

"Just final steps," Cuse said. Jutie moved quietly in, hiding behind a counter. From there, he could see Cuse stirring something over the stove while Enzin paced about impatiently. Erno leaned against the wall, and next to him were a couple of bottles of some red liquid, glowing like lamps.

Blazes, could Cuse do magic?

"Ladies aren't even here yet," Erno said.

"Blast them, they miss it, their fault!" Enzin said. "We're better off without."

"And here I thought we were in this together," Magpie said as she and Jackdaw came in. "Sorry it took us a bit longer to sneak over here."

"You're right on time," Cuse said. "Not a worry at all."

"Good," Jackdaw said. "Then I don't have to be upset."

Cuse pointed to a blue bottle on the counter Jutie was hiding behind. "Take a slug out of that, or you're going to be very unhappy in a minute, and then you will really miss it."

Jutie slunk down as far as he could as the ladies came over. Magpie uncorked the bottle, sniffed at it, shrugged, and took a sip, handing it over to Jackdaw, who just poured some into her mouth before slamming the bottle on the table. They went back over to the stove, Magpie palming a few eating utensils from a bin.

"We ready?" Enzin asked.

"As a rooster at sunup," Cuse said. "Grab those red bottles and let's move."

Erno grabbed the bottles and tossed one to Enzin, while Cuse gestured to Jackdaw to come carry the pot he had been using. He led them all down the hallway.

Jutie grabbed the blue bottle and took a drink from it. It tasted like how his brother would smell every day coming home from the tannery, but if they were drinking from this thing, so would he.

He followed them down the hallway to Ward Three in time to see a pair of guards shout at the quintet that they better hold fast. Immediately Magpie jumped in front, throwing two forks. They both struck true in each guard's right eye.

But the cry had gone out, and guards came running from several directions. Two came up to Jutie and grabbed him.

"Stop!" one guard shouted. "Put that down!"

"Here's as good as anywhere," Cuse said. Jackdaw put the pot down on the ground, and Cuse poured something into it. The pot bubbled and steamed, and then a dark green smoke poured out of it, filling the hallway. When it rolled over Jutie, the smell of it was rancid and horrid, but the guards holding him both screamed, vomited, and clawed at their eyes like they were burning.

"Saints above," Jutie whispered. Through the smoke, he saw the five of them move on, walking through it like it was nothing. Jutie chased after them, seeing all the guards were on the floor, retching and wailing. Poor bastards.

"This wall," Enzin said when they reached one junction.

"Throw your bottle," Cuse said. Enzin did, and the wall was covered with the glowing red liquid. Enzin looked disappointed.

"That's it?"

"Now the other," Cuse said. "And take cover as they mix."

Erno whistled jauntily as he wound back his arm, and threw the bottle at the wall. It shattered, and as its liquid started to ooze down the wall, it mingled and shimmered with the first. The glow sparkled and danced like the embers of a dying fire, and then crackled.

Cuse ducked behind the corner, and the rest scattered as that crackle turned into a drumbeat, and then burst like thunder.

Jutie looked back, and the wall had a giant gaping hole in it, open to the night and the city beyond.

"Brilliant," Erno said. "Let's not tarry, hmm?" He dashed out the hole.

"Not a chance," Cuse said. "We need to make the Thorn pay." He went out after Erno, and the rest followed right behind.

Whistles were blowing all around, and the sickening smoke was starting to thin out. Guards would be here shortly. Jutie only had one chance, he had to move if he was going to help the Thorn from whatever revenge these five had planned.

He ran out through the hole, into the cold, dark night. He had to warn the Thorn, wherever, whoever he was.

CHAPTER TWO

"VERANIX, WAKE UP."

Veranix wasn't sure if there had been a significant amount of time between the words being said and the slap across his face, but he was certain that he had not been given anywhere near the adequate amount of time to react to the words and rouse himself.

Besides, he had been rather happy being asleep.

"What, what?" he muttered, opening his eyes to the lamplight that felt far too bright. "I just closed my eyes for a moment."

His eyes focused on someone standing over him with the lamp. No, three someones: Kaiana Nell, Delmin Sarren and Mila Kendish. All three of them were scowling.

"What time is it?" he asked. The fact that all three of them were looking down at him was not a good sign. Last he remembered he had gotten back to campus after cracking up the dealer's count room under Rosy Nan's Tea Shop, with a pass through Orchid Street on the way home. He had gotten back to the Thorn lair—"safehouse," Mila insisted on calling it—put his gear away and had lain down on the bunk in the back for a just few minutes.

"It's nearly nine bells," Delmin said.

So not just a few minutes.

"Huh," Veranix said, rubbing his eyes. "Must have fallen hard asleep."

"You think?" Kaiana asked. She shook her head and walked away from the bunk. "I think we need some new rules with you operating out of this bunker now. Namely, you shouldn't be alone out there on the street, and you should definitely check in with someone when you get back in."

"I've been saying," Mila said.

"We're doing rules now?" Veranix asked.

"It doesn't work here like it did with the carriage house," Kaiana said. "When you were checking in with your gear, I was always there."

"Don't you like it better that my stuff isn't where you're sleeping?" Veranix asked. He'd grown quite fond of this new location to base his Thorn operations from. Kaiana had found it for them, now that she was the head of grounds for the University of Maradaine. Her new job had not only given her a proper staff apartment, but an office with charts and records of all the buildings and structures over the entire history of the campus. She had pored over those, finding this abandoned subbasement for a dormitory that had been built and torn down a century ago, as well as half-finished tunnels leading from it to other parts of the school. She and Veranix had done a fair amount of work over the summer and the beginning of the autumn semester, cleaning it out, finishing the tunnels, and creating hidden entrances all over campus.

"So much," Kaiana said, looking over his Thorn outfit, which he had hung back up in its cabinet with his staff, rope, cloak, bow, and quiver of arrows. His arsenal as the Thorn. The staff had been part of his mother's performance as an acrobat with the circus; he had learned as early as he could walk how to use it as an extension of his body. The bow had been his father's skill, with his trick-shot show. This particular bow and its arrows had been a gift from Mila's friend and mentor Verci Rynax, the west-side gadgeteer who made all sorts of delightful inventions, including the set of arrows with special heads that could be filled with smoke powder, boom powder, acid, and a variety of other options of chemicals that Mila acquired from one of her other deviant associates.

And then there were the rope and the cloak, the napranium-laced items he had taken from the Blue Hand Circle, and which Fenmere was smuggling into the city for nefarious purposes that Veranix never fully understood. It didn't matter what they had been made for, he had made them his own. The mystical metal woven into the fabric gave them a powerful capacity to draw and focus the magical energy *numina*, and when wielding them, Veranix's already formidable knack for magic was greatly enhanced.

And when you take them off, you're exhausted, Veranix reminded himself. He hadn't even pushed himself that hard last night, but it had been enough to knock him for a run for the rest of the night.

"That means no one is here to make sure you don't fall asleep here when you get back," Mila said. "I would stick around if I could, but my roommates are far too nosy about my comings and goings. They would report me to the prefect if they realized I was out of bed after curfew."

"And you're lucky that I'm your prefect," Delmin said. "But if anyone else paid close attention to your comings and goings . . ."

"No one is," Veranix said. He realized that he was still standing about in his skivs. Not that it was anything that anyone here hadn't seen before. His school uniform was hanging by the bunk, and he quickly started dressing.

"How did you do?" Kaiana asked, still looking at his tunic. "You got some blood on this, and you're short four arrows."

"The count room under the Rosy Nan is out of commission."

"They dead?" Mila asked.

"Not when I left them," he said. She sighed, clearly disappointed in him. She kept insisting he ought to be more . . . final . . . in his measures. "But tied up, money, books, and product gone. I imagine that Fenmere won't leave them breathing long." He pointed to the takings from last night that he'd left on the table.

"Enemies left alive are enemies that come back," she said.

"Anything good in the books?" Kaiana asked, glaring at Mila.

"Haven't looked at them yet," Veranix said.

"And you can't now," Delmin said. "We've got to get to drills in ten minutes."

"I haven't eaten."

Delmin pointed to the paper sack on the table. "I have you covered. Just like I covered for you in the dining hall to get those."

"Blessings of every saint," Veranix said. "Books and the money?"

"I have work," Kaiana said. "But I'll go over it this afternoon."

"And I'll destroy the product after my classes this morning," Mila said. "Get going."

Veranix grabbed the sack and followed Delmin down the tunnel to the exit closest to their magic class.

"What did you score me?" Veranix asked, digging into the paper bag.

"Itasa rolls," Delmin said. "Is it me, or are they really leaning on those this semester?"

Veranix took one out—dry lamb sausage and cheese wrapped in rich pastry—and took a bite. "I think there's a new baker in the kitchen, and this is their favorite to make."

"And they're good," Delmin said. "We're just getting them a lot."

Veranix had already finished the first and was working on the second. "We're about to go into a Magic Drills class. I'd eat dry flour right now if that was all there was."

"You're doing fine in drills," Delmin said. "This is shaping up to the be the first class where I do not receive full marks."

"We're going to get you through it."

Delmin grumbled. They came out of a shed that hid the entrance to the lair, which itself was out of line of sight from the campus walkways, and joined in easily with the throngs of uniform-clad students who were making their way to morning classes.

Delmin had been struggling all semester with the new curriculum of the magic program—the Altarn Initiatives—which took their magic classes far from the academically driven studies they had been to a style that could only be called militant. The classes weren't even called theory and Practicals anymore, but methodology and drills.

And drills was a perfect name for these sessions.

They came up on Curtin Forum, the large building that had been used for sporting events over the summer, but had now been appropriated by the magic school for the drills. Practicals used to be done in a professor's office, in a small group, if not one-on-one. Drills brought everyone in the magic school together—there were fifty-five third- and fourth-year magic students—so the larger space was necessary for what they were doing.

"Coming up on nine bells!" Lieutenant Goodman called out. "Get with your squad, folks. First- and second- years, take places in the upper seats." Goodman couldn't have been more than a couple years out of university, but he had a drawn and weary quality to him, like a man who had been through too much. He was one of the new guest faculty as part of the Altarn Initiatives, always in his gray Druth Intelligence uniform, and usually the one getting things started at the top of drills.

Almost the entire magic faculty, save Professor Alimen, was present for Drills, but Goodman, Missus Jacknell—who had the military bearing of an Intelligence officer, but not the uniform or rank, as far as anyone had been told—and Major Dresser were the ones who ran every class.

"You heard him!" Missus Jacknell snapped. "Squad up!"

Delmin and Veranix were together on the Violet Squad—they had made a point of being together, thanks to Delmin quickly determining how they were breaking people up and standing in the right spot to end up with Veranix—with one other fourth-year student and two third-years.

The fourth-year was from the women's college, Anduette Nessick. It wasn't until their third session together that Veranix realized where he had seen her before. She was the magic student who had done the color announcements during the tetchball games of the Grand Tournament. She had solid magical talent, and held her own in their drills, with a real knack for manipulating sound with her magic.

"You boys look a mess," she said as they came up. "You sleep at all last night, Nix?"

Veranix was not crazy that she called him that, even if it had provided an easy alias for him to use with the Rosy Nan crew. "Of course I did."

"And you," she said, tapping on Delmin's chest. "Maybe you slept too much? But you look like you just fell out of bed."

"I've been up for hours."

"You need to mind your hair, friend," she said, her hand brushing a stray lock from his face.

"My hair?" Delmin frantically pawed at his stringy mop.

"He's too easy," she said, winking at Veranix.

"You ready for today's tussle?" he asked her.

"Depends what they give us. These assignments are—I don't even know. They're fine, I'll go with whatever they want us to do, I suppose. I just wish I could see the overall value over these very specific exercises." Drill classes had two forms: repetitions and challenges. In rep classes, they did the same magic action over and over, and Veranix found it dreadfully boring. Today was a challenge class, which Veranix found exciting and competitive, even if they were often completely impractical if they were some form of martial exercise to train someone to use magic in a combat or militant situation.

But that did seem to be exactly what they were training for, which Veranix found more than a little troubling.

"You did well with those light sculptures in reps last week," Anduette said.

"About the only one I did, and that was with your help," Delmin said. "And that one was less . . . martial. Most of them have us running about as much as anything."

"They're oddly specific," Leon said as he came up. Leon Fetsler was a third-year, but he looked like he was twelve years old, and had a thick north country accent. From around Hechard, though Veranix never sat him down and asked. Bright kid, good with theory.

"Specific goals to force us to think in creative, problem-solving ways." Jemica Sine was a serious, studious young woman, the other third-year on Violet Squad. She pushed her spectacles up as she came close. "Good morning, Delmin."

"Morning," Delmin said, clearly oblivious to the eyes Jemica was making at him. "Vee, ready?"

"I suppose I need to be." Veranix didn't want to admit it, but when it came to practical magic, especially in crunch situations like they kept working in drills, he was the one carrying the most weight. Anduette was the only other one who had any real knack for the exercises. Though she had proven quite useful in several so far.

"Morning, squads!" Major Dresser called out as he strode into the lecture hall.

"Good morning, Major!" everyone called back in unison. That was one of the first things Dresser had insisted upon when he took charge of drills, and Veranix found it more than a little chilling.

"Today's challenge is a unity course," he said. "Each squad will go through, and you will be scored on time and points. There are five stones on top of each of those towers. Each member of the squad must get a stone. Throughout the course, you'll note the swinging bottles."

He pointed to one of them, a wine bottle with another one inside, hanging on a rope. "Note carefully, every bottle is in fact, a double bottle, a red one inside a green one. Each member of a squad must destroy a red bottle without destroying a green bottle."

"How?" someone from one of the other squads asked.

"Between the last two method classes, and the exercises of the last two reps, you *should* know exactly how. Provided, of course, you have been paying attention and understand how to apply that knowledge."

Veranix frowned. He had no rutting idea. At least, not from that. What were the last repetition drills about? Something with pushing coins, which he did easily but didn't understand how it applied to this. He looked to the others. Delmin, Leon, and Jemica were all screwing their faces in thought. Anduette, though, looked fairly calm.

"Each additional red bottle broken in the time allotted is another point, each green broken, you lose two points. If you get struck by a swinging bottle, you lose two points. Each of you with a stone in hand is five points. Each squad will have five minutes. Yellow Squad, you're up first!"

That was, at least, a small blessing. They would have a chance to watch at least one of the other squads blunder through first. They took their places on the stands while Yellow Squad stepped up to the start line.

"You know how to break the bottles?" Veranix asked Anduette as he sat next to her.

"I know how I would do it," she said. "I don't think it's the way they want, though."

In that, Veranix had noted, Anduette was like him. She was more interested in getting something done, rather than necessarily how she was supposed to do it.

"Well let's see what they do," he said. "Delmin, stay sharp to what's going on, hmm?"

"Sharp, right," Delmin said, looking back up. "You coming up with a plan for how we tackle this?"

"A plan?" Veranix asked. "You know me."

"Right," Delmin said. "So, no plan."

DELMIN HAD NO IDEA WHAT RUNNING AROUND, BREAKING BOTTLES AND collecting rocks had to do with proper study or academic practice. He was damned tired of this drill process, and dreaded the idea of this being the cornerstone of his education for the final terms.

Violet Squad was up fifth, which at least gave him some opportunity to watch other students try—and fail—to make it through the course. Four squads had gone, and not one of them had managed to each collect a stone and break a red bottle.

There were a lot of green bottles broken, though.

Delmin did have one thing working for him as they stepped up to take their shot—this room was loaded with *numina* flying all over the place, and that gave his magical senses something interesting to work with. That had been one advantage to these large group drills—at first all that *numina* had been just so much noise, like a blinding sun—but now he was growing adept at hearing the melodies through the noise.

"All right, Violet Squad, step up!" Lieutenant Goodman snapped. "Let's see if you measure up any better than these fools."

"Ready?" Veranix asked the squad.

"It's a snap and a whistle," Anduette said. "At least for me." She was always a little too excited about running drills, but that was probably because she wanted to play tetchball but was barred from it since she was a mage. These gave her an outlet for her competitive nature. He had to admit, it didn't hurt having one of the more athletic, competitive magic students on the squad with them.

"Is this going to be a moment where you show off?" Delmin asked.

"Can't let Nix get all the glory. And you—" She tapped him on his temple. "Open your ears. We went over it in methodology two days ago."

Delmin thought back. "*Numinic* resonances and amplification of ambient energies?" Lessons on doing more with less, not wearing yourself out by drawing *numina* smarter instead of harder. Not that Delmin was very good at that sort of thing.

"Go!" Goodman shouted, and he, Jacknell, and the rest of the faculty pulsed their magic, sending all the bottles swinging wildly around the course. It would be nearly impossible to move through the floor to the towers without getting clipped by one of the bottles.

But those pulses of *numina* were doing something very interesting, not just sending the bottles flying about. The *numinic* forces bounced off the green bottles, the red bottles inside, the copper towers, and the marble stones on top of each one.

Delmin almost got clipped by a bottle as he realized that he could tell the towers were copper and the stones marble. He could feel how the *numina* bounced and echoed off each of them in different ways, making each distinct, and easy to recognize.

Veranix dashed forward, like the damned fool that he was, and flashed the floor with grease as he dropped low, sliding under the swinging bottles toward one of the towers. It got him through the barrage of bottles without getting hit by any of them, which Delmin had to admit was pretty clever.

Veranix, of course, was used to facing adversity. People were always trying to kill him. So this was duck in the water to him.

"On me," Anduette said. "Cover your ears and follow tight."

She put her fingers in her mouth and whistled—with a *numinic* surge from her—and that whistle was louder than anything Delmin could imagine. He had barely got his hands over his ears in time. Veranix, at the base of one of the towers, winced as he covered his head.

But that had been effective—a wave pushed the bottles away, cutting a path to a tower. Anduette ran through, and Delmin was right on her heels. As they approached the tower, she snapped her fingers at one of the bottles that was coming for her. Magic surged, and the red inner bottle burst.

Delmin felt that explicitly. There was a flavor—no, a resonance—

that the red bottle had, but which the green bottle didn't. Anduette gave him a knowing look.

"You felt that?"

"Yeah."

"Now you know."

Veranix, at the base of one tower, reached up, *numina* surging from his hands. But that energy stopped halfway up the tower. He tried again, scowling in frustration.

"Something isn't right."

Delmin couldn't identify it, but there was something, not unlike dalmatium—the magic-blocking metal used in mage shackles—that scattered magical energy halfway up.

"You can't just reach up and pull down a stone with magic," Delmin said.

"Not directly," Anduette said. She snapped again, and sent a sound vibration up the copper tower to the stone up top. As it dropped into her hand, she said. "Like I said, snap and a whistle."

Leon and Jemica were pinned up against the wall, trapped by the bottles. Delmin hadn't seen how they got over there.

"We each need to get a stone," Delmin said.

"How do we define 'get'?" Anduette asked, dropping her stone in his hands. "You got one."

Delmin had an idea—how to solve the bottles, maybe. "Do what you did to clear a path for them, get them to another tower, help get them stones. I'm moving to Veranix."

She nodded and with another whistle vibration, raced off to them. Delmin sent out a pulse of *numina*—he couldn't waste more than that without quickly wearing himself out—and tagged the bottles with *numinic* vibrations. They were still swinging wildly, but in a moment, he could feel the pattern, feel a path through them all, to make his way to Veranix. He ran so fast, he collided right into him.

"Easy," Veranix said. "What's up?"

"Let's crack some red bottles," Delmin said. "I know how, at least I've got a wild theory."

"I'm all for wild theories."

Delmin turned around and pressed his back into Veranix's body, and took Veranix's hand and pressed it on his chest.

"Del, what—"

"I'm going to attune myself to the red bottles," Delmin said. "And you, focus *numina* through me."

"Can that work?"

"Use me like the rope," Delmin said, almost confident in his idea. The theory was sound—he didn't have the knack for channeling raw power than Vee did, but he would be able to tune that power. "I'm as much a conduit for *numina* as it is."

"Like you're the rope," Veranix said. "Got it."

Delmin closed his eyes, let his magical senses focus on the resonance of the red bottles. Shut out the rest. He pushed out lightly with a wash of *numina*, let it harmonize with the red bottles. He could feel each one, swinging back and forth throughout the chamber.

"Now!"

Veranix sent a pulse through him, and it was like a fire had been set in his chest. The sheer power that Veranix seemed to be able to channel was astounding, and to think that was his normal capacity. With the *numina*-enhancing powers of the napranium woven rope and cloak, it was no wonder he was a force to be reckoned with as the Thorn.

He fought monsters, while you hid in the church.

The surge passed through Delmin, and he was able to hold it to the resonance he had formed with the red bottles.

They all shattered, green bottles still intact.

"Well done," Veranix whispered in awe. Delmin didn't have time to be impressed, as his legs dropped out from under him. Veranix caught him before he crashed, face first, onto the concrete. "You all right?"

"That was a lot," Delmin said.

"Now the stone," Veranix said.

"You have a plan?"

"Just the boring way," Veranix said. "Muscle and bone."

He grabbed hold of the copper pipe and shimmied his way up, like a spider climbing a line, like he was born to it. While Delmin still struggled to catch his breath, Veranix climbed to the top, grabbed the stone, and slid back down.

"And now we're—"

"Time!" Goodman shouted.

"Stand down, Violet," Major Dresser said. "Three stones, no strikes, but twenty red bottles without fault. Not a completed trial, but at least notable in the failure."

Delmin stumbled back over the start line, not wanting to show how draining the whole thing had been to him. Veranix must have sensed how bad off Delmin was, because he kept close, holding back but in position to catch Delmin if he fell.

Anduette came over with Leon and Jemica, who both looked put out.

"While we reset, what did they do right?"

"Have Andi on their squad?" someone called out.

"Miss Nessick was individually very successful, yes," Dresser said. "And used her advantage of sound-based magic to overcome the elements of the towers designed to prevent using it to get the stone."

"Vee and Del seemed to be ready to roll each other!" someone else shouted.

"Easy," Dresser said. "Let's not be crude. Who understands what they really did?"

Uneasy murmuring in the crowd of students. Mackim—a fourth-year from Blue Squad who rarely offered opinions—raised his hand. "They merged their magic?"

"Not exactly," Dresser said. "But they did use excellent teamwork. Mister Sarren could use his knack for sensing *numina* to target the red bottles, but he lacked the power to also shatter them. Mister Calbert had that power, so he channeled through Mister Sarren."

"That looked like it hurt," Hartman, on Yellow Squad, said.

"Like blazes," Delmin said.

"And then Calbert was a damned cat!" This from Anjal, a third-year girl of Tyzanian heritage. She was on the Blue Squad with Mackim.

"His solution was unorthodox, and—"

"A very important object lesson there. Magic cannot solve all problems." All eyes turned to that voice, because everyone immediately knew who it was. Professor Alimen, stood in the doorway, looking far too tired. This was the first time Delmin had seen him since the first class of the semester.

"But it's a magic lesson," Anjal said. "We're supposed to be using magic."

"It's critical to also have the wisdom to know when magic is not the solution," Alimen said. He turned around and left the room.

"Indeed," Dresser said, frowning at Alimen. "All right, Violet stand down. Crimson Squad is up."

Veranix and the others went to sit down, but Delmin went over to the doorway, hoping to get a word with Professor Alimen. He had been nearly distraught over the summer, and was reclusive now. It was clear he had been distressed over the Altarn Initiatives, and now could barely stand to participate in the magic program.

Delmin reached the doorway, but Professor Alimen was already gone.

CHAPTER THREE

AS HAD BECOME THE NORM after drills, almost every magic student went directly to the closest dining hall—which was Holtman—for lunch. There had been a new policy this semester, one which had caused quite an uproar, that every dining hall on campus was open to every student. Holtman was no longer only for male students, and at first a few people really lost their minds over it. But now, a month into the semester, that had cooled down.

In no small part due to some of the Ladies' College magic students brooking no nonsense from the boys. There was a fellow named Chadlin who once had attempted to pull Anduette into his lap once, and Veranix had it on good authority that the ringing in Chadlin's ears still hadn't stopped.

Veranix wasn't sure what had prompted the change on campus—he had thought at first it had been connected to the Altarn Initiatives, but that seemed to be connected only to the magic curriculum. Mila had discovered the answer—as she was very good at finding answers one way or another—there had been a suit filed against the University that the segregation of dining halls placed an undue burden on the Ladies' College students, as they had to walk all the way back to the north side of campus for meals.

The upshot of this was Mila would usually meet them for lunch, which Veranix was quite happy about. He hadn't quite figured out what the nature of his relationship with Mila was, but it did involve occasional kissing, so he wasn't going to complain one bit. Many of the fellows from the third floor of Almers Hall did give him some flack about it, since he was a fourth-year student and she was a first-year, but Mila was older than most of the other first-years. He was only a few months older than her. Anyway, it wasn't like they were seriously talking intentions.

At least, she adroitly dodged anything resembling conversations like that whenever he hinted in that direction. So he let it be, because occasional kissing was involved, and it was better to not ruin that.

"Have you ever actually read Parliamentary Declarations?" she asked as she sat down with Veranix and the rest of Violet Squad. As she did anytime in public at the University, she spoke with her affected, refined accent that she called her "Jendly Marskin" voice, as opposed to her natural West Maradaine one. Veranix was pretty amazed at her ability to create a character and embody it, a skill she had used to be "Jendly," the persona of a young, harried city clerk she used to charm her way through bureaucrats. There was a whole part of her life before coming to the University—a life that involved heists, revenge ploys, and the West Maradaine underworld—that Veranix had only gotten a small glimpse of when he pursued Fenmere's drug enterprise spreading out west this summer. With help from Mila and her former crew, he had been able to block that expansion.

"I can't say that I have," Veranix said.

"Fascinating. Infuriating. It's like an exercise to say the least things in the most words, while at the same time twisting words to create iron-locked intention, but filling every sentence with traps to escape from."

"Did you say traps?" Jemica asked.

"Like a puzzle box of words," Mila said. She leaned in closer to Veranix. "The real thieves in this city are the crafters of law, let me tell you."

"Especially the ones who protect the worst people," he said. "So your class went well?"

"Frustrating, but . . ." Her smile lit up. He knew how happy she was to be here, to be a proper student, to change her life. "You all look like the cat dragged your tails."

"The what?" Anduette asked.

"You all look very harried," Mila said with slightly over-emphasized words.

"Rough go with our drills," Veranix said. "Everyone's, really. No squad actually succeeded in the course, but we were one of the top scorers."

"Should have been the top," Anduette said. "Gray Squad went last and cribbed all our tricks."

Delmin was eating heavily, even for him. His plate was piled high with cured meats and pickled preserves. "They didn't score much higher. Quite the drubbing all around today."

"So this is where all the food is going today." Eittle, the tall Natural Philosophy student who lived on the third floor of Almers Hall, sat down with them. "How's your day been treating you?"

"Fine," Veranix said. "You been all right? Haven't seen much of you lately."

"More time in the library, researching my Letters Defense. But also been going out to Lower Trenn Ward most days to see Parsons."

That made Veranix twitch—and noticeably enough that Mila's hand went to his leg with concerned affection.

"I take it Parsons hasn't been any better," he said, trying to bury his annoyance. Parsons had been Eittle's roommate—and probably more than that, given Eittle's continued devotion, Veranix assumed—and had overdosed on *effitte*, putting himself into the burned-out trance he had been stuck in ever since. The fifth floor of Lower Trenn Ward was full of *effitte* victims, including Kaiana's father.

And Veranix's mother.

But unlike Parsons, Verona Aylixi Calbert had not chosen to take *effitte* and destroy her brains. Fenmere had done that to her, and left her there in the ward. As warning, to whoever else might cross him. As bait, to whoever else might love her and Cal Tyson. She'd been there for four years, and surely Fenmere was still waiting for someone to come.

Veranix hoped Fenmere knew that the Thorn was exactly that some-one, even if he didn't know who the Thorn was. If he knew that Veranix

Calbert, fourth-year magic student at the University, was the son of Cal Tyson, as well as the Thorn . . .

Veranix doubted that anything would keep Fenmere from bringing every ounce of pain he had at his command upon him.

"Not yet," Eittle said. "But I'm going today to meet Parsons's parents."

"They're like, *Parsons*, as in Parsons, Parsons & Toll," Delmin said. "I thought they had written him off."

"They had, yeah," Eittle said. "But I heard from them the other day that they found someone who was a specialist, who could really treat him. So they're bringing that guy in today."

Veranix's heart almost stopped. The idea that there even could be a treatment, that his mother could possibly be anything more than the withered, hollowed shell she had become, he had never even permitted himself that luxury.

"I . . . well, that . . ." he stammered, not sure how to respond. "That's really incredible. Do . . . do you know more about this specialist?"

"I don't," Eittle said, his rural accent growing a bit thicker. "I'm just glad they told me about it. I think—" He stopped for a moment, holding up his forkful of food. "I think they're going to do whatever they can to get him better, but they have no intention of being around for him if he is better. So they want me around just so they can pawn him over to me once it's done. If it works."

"It's an if, then?" Delmin asked, his eyes darting to Veranix.

"That's what I know."

"Listen," Veranix said, almost forcing the words out. The idea of what he was about to say terrified him, but he knew he had to say it, while the opportunity was here. "I know we've not been all that present for you, in terms of Parsons."

"I know you were fired up mad," Eittle said. "Don't think I didn't feel the same damn way. When he's up and about he's getting a piece of my mind."

"Right," Veranix said. "But, if you want—" He faltered.

Delmin picked up the cue, bless him. "Vee and I can go down there with you. Show of support."

"Mighty kind, fellows," Eittle said. "I was going to leave around three bells. You can do that?"

"Absolutely," Veranix said. "That's when I'm done with my special training session."

"Why ever did you volunteer for that?" Anduette asked. "Everyone else knew to stay clear."

"What's this special training?" Eittle asked.

"There's this Uncircled mage," Anduette said. "Older fellow who never properly trained, didn't go to university. None of it. And he's a constable. For some reason, Lord Preston's Circle wants to go through the motions of trying to give him a full experience of his Letters of Mastery in, like, a few months, every other afternoon."

"So, teach him, let him get Circled," Eittle said. "There a problem?"

"Can't be done," Leon said. "And . . . it'd be one thing if he resigned. But you can't trust a constable to be fair to mages."

"Even if he is a mage?" Eittle asked.

"He's showing where his loyalty is by keeping that coat on," Anduette said.

Jemica chipped in. "I think the Circle is just wanting to show that they tried. That's it."

Anduette went on. "So, the Circle brought it to the professors, and none of them want to be in the same room as this stick. So they ask the fourth-years for a volunteer. No extra stipend or credit or anything. Just one of you waste your time working magic with an untrained stick who'd just as soon lock you up."

"And you stepped up?" Eittle asked Veranix.

"Raised his hand right away," Anduette said. "Never seen him do that any other time in class."

Eittle shrugged. "I don't get why it's a problem, I'll tell you. But, see, I knew you were decent people, Calbert."

Veranix took a last bite of his lunch. "And I should get going. See you at Almers at three?"

"Yes, sir," Eittle said.

"All right then," Veranix said. "Can't keep Inspector Welling waiting."

Lieutenant Benvin could not believe what he was reading.

"This is real?" he asked his squad as he held up the report. "Not some twisted joke you all cooked up?"

His squad—Tripper, Pollit, Wheth, Welling, and Saitle—all nodded. "Swear, Left," Pollit said. "Wheth and I went out to Old Quarry to check it out."

"They were not happy at all out there," Wheth said. "Apparently they had tried to keep things quiet, so they were vexed we even knew."

"And we knew because?" Benvin asked, even though he was certain he already knew. All the other eyes went to Jace.

Jace Welling, youngest patrol officer on Benvin's squad—he and Saitle had only just gotten their brass a few months ago—sat at his desk with an infuriating grin. "So, my cousin Davis, he's an examinarian, and he just got moved to the Southwest stationhouse. Hates it."

"I can imagine," Tripper said. Southwest was the new house that covered Wheaton, Trinital, and Old Quarry, with the old stationhouses shut down and consolidated. It was decidedly a mess, and every constable in the city wondered what such a change heralded for the future of the Maradaine Constabulary.

"And he was brought in last night, middle of the night they sent a page to pound on the door, they need all hands. At least, all hands who can treat people. He grabs my cousin Ferah—she's a Yellowshield—and they're off. They get back before breakfast with a story about how everyone in the 'gate is sick. Puking their guts out sick. Stench like month-old sewage in the place, they got to cover their faces just to—"

"Less story, Jace, more point," Benvin said.

"Breakout at Quarrygate, and the perpetrators—at least the ones who are unaccounted for—are six folks we brought in."

"We as in Aventil or our squad?"

"All but one, our squad," Tripper said. "And that one, brought in by University cadets to our house for processing. That one is Cuse Jensett."

"The 'prankster' working with the Red Rabbits," Benvin said. "And that name—"

"Yeah, he was a nephew of Reb himself," Tripper said. "Got kicked out of Uni back in '12, puttered around and started making magic bombs, or something like that?"

Benvin thumbed through Jensett's file, and a good mess of it went over his head. "And the one we caught as the Thorn? Arno?"

"Erno Don," Pollit said. "Turned out to be a mercenary for hire, as well as a wandering troubadour."

"And he is the bastard who killed Mal," Tripper said.

"Nearly me as well," Benvin said. "And Enzin Hence, he was the one your brother brought in to us from campus. The Bird killer, the one who was selling Soldier's Fist from Kyst?"

Jace nodded. "That's the one. Which makes us wonder why he was working with two of the Deadly Birds."

"Magadina Kend, called Magpie," Pollit said, holding up a file. "We took her in when there was that dustup with the Thorn, the day the Trusted Friend collapsed."

"Which was the same day Jensett tried to blow up the Uni," Tripper said. "Maybe they were working together."

"But also Kat'rick-Ra, otherwise known as Jackdaw. She was one of the ones you all caught in that botched attempt to get the Thorn."

"All these folks seemed to have a grudge against the Thorn," Jace said. "He tussled with Jensett when that stampede got started. He put down the Birds, as well as Hence. And Don was pretending to be him."

"All of them except Higgs." Juteron Higgs, a minor rat in the Rose Street Princes. He got arrested helping the Thorn, in that fight where Magpie was pinched. If anything, Higgs was an ally of the Thorn. "He doesn't match the rest of him."

"Maybe he got lucky?" Saitle asked. "The other five planned a breakout, and he was just in the right place when it happened?"

"Maybe," Benvin said. "So, we've got six dangerous people out in the streets, and we have to guess they're coming to our patch here."

"Coming for the Thorn," Jace said.

"Maybe we should let them get him," Tripper said. He was still quite salty that they hadn't gotten the real thing when they arrested Don. Benvin understood—he was mad as all blazes when he read that pamphlet telling the crazy story of the Thorn fighting in Seleth. But there had already been other reports, unconfirmed sightings. They knew they hadn't gotten him. It ate at Benvin, but not like it did Tripper.

"Then who would stop them?" Wheth asked. Tripper and Pollit both scowled at him. "Hey, I don't like the Thorn one damned jot, but let's not pretend that those aren't all very dangerous folks, and we likely never would have brought in any of them without him."

"Not Jensett," Tripper said. "It was someone on campus who took him down, right? Some woman on the staff?"

"Kaiana Nell," Benvin said. "He might have a grudge on her as well. And we have to assume that Captain Holcomb and the rest of the house here aren't going to be to engaged in this." Somehow, the captain had grown even more complacent since autumn started. Plenty of the regulars were likely taking lookaway money from some of the gangs, too. Benvin couldn't stand it.

"So what's our play?" Pollit asked.

"We're going to get on the street, talk to the people who will talk to us. We all have a few ins with some of the street captains, let's use them."

"Hence was in town for the Grand, living on campus," Pollit said. "I know a few people in the cadet corps there, I might get some answers."

"Good. Take Jace, and see if you can find that Nell woman. She might be in danger, least we could do is tell her to keep her head down. But be discreet, hmm? Uni doesn't like it when constabulary comes on campus."

VERANIX REALLY WISHED MINOX WELLING WOULD NOT INSIST ON wearing his uniform when coming to these trainings, but he already knew the man well enough to know Minox would not be dissuaded from it. "I am here in an official capacity," he would say. "Even if I am on restricted duty."

Minox was waiting for him in the classroom in Bolingwood Tower that had been set aside for these trainings. Veranix hadn't even realized there were classrooms in the tower—he had gotten used to just climbing up to the top where Professor Alimen's offices and apartments were. Apparently these rooms had been the original setting for magic classes —the tower was reinforced with steel when it was built, according to the story, so it could handle the magical energies being used within.

Veranix had realized one thing early on when he had volunteered for this: the professors, including the new militant ones, were terrified of Minox. He had initially thought this was some sort of bizarre prejudice against Uncircled mages—an attitude that Veranix had always found unfathomable—but after a couple weeks, the real source of their fear was clear.

They were terrified of Minox's hand.

Veranix had to admit, there was good cause for that. He did not understand what had happened to Minox that transmuted his hand into something inhuman, but he had seen and felt the power that rested within it. It was that power, in part, that both fueled and resolved the horror the Brotherhood had unleashed out in Seleth. It wasn't just teeming with *numinic* power, but somehow a pure source of it. The one time Delmin had come to these sessions, he said being too close to Minox, and his hand, was like staring at the sun.

Veranix could feel that power when he came into the room. It had grown stronger over the months, and today it was crackling and leaking all over the room.

"Bad day?" Veranix asked. Minox never looked actually happy, at least in Veranix's presence, but today his face was a thundercloud.

"Not in any way that you need to concern yourself with, Mister Calbert."

"I ask because your discipline has regressed," Veranix said. "Your hand is particularly noisy today."

"Hrm," Minox said, turning his attention to his hand. In a moment, the roar of *numinic* energy hushed to a whisper. "That was unfortunate. My household was disrupted in the night, and that led to moments of heated tempers with my brother, Oren."

Veranix chuckled. "I know a few things about heated tempers with brothers."

"I wasn't aware you had brothers."

"Brother, one," Veranix said. "I haven't seen Soranix for years. He left the family, the whole circus, about a year before I came to the University. And he and I would—" He stopped, the sudden realization he hadn't ever considered hitting his heart like a hammer.

"Mister Calbert?"

"Sorry, I . . . I just realized that Soranix probably has no idea that our father is dead, or that our mother is . . . where she is." He had given so little thought to his brother in the last four years—when Soranix left the circus it had been so rancorous, so final that Veranix had long since resigned himself to the idea that they would never see each other again. "Blazes, I have no idea where he even is, how to reach him, anything."

"I understand," Minox said. He pursed his lips for a moment, and then said. "We were arguing about the fact that we don't know what happened to my sister Corrie. He wants us to accept that she's dead, and I am not ready to cross that bridge."

"Nor should you be," Veranix said.

"Thank you," Minox said. "Also, I have news that should concern you."

"Oh?" Veranix asked. "Something to put another nail in Fenmere's coffin?"

"Sadly, no," Minox said. "There was a breakout from Quarrygate Prison last night. Cuse Jensett, Erno Don, Enzin Hence, Magadina Kend, and Kat'rick-Ra."

Veranix startled at that. The Alchemist, the Jester, and the Hunter, all escaped together. That didn't sound good at all. "I don't know the last two."

"Deadly Birds known as Magpie and Jackdaw. You do recall we subdued the latter together."

"The Ch'omik one with the weapon that looked like a rowing oar?"

"Her, yes."

"This sounds like very bad news," Veranix said. "Is Constabulary on it? Or should I . . ."

"I would never explicitly advise you to take vigilante action. But you should be on your guard. It's not unlikely that any—or all—of them might seek to target you. Manage your risk."

"Never my best skill," Veranix said.

"I have noticed that," Minox said. "I think we've dawdled as much as we can dare. I require as much proper practice and training as I can manage in these sessions."

"Right," Veranix said, going to one of the boxes in the corner of the room. "I've been thinking about what you need to achieve with this, in the time we have to work with. Which is how long?"

"My probational period ends in fifty-four days, at which time I will be assessed to determine if I can be allowed to resume my duties as an inspector, or cashiered from the Constabulary."

"Fifty-four days," Veranix said, shaking his head. He couldn't believe how none of the professors were even interested in properly solving this problem, or anyone in Lord Preston's Circle. Putting the box on the worktable, he said, "Here's what I'm thinking. The main thing that they're going to be looking at is making sure you've got that hand under control. You even move a finger right now, you make a mess of *numinic* noise that even I can sense, let alone those fellows. So rather than trying to cram an entire magical education into less a couple months, let's focus on fine control."

"So I have enough mastery to quell their fears," Minox said. "Reasonable. How do you propose we do that?"

Veranix opened the box, taking out needles, thread, and cloth. "You're going to sew."

"I fail to see how that would be useful."

Using barest hints of magic, Veranix raised one needle off the table, letting it float in the air in front of him. With another wisp of control, he brought up the thread. "Your hand is a like a mining sledge, and most of what you do is hammering. But threading the needle, controlling it through the cloth, that takes finesse and focus. You can't do it slamming things around."

Minox nodded, sitting down at the table. He held out his hand and a rush of *numina* came from it.

The needles, thread, and cloth all went flying across the room, slamming against the wall.

"Not ideal," Minox said.

"That's why we keep trying," Veranix said, picking the mess up. Just like running repetitions. Veranix had to admit the militant discipline had its uses. "Again and again, until you get it."

"I will endeavor," Minox said. "Though I fear it will continue to be unsuccessful."

"Just pretend you're me," Veranix said.

"In what manner?"

"Too stubborn and too stupid to quit."

Minox laughed—in that dry, almost mirthless way of his. "I think I can definitely emulate the stubbornness, if nothing else."

"It's gotten me this far," Veranix said. That was how he had learned archery, again and again, day after day, insisting he could trick shot as well as Dad and Soranix could. *You had been a patient teacher, Dad. I'll be damned if I don't do the same thing now. I'll be as good as you were.*

CHAPTER FOUR

MILA KENDISH WAS NOT DOING what she was supposed to right now. She knew she had been fortunate that strings had been pulled to get her into the University of Maradaine, despite no proper schooling before this. She had been given a tremendous opportunity, and she should be focusing all her energy and time on her studies. She had a full docket of classes, she had two roommates who were far too curious about her comings and goings, she had a whole dorm floor with whom she was expected to engage socially. She had a part to play: the good, attentive first-year student, complete with the expected accent of a well-educated, stable-familied, central Maradaine girl who had never faced adversity greater than a social house boy who had forgotten his manners.

But that was not who Mila Kendish was. She was a westtown girl. She had spent plenty of nights sleeping in alleys or abandoned shops. She had lost her parents when she was young, and fled her uncle shortly after that. She had scraped and stolen and done whatever she needed to keep herself and her sister alive. And when she lost her sister, she fell under the wing of Asti Rynax, and learned a whole new set of skills from him.

The skills that let her fake her way into being the Mila Kendish she was supposed to be here.

But she was still the same Mila Kendish she had always been, and she didn't shy away from a fight. Veranix and his friends had a blazes of an impossible fight on their hands, trying to stop Fenmere and his empire of drugs and other vices. Fenmere's people had already tried to push into her old neighborhood, and Veranix had helped her out there, so she felt the obligation to help him now.

Plus, they had something going on which did involve regular kissing. She had no strong urge to further define that, but was definitely interested in continuing for the foreseeable future. That future was hard to foresee if he got killed by Fenmere's goons, so she was going to help him.

That help, today, meant poring over the ledgers Veranix had snagged from the last crew he had busted up, and going over the neighborhood map and the Constabulary files he had somehow acquired.

What she had found fascinating was that Veranix had an absolute trove of useful information about the whole Fenmere operation—especially the aspects controlled by a lieutenant named Bash Jullick—but he was terrible at knowing how to use that information. At best, he only saw the next address or drop spot to hit. No sense of long plan or integrating that information for a larger purpose.

Thankfully, there was Kaiana.

"So," Mila told Kaiana as they worked in the safehouse—Mila *refused* to call it a "lair"—over the map and slateboard. "We've got the drophouse beneath the Rosy Nan neutralized, at least for the moment, since he left them alive."

"A room full of dead bodies gets Constabulary's attention," Kaiana said. "Especially if the bodies are Fenmere's people. The constables in Dentonhill are fully in his pocket."

"Hmm," Mila said. "Still, you know this isn't the sort of business where leaving people alive is good sense. You don't want folks coming back for revenge."

"And I suppose you know something about that?"

"Vengeance or killing?" Mila asked. The answer was yes either way, and her expression must have made that clear, as Kaiana turned away and went back to the slateboard.

"I think Vee tries to let people have a second chance, when he can."

"Second chance to kill him back," Mila said under her breath. "Anyway, with the Rosy Nan crew neutralized, that's the main hub of *effitte* and *efhân* for these two blocks. Presuming that the demand is going to remain . . ."

"Someone needs to move in to the hole."

"Right," Mila said. "And based on these notes, that will be handled by these two: Avi and Bobba, who handle delivery of goods and collection of money. And both of them report right to Jullick."

Kaiana looked over the logbook Mila was referencing. "Right. We have those two as his captains."

"So today, they'll need to be moving about, setting things up."

"That's probably true."

"And from the Constabulary files, the work we've put together, we have a sense who else we need to keep an eye on."

That stopped Kaiana. "We do?"

"Look," Mila said, going to the map. "We've figured out that Jullick is the overboss for these seven blocks. He runs street captains and dens all throughout here. But from where?"

"That's what we don't know."

"But we do know who his other captains are. Veranix has a list." She put up a handful of charcoal sketches. "First Avi and Bobba. Then these two—Bryce and Gamm—who operate their storehouses somewhere here—" She pointed on the map. "They're all going to have to shuffle to fill up that hole. Plus they'll need to replace the product Vee destroyed. To do that, they'll want to move product from the main storehouse in the Jullick blocks. We still don't know where that is."

"Right, and?"

"I would bet, given the bloody nose they took, those captains are on the streets now, or will be soon, either working through Jullick's main storehouse, or going to him in wherever he makes his office. So this is the key time to put eyes on him, and so we're able to plan for Vee to make a move against him."

"Make a what?" Kaiana asked.

"Listen, I know Vee is supposed to be cautious, not going out as the Thorn and making another big hit right after going out last night, but . . ."

"But?"

The idea fully clicked. "Tonight might be a perfect opportunity to cut Jullick's legs out."

"How so?" Kai now looked very interested.

"I could be wrong," Mila said. She went over to the trunk she had already set up down here with some of her gear and supplies, and a healthy amount of costumes, wigs and face paint that no one in the University Theatre School was likely to miss. "But the only way to find out is to get some feet into Dentonhill right now."

"What did you have in mind?"

"I want to find out if it is worth Vee risking another bout tonight. So I'm going to scout through these blocks. Be inconspicuous, eyes and ears open."

"You aren't worried that's dangerous?"

"Of course I am," Mila said. She picked out a few things that would make her look like a chicken factory girl. With the right makeup, she could easily look a little older, a little underfed, and maybe even hurting for a dose of the violet. That will be perfect. "But it shouldn't be too dangerous for me. I can blend in."

"And I can't," Kaiana said sharply.

That seemed to be something Mila had stepped in. "I didn't mean it that way."

"You know Veranix and I were doing this, just the two of us, for some time."

"You were. But we're a bigger crew now. And we each do different things for the mission."

"And what is the mission to you?" A snap from Kai. Almost a threat.

"Stop Fenmere and his empire," Mila said. "You know he moved in on my old neighborhood. He tried to push at my home, my people. Boys who had been under my care were swept up in his nonsense."

"Fine."

"You don't doubt I have a stake in this?"

Kaiana sighed. "I just want to know this isn't some lark for you. Extra excitement so you don't get bored in class. Or that you're just doing it for him."

"I mean, I am here for Veranix," Mila said firmly. He was the face of it. "The Thorn." Back when he came out to Seleth, she had gone into a couple scraps at his side in a similar disguise as "the Rose." She'd have kept it up here, but the reality of her studies made that challenging. "I won't pretend otherwise. But that doesn't mean I'm doing this frivolously. I've got my own scales to balance. And if you have a problem with my—"

"I don't," Kaiana said quickly and firmly. "I just . . . I'm still dealing with all the changes. You have a good idea. Do you need anything from me for it?"

"No, thank you," Mila said. "I'll be quick and quiet, and if what I'm reading between the lines on these reports is right, I'll know exactly where we can hit for Veranix to take down Jullick."

"And that's the goal?"

"I think that's a very good goal. If we're going to dismantle Fenmere's entire empire, it needs to be piece by piece."

"Not just kill Fenmere? When I get a snake out of the garden, I cut off its head. I don't go digging around in its den."

Mila held back the urge to snap. Veranix and Kaiana, they were clever and well-meaning, but they sometimes were idiots who didn't know how things worked. "You ought to, though. You need to find the whole nest, filled with baby vipers. You kill just Fenmere, I guarantee, within months you'll have chaos. All the petty street lords will try to be the new king of Dentonhill. So let's tear down the kingdom first, so there is nothing left to rule."

KAIANA HAD LET MILA GET TO HER, AND SHE NEEDED TO STOP DOING that. She knew that Mila brought knowledge and experience that Kaiana, as well as everyone else on Team Thorn, simply lacked. But she still found herself getting upset that Mila would keep coming up with plans and ideas, plus understanding exactly what things in ledgers meant.

It had almost nothing to do with the fact that she and Veranix would spend some of their time kissing. Almost nothing. And most of that was how she felt they were being very unfocused when they were kissing. Something could go wrong. That was the only reason. She had the completely reasonable concern that they would be far too distracted at a critical moment and both get killed.

Completely reasonable.

Also, Kaiana still had to get work done. The summer had been hot and dry, and it had been brutal for most of the trees on campus, and the grass was a disaster. She had been focused on saving the flowers along the eastern wall, and put her crews on keeping the lawns, if nothing else, neat. Green wasn't even an option. The rain barrels were all empty, and there had been several letters from various offices around campus about conserving the water from the spigots. "We understand the struggle, and a vibrant lawn cannot have priority over the students drinking and bathing."

Kaiana was checking on the violets that bordered the south wall when they came up to her—two constables, both with very boyish faces. Neither of them looked like they were even capable of growing a beard.

"Miss Nell, ma'am?" one of them asked, talking as if they were trying to make their voice sound deeper.

"Can I help you with something, officers? I don't believe you're supposed to be here on campus without blessing of the campus cadets."

"Yes, ma'am. I'm Officer Kendall Pollit, and this is Officer Jace Welling—"

The other one did look a bit like a younger version of Minox, with a bit more life in his cheeks.

"Are you related to the Inspector Welling from Inemar?" she asked him.

"That's my brother, yes," he said.

"So you know about clearing your presence on campus with the cadets?" she asked.

"Yes, ma'am," Pollit said. "We have already spoken with them, they directed us to find you."

"And what are you seeking me for?"

"We're aware of your role in apprehending one Cuse Jensett when he was attempting some mischief on campus," Pollit said.

"That was the fellow who tried to destroy the commencement,

right?" she asked. Why would they ask her about him? Did they know about her connection to Veranix? "I just saw trouble and did what I could to stop it. I don't know much more than that."

"We're here to warn you," Pollit said. "Mister Jensett, as well as a few other miscreants, recently escaped from Quarrygate Prison, and it is considered highly likely he might seek some form of revenge on you."

"On me?" Kaiana asked. "Because I caught him?"

"It's very possible," Jace said. "He escaped with a few others who were . . . notable arrests."

"Notable how?"

Pollit looked a little annoyed with Jace. "All of them had entangle-ments with the vigilante called the Thorn, as well as one other who was apprehended on campus."

"Was one of them Enzin Hence?" she asked. The "Hunter" who had been selling and using drugs that enhanced his strength.

"Yes," Pollit said cautiously. "Is that notable to you?"

"I was present in his attack on campus when Mi—your brother caught him. That's how I'm familiar with him."

"And then two assassins called Magpie and Jackdaw, Mister Erno Don and Mister Juteron Higgs. Do those mean anything do you?"

Not that she could specifically think of, but she had her guesses. Not guesses she would speak in front of the Constabulary, though.

"I can't say they hold much meaning for me. But I appreciate the warning about Mister Jensett. I will stay on guard."

"We can keep you in protective custody, if you wish," Pollit said. "Either at the stationhouses, or in a safehouse we have in the neigh-borhood."

"I appreciate that," she said. "But I will decline."

"If he comes after you—"

"I stopped him once," she said. "And I'm forewarned. If he is inclined to come for me, I'm ready."

"Let us help you, Miss Nell," Officer Pollit urged.

"I've been clear," Kaiana said. "I am fine. Thank you."

The two officers looked at each other with a bit of confusion. "As you wish. You have a good day."

She watched them go, and got back to work pruning the hedge. Her mind was no longer on the work at all, but on what she would tell Veranix when she next saw him.

VERANIX FELT HIS PULSE QUICKEN THE MOMENT THEY STEPPED INSIDE the Lower Trenn Ward. The idea of even being in here felt wrong. Veranix couldn't risk coming to see his mother, no matter how much he wanted to. Fenmere had her put here when he broke her mind, and he presumably had eyes on her. Veranix knew this. A wrong step could put her and him in danger.

The last time he came here with Eittle was far too close. He had to be more careful this time.

But if this was true, if there was some way to cure Parsons, then there was hope for his mother as well. That hope burned in his heart like the dying embers of a fire, but he was determined to hold on to it. He had to be here, to see it with his own eyes.

Thankfully Delmin had come along as well. It made Veranix far less conspicuous. Eittle had brought along Parsons's friends, which was very normal. No one would think anything odd.

"There they are," Eittle said, pointing to three people standing by the front desk. Two of them were obviously Parsons's parents—a pair in well-appointed clothes, both looking around skeptically at their surroundings. They looked like they had never before stepped south of the river, incredibly out of place and deeply uncomfortable.

The third person, though, despite his rich coat that looked like the ocean, seemed completely at ease. He leaned against the front desk like he owned it, his gaze off to the middle distance in a show of bored disinterest as he hummed tunelessly.

"It's him," Parsons's mother said, as if Eittle was a walking source of filth. "And he brought people."

"It's good that Kendall has friends who support him," the father said. "He'll need them if this works out."

"Sir, ma'am," Eittle said as he walked up. "It's a genuine pleasure to finally be meeting you, though I wish it was in happier circumstances."

"We all wish for a world where foolish choices were not made," Mister Parsons said. "But nonetheless, this is the world we find ourselves in, Mister Eittle."

"These are two dear friends from Almers Hall," Eittle said. "Calbert and Sarren."

"Sarren," Mister Parsons said. "Any relation to Oscren Sarren?"

"That's my uncle," Delmin said.

And with that, Parsons's father's shoulders visibly relaxed a little. "Good, good. I know of him more than know him, but we are in a couple of the same clubs together."

"And what sort of name is Calbert?" the mother asked. "Are your people here? Or in the Little East, you do seem a bit dusky."

"Not from here originally," Veranix said, desperately wanting to pivot away from wherever she was leading this conversation. "But happy to be a proud student at the University of Maradaine."

"Hmm," she said. "And what do you boys study?"

"Magic," the third person said, though his attention was firmly focused on his own fingernails. "These two are most definitely magic students."

"So, you can . . . sense that, can you, Mister Rassin?"

"Not exactly," this man—Mister Rassin, apparently—said. "But it is rather obvious to me."

"Magic students?" Parsons's father asked nervously. "What sort of opportunities are in that?"

"Quite a few," Delmin said. "But I find—"

"This is tedious," Rassin said. "We should go upstairs rather than prattle on. Or I'll have to charge you more."

He went to the stairwell, and the Parsonses gathered themselves up to follow.

"Who is this fellow now?" Eittle asked as they all followed. "Some kind of specialist? An expert in drugs, an apothecary of some sort?"

"Not exactly," Missus Parsons said. "Certainly a specialized person."

Rassin stopped mid-step and spun around on Eittle. "Look at all of that, those theories spinning through your head with such . . . glorious rapidity and complexity. And yet . . . ." He stepped closer to Eittle, looking him up and down. "It's fascinating, this whole presentation of yours, never wanting the world to know exactly how smart you are, how fast your mind works, and . . . oh . . ." He chuckled. "Yes, of course. Our little secret, Mister Eittle."

"What the blazes?" Eittle asked.

Veranix bounded up two steps, putting his body between Eittle and this Rassin fellow. Rassin stepped back from that, a sly smile across his face.

Eittle recovered himself. "Pardon me, ma'am, I didn't mean to—"

"Quite all right," Missus Parsons said.

Mister Parsons asked, "Can we continue, Mister Rassin? You said you didn't want to dawdle."

"No, indeed, I do not," Rassin said, pivoting again and returning to his ascent. The Parsonses followed, but Eittle stayed rooted in place.

Veranix touched him on the arm. "Hey, Eittle. You all right?"

"What . . . I don't even know what that was."

Delmin leaned in and whispered. "I think Mister Rassin is a telepath."

"That's real?" Veranix asked.

"Yes, that's—do you not even read the assignments?"

"I skim them."

"He . . . he just knew what I was thinking?" Eittle asked. "Read it out of my head like reading a book?"

"More or less," Delmin said. "Let's stick with them."

"He can do that to all of us?" Veranix asked.

Delmin shook his head. "Read the damn assignments, Vee. The short of it is, he'd have a harder time with mages. Not impossible, but harder."

"Good."

They reached the fifth floor, to find Rassin stopped in the middle of the hallway, arms outstretched. "Oh, my, this is fascinating. Like shattered windows everywhere. Fascinating."

One of the doctors, attending to one of the dozens of patients sitting motionless in chairs, came up to them. "Pardon me, what is this? Who are you?"

"Me?" Rassin asked. "Tor Rassin. A specialist for hire, if you will. I'm here to consult on the recovery of one of your patients."

"Doctor Browning," the doctor said. Veranix realized this doctor was the same one he had seen here, months ago, when he brought that *effitte*-addled doxy to the ward. "I was not told about any sort of specialist."

"Didn't you tell them?" Eittle asked the Parsons.

"We're here right now. Let's just see if this works."

"Wait a damned minute," Doctor Browning said. "I need to know something about your credentials, Mister Rassin. Are you a doctor or what?"

"Of course, doctor," Rassin said. He reached into his pocket and took out a calling card, handing it to the doctor. "Does that make it clear?"

"Oh. Oh!" Doctor Browning said looking at the card. "I'm so sorry, sir. Let me know if you need anything."

"Thank you, doctor," Rassin said, taking the card back. As soon as he had taken two more steps, Veranix moved up and snatched the card away.

It was blank.

"What was that?" he asked Rassin.

"Simplification," Rassin said. "And call me Tor, please."

"What?"

"In your head, Veranix, you've got me as 'Rassin,' and that's so very boys' school, isn't it? Saints, you think of him as 'Eittle,' like he doesn't have a given name."

"Stop that right now," Veranix said.

"Or you'll what?" Rassin asked. Then his eyebrow raised. "Well, I didn't quite get all that, but it was interesting."

"Ease off, Calbert," Eittle said, pulling Veranix away. "He's here to help."

"Is he?" Veranix asked. Just out of raw instinct, he didn't trust a word out of this Rassin fellow's mouth. "I don't even see how this guy could help. He seems to just be tricks and scams."

"Not just," Rassin said. "And you already know that."

"Do you have any training or accreditation?" Delmin asked.

"And no blank card tricks," Veranix added.

"Please, don't upset him, boys," Missus Parsons said. "We just want to get Kendall the help he needs."

"I actually would like to know, Maira," Mister Parsons said. "Answer the boys."

"Oh, let's see. Graduated from the Royal College of Maradaine, Letters in Literature and Music. I've played Prince Halitar in *Demea* and Tristan of Erien in *A Trio of Travellers Called Tristan*, and I've been bonded to the Collective of the White Rose from *birth*, just like my sister and father, may the sinners dance on his soul, and let's not forget that I can pluck your worst memory and make you live in it for the rest of your pitiful life." His voice rose in a rising crescendo as he directed the end of his speech to Delmin. "So, Mister Sarren, tell me. Is that accreditation enough for you? Or do we have to talk about Davis Kell?"

"No," Delmin said, swallowing hard. "I think you have excellent credentials, clearly."

So that's who this fellow was. A bully.

"So that's what you'll do?" Veranix asked. "You're going to reach into Parsons's head and just . . . put him back together?"

"Crudely put, old boy, but apt," Rassin said. "Each mind is something like a symphony, and this room . . . it's all discord, out of key. And the question is, can I . . . tune the orchestra?"

He walked into the room, filled with patients in rollerchairs, on cots, or for some, wandering in a stupor. All of them lacking expression, glassy eyed.

And there, one of the walkers, Veranix's mother.

She looked so thin, so impossibly thin, her once muscular arms now just twigs in her loose gown. Her hair was cropped almost to the scalp, and her face . . . so drawn, pale, and devoid of any spark.

Veranix's heart shattered, and as much as he kept that off his face, held his body still and together, he let something come through, as Rassin turned to him, tilting his head.

"Now," Rassin said slowly. "I will be honest, I have not done anything quite like this before."

"Quite?" Mister Parsons asked as he went over to Parsons, slumped in his rollerchair, drool falling from his mouth.

"I have worked on repairing a mind ravaged by a telepathic attack,"

Rassin said. "This is similar in appearance, but definitely different in practice." He crouched down and ran his fingers over Parsons's face and head. "But those differences are enticing."

"Can you do it, Mister Rassin?" Mister Parsons asked. "I'll remind you we have been quite generous with you."

"Because you know you'll never find anyone else who would even attempt this," Rassin said. "People of my skill rarely are as coldly mercenary as me."

"Can you?"

"I think so," Rassin said, standing up. "But I do want to give you your money's worth, so perhaps it is best if I practice on a few of the little ones in here first, before I help your son. You know, just to get the kinks out of it."

"Yes, that makes sense," Mister Parsons said.

"You will still pay for my time, of course. Now . . . who shall I try this on?" He circled the room like a hawk over prey. "I might be saving one of these poor souls. Or I might just shred what is left of them in the attempt. Which shall be the lamb I take to the slaughterhouse?"

"Please, sir," Eittle said. "No need to be crude."

"Hmm," Rassin said, stopping next to Veranix's mother. "But maybe I'll be doing a favor either way." He looked closely at her, and Veranix held silent screams in his heart. Saints, he wanted nothing more than for his mother to be fixed, to be well, if this fellow could do it, that would be—

But if he failed, would she be worse off?

Veranix couldn't decide if he wanted Rassin to try or not, though he desperately wanted her back, and just as desperately wanted this disgusting man to take his hands off her.

"This one seems a bit fragile, no?" Rassin said, walking away from Veranix's mother. He approached one of the cots. The man lying there was in the same loose gown as everyone else, but his arm was marked with tattoos. "But here we have an army man, a soldier."

Doctor Browning approached. "Yes, that's Mister Nell, served in the island wars, got hooked on the original stuff out there."

Now Veranix's heart all but stopped. Kaiana's father.

Rassin knelt down next to him. "A man who was ready to serve and sacrifice. A perfect possibility." He put his hands on Mister Nell's face. "Now, let's not do anything to disturb or disrupt me, hmm? I would hate to be startled and tear something I couldn't repair."

He took a deep breath, and then leaned in over Mister Nell. Veranix didn't think he could watch, so he turned away, and found himself facing his mother. Her dead eyes staring emptily at him, no sense of recognition in them.

He allowed himself the luxury of, for once, just looking at her. While Tor Rassin worked, there was no reason he couldn't.

CHAPTER FIVE

MILA HAD WALKED THE CIRCUIT through the "Jullick blocks" of Dentonhill—the triangle of Waterpath, Oscana Avenue, and Curtis Road. She went through, head down, inconspicuous, while she kept her eye on the places she had already suspected, pausing idly when the opportunity arose to catch a bit more information. She was ready to check out the last target on her list, a grocer—and more specifically the office above it—where she noted four fellows who looking very concerned about what was going on in the street. She spotted one of them—Bryce, he was called—having a quiet word with a pair of Constabulary footpatrol, saw coins and handshakes that no one was supposed to see, and caught a few whispered words as she went by. Carts being loaded in one back alley. A couple chaps frowning while muttering about the Rosy Nan.

She slipped into an alley backhouse, flipped around her outfit, swapped her wig and scarf, and went back out for another pass through there.

This pass, she spotted Miss Jads—looking as petty and awful as she had the last time Mila had seen her—going up to the office above the grocer. So Mila milled about in front, examining produce and looking like she had every intention of purchasing something. Head down, ears open, she found a place she could stand, look at the meager assembly of spotty apples, and hear a few choice words through the open window above her. Thank the saints it was still hot, even this late in the autumn.

"—these records need to be cleared—"

"—have to assume—"

"—we'll be finished tomorrow morning—"

"—he wants this clear tonight by eleven—"

That was enough for her, the final detail to confirm, so she bought a couple apples and went on her way, back across Waterpath, into Aventil. She had worked out the key points of Fenmere's operation in this patch of Dentonhill, and now she also had a timeline. Now to get back to campus, tell Veranix what she had figured out, and see what he wanted to do with that information.

She knew damn well what she would do, were she him. Tonight was the ripe opportunity, it had to be now. There was no substitute for ripe opportunity. All the planning in the world didn't make a difference if you didn't have the moment.

Tonight was the moment, she could convince Veranix of that.

"Hey, girl, what do you think you're playing?"

She looked up. She was in Aventil, out of the Jullick blocks and Fenmere's range. No, not any of his people. A couple of Aventil street rats standing in front of her.

"What do you think I'm playing?" she asked. She went for her natural West Maradaine street girl accent, perhaps thickening it up a bit.

"You can't just slip in here from across the 'path. You think you can waltz from Denton to our patch?"

"You think I can't?" she asked.

"I think we know you shouldn't."

Mila knew she should just back off, go back across Waterpath, and approach campus from the east gate.

She should, but she wasn't going to let tossers like this get in her way.

"I don't think you boys know much of anything," she said. "Else you'd know just to let me be on my way."

"Your way is apparently through our patch, girl, and that's something we don't brook."

"Your patch?" she asked. "You got a scar on your cheek, and you got a burned tattoo on your arm. So whose patch is this? Princes? Orphans?"

"You should know whose patch this is, tart," one of them said.

This fellow was just begging for a knife in the throat, but that wouldn't suit her needs right now.

"Oh, sorry," she said, deliberately goading them. "I don't know who your little gang of pissdrinkers are. I have places to be."

She took a step further and they both closed off in front of her.

Scarred face said, "Denton tarts need to pay a toll if they walk through Orchid Street, because that's home of the Sons of Tyson."

The one with the burnt arm said, "You don't disrespect with the Sons."

One of them grabbed for her, but she stepped to the side, kicking him hard in the knee. A solid knee shot always put a boy like that on the ground. When his friend made to grab for her, she whipped off the scarf and wrapped it around his neck, twisting it tight while driving the heel of her boot in the tenders of the man on the ground.

"Now," she said in a quiet whisper. "I've laid low Scratch Cats and Potato Boys and men whose names would chill your blood if I said them out loud. So don't think you boys are going to give me grief that I've not beaten down before, and from better than you."

"Stupid . . . slan . . ." the one she was choking eked out.

"I told you, I had places to be. But you had to hassle me, and—"

"Let them loose."

She looked over to the speaker, someone who had just stepped out of the pub they were in front of. This one looked like a real brawler. Reminded her of Asti Rynax, were he a foot taller.

"They hassled me," she said. This fellow looked like he deserved a hint of respect, so she let the one she was choking free, and took her heel off the other one's groin after getting in a final grind. "I didn't seek any trouble."

The bruiser looked to those two. "Walk it off. Out of my sight."

They scrambled away.

He looked back at Mila. "Are you going to be a problem for me?"

She put her scarf back on. "Depends on how things run when I come through. You have your boys hassle me for walking across the street, then I'm an applecart full of problem."

"I can't have someone who embarrasses my boys walking through here like that. I have a reputation to uphold."

"Maybe I do as well."

"You definitely do," he said with a smile. He came in closer to her—a little too close for her liking, and for a moment she thought he was going to try to kiss her. "You tell Veranix I need a word with him, sooner rather than later, hmm?"

"How did you—"

"I do make a point of knowing what's going on with him," he said, stepping away. "And who with. It's what family does."

This was the cousin on the street. Colin? That was his name.

"I'll let him know."

"Tonight if he can."

"Tonight might be busy."

"All the more reason."

She took that in. "Sorry about your boys."

"They need the learning. Now move on."

She nodded and went off. She had to get back to the safehouse quick, and tell Veranix everything. Tonight could be a very big night indeed.

KAIANA DID NOT MISS THE CARRIAGE HOUSE. HAVING HER OWN OFFICE and her own proper apartments on campus, with the latter having her own private water closet, was an absolute joy.

It also let her keep her sleeping life—her personal life, by every saint, she could have one—separate from all the Thorn business in the underground lair. She gave Veranix one hard, unbreakable rule that her apartment was *sacred* and he should not go there for any reason. She regretted that sometimes, because there were bound to be moments where Veranix needed immediate help. That had been the case far too many times when she had been in the carriage house. At minimum, he needed sew-up work on a fresh set of injuries.

So she set up a compromise. Since her apartments were part of the staff facilities, there was a series of bells and pullcords with very clever and intricate engineering so members of the staff could be summoned or woken by one of the campus ushers, should the need arise. With a bit of ingenuity—and Mila had helped with this one, Kaiana couldn't ignore that—they had managed to rig up a pull cord from Kai's apartment to the underground bunker, so someone in there could reach her at any unsaintly hour they might need.

Veranix promised not to pull it unless it was an emergency.

Kaiana had just returned home, washed off her hands, face, and feet, and settled into making herself a cup of tea when the bell started ringing. Not just a ring, but an almost frantic, wild ringing. Whoever was in the lair—it had to be Veranix—was pulling the cord like a madman.

She quickly got her shoes back on and went out, slipping down the back way to the bunker, to find him and Delmin down there, still pulling on the cord.

"Saints and sinner and idiots!" she said coming in. "What has got you so—"

"Kai," Veranix said, racing over to her, grabbing her shoulders. His face was filled with a thousand emotions, one racing after the other. "It . . . the guy . . . he . . . it works. It works!"

"What works? What are you on about?"

"Your father's awake, Kai," Veranix said.

She felt her legs go out from under her, but Veranix caught her before she hit the floor. He helped her over to a chair. Her whole body had just stopped functioning for a moment while her mind caught up with what he had said.

"How . . . he's . . . I don't understand."

Veranix took her hand. "Eittle told us that Parsons's parents had hired some sort of specialist to help him, and he was going out to the Lower Trenn to meet them. Delmin and I went along, because I . . . I had to know."

"Of course," she said, if only to force some words out of her mouth. Her mind was numb, but Veranix's seemed to be on fire.

"And this guy—total jerk, absolute pig—he was a telepath, apparently, that's what he was, right, Del?"

"I'm pretty sure," Delmin said. He was leaning against the wall, quiet and drawn in, even for him.

"He's all, 'oh, maybe I should practice on someone first before I do it to Parsons' and he looks around and first he's going to my mom, but I think that was because he knew—that little bastard just rutting knew—and he was trying to get at me, because he went to her and was all, 'oh, no, I don't think so, but this guy was a soldier, he'll do.'"

"My dad?" she asked, able to find the words finally. "He used my dad for a test?"

Veranix's eyes went wild. "And it worked, Kai. It rutting well worked!"

"Worked how? He's awake? He's talking?"

Delmin came over. He was far more rational than either she or Vee could manage. "He still seemed groggy, like he was coming out of a fog or something. But he was definitely coming out. He asked for water, he said he was hungry."

He was speaking. He was awake. This was . . . Kaiana wasn't sure how she felt but she had to go see him. She had to talk to him.

She hadn't even realized that she had said that out loud and was halfway down the hall before the boys stopped her.

"You can't visit now. It'll have to be tomorrow," Delmin said.

"The whole thing made a stir in the ward, and they wanted to check him out. And the smug jerk Rassin was all, 'That was exhausting, I must recenter myself before trying again.'"

"But . . . he did it?" Kaiana asked. "It really works?"

Veranix nodded. "By what we saw . . . yeah. It really works."

"What did he *say*, though?" she asked. She couldn't think of any answer that would have satisfied her. Nothing that Veranix could say right now would actually give her peace of mind or any ease. She wanted to go see her father, to hear his voice, tell him . . .

Tell him what a damned idiot he was.

And just be with him again.

"He just asked for water, then said he was hungry, and . . . we were ushered out," Veranix said. "It's not like he knew who we were, or the staff there knew who we were, or—"

"Right, right," Kaiana said. They had told her that already. She couldn't keep words or memory in her head right now. "But he's all right?"

"He's awake," Veranix said. "And that means . . . maybe—"

Kaiana couldn't hold back tears further, burying her face in Vee's chest.

"Everything all right here?"

Kaiana looked up. Mila was in the entranceway in one of her disguises. She looked a bit put off by what she was seeing, but Kaiana could not care less.

Her father was awake.

"It's fine," Veranix said. "We just had some good news."

"Well," Mila said. "I've got some good news, too. I think we can take out Jullick's entire wing of Fenmere's operation. But it has to be tonight."

Veranix was still trying to find his feet in everything that had happened today. Now with a sliver of hope about his mother, that she might someday be *whole* again, his heart was soaring. It didn't matter that Tor Rassin was a complete jackponce, who cost far too much for Veranix to ever afford. He would make it happen, he would make it work, he would get his mother back.

He would get something back that Willem Fenmere had taken from him. Then he would take everything away from Fenmere.

"Jullick's whole branch?" Veranix asked. "How?"

"Your hit on the Rosy Nan spooked them, as well it should. From the ledgers you took, Inspector Welling's files, and my own nosing about this afternoon, I've sussed out the lynchpins of the operation for Jullick's blocks."

"Saints," Delmin muttered as he looked over the notes she had made. "Every research department on campus should be climbing over each other to get you in their ranks."

"Damn right they should," Mila said. She went to the map. "His office, with his main ledgers, is here, over the Hebutt Grocer on Brown and Willett. Primary target. Next, there are two key storehouses for *effitte* and *efhân* here on Shade, and here at the corner of Vinny. One's a tenement basement, the other is a livery stable. And finally, Jullick's countinghouse, where they keep goldsmith notes and coin, is here on Prince. If we strike at those spots, we can cripple Jullick."

"And hobble Fenmere in the process," Veranix said. He had had his eye on the livery stable—he had seen a few suspected dealer bosses near there, and he had scouted it the other night. The place held far fewer horses than a stable that size could manage, and it felt like a front for Fenmere's operation. "So why do we have to go tonight?"

"Because they're spooked. I heard Jullick and Jads in their office, and they're going full scrub and vinegar."

"They're going what?" Delmin asked.

She sighed. "They're emptying those locations and abandoning them. That move is going to happen tonight. By tomorrow morning they'll have cleaned everything out, and moved the whole operation to new storehouses and offices."

"So if we don't go tonight, everything we've learned is useless," Veranix said.

"It's more than that," Mila said, patting his cheek with a hint of condescension. "Those locations would normally be fortified, guards that could dig in, alarms and traps. I saw a bit of that. But moving fast means their defenses have to be lowered. They're soft targets."

That was all Veranix needed to hear. He stripped off his school uniform and started getting into his Thorn clothes.

"Even if that's true," Kaiana said, taking Mila's notes from Delmin. "He can't hit them all. Surely if he strikes at one, the others will all lock up with more guards, be ready for him. Not to mention he could get swarmed."

"That's why my plan is he doesn't do it alone," Mila said. "And he doesn't do his usual stupid thing of 'jump in with no plan and hope the saints smile over him.'"

"Hey!"

"Am I wrong?"

Veranix, half dressed in his Thorn outfit, didn't have a response to that.

"What do you mean by 'he doesn't go alone'?" Delmin asked. "Like, all of us go out there? I'm not sure what good that will do."

"You're a mage, you don't know what good you'll do?" Mila asked. "Please, I've already come up with a plan with the four of us."

"The four of us doing what?" Kaiana asked.

"I'll be out there as the Rose," Mila said. "High time she made a proper appearance in Dentonhill."

"And what are we?" Delmin asked. "The Vine and the Seed?"

"Not terrible," Veranix said.

"If you think you're calling me the Seed I'm going to crack your head open," Kaiana said.

"I thought he was the Seed," Veranix said.

"We don't actually all need names," Mila said, rubbing her temples. "What we need is for you all to listen to the plan and calm down."

"I still want to know why I need to be there," Delmin said. "I'm not a fighting mage."

"But," Mila said, "you can get very tiny."

This was news to Veranix. "What was that?"

"That happened once and it was an accident." He sputtered about. "How did you hear about that?"

"I hear about lots of things. Can you do it again?"

Delmin shrugged. "I don't know, maybe?"

"And when you did it, you did your clothes and everything?"

"Yes . . ."

"So," Mila said, "we've got an excellent supply of the refills for your smoke arrows and boom powder arrows. And we've got someone who can sneak that stuff in like a mouse."

"I . . . what?"

"And what do you want me to do?" Kaiana asked. Veranix wasn't sure from her tone if she was interested or upset.

"Eyes on the streets. There's a tenement where Shade and Brown meet Price. From the roof, you should be able to see all the targets, all of us in play. They're going to have wagons moving, people ready to strike. You're there to keep watch on stuff, signal warnings. Pull any of us out if things turn left."

"I don't see how it will work," Kaiana said. "We don't even know how many guards they have, and if it's not all four places at once, then whatever we hit will become the center of all their folks." She looked to Veranix with disapproval. "We'd need an army."

"You're right," Mila said.

"And where am I going to get an army?" Veranix asked.

"What about Colin?" Mila asked. "Doesn't he have one?"

IT WAS SUPPOSED TO BE A RESPECTABLE DINNER PARTY, THE VERY SORT of thing Willem Fenmere had been lacking this season. Some old friends, some new friends, and a few choice people from prominent families in the neighborhood. His chef had prepared sets of lamb ribs, dressed in mint and garlic, duck-seared potatoes, roasted root vegetables, bread in the Lacanja style, a case of wine from the Nitaria region of the Kieran Empire—all to perfection.

But just as they were about to sit down, Corman came and whispered to him about the problem. He could not believe that such a thing would come into his home, on a night like this. The audacity. He would deal with it—he had to deal with it—but the fact that he had to raised his ire immensely.

"Please, start without me, I insist."

He made polite excuses to his guests and stepped out from the dining room, through the sitting room, past his study, down the steps into the cellar, and past the wine racks.

To the bleed room.

A group of Kenny's men—who were affectionately called the Bone Crew—gathered around these five intruders who had come to his gate. These five—three men, two women, one of them a chomie—sat surrounded by the Bone Crew, bound in wooden chairs, looking tired. And bored.

Anyone who found themselves in this room, with the meat hooks on the ceiling, selection of blades on the wall, sluices and drains on the bloodstained floor—they ought to at least have the common sense to be afraid.

No, these five looked mostly put out.

"This the man?" the one in the center asked as Fenmere came in. "You're the boss of all this?"

"I told you," the blond woman said.

"And who are you?" Fenmere asked. "Who the blazes are any of you, and why did you come to my home?"

"You need us, we need you," the one in the center said. "And we can be good for you."

"I doubt that," Fenmere said. "I don't have time for this. Name."

"Cuse Jensett," the one in the center said. "That's Erno Don and Enzin Hence, and the ladies are Kat'rick-Ra and Magadina Kend. You're going to want to hire us."

"This is absurd. You called me away for this? Just kill them."

"Hey, hey," Erno said. "Why would you want to do a thing like that? Before even learning how useful we are."

"How in any name are you useful?" Though they all certainly had a bearing of capability, he could see that. But capable folks were far too common, common enough not to waste time with these five just for that.

"This is a waste of time," Enzin said.

"They were easily subdued," Corman offered.

"We weren't subdued, we came willingly," Jensett said. "We wanted to talk to you."

Wait. Jensett.

No.

Fenmere crouched in front of that man, got a real good look at his face.

"What are you to Reb Jensett?" Fenmere asked.

"Nephew," he said.

"So you're a Red Rabbit?" Even after all this time, Fenmere would still relish the opportunity to cause a bit of pain to any one of the Aventil Nine, or any of their remaining kin.

"I hear there are no more Red Rabbits. This guy made sure of that."

He gave a nod to Erno. "But I've got no grouse with him. Or with anyone who wants to cause pain in Aventil."

Fenmere looked to Erno. "What does he mean by that?"

"Right," Erno said. "I did kill off the Red Rabbits, didn't I? That's what your man hired me to do, why I thought you'd be interested in chatting with us." He glanced back at Jensett. "That was nothing personal, Cuse."

"My man?" Fenmere asked.

"If I may elucidate, sir?" Corman said. "Over the summer, Mister Bell had hired a mercenary to pretend to be the Thorn and hunt the last Red Rabbits."

"This fellow?"

"I have my moments," Erno said.

"I'm not impressed," Fenmere said. "Like I said, kill them. And make it hurt a lot for the nephew of Reb Jensett."

"Hey now—" was all Enzin said before the Bone Crew fellows came up behind them all, ready to slit throats.

All chaos broke out, a flurry of fists and feet, and before Fenmere had even realized it—Corman had put his body between Fenmere and the rest, so he didn't even see what happened—all the Bone Crew were on the floor. Maybe it was just a trick of the light, but when Enzin grabbed a member of the Bone Crew, Fenmere would have sworn that the greenish veins in the man's arm pulsed and throbbed. His whole body seemed out of sorts, like the proportions were all wrong.

"We came here for your help," Jensett said calmly, still in his chair. "We don't have resources right now, we were hoping for your help along those lines. And then we want to help you. As you can see, we have a few worthy skills."

Fenmere looked at the two women. They had been the most brutally efficient in the little brawl with the crew. "You're Deadly Birds, aren't you?"

"We had been," the Ch'omik woman said.

"Why come here to me? Go to Laira."

"You get arrested, you're burned," Magadina said. "We need to re-earn our place."

"Arrested?" He remembered the news. It made sense now. "You five are the ones who escaped Quarrygate. And for some reason you came to me. Pointless."

"I don't think so," Jensett said. "If we can be supplied and—"

"Supplied? Are you mad? I should still have your throat cut. Instead, I'll let you back out into the street to find your own way."

"That is a mistake," Jensett said with an insufferably smug air.

"And it's one I'm comfortable with. I don't want you here, and I don't want to see any of you again."

"I did notice the dalmatium pylons around the house. To keep out the mages. Or one mage. Crude, but not ineffective. I could improve those."

This fellow was earning having his toes fed to him.

"I don't want to hear another word from any of you. Leave while I let you."

"One thing—"

"Shush."

"I'm going to tell you something," Jensett said, undeterred. "And when I tell you, you will give us rooms, equip us with weapons and supplies, and you will pay us handsomely to work for you."

"Mister Jensett," Fenmere said. "I cannot imagine what you could say that would endear me to you so. And even if I was somehow, in a fit of madness, inclined to be charitable to you, I have an air of respectability to maintain, guests of some note to attend to. I cannot also be playing host to escaped prisoners. Go with peace, and do not trouble me again."

He started to walk away, hoping that the lamb had not chilled too much.

"I know who the Thorn is," Jensett said. "I've seen his face."

Fenmere stopped and turned around.

"You have my attention."

CHAPTER SIX

"Why do you order those and not eat them all?"

Colin slid the plate of rackers and crisps over to Sella. "Because I know you'll want it."

"I mean, I got to do something," she said. "The damned sew-up doesn't have any *doph* anymore."

It wasn't that he didn't have any more, it was that Colin had told him if he gave any more to Sella, he'd cut the fellow's tenders clean off. That man was especially fond of them, so he complied. He could tell Sella was going to lose her fight against staying off the *doph*, so it was best to cut off her supply. Sella was a good lieutenant when her head was clear, so Colin made a point of keeping it clear.

"Finish eating that, and then go check on our people in the flop under the barber. Haven't heard from them since yesterday."

"If you say, boss, but—"

She was cut off by a flash of red light, and a boom that rattled the windows. When Colin's eyes cleared, Veranix was standing right in front of him with some bird at his side.

No, not Veranix. He was fully there as the Thorn. Burgundy cloak and hood, face hidden in shadow. The woman with him was decked out in reds and crimsons, her face masked, knives at her belt.

Sella and the other Sons of Tyson in the Old Canal were gawking. Colin got his wits back quickly, time to show some authority.

"Thorn," he said firmly. "Good to see you about here. You and—"

"Rose," the girl said coolly. It was the same girl from earlier today, but Colin only knew that because he was already aware that Veranix had done a few runs with her at his side. First time he had seen her in this getup, and he had to admit, she was unrecognizable from how he had seen her a few hours ago.

Veranix offered his hand to Colin. "Good to see you, cousin," he said, his voice deeper and echoing just a little. Rutting magic. "Glad you're holding the line here."

"Representing the Sons of Tyson," Colin said.

"The true heirs of Aventil's streets!" one of the other boys—Tevvy? Saints, he was losing track—shouted.

"You here to knock those Orphans down?" another asked. "We gonna tussle with the Thorn on our side?"

"Hey, hey," Colin said. "Easy all. Thorn's a busy man." Though he was shocked that Veranix showed up like this, so openly, so public. What the blazes was this about?

"Can we talk?" Veranix asked Colin.

"Back here," Colin said, pointing toward the kitchen. He went back without further confirmation, ordering the Canal's cooks out when he got there. They scurried, probably more because they saw Veranix and Rose coming in.

"A little theatrical, no?" he asked Veranix.

"I thought you needed some dramatics," Veranix said. "So your people could really see us together."

Colin nodded. "Yeah, it probably helps. They've been starting to get itchy about you."

"That why you needed to talk to me?"

"In part," Colin said. Realizing they both had a serious air to them, he added, "But that's not why you're here right now."

"Rose thinks we have an opportunity to really hit Fenmere hard tonight."

"Are you crazy?" Colin asked. "I mean, even if—I mean, of course you are, but if you can do that why—oh. Blazes."

There was only one reason why Veranix would be coming here before trying to hit Fenmere.

"You've figured it out."

"Yeah," Colin said. "And if you need my help, you need to tell me more."

Veranix looked to Rose, who started into it. "Thorn's action yesterday got the whole Jullick organization spooked, so—"

"Jullick is?"

"One of Fenmere's main captains, controlling the south triangle of Dentonhill," Veranix said.

"He's the center of the *effitte* trade in that whole part of the neighborhood," Rose added. "I've worked out his main centers, but they're scrubbing and running tonight."

"You think you can knock them while their windows are open," Colin said. "How many spots?"

"Four."

He shook his head. "And there's three of us."

"We've got a plan for Kai and Delmin to be in the mix," Veranix said.

"Your skinny friend, in this? Can he handle it?"

"He's tough," Rose said. "And he's got a specific job. So will you and yours."

"Mine?" Colin asked. "You want all the Sons of Tyson?"

"I really wish you hadn't chosen that name."

"I didn't, really, but it's done."

"How many of your folks can you spare?" Rose asked.

"Honestly, none," Colin said. "Listen, we're already in the squeeze here. We're basically holding on to a few blocks that were the Rabbit's, or the Princes', and the war is coming. We're not part of the truce, so—"

"So you're free to help us knock Fenmere in the nose."

"And we'll get crushed on both sides, then."

"What if the Sons don't get any blame from Fenmere?" Rose asked. "Or give him any sense that the Thorn is working with you?"

"How would you do that?"

"I have a plan."

He looked to Veranix. "I didn't think plans were your thing."

"She's got a knack for them, and I'm learning to listen."

"Then I'll listen as well. But I don't know—"

"How can we convince your people to join in?" Rose asked.

Colin laughed. "All we have to do is say, 'help the Thorn' and they'd be in. But they're not seeing the whole picture. That's what I got to do."

"So what do you need?" Veranix asked him.

"I told you, a war for Aventil is coming. The other gangs are going to press us soon. I'm going to need the Thorn's support for that."

"I'll be there."

Colin nodded. "I shouldn't ask. I made a promise to your father to keep you out of all this. To get you to finish your schooling. So I need you to . . . I need you to not . . ." Colin wasn't sure what he would need. Or what he wanted Veranix to do. But he knew that a good portion of the loyalty to him right now was balanced on a knife edge, based entirely on him having the Thorn's ear. When the war came, he would need to leverage that to his advantage. "But I may need you, as much as I hate the idea of it."

"We'll work it out," Veranix said. "And tonight?"

"Tell me this plan," Colin said. "And we'll bring it to the crews."

Jutie had to move through South Maradaine carefully, block by block, dodging constables every other step. He had managed to filch a pair of shoes that didn't fit too badly, and grabbed a coat and pants off of someone's rooftop wash line. He had taken most of the morning just getting through Wheaton and halfway across Laramie, until he was too exhausted to keep at it. He found a tenement with signs for apartments for rent, the whole place tumbledown and neglected, easy to see why half the flops were empty. He broke the lock on one door, hid in a closet and let himself sleep for a few hours.

The sun was all but down when he woke up, and he finished the trek past the creek, and into Aventil.

Hallaran's Boys patches.

Head down, keeping his arm covered and paying no one any mind, he crossed through their blocks and made a point to not give anyone a reason to start something with him. Last thing he needed right now.

It was well past nightfall, still bright with the nearly full white moon, the light just kissed by the sliver of red from the other moon, when he got to Rose Street and the Turnabout.

He slipped into the alley to the back door. Perhaps a bit too cautious, but there were a few sticks milling about near the front door. Were they looking for him? If they knew he had escaped, if they knew who he was, surely this would be the first place they'd look.

But he had to get to the Princes. The only place he'd be safe.

Through the back door, he crept down the hallway to the taproom, so he could check if there were any sticks around, and still run if he needed to.

Taproom was full of Princes. And two faces he knew well enough. He went to their table and sat down.

"Deena, Tooser. Good to see you."

Tooser's eyes went wide, and he grabbed Jutie in a great embrace, lifting him off the ground.

"Jutes!" he shouted. So much for being discreet. "You rutting got out of the Quarry?"

"Shush!" Jutie said, waving Tooser down. Tooser put him back on the ground, let him sit back down. Deena slid a beer and striker over to him.

"I take it you didn't exactly finish your stint," she said.

"No," Jutie said, eagerly taking up the sandwich and shoving it into his mouth.

"You broke out of the Quarry?" Tooser asked. "How the blazes did you do that?"

A couple more Princes sat down. "What, he broke out?"

"How'd you do it?"

"Easy, easy," Deena said, waving them down. "Let the boy breathe." That was when Jutie noticed she had captain stars on her arm. She must have moved up since he'd been gone.

"I didn't so much break out," Jutie said. "As I was in the right place when a breakout happened."

"I heard word of that," A Prince Jutie didn't know said. "A few real blockers blew out the wall, something like that? Like some real nasty fellows."

Jutie told the story quick of how it all went down, and was interrupted with questions again and again, as more beers and strikers were brought to him.

"Listen," he said when a fourth beer was brought. "Those five, they all got a grudge against the Thorn. We need to warn him."

Everyone went a bit quiet.

"What's wrong with you all?" he asked. "Listen, where's Colin, he'll know—"

The silence shifted to awkward looks, everyone suddenly paying attention to the ceiling or the floor.

"The blazes?"

"Listen, Jutie," Deena said. "We're not exactly square with the Thorn and . . . and Colin . . ."

"Colin betrayed us, Jutes," Tooser said. "I wish it weren't so, but he stood right here, in front of all of us, and admitted to it."

"What?" That was rutting impossible. "What did he do?"

"Broke the truce, crossed Waterpath with his arm showing."

Tooser added. "Went to some of Fenmere's boys and beat them to the rutting bone."

Deena scowled at Tooser, and then said. "Made a whole mess of trouble for all of us here."

"So where is he? What happened?"

"They burned his stars off," Deena said. "And he walked out of here, started his own patch of misfits, but with the Thorn by his side."

"We gotta let them know—"

"Jutie," Deena said fiercely. "We don't gotta do anything for that traitor. And the Thorn is not one of ours."

"No, he—"

"Maybe once, we saw him as an ally. But he's with Colin, and they are *not* with the Princes. But you are, aren't you, Jutes?" She took his hand and squeezed.

"Of course I am," he said, though he was still very confused. How could Colin, of anyone, betray the Princes? And with the Thorn? They had a new gang here? He had had too many beers already to think through all this clearly.

"We're real glad to hear that, Jutie," she said. She looked up and nodded.

Two pairs of hands rested on Jutie's shoulders.

"Juteron," someone said from behind. Jutie couldn't turn around because the strong hands were keeping him in his chair. An old man came around into his view—one of the Basement Bosses, but Jutie wasn't sure which. Giles? Nints? "We're really happy to see you come home. And the Turnabout, the Princes, they are your home, yes?"

"That's what's on my arm," Jutie said, though only because he knew it was the smartest thing to say. He needed to keep his head about him, especially now.

"So happy to hear it. So why don't you come down with me, and you can tell Vessrin and the others everything that's happened to you. We want to hear every detail."

"Sure, sure," Jutie said, standing as the two bruisers behind him let him get up. "Happy to." He'd never been asked to talk to the bosses before, and, right now, it was the last thing he wanted to do, but he knew the score.

"Good," the boss said. Blazes, which one was he? "We need you safe and out of sight for a while. Until things cool down. You understand."

"Sure, sure," Jutie repeated. He had no idea what this was all about, but he'd tell the bosses everything they needed to know.

"Deena," Giles-or-Nints said. "Take a crew and make a pass around Cantarell Square. Just in case there's any noise out there."

"On it," she said, getting to her feet. She signaled to some folks and they went out. Tooser gave Jutie one last wave as he left with her.

"Let's go, Jutie," the boss said. "And we'll have a good, long chat."

As they took him down to the basement, Jutie started to wonder just what went down with Colin and the Thorn, and where they were right now. He was a Prince, loyal to the mark on his arm, but even still, Colin was his cap, and he knew the Thorn was the right sort. What could have made Colin turn against the Princes, start his own patch? If Jutie had been out, would he have stayed like Tooser and Deena? Or would he be next to Colin, elbow to elbow in whatever fight he was in now.

"AND AS YOU GO OFF INTO YOUR EVENINGS, TO YOUR HOMES, YOUR families, or whatever else you might have planned, take with you, not just the blessings of Saint Julian, who stands watch over your souls in your troubled days, but hopefully the wisdom he imparts. Take with you the choice of peace. There is no end to what you can accomplish if you put peace, and your capacity to open yourself to it, at the forefront of every choice you make. Blessings be with you."

This was Reverend Pemmick's typical ending for evening services, and every night he hoped to reach certain members of the congregation with it. Every night there were a few youths from the so-called Knights of Saint Julian, a gang that had evolved from a former reverend's personal muscle. That reverend had, apparently, not taken his vows as seriously as most of the clergy of the Church of Druthal.

Tonight there was a typical scattering of the Knights among the congregation, and a few representatives from the other gangs in Aventil. Pemmick knew most of them by name, learned each of their struggles as best he could, and offered whatever counsel he felt comfortable with. If he could get any of them to move on to a stable, law-abiding life, that was a victory, of course, but the best he let himself hope for was comfort and a chance at absolution for their souls.

It was what everyone who walked through those doors deserved.

Today there was an uncommon visitor, hanging in the back of the pews during his sermon, and staying there as many filed out. Uniformed members of the Constabulary rarely sat in, and this lieutenant had never taken the time. As more folks left—though Pemmick did note that Fortill and some of his closest crew were hanging back—Pemmick approached the lieutenant cautiously.

"Always grateful to see someone new come in for worship," he said. "Or are you here for reasons beyond your own spiritual guidance?"

"I'll accept guidance from wherever it might come, Rev," Lieutenant

Benvin said. "Though I can tell you, listening to that speech, I don't know if you have it to give."

"You take issue with a message of peace?"

"Issue with the idea that we have a choice," Benvin said. "Too often, the choice is made for you."

"I am aware. But every day we can choose to try."

"That what you're up to with these washes?" he asked, gesturing to Fortill's group. "Or the Thorn?"

"I tend to every member of the faith who comes in here," Pemmick said.

"Please have the decency not to insult my intelligence," Benvin riposted, pointing a jabbing finger. Pemmick saw Fortill jerk forward at that, but only a bit. Good. The boy was learning patience, awareness, even through his hot temper.

"Would you have me deny that to any member of this community?"

"I would have you not harbor or protect the lawless."

"I would argue that the laws of Druthal do not supersede the mandate of the church. 'Souls come be—'"

"'Before the standing of man, for the judgment of God and their saints will stand forever, while mortal man must struggle his finite time.'" Benvin sighed. "I do know my studies."

"Very good. And that is why you came? For further study?"

"Listen," Benvin said. "For what it's worth, while I would just as soon iron the Thorn and have him face the justice of the bench and throne, I do know what isn't justice."

"And that would be?"

"That would be getting killed by the folks he put down before. The five who just escaped Quarrygate."

"Former enemies escaped the prison?"

"So, if you see him, Rev," Benvin said. "If he comes to you for . . . spiritual guidance. Let him know that trouble is coming his way. And either way, I'll still see him soon." Benvin gave a casual nod of his head and put his cap back on as he left.

Fortill scurried up. "Rev, you sure you don't want us to give that stick what for?"

"Fortill, the man is doing his job and serving the community, in the way that his ethos tells him he must. As do I, as do you."

"I don't rightly know what that means, Rev."

"That means he is being the best good man he can be, as I strive to help you be."

"Yeah, yeah," Fortill said. "But that stick shouldn't be giving you business, no. Not for."

"He was not," Pemmick said. "You can do me a service, though."

"Name it, Rev, the Knights are here for you."

They said that so often, and Pemmick wished it brought him comfort.

"Some dangerous fellows have escaped from Quarrygate. Let me know if you hear word of their whereabouts or intentions."

"Sure thing, Rev," he said. With a wave, he signaled his crew to head out.

Pemmick went to the Absolution booth, in case anyone came seeking the rite from him. It would also let him be prepared in case Veranix Calbert came to him tonight, for either guidance or aid. Regardless, in the quiet moments of the evening, Pemmick would continue to focus his prayers for the saints to aid the angry, blessed young man on whatever troubles he faced tonight.

THE OLD CANAL WAS THE PUB THE SONS OF TYSON USED AS THEIR clubhouse, but Colin had Veranix wait with Mila up in a flop above a sew-up office while he gathered his folks up. This seemed to be the real home for the Sons of Tyson, and where Colin and few others would crash for the night. Mila paced about nervously, having put down the sacks she had brought along as part of her plan.

"You all right?"

"Yeah," she said. Even through her Rose masking, though, her face told a different story. Why was she spooked? This was her plan. "What is this gang to you?"

"They're Colin's," he said.

"Yeah, but, they're called the Sons of Tyson. I take it that's your old family name. You and Colin."

"Our dads were the Tyson Brothers back in the day, I'm given to understand," Veranix said. "Not too unlike your Rynax friends."

"So it's a name that means something to you. These folks in the Sons, they're literally fighting in your name."

"It's not like I've ever been Veranix Tyson, if that's what you mean."

She moved around to force him to face her; he hadn't even been aware that he had been avoiding looking right at her.

"My point is, these folks, they didn't just bond together under Colin. It's not *his* legacy that excites them. It's yours."

"I don't have a legacy," Veranix said. "I don't even know what you mean."

"Of course you do, don't you—" She shook her head. "You didn't grow up on these streets, right?"

"I grew up on the road," Veranix stressed. "Town to town, city to city."

"Legacy, family, it's everything. Do you know why Asti Rynax first trusted me, instead of chasing me off? Because he knew who my father was. My name, my legacy opened that door."

"I'm not—"

"And he—your cousin—he acknowledged you, the Thorn, as his kin. That you *come from here*. That's what matters to them, and why they gather under his banner."

"It's a street gang, not a duchy."

"It's the same to them." She took his hand and squeezed. "I'm saying this because in a moment, Colin's going to bring them in here, and they're going to do a thing you need. I saw how they looked at you in the Canal."

"And that's the idea, right?"

She nodded. "They're going to let you lead them. That's a serious responsibility you're going to take on."

"What are you—" Veranix did not understand. "This was your plan."

"You remember Tarvis? Peeky and Nikey?"

He nodded. The kids in Seleth who had helped them out when

Veranix had been exhausted and they needed a place to rest. "They called you Miss Bessie, right?"

"They were Bessie's Boys. I was supposed to be in charge of them, to lead them, and I failed. Some got killed, some got hurt, and some went to whoever would take them. I lost them, and most of them lost each other, because I didn't take care of them."

"So what are you telling me to do?"

"Take this seriously. Take *them* seriously. Some of them could get hurt tonight. Or killed. And you 've got to lead them, and that means *being* a leader to them."

"I . . . no, that's Colin's job. I can't . . . he's the chief of this gang. I've got to give him that authority."

"But—"

"He's already lost so much protecting me. It's Sons of Tyson because he's protecting me. He stood up against the Princes, broke the truce, all that . . . for me. If anyone is Bessie, it's him. And I'm . . . I don't know. Tarvis."

She laughed at that.

"Far from."

Colin came into the loft with about two dozen folks, almost all of them with a burn scar on their arm or cheek to match Colin's burnt Prince tattoo. Former Princes or Orphans or Kickers or what have you.

"It's really him," one of them whispered.

"Told you," another said.

"We don't have a lot of time," Veranix said, using a hint of magic to alter his voice. "Rose and I have a plan to hit one of Fenmere's top captains, and hit him hard, but it's got to be tonight. And I can't do it without you all."

"We're with you, Thorn!"

"I appreciate that," Veranix said. "And Colin, I'm happy that you've brought your people here to help out with this. Couldn't be done without you."

Colin looked a bit perplexed. "We do what we need to, right?"

"We do," Veranix said. Then he understood the point Mila was trying to make, what she was trying to tell him. He had to take care of these people, like they were his own. They were about to go fight for him out of loyalty to Colin, loyalty to his family name, loyalty to an idea of what Aventil had been. He had to pay that loyalty back. "So when we go in there, there's going to be Fenmere's drugs, there are going to be ledgers and papers, and there's going to be cash. Here's how it's got to go. The drugs will need to be destroyed."

There was an air of disappointment in the room at that. Not clear if some of them wanted the drugs to sell themselves, or to use them. Either way, Veranix wouldn't have that.

"Destroyed how?" one asked. The woman who had been sitting at Colin's right arm in the Old Canal.

"Rose and I will handle that," Veranix said. "We're also taking the books and ledgers. But the money, that's all yours."

That got nods and murmurs of approval. Especially from Colin.

"So you say you got a plan," Colin said. "Big part of that plan needs to be to make sure grief doesn't come back on us, or across Waterpath at all. Because as soon as any crosses the 'path, the other gangs will know it was us and all crack down together."

"Got that covered," Mila said. "No one will know that the Sons of Tyson helped us out."

"Or blame it on any other gangs in Aventil," Colin stressed. "Any fire poured on them will flash back on us."

"Or that either," Mila said, picking up one sack, dumping its contents on the floor. "Like I said, there's a plan."

She picked up the other sack and dumped it out as well, making a messy pile of University of Maradaine school uniforms.

"Suit up, kids, you're going back to school."

CHAPTER SEVEN

KAIANA DID NOT ASK QUESTIONS—nor did she even want to ask—about how and from where Mila had managed to steal a few dozen school uniforms with only an hour's notice. When Delmin pressed, Mila made it clear that this had not been something she had just come up with off the top of her head.

"First off, the security of the campus launderers is pathetic," Mila had said. "The staff is constantly just picking up dirty uniforms and bedding, dropping off clean ones, and no one pays them any mind, nor are they paying serious mind to their inventory. There's a lot of assumption with anyone going in, picking up, dropping off, that they're supposed to be there. You throw on a work smock and grab a bundle of clean uniforms, no one questions you. So I've been building up a stock in case we needed them."

"Yes, but . . . why did you think we'd need them?" Delmin asked.

"You never know what might be useful. And uniforms are a terrific tool for anyone planning a job. Someone's wearing a uniform, most people see only that. They don't remember faces, just someone in a school uniform. Perfect anonymity."

Despite that assurance, Kaiana felt as conspicuous as all blazes wearing a Ladies' College uniform as she left campus out the east gates into Dentonhill. She was a still a brown-skinned girl with Napolic features, and no anonymity of a uniform would hide that.

It did not help having a tiny Delmin in her coat's breast pocket.

"I need to study this more, because this is fascinating," Delmin said as she walked. "I'm carrying a good ten pounds of boom powder, and I weigh about a hundred thirty pounds, yet clearly neither I nor what I was holding in shrinking still maintain that weight."

"Will you shut it?" Kaiana whispered. "This is already strange enough without your voice coming out of my clothes."

"I'm sorry, it's just . . . my mind is reeling."

"Reel quietly," she said. "And haven't you done this before?"

"That was an accident, and in an urgent situation. I didn't really have an opportunity to reflect on it."

"Shush." Kaiana nodded and smiled as she passed a pair of men she hoped didn't think she was a complete madwoman. Of course, it would be better that they thought her a madwoman rather than assume she was walking through Dentonhill as part of a wild, insane scheme of a coordinated attack against one arm of Fenmere's drug empire.

It was insane, but she was letting herself believe it could really work. That they could, in one night with a well-executed strike, cripple a large section of the *effitte* trade in Dentonhill. They could remove an enormous amount of the vile junk from of the neighborhood, protect the people that it would hurt from themselves.

That was worth a bit of madness.

Saints, in moments like this, she realized how well she understood Veranix. As much as he infuriated her, the foolish risks he took, here and now, she was just as willing to jump in with both feet.

Because tonight they could win.

And her father was awake.

"Is it clear?" Delmin whispered.

"If it wasn't, that would have been disastrous," she told him. She stepped into an alley, bending down as if to lace her boot. "I'm about a half a block from the stable. Let's move you to my hand."

"Happily," he said, climbing out of her pocket. He was not wearing a school uniform, as Mila had insisted that it would be a terrible disguise for someone who is supposed to be wearing one. Mila had dressed him in a buckled vest and tight slacks, the same crimson as she and Veranix were wearing, as well as a scarf masking his face. Delmin had said he looked ridiculous, but she caught him admiring himself when he thought she wasn't looking.

"The three of us in the same colors makes it easier for us to spot each other," Mila had said. "Especially if chaos breaks out."

Matching colors was why Kaiana's uniform had the crimson and white hat and scarf of a finance student. Not that she would be hard to spot in a crowd.

"What's the time?" he asked.

"I just heard them ring quarter before eight bells. Assuming Vee and Mila are in position, as well as Colin and his people, everything is set to go at the eight bells ring." She glanced around, and spotted a few other folks in university uniforms. Colin's gang. Things were ready. "Can you get in place and back out in time?"

"Think so," he said, hopping onto her bare knee. Why were the skirts of the Ladies' College uniforms so short? He looked down and seemed to realize he was on her skin, and his tiny face turned bright red. "I, uh . . . sorry . . . that is . . ."

"Just breathe and calm down," she said.

"Yes. Sorry."

She picked him up and stood back up. He grabbed onto the cuff of her coat while she cupped her hand. "You'll be great. Don't worry."

He said something that was too muffled for her to hear, which she hoped didn't matter. She had to start walking, as there were a couple tough bruisers who had come out of the stable coming in her direction. Definitely the type who worked for Fenmere.

Her heart jumped to her throat as she walked, and her palms began to sweat. Having Delmin cupped inside her hand didn't help at all. She nodded and smiled as she passed them, hoping that she looked just like a normal college student—as much as she could—and they wouldn't really make any note of her.

"Coming up on it," she whispered. The stable door was shut, but it had a drainage sluice at the bottom of the door. Saints only knew how nasty that was, but it was an open path for someone Delmin's size. "Get ready."

Three more steps, and, after giving him a tap as a final warning, she let him go. She felt him jump from her hand, bounce off her skirt, and then he was gone. She took a few more steps before daring a glance back.

No sign of Delmin. Good.

She kept on walking, to put herself in the position Mila had assigned her. The oddly shaped tenement wedged into the tiny triangular lot between Price, Brown, and Shade. The building loomed imposingly, an eyesore of gray stone covered in years upon years of paint and paper jobs. The main door into the building was broken on its hinge, hanging limply open and plastered with remnants of papers whose purpose had been lost to time. Nothing and no one impeded Kaiana's entry into the lobby, and the only thing slowing her ascent to the roof was the disgraceful state of the stairs. Every few steps were cracked or broken, and on the third floor there was an impossibly thin girl lying insensate across the stairwell, somehow looking far too young and incredibly old all at once. The vial in her pale fingers confirmed what Kaiana suspected: she was deep into the *effitte*. Kaiana wanted to help the poor girl and kick her down the steps at the same time. She was a victim of her own villainy, Kaiana knew.

Your father is awake. The thought drummed through her head. She still didn't know how to deal with that. A problem for tomorrow. But tomorrow she would have to go out to the Lower Trenn and see him. That was without question.

The roof was only a tiny space, with the bare posts for a drying line that didn't exist. A satchel hung on one of those posts, with a tiny card attached.

For The Vine.

Kaiana's grudging admiration and gnawing annoyance with Mila were both continuing unabated.

The satchel contained a change of clothes, including a heavy coat, cap, and scarf in the matching scarlet. It also had a lensescope, a whistle, a handful of labeled boom powder balls, and a couple of gardening tools that could serve as a truncheon in a pinch.

Saints, the girl did know how to prepare.

Kaiana changed clothes in a hurry—the night was sultry hot, and she didn't want to wear the coat, but it looked like it could keep a knife from finding her ribs, so she decided to put it on. She crouched low so she could just look over the ledge to the streets below.

As promised, she was in an excellent position. To the west of her, Brown stretched out to Waterpath, and halfway down she could see the grocer, and the office above it. To the southwest, down Shade Street, the livery stable where she had left Delmin. A few folks in Uni uniforms were clustered about down the street, including one standing watchfully at the corner of Shade and Price. Kaiana looked through the scope and confirmed: Colin, in a place to move in whichever direction he was most needed.

To the south, Price stretched out, with the last two targets in sight: the stationary post that was the front for the counting room, and the dry goods shop that held a storeroom of *effitte* in its basement. More Sons of Tyson in school uniforms scattered up and down the street.

No sign yet of Veranix or Mila. But both were supposed to be out of sight until the moment.

Church bells from Saint Olivar's rang out, off to the north. Eight bells.

This was the moment.

EVERY STEP DOWN THE STAIRS FROM THE SLEEPING ROOMS AT THE Buck's Point was absolute agony. The sew-up had told Nags that her foot wasn't broken, and she should walk on it. "It's just fear that is keeping you off it."

Fear of the fact that it rutting hurt like blazes.

So the owner of the Bucks—who could barely stand a Jelidan girl like her staying under his roof—he said he wasn't bringing meals up when she could walk just fine.

He was bringing up to her boys, who could not get out of their beds. Burt might not ever get out, they said.

"Heya, markie," she said to the man behind the bar as she eased her way onto the stool. "Serve me whatever you got in a pot, hmm, and a crack of bread?"

"I didn't understand a word of that," the barman said. "Everything out of your mouth is just—"

"She said stew and bread, don't be a tosser," a man said as he took the stool next to her. "Bring beers all around as well." He pointed to himself, her, and the man sitting on her other side.

"I know you bents?" she asked them.

"Nah," the one on the other side said. "I'm Jendle, he's Lemt. We used to deal and hash a few blocks up, out of the Dogs' Teeth."

"Good and joll for you both," she said. "Why're you boxing me?"

"Heard you and your boys got a real crackdown from our mutual friend," Lemt said. "Thought you could use a drink on someone else, a kind word?"

"You baiting a hook to dance in my skivs or something?"

"Wouldn't be opposed—" Jendle started.

"Hey, no," Lemt said firmly. "We ain't looking to make you no trouble, Miss N'gašbhi."

She perked up. He hadn't mangled her name too badly there, and at least he tried. "Look at you, Mister Lemt. Wooo, I almost thought I was back in Tisa Ahcke."

"We just want to be polite," Jendle said.

"Just buy my dinner and beer it is?"

"And hear what happened. Your story," Lemt said. "The Thorn has cracked up a bunch of us, especially the two of us, and we just—"

"Wait a breath," she said. "Oh, I have heard your story. The Dogs' Teeth, mmm-ha, yeah." These two got thoroughly thrashed by the Thorn twice, and the first time they gave up their boss, who also got thrashed by the Thorn.

Beers got put in front of them, with the barman scowling hard at Nags as he put her bowl of stew in front of her.

"So we've been where you are," Lemt said. "We're trying to—"

"What, get back in the grace of the bosses?" She laughed hollowly as she spooned up some of the stew. Bland as anything, like everything else in this town. "That's a dream of a dying man."

"Maybe it is," Jendle said. "But we're thinking of how to get the Thorn, and that would put us in a good position, you know?"

"Sure, if you got him," she said. "I mean, the stories on him are true. Blazes, you know better than any. My boy Burt is the toughest cliker I know, and the Thorn put him down like an rotten apple. He's up there in a bed now, we'll see if he makes it another sunrise."

"We know," Lemt said. "But we've been talking to everyone who tangled with him, putting things together. The where and when, what he said, what he did, all that wash."

"He got into your bunker looking to get hired, right?" Jendle asked. "You saw a face that wasn't his, right?"

"Saw a face that melted away when he became the Thorn in front of my eyes," she said. She took another bite of flavorless stew.

"Eye color?" Lemt asked.

"Umm . . . blue," she said after thinking about it for a moment. "Yeah, he had blue eyes that really stood out."

"Hair?"

"Dark. Real short and scrappy. But that's not his face."

"Yeah," Jendle said. "But we've heard stories of a lot of not-his-faces."

"And we figure," Lemt said, opening up a charcoal sketch notebook, "with enough of a sense of what his face *isn't*, we can figure out what his face is."

"You're wasting time," she said. "Drink your beers and be grateful you still get to draw breath."

"One last thing," Jendle said. "He use a name with you all?"

"Yeah," she said. "Nix."

That seemed to mean something to them both, to the degree they slapped hands over her head.

"Rutting Racquin bastard!" Lemt said.

"Wait, what?"

"All right, listen," Lemt said. "From all we put together, the Thorn might be a student or a teacher at the Uni, or someone living in Aventil."

"And a couple of times he made one of his little jokes while knocking someone down," Jendle went on. "And from that, someone thought he sounded Racquin or Kellirac. Another bloke said he even said 'by Jox' once, which is a real Racquin thing to say."

"All right," she said.

"And so we've been keeping eye on some folks in the campus lists, in the neighborhood, who are quins. We got it narrowed down, and 'Nix' just cinches it."

"So now we know," Jendle said quietly. "That the Thorn is—"

Whatever name he was about to say was lost to the great booming sound outside, so loud it knocked all three of them off their stools. Nags landed on her bad foot, which twisted as she fell. She screamed in pain, but no one noticed. She could barely hear herself, her ears were ringing so bad.

Lemt helped her up and onto the stool. The rest of folks in the Buck's Point were all staggering to get to their feet, looking about in confusion.

"It's *him*," Jendle said. "Let's get in the mix."

"Right," Lemt said. He looked to Nags. "You all right?"

"I'll manage," she said.

He dropped a ten crown note on the bar. "You take care of her, hear?" he told the barman. He drew a long blade out from under his coat. "And don't let me hear otherwise."

Jendle smacked Lemt on the arm. "Let's get on it."

"Right," Lemt said, and the two of them dashed out.

The barman rubbed his face as he snatched the note. Looking around cautiously, he asked, "So you need anything else?"

She took another bite of stew. "Another beer, for one," she said. "And maybe for you people to learn how to spice things proper."

THIS NIGHT WAS GOING TOO SLOWLY.

Jullick had no idea how this office had even collected so much paper, nor did he honestly understand why they made a point to hold on to it, keep it orderly, especially since it was so incriminating.

But it had been made perfectly clear to him that the office needed to be emptied, and the papers needed to be packed up and brought to the new office tonight, as well as clearing out his drophouses and counting rooms.

It would have been a laborious evening, regardless, but one his fellows could have done with a certain amount of speed if Jads hadn't been hovering the whole time.

"Your files are an absolute mess," she said. "Who taught you how to organize these?"

"No one," he said. "We didn't all have fancy educations."

She rolled her eyes and waved for him to get back to the file drawer. "Get this sorted. We're burning off moonslight."

"You don't need to be here," he told her. "My people have this."

"Your people were the ones who apparently recruited the Thorn and brought them into their drophouse," she said. "So forgive me if I am not too impressed with either them or their acumen."

"Acumen," he replied with a heavy sigh. Jads had far too high of an opinion of herself, and her role in the Fenmere organization. Jullick was fairly certain she did not have any authority over him.

But she had been sent—*sent!*—by Corman and Gerrick to oversee the evacuation of the offices, storerooms, and countinghouses he controlled.

He understood, of course. The Rosy Nan's crew had been careless, and that compromised things. Bobba was furious, both that her people had been tricked, but also that they had been so thoroughly whooped. All of them except one were laid up, barely able to stand, and that one— Nags—was limping about pretty badly. She was the only one able to walk into his office and explain what had happened.

The Thorn had crushed them and taken everything. Not just the coin and drugs, but their ledgers and books. Which they all knew meant it was just a matter of time before he came crashing through the doors of this office, or the storerooms. Had to move tonight.

"Connie!" he called out.

Contanik, Jullick's usual right hand, came in from the outer office. "Yeah, boss?"

"Get one of the wagons ready at the back door, and bring in some boys to get these crates."

"Sure thing, boss," Connie said.

"We got word where the new storehouses are?"

"Last I heard they were loading crates up, but wanted to wait until it got a bit darker to roll."

"No, we should roll now," Jullick said. "Or as soon as we can."

"Streets are a bit crowded out there," Connie said. "Was there a Uni match of some sort tonight?"

"Not that I know of, but I don't follow that sort of thing," Jullick said.

"Why?" Jads asked.

"Lots of Uni kids about in the street. Thought there might have been a thing and they're looking for a pub to crawl through."

"Maybe," Jullick said with a shrug. "Either way, we can't be sitting around, we need to . . ."

Jads was at the window. "This isn't right at all."

"What do you mean?"

"You *never* see Uni kids like this in Dentonhill, not in this patch. When I was there—"

Rutting blazes, Jads was about to go on one of her "when I worked at the Uni" tears. Jullick didn't know how much of it he could take.

"Students wouldn't come out to here for anything. Not in droves."

"Why not?"

"Because the pubs here are run-down, serve sewage, and dangerous," Jads said. "Which is why they go into Aventil or Gelmoor. Maybe a few brave souls, but . . . there's a couple dozen down there."

He came and looked out the window. Like she said, groups of Uni students were milling about. They were in groups of three or four, but there were too many groups for it to be a coincidence.

"Blazes, I don't know what that is, but I know that can't be good."

"What do you want to do, boss?" Connie asked.

"Who do we got in shouting distance who's ready to scrap?"

"I got four boys here, to load up the wagon. They'll scrap fine in a pinch, but . . ."

"They'll do. Send someone to run to the stables, tell them to get ready to punch out and move hard, and—" There was something else.

"Sticks," Jads said quietly.

"We already greased them, they're out of our hair for the night."

"We need them in here, in *their* hair," Jads said. "The whole point is to not draw undue attention to what we're working in these blocks. That's why we're clearing out. We can't be starting scraps in the streets now."

"But—"

"Try to keep up," she said. "If we get the sticks in here to clean out those Uni kids, or whoever they are, then we just have to be patient and move out before—"

A deafening boom rocked through the street, and the windows shattered, glass flying into the office. Jads screamed, but Jullick was in too much pain to care. Shards had sliced his face and coat.

"Move, move!" Connie shouted. He and two other guys stormed in, grabbing Jullick to pull him out.

"Get the boxes!" Jads snapped, blood dripping from her arm, scrapes all over her face. "This is going to be a real scrum."

"But—" Jullick said.

"This is a hit," she said, grabbing a box. "Contanik, get everyone you have to start knocking down anyone in a Uni uniform. Don't care. Jullick, grab a box, load it in the cart, and then run to the counting room."

"Why should I—"

"Priorities!" she snapped. "Evidence, money, product. In that order. Our own survival is well below that. If we live but lose any of those, we won't enjoy survival."

"Don't you shout at me, Jads, I—"

She dropped the box and grabbed him, pulling him to the ground. Before he could scream at her, there was a terrible crack. An arrow lodged into the far wall, then another right behind it.

"What—"

"The Thorn!" she shouted.

"Connie!" he called out.

Connie raced in, drawing out a club. "Boss, we got to—"

"Boss? Oh, that's lovely."

Jullick looked up and saw him perched in the hole that had been the window. Saints, it was really him: the Thorn, cloak flowing in the breeze, bow drawn, and that infernal rope everyone talked about coiled around his arm.

"Don't get up," the Thorn said. "Tonight's your reckoning."

CHAPTER EIGHT

DELMIN HAD REALIZED HIS ERROR far too late.

Of course, his real error was agreeing to take part in this wild scheme, but he had long since abandoned any hope of being a voice of reason with Veranix and the others. He doubted he could even call himself the reasonable one anymore. He was talked into doing this, after all.

Shrinking himself intentionally turned out to be relatively easy. He hadn't been entirely honest with Mila—while the first time had been an accident, he had instinctively understood how he had done it, and done further research into the theory behind it. Getting small, that was not a problem. Hiding in Kaiana's coat as she delivered him to the livery stable was oddly pleasant, while also kind of terrifying, and it had given him a chance to recover from the magical toll of shrinking. Even sneaking into the livery was a very simple matter, though he had under-estimated the time it would take him to cover the distance across the stable floor, or even what a stable floor would look like at this size. That was a particularly horrifying journey, but at least he had no trouble finding the stores of *effitte* that were being loaded onto wagons. This was the place he needed to be.

No, the error was that he had four canisters of "boom powder" attached to his body, which were also tiny, and he had no idea how he was going to deploy them and get them back to "normal" size without being spotted, or caught in the ensuing explosion.

He could throw them, but at this size he couldn't throw very far.

The bigger problem was if they exploded at their current size, in theory they would be nothing but a little pop. Making this entire venture fruitless. At least, that was consistent with how Delmin understood the theory.

Absolutely nothing of what he had read about shrinking magic gave insight into how it would affect the efficacy of boom powder.

"Boss, where are we going with these?" someone called out.

"Are the wagons loaded?" the man who appeared to be the boss asked.

"First one is," the man responded.

"Then we roll out the first," he said. "It's better if we don't got three wagons going together to the new spot."

"Yeah, but where is the new spot?"

"That's for me to know."

"Damn it, Bryce, don't be a tosser about this."

"I'll ride out with the first," Bryce—the boss—said as he walked over to the wagon. "Get the rest ready to roll, and I'll be back."

Delmin swore quietly to his tiny self. One of the wagons leaving, and they would lose it if he didn't figure out how to do this quickly.

He thought back to one of the passages he read in *Cannel's Handbook for Practical Body Magic*, which had been the most informative text on the subject.

Objects whose size have been altered with you, just like your own body, retain a fundamental "memory," for lack of a better word, of the size they are supposed to be. Magic alterations are in opposition to the natural order, and in the absence of active numinic *infusion, they will revert to normal size in due course.*

"Due course" was doing a lot of work in that passage. Presumably the *numinic* infusion was coming from him—he was keeping himself and everything he was holding at this size, like a tensed muscle, and returning to full size, according to the reading he had done, required just a minimal "push" of *numina* to trigger the action.

That was how he was able to visualize it in his mind, at least—he "pulled" himself in to shrink, and would "push" back to his normal size.

But if he just left the canisters on the wagons, they should revert in short order. However long "short order" was.

"Let's get rolling!" Bryce shouted, and men started to hitch horses to the first wagon, while other men loaded the second and third. No time to waste.

Four canisters, three wagons. So, one for each wagon, and one more for whatever emergency might turn up. Or to not use and return to Veranix's inventory of supplies. No need to be wasteful.

Not much time. Delmin scurried—at his size all he could do was scurry—in the shadows along the stable wall near the second and third wagons, which folks continued to load up with crates presumably filled with *effitte*. He pushed the spring lever on the tops of two of the canisters, which activated the ingenious device inside of clockwork and springs that would trigger the powder in, according to Mila "about four minutes."

That estimate did not fill him with confidence.

He rolled the two canisters, like he was playing eight pins, under the wagons. By a fortunate bit of luck, and perhaps also a hint of skill at eight pins, they stopped rolling in good spots under them.

No time to waste, he ran over to the first wagon. Bryce was about to climb on, and lacking better options, Delmin jumped onto the man's boot and climbed up into the cuff of his slacks.

Madness, madness, madness. How did he get talked into this? How did Veranix do this sort of thing all the time?

As the first wagon started rolling toward the stable door, Delmin scrambled off Bryce and into the wagon bed, glancing back to notice Bryce slapping at his leg.

"Something wrong?" the driver asked.

"Fly or something on me," Bryce said.

The wagon moved into the street, while Delmin kept his attention on the canisters under the other wagons. He couldn't see them at all anymore, they were too tiny.

They were still too tiny.

Blazes.

He clicked the trigger on a third canister and dropped it into the bed with the crates of *effitte*. One less thing to worry about right now. But the other ones hadn't snapped back to full size yet.

Due course. "How bloody long is 'due course,' Cannel? Did you even measure it?"

The mages of the eleventh century who wrote all the textbooks had no sense of rigor.

Time was running out, and those canisters would be useless if he didn't take action.

Just a push, he thought. He could send a wave of magic out, snap them back to normal size before they blew.

The wagon started to turn out into the street. No time left. He drew in the *numina* around him, focused it as best he could, and pushed it out at the wagons.

Everything shifted, and there was a horrible crunching sound as Delmin fell over. He caught himself on the ground before he landed on his face.

The ground.

The cobblestones of the road looked very wrong, and he shouldn't even be near the ground, unless he had fallen off the wagon.

He turned around, and realized that he hadn't fallen off, the back wheels had collapsed under him, and to his horror he understood why.

He was easily twenty feet tall.

Which explained all the screaming in the street around him.

"What the rutting—" Bryce said as he jumped off the rutting wagon. "Who the blazes you think you are?"

"I, um . . ." was all Delmin could think to say as he tried to get on his feet, but the act of standing made him incredibly dizzy. As he attempted to find his balance, he glanced back into the livery.

The other wagons had tipped over, and the canisters were now the size of a large dog.

"Oh no," was all he could say as he ducked—as much as he could— covering his head while attempting to summon enough *numina* to pull himself back down to normal size.

The canisters in the livery exploded in a deafening roar.

THAT BOOM WAS MUCH LOUDER THAN IT SHOULD BE.

Veranix knew he needed to have his attention fully on what was in front of him—Jullick and Jads, two ripe plums ready to be plucked—but the nagging thought that something must have gone terribly wrong for the explosion to have been that loud, for it to have shattered the windows here, a block away.

Damn it, Delmin could have been hurt, or . . .

Further thoughts were put on hold as the fellow with the club dove in at him, swinging hard and true. Veranix was forced to loose the arrow as he jumped out of the way of the blow, not even seeing where it went.

"Get that bastard!" Jullick shouted.

"See, that was my plan for you," Veranix said to Jullick, dodging further swings from the fellow with the club. With a nod to Jads, he added "But I get the both of you for my efforts."

"Not a chance," Jads said.

"I think I have a bit of a chance." He switched his bow for his staff, and blocked the next blow from the club. With a quick parry and sweep, he knocked the man off his feet.

"Guards!" Jads shouted with an impressive roar. "The Thorn is here!" She reached into her coat and threw out a trio of darts, only one of which found its target as the other two went wild. That dart stuck into Veranix's vest without penetrating further.

"Your aim needs some work," he said, whipping out the rope to ensnare her and Jullick together. "But I don't know if you'll have the time."

"I'm not the one out of time," she sneered. "Get him!"

At least half a dozen men charged into the office, all rushing at Veranix. There wasn't space to maneuver in the office, nowhere to dodge, nowhere to go.

Except back out the window.

"Time to fly," he said, jumping backward. He kept hold of the rope, still ensnaring Jullick and Jads, pulling them with them as he dropped to the ground, using just enough magic to sweeten the fall. He landed hard, but not hard enough to hurt himself. He had pulled Jullick and Jads half out the window with him, but they had managed to hold on to the ledge, and those half-dozen men grabbed a hold of them to keep them from falling.

No, he wasn't letting those two go.

With a pulse of magic, he tightened his grip with the rope and yanked, enough force to pull Jads, Jullick and a few of those guards out of the window and crashing them onto the vegetable cart below.

"Get him!" one of the men who had stayed in the office shouted. "The Thorn is here!"

Veranix suddenly realized the street was full of folks with knives, truncheons, and knucklestuffers, all looking at him.

"Hey, now," he said, coiling the rope back to himself. "I know this is a party, but I can't dance with everyone." He readied the staff.

A few of those folks did not hold back at all, jumping at him right away. Veranix knocked them away with relative ease, and that gave the rest a bit more pause.

"A hundred crowns to whoever takes him out!" Jullick yelled as he was helped to his feet. "And get those wagons loaded!"

"Wagons, now?" Veranix asked. "That is very interesting."

Jads was on her feet, pushing the guards toward Veranix. "Kill him!"

Veranix swapped back to the bow, nocking and loosing three arrows quick and hard at the guards around Jads and Jullick. At the same time, a couple of the uniform-clad Sons of Tyson jumped into the fray with the other heavies around Veranix. In a few breaths, the whole of Brown Street was in a full on rumble. Veranix had to tussle with a few more who came at him, which kept him from closing in on Jullick before the hateful little man was able to hobble into an alleyway. Veranix was tempted to blast out with a pulse of magic, flatten the street, but that would probably drain him too hard. Also, surely not every one of these people in the rumble, even the ones coming after him, were really Jullick's people. Some of them might be just innocent folks who couldn't pass up the hundred-crown bounty. He couldn't blame them, and did his best not to hurt them too badly as he knocked his way through.

"Oiya, Thorn!" he heard someone shout. "Get ready to settle up!"

He looked over to see a woman—she looked not unlike Kai, so possibly of Napolic heritage, but easily six feet tall and arms that looked like she could throw a horse—knock two of the Sons to the ground with a single arc of her fist.

"I never opened a bill with you, friend," Veranix said. "Nothing to settle."

"You knocked down my crew at the Rosy," she said as she stalked across the road to him. "All four of them, so I'll knock you down four times!"

Veranix launched an arrow at her, which struck true in her shoulder but didn't slow her down at all. He flipped backward while swapping back to the staff.

"So you must be Bobba," he said when he landed. "Your boys there did warn me about you." He spun the staff and struck at her head.

She caught the staff with her bare hands and ripped it out of his grip.

"You should have listened."

She whipped his staff back at him, cracking him across the jaw. He crumpled down, spitting out blood onto the cobblestone. Another punch from her monster of a fist was coming his way, but he rolled out of the way before she could land it. One hit from this woman was enough, no need for more.

"I really don't have time for this," he said, continuing to put distance between him and her. "Pressing matters and all."

She pulled the arrow out of her shoulder, with as much concern as removing an uncomfortable hat.

"Oh, the matters are going to be pressing, son," she said, putting a knucklestuffer over her fist. "Have no doubt."

EVERYWHERE COLIN COULD SEE, THERE WAS FIGHTING. IT WAS actually pretty incredible. He had heard stories of brawls like this, especially in the neighborhood wars of '94, but he had never seen anything like it.

This is what the truce has been preventing all this time.

"Take out the students!" someone shouted.

"They ain't students!" someone else called out, and when Colin tracked the source of that voice, it was someone who was charging into one of the uniform-clad Sons, spiked knucklestuffer over his fist. Colin, knives out, dove into that scrum, taking down the attacker after they had gotten one punch in.

"You all right?" he asked the kid—Bortie? One of the former Kickers.

"Been hit harder, boss," he answered through bleeding teeth.

"Hit harder back," Colin told him as he pulled Bortie away from another swing from a new attacker. Folks were pouring out of a couple pubs—the Buck's Point on this corner, and the Damned Shoe a bit farther south on Price. The Shoe was where he was trying to get to— Sella and Cainey were leading a few of the younger ones as they beat their way through the thugs and heavies pouring out the doors and alleys.

The countinghouse, and with it the money Veranix had promised the Sons they could keep, was above the Damned Shoe. If nothing else, they needed to take that, or the whole enterprise would be a waste of time.

Bortie was at his right arm, stomping another heavy that had come out of the Buck's. Two more of them came out, one flipping his knives, the other with an old army sword.

"That's him!" the one with the sword said, pointing at Colin.

"Too old, but looks the part," the other said. He flipped one knife and threw it true to Colin's heart in a swift, fluid motion. Colin stepped to one side to dodge it, hoping the knife wouldn't find its way into the back of one of his people.

His people did jump on those two fellows, which let him turn back toward the Damned Shoe. There the fighting was brutal, but he could see Sella was out in front of it. She hadn't seemed like much of a scrapper when he first met her, but here she was knocking fools up and down. In as much as anything could be handled in the here and now, she and hers seemed to have it handled.

He glanced to his right, down Shade Street, and there it was ugly. That's where the whole stable had blown up, and several folks were laid out on the ground amid the smoke and ash. One wagon was tipped over in the middle of the road, and one of his boys was in there, trying to hold off four blokes on his own.

Blazes, his man was standing over Veranix, trying to keep folks off him. Wait, Veranix was supposed to be a block away from here. That wasn't him, but his skinny mage friend. Delmin. Why had Veranix even brought that kid into this, dressed in the same colors?

Colin had to get in there. Running full tilt, he charged up the broken wagon and drove both knives into one of Fenmere's men, just as that bloke had gotten his knife into the Son he was fighting.

Damn, it was Cober.

Cober took a wild swing at one of the other ones, stumbling back as he did. "You think you're gonna stop me?" he shouted.

"All of you are going to wish you didn't wake up today," one of Fenmere's boys said. Colin jumped on him before he could stick another knife in between Cober's ribs.

"You keep your rutting hands off," Colin said, knocking him in the neck. He put that bastard down and got himself in between Cober and the other two. "You holding up?"

"I got my feet down and chin up," Cober said weakly. Colin took that as a sign he was good enough and got to the mage.

"Kid!" Colin said to Delmin. Saints, he was just like Veranix, with his face covered, but that mop of stringy hair was easy to spot. "Can you get up?"

"If I could just fundle some flepping . . ."

He wasn't all right. Time to get him out of here. Uni kid shouldn't even be in a scrum like this.

"Get the kid and yourself out of here," Colin ordered Cober, while fending off the last two of Fenmere's heavies. Knives and clubs came at him, and he got out of their way as best he could, hitting back hard as he could. Something got past his defenses, a sharp slice to his side.

He pushed through the pain, putting down these last two. He glanced back to Cober, who had fallen to one knee, holding the gushing wound in his belly.

"Boss, I . . ." he managed to say.

Damn and blazes.

"Kid, I need you on your feet," Colin said to Delmin. He had to turn back to the rest of the street, as more of those bastards were moving in, and all of his people were down or elsewhere. "Get your magical ass together and get out of here!"

"Boss—" Cober gasped, pointing down the block.

Down on Price, where the worst of the fighting was going on, smoke filled up the street. Was Veranix doing that? Or that girl, Rose? It didn't matter. Colin was hurting, Cober was in a bad way, and the kid—

The kid was gone. He was just here, but now Colin couldn't see him anywhere. And with the smoke clouds drifting onto Shade, there wasn't much seeing anyone.

"Come on," Colin said, grabbing Cober's arm. "We gotta move before—"

Constabulary whistles pierced through the air.

Before that.

CHAPTER NINE

MILA'S SMOKE BOMBS WEREN'T GETTING her anything but confusion. She had gotten in the front door of the tenement, thrown out her smoke, and made her way to the basement where the *effitte* and *efhân* was stored. At least, she had tried. The basement door was more secure than she had thought it would be. When she had scouted through here this afternoon, it looked like a normal door, but it had serious locks and bolting on it, and her attempts to get it open had failed.

Failed long enough that several of Fenmere's guards had come for her. Fellows who were bigger and stronger than her, but she was fast and the tenement hallways were narrow enough to work to her advantage. She slipped past two, kicked open an apartment door as she dropped another smoker. She ran through the apartment—scaring some girl and her cat who were squatting here—and dove out the window.

"Damn, damn, damn," she muttered. Where were they unloading the drugs? How were they doing it? Maybe they weren't even abandoning this storehouse.

Whistles came through. Constabulary. A lot more reactive in this neighborhood than back west. More whistles. She came out the alley back onto Shade Street, which was now a mess of smoke and brawling. No way back into the tenement—not that it would do her any good—

and a bulk of the brawl was around the Damned Shoe. Jullick's people were doing too damn good a job holding their place, and Colin's gang were getting beaten back.

Whistles again. South and east. She saw at least a half-dozen footpatrol regular coming up the street in lock step up Price, and more coming from the side streets. All of them with crossbows up, handsticks at the ready.

"Take 'em all down!" one of the constables shouted, and blunt-tips started flying. One of them cracked into her side, knocking her to the ground.

She swallowed the urge to cry out, but that hurt more than she had been ready for. Even through her thick-lined Rose coat, that hurt like blazes. She clutched at her side as she stumbled getting to her feet.

One of the constables charged her, ready to bring his handstick down on her head. Mila managed to get on her feet and dodge that first swing, but then the next one came across her shoulder. Pain and instinct took control, and she drove a knife into the stick's leg.

He screamed, his own face filled with panic and fear.

"I'm sorry!" she said as she backed away. She didn't know why.

Mila ran.

She bolted away from Price Street, dropping the bloody knife as she ran.

She heard more blunt-tips fly past her head, saw constables clubbing their way through folks out of the corner of her eye.

This wasn't right, it shouldn't have gone like this, she had a *plan*. It was a damned good plan, and yet she couldn't get her job done. Constables pounded on everyone along Price Street, especially the crowd in front of the Damned Shoe. Aventil folks in uniform, Dentonhill toughs, all of them. The sticks knocked everyone down.

She had three smoke shots left in her coat pocket. She hurled them into the street as she kept running, shouting, "Get out, get home!" as she went. The smoke filled up the road, and in moments she couldn't see a damned thing, and hopefully no one could see her, either. She cut left and dashed down Lea Street.

What the blazes had gone wrong? Her plan had been great. Though the sound of the explosion after the eight bells signal *had* been a bit louder than expected. She didn't think she would have felt it like she had down at Price and Vinny. Or that windows would have blown out.

Had she put in too much boom powder? What else had she gotten wrong?

Was it just that Veranix couldn't handle a plan? Was that all it was?

More sticks pressed in from Waterpath, blocking her route. A couple of Sons of Tyson in their university uniforms ran past her, and a few of the Dentonhill heavies were right behind them. The Sons stopped cold when they saw the press of constables, and turned around to have Fenmere's muscle be right on them.

Short work with knives and clubs, blatantly in front of the constables, put and end to those Sons. They didn't even have a chance.

Mila contained her urge to scream as she forced herself into the alley next to, of all things, Rosy Nan's Tea Shop. She had messed up, and now those two were dead. That constable might die. Who else had? Who else would? What had she gotten wrong?

Get a hold of yourself, Mila. She felt that, almost as if it hadn't come from her own head. Almost not her own voice.

It was Asti's voice in her head, reminding her what she needed to do. What had the Rynax boys always said? When the job is skunked, you've got to drive forward. This was skunked, beyond all reckoning. What could driving forward even mean right now?

How could she make it right now?

What would Asti do?

Take care of your family.

That was it. Find the others—Kaiana, Delmin, Veranix—and help them. Get them out, get them safe. Live to fight another day.

"There's that one!" she heard someone shout. At the mouth of the alley, two of Fenmere's goons. She turned around to run the other way, but two more were on the other end.

"The blazes is she?" one asked.

"Dressed like the Thorn," the other said. "Who do you think you are?"

She took her rope off her belt, glancing back to the two coming up behind her, and back to the two in front.

"Every Thorn has a Rose," she said. These bastards were between her and her family, and if nothing else went right tonight, she'd show them what the cost of that would be.

It had been only five minutes, but to Kaiana it had been an eternity, and the blink of an eye. Her knuckles were white from gripping the ledge of the roof, as the chaos and carnage unfolded below her. The explosions were out of control, smoke everywhere. Where Kaiana could see, she saw fighting, all of it horrible.

Mila had been right about one thing—uniforms and costumes did help Kaiana spot her friends and their allies on the ground. Veranix was surrounded on Brown Street, barely holding his own as Fenmere's people came at him from all sides. Delmin had grown to a giant size, and then back to normal as the street blew up. Colin and his people were getting hammered, especially as the constables rolled in. And Mila . . .

Kaiana had lost track of Mila in the smoke.

It looked like the only part that had gone remotely correctly was the stable livery blowing up, but even that was clearly a larger boom than intended. Veranix hadn't stopped the people in the office, the Sons hadn't gotten in the countinghouse, and the constables were beating and arresting everyone.

Gathering herself from the horror of what she was seeing, she reached into the knapsack for the tool she had that might be able to stop it. The point of her placement up here was that she could see everything, and, at least according to Mila's plan, be in a position to signal folks if things were going wrong.

This was pretty damned wrong.

Two of the boom powder balls were labeled "retreat." What were the instructions? Twist the spring on the top, count to five, and throw before it gets hot. She twisted both the spring triggers, counted, and threw the balls as high as she could.

They hadn't gotten hot in her hand. Had she done it wrong? Had she messed up the—

Deafening blasts of green light in the sky disabused her of the notion. The light burst into a hundred pieces that rained down and faded to the streets below.

No one in a ten block radius didn't see that. Which meant that Veranix, Delmin, and everyone else got the signal: time to run.

As she pulled her scarf over her face, Kaiana ran down the stairs, bounding three or four at a time, not letting up until she reached the street. She had to move, had to get out, get back to somewhere safe, and quick. But she couldn't just run. Veranix was in trouble. Delmin was in more trouble. She had to help at least one of them.

She swore profusely as she reached the street. Between the smoke, the fights, and the constables, she saw no way to get through the crowd on Brown Street to Veranix. No way to get to him from here.

There was a path through the mess to Shade Street, especially with several of the Sons of Tyson making their run for it. Kaiana tightened her grip on her truncheon and ran for it, clubbing anyone whose hand got too close to her. She could barely see more than ten feet, but she had to get through.

Someone came out of the smoke, right at her, and she brought down the truncheon hard on whoever it was. She knew she didn't have time to waste on whoever might be coming at her, and it didn't matter who it might be.

Colin caught her arm as it was coming down, and had his knife halfway to her belly before he caught himself.

"Blazes you doing?" he asked. He pulled her out of the way against one of the buildings.

"Getting out!" she said. "Why are you running the wrong way?"

"I've got people here. But you need to get out. Get the Thorn out too."

"He's up on Brown, I . . ." She shook it off. "Delmin. Where is he?"

He looked about. "I pulled some folks off him, but I lost him in the chaos. I need to get to my folks, get them back across the 'path."

She nodded. "Good luck."

"Same."

He went back toward Price, and Kaiana pushed on.

"Del!" she called out. "Where are you?" She couldn't see a damned thing. And she couldn't stay here much longer without getting arrested or killed. "Del!"

A hand grabbed her ankle. She brought up her truncheon but saw immediately it was Delmin, splayed out on the ground in the mouth of an alley. The same alley where he had been perched on her knee not a half hour ago.

"Hey, hey," she said, kneeling down to him. "You all right?"

"Water summon lights to harbor," he mumbled.

She dragged him deeper into the alley. "Can you walk, or—"

"I read," he muttered. "The pull of . . . the system . . ."

Saints, that was not good at all. She had to get him out of here on her own, that was clear. Veranix would have to fend for himself.

Bobba hadn't given Veranix the chance to catch two breaths, let alone focus any magic, or even waste a second drawing his bow. He couldn't even get distance from her. She was strong and stocky, but saints, that woman could move. Any time he got three steps away, she closed the distance and had her meaty fist in his face. He had barely managed to dodge most of her blows, and the ones that landed were brutal.

"Yeah, take him down!" someone shouted.

"She's killing the Thorn!"

Blazes, they might be right.

He took two steps and drew his bow, hoping to be able to get farther away and take a shot, but again she was right on top of him. She ripped the bow out of his hand and tossed it to the side.

"None of your toys," she said.

Whistles shrilled in the distance, Constabulary on their way. And through the smoke and haze, he saw the green fireblasts in the sky. Kaiana called for folks to retreat. The rest of the fight out here must be going just as badly.

The glance upward at the fireblast had been a hint of a mistake, as it put him a half step behind where he needed to be, and Bobba's metal-sweetened fist cracked against his jaw, sending him down.

"Not so tough without your tricks," she said, spitting on him. "Now let's—"

A uniform-clad Son of Tyson leaped on Bobba, screaming wildly as he tried to pummel her head and shoulders. She just scowled, grabbed the fellow by his hair, and hurled him onto the cobblestone headfirst.

Veranix's heart dropped with the sickening crunch of that kid's skull. He had to get out of here, get out of this fight before she did the same to him.

She pushed the Son out of her way and grabbed Veranix by the front of his tunic, taking his right hand and squeezing so he couldn't move. "You got anything left, Thorn?"

"Yeah," he said, grabbing an arrow with his free hand, and praying that he hadn't lost count of what he hadn't used yet. Flipping it in his fingers, he brought it down on her shoulder, feeling the nicks on the shaft to confirm it was one of the special arrows Verci Rynax had made for him.

The blast from the boom threw him across the street.

He managed to land on his feet, though, and take a moment to gather himself to see where things stood.

Bobba was laid out on the cobblestone.

Several other thugs and heavies were still gathered about, but most were in a haze and dazzle of what just occurred. Who wasn't in sight, though, were Jullick or Jads. Down the alley behind the grocer, he spotted a wagon just taking a corner out of sight.

Veranix's hand went to the rope as the heavies in the street started to focus their attention back on him.

"Friends and neighbors," he said as he used the rope to recover his bow and staff from where Bobba had thrown them on the street, while also gathering *numina* back into his body to charge himself with magic. "I would love to stay and dally through the evening, but there's riper fruit to pluck."

They charged at him, but he had pushed the magic into his legs and leaped over them all, into the alley, through and around the corner. The wagons were continuing: two of them, loaded with crates, boxes, and Jullick and Jads.

Kai had given the signal to retreat, but he had them, they were right there. The rest of the team could run away, fine. He'd do it alone. He was going to make these bastards pay. Pay for his mother, for Parsons, for Kai's father, for his father. All of it. He had them running right now, and he couldn't give up that chance to tear all of them down to the ground.

CHAPTER TEN

V ERANIX WHIPPED OUT THE ROPE as he landed right behind
the rear wagon, magically willing it to wrap around the axle.
With a sharp pull, feet planted, sweetening the power with his magic, he
tore the wheels right off the back of the wagon. The contents—crates
and men—tumbled into the street as the horses continued to drag the
collapsed wagon down the cobblestones.

"Hold right there, fellows, while I tend to your boss," Veranix said.
Jullick was still on the front wagon, almost out of sight, no time to
waste. He pushed magic back into his legs and jumped, ready to soar
over to Jullick's wagon.

Instead of soaring, his foot snagged. He only managed a few feet
before being yanked back down, crashing onto the cobblestones. He
flipped onto his back to see what had happened—a rope noosed around
his foot, and holding tight to the other end of the rope was a woman in
dark leather, her hair and face covered with Racquin dancing veils, so
only her heavily painted eyes could be seen.

"I don't think we've met," Veranix said.

"But I know you, killer," she said, drawing out a *dektha*—a Kellirac
throwing blade—and hurling it straight at him.

Veranix pulled himself backward, using a bit of sloppy magic—too
hard, too fast—to pull her and her rope with him, bringing up his leg so

the blade hit the rope instead of him. Razor sharp, it sliced straight through the rope and whistled past his nose. He scrambled away and got on his feet, bow out. The *dektha* arced about and returned to the woman, where she caught it gracefully just as Veranix took his shot. She used her weapon to deflect the arrow with an effortless air.

"Look, I'm not sure what you want," he said as he drew and fired two more arrows—the last two in the quiver—walking backward as he went. "But right now—"

"I'm here for revenge," she said, throwing the *dektha*, and then following up by throwing two more in rapid succession.

"Well, take a spot in the queue for that," Veranix said, dodging out of the way of the first, second, and third, but he wasn't ready for the first to clip him on the arm as it returned to her. Biting back the urge to cry out, he added, "Tonight's a very busy night."

"I think we can all have a turn," one of Jullick's men said, stalking over to Veranix. The rest were back on their feet and forming a ring around him.

"Everyone is so impatient," Veranix said, flipping back to get space to maneuver, while swapping the bow for the staff. "But if you don't mind sitting together."

One of the thugs moved in, swinging with a monster punch. It was slow and heavy enough to ably dodge, letting Veranix knock him twice with the staff while continuing his retreat. Crack, step, crack, step.

Another *dektha* just missed him, embedding in the shop wall behind Veranix. The Racquin Revanche jumped in while the other two brandished bladed knucklestuffers. Veranix's back was to the wall, nowhere else to go. The Revanche in front, Jullick's men on either side, and his wagon out of sight completely.

Pinned, he'd have to fight his way out of this.

The Revanche came in strong, swinging her weapon, when with a sudden clang, it flew out of her hand, clattering on the ground with a blunt-tip bolt.

"City Constabulary!" a far too young voice called out. "Stand and be held!"

Jace Welling's shift in the Aventil was supposed to end at six bells in the evening. He rarely actually logged end of watch before seven, if not later. That was the same for everyone in Benvin's squad, though most nights the lieutenant made sure Jace was logged out and walking home by eight. This was in part because Benvin knew the family—he had even come to dinner once—and told Jace, "They all deserve to see you at the end of the day, so they know you're all right."

The rest of the squad all lived in Aventil now, and as far as Jace knew, the rest didn't have anyone else to go home to. Blazes, no one in Pollit's family even spoke to him anymore.

Jace was sometimes tempted to join the rest of them in the flops they had moved into on Drake and Clover, if for no other reason than to shorten his walk home at the end of the night. More and more, Aventil felt like "his" neighborhood, certainly more than Keller Cove where the Welling household was. But even though he was in the house less and less, he couldn't bring himself to actually move out. The family was still hurting from Corrie's disappearance—blazes, the fact that they were still calling it that, when she was surely dead—and he couldn't put another blow on his mother.

Plus if he moved out he'd have to make his own meals and learn about laundering and a dozen other things he was completely ignorant of. All that was worth the long walk to and from work.

So Jace Welling was halfway through Dentonhill at a bit past eight bells when there were a few thunderous booms to the south. He paused when that happened, and calmly started to stroll toward that noise, in case anything else happened.

Of course, Dentonhill had plenty of constables on duty in the evenings. His cousin Edard was one of them. Constables, fire brigade, Yellowshields—like his cousin Ferah—all fully staffed here. They had it covered.

Still, Jace stayed alert. Just in case.

Then the whistle calls came. Alarm calls, danger calls, help calls. Jace walked a bit faster, getting his whistle out.

Then the return calls came in. Dentonhill sticks responding. They were on their way. And quite a few.

They had it covered. He should go home. They didn't need him. He could just go home.

But he didn't take a step in that direction, not just yet.

The sky lit up with a booming green fire, south by Brown Street. There was no missing it—anyone in Dentonhill with working eyes would have seen it. Blazes, anyone in Aventil or Inemar, even, if not the whole south side of the city.

You signed out. They've got it. Two more hands won't—

A wagon ripped around the corner, and there was a horrid crunching sound from down the street. Then another wagon—or at least the horse team of one, dragging a wagon with no back wheels—continued behind it.

Jace dashed to the corner, not sure if he should chase after the wagons or see if he was needed where the wheels came off. Once he reached the intersection, it was painfully clear where he was needed.

The Thorn was in the midst of a fight. There were a handful of men, most likely working for the drug boss of Dentonhill, all surrounding him, while a woman in Racquin leathers and dance veils came at him with a relentless barrage of attacks with curved blades. The woman moved like lightning, throwing and catching her blades with lethal assuredness.

She'd cut him to ribbons in moments.

Jace didn't even think, closing in while he brought up his crossbow, snapping off a shot at this woman who was about to slice the Thorn's throat open. His blunt-tip hit her weapon—damn, that was a good shot —knocking it out of her hand.

"City Constabulary!" he shouted as he reloaded. "Stand and be held!"

The woman stepped away, glancing back and forth between Jace and the Thorn. "Another time, killer," she sneered, and dashed off. The Thorn vanished from sight, as if he melted into the wall behind him.

The other men, who all had knives out at the ready, grumbled and went to pick up the crates that had scattered on the ground.

"Hey!" Jace shouted. "What did I say?"

One of them scowled at him. "You can go now, hmm?" They kept at their work.

"I said stand and be held," Jace said. "All of you, up against that wall."

"Is he serious?"

"What's with this kid?"

"Run along," one of them said. "This doesn't concern you."

Jace kept his crossbow trained on that one—he seemed to be the leader—as he took out his whistle. "I told you, stand and be held, or you'll be further charged—"

That was as far as he got before two of them grabbed him, pulling his arms back.

"Must be new, or—oh, he's not from this neighborhood," the leader said, coming up and flicking the pin on Jace's collar. "Get rid of him and let's clean this rutting mess up."

"City Constabulary!" Jace shouted as another of them pulled out his knife and came up to him. He tried to get himself free of the two who were holding back his arms, to no end. "Officer in danger!"

"Ain't no one in this patch who would yell that," the man with the knife said. He flipped the blade over to bring it down on Jace's chest. "Sorry, kid, but, it's business—"

The knife nearly brushed the front of Jace's uniform when a flash of crimson intercepted it, and the man with the knife went down to the ground with his attacker. In a rapid fire of hits and blows, that man was knocked senseless. His attacker—the Thorn—popped back up, quarter-staff in hand.

"Bad business to be in," he muttered, whipping his staff around to crack the skulls of the two men holding Jace tight. They both crumpled to the ground.

"Came back for more?" the leader shouted, his own knife drawn. "You think you scare us, Thorn, you think this—"

The Thorn threw out his rope, which wrapped around the man's neck, and pulled him down to the cobblestones with a very satisfying crack.

"We need to stop meeting like this, cadet," the Thorn said as his rope came back to him. He glanced Jace up and down. "Officer, now. Congratulations."

"You already knew that," Jace said. "But thank you. You need to—"

"We need to both get out of here," the Thorn said, clutching his side as he walked away. "At least I do, before—"

"You got hurt?" Jace asked, noticing blood dripping by his hand. He kept after him.

"It's nothing, that one got a piece of me," he said. More blood was seeping from his side, leaving a trail as he walked. Hurt worse than he wanted to admit.

"You can't just—"

"Another time, Mister Welling," the Thorn said as he flickered into a blurry shadow, but that only lasted for about two steps. The Thorn became fully visible as he stumbled and fell.

"Don't be ridiculous," Jace said. He caught the Thorn before he dropped. "You won't get two blocks like that. We need to get you patched up."

"I appreciate the thought, constable, but I don't think you can bring me to a ward or a sew-up in this part of town. Can you imagine? 'Oh, hey doctor, can you check on the Thorn before you call Fenmere's men?'"

"Do you ever hush?" Jace asked. He pushed the Thorn up against the alley wall and squatted down to get a look at the injury. More than a little deep, and despite the Thorn holding on to his side, the blood kept coming.

That knife would have gone right into Jace's heart if it wasn't for the Thorn. Yet again, he was still alive thanks to this man.

This kid. The Thorn was definitely the same age as him. Which was clear, as the shadow over his face had faded. Not that he hadn't seen the Thorn's face before—the night he saved him on the bridge. But now seeing him, all the color was drained from his face. He was in real trouble.

"Gotta keep talking," Thorn said. "Stay thinking, stay awake or I'll—"

He slumped down. Jace got under his arm and hauled him—saints, he barely weighed a thing, so skinny—into the tenement next to them. It looked half abandoned already, and the first apartment in there had the door already busted open. Jace carried the Thorn inside.

"Anyone here?" he called out. "City Constabulary!"

No response. He laid the Thorn down on the ground.

"You still with me?"

"Reporting for duty, constable," Thorn said, weakly putting his hand to his head in a salute.

"We need to get you a doctor, or—"

"Or, what? Call a Yellowshield? You know one in Dentonhill you can trust?"

Of course. "Yes, as a matter of fact I do," Jace said. He moved the Thorn's hand to the wound. "Hold it tight, I'll be back as fast as I can."

"Where are you—"

"Like you said," Jace said as he went to the door. "A Yellowshield I can trust."

KAIANA GOT DELMIN OVER HER SHOULDER, THERE WAS NO WAY HE could walk, let alone run. "Hold up, we'll get you out of here."

"Got class in the morning," he said weakly.

"You'll make it."

All she had to do was get a couple blocks to Waterpath. Then she'd be out of the worst of it.

She came back out of the alley and almost crashed into two muscle-bound thugs.

"That's the guy who got big," one of them said, pointing at Delmin.

"The Thorn?" the other asked.

"Maybe." The first pulled his knife and moved closer to Kaiana. "And this must be the Thorn's little friend. That right?"

"Back off," Kaiana said, brandishing her weapon as best she could with Delmin over her shoulder.

"She sounds scared," the first thug said. "What do they call the Thorn's scared friend? You the Rose?"

"No, that's me."

Mila came out of nowhere, leaping on the first one and stabbing him several times, her blade moving like a hummingbird's wings. She was off him and wrapping her rope around the other one's neck before the first even landed on the ground. He tried to futilely keep her off him, but she had him noosed, and then jabbed him twice with her knife before he really had a chance.

"You all right?" she asked as she tightened her rope on his neck. He kept gurgling, eyes bulging as he clawed at empty air.

"I . . . uh . . ." Kaiana stammered.

"Can he walk?"

"No." Single words were all she could manage.

Mila glanced around as she uncoiled her rope from the very dead man's neck. "One tick." She dashed off and returned before Kaiana could even ger her thoughts around what had just happened. She knew Mila could fight, had grown up harder than even Kaiana had, but she hadn't expected her to be so capable of such . . . brutality. Kaiana could fight—had fought—when she needed to, but Mila just killed two men like she was drinking a cup of warm tea.

"Here," Mila said as she came up with a pushcart. "Get him in, then follow me through that alley. We get to Vinny, should be clear of sticks, and cut west across Waterpath. You lose me, there's a shoemaker shop on Hedge between Lily and Vine. Go to apartment Two-East above that."

"Whose apartment—"

"Mine," Mila said. "Follow me."

Mila was off like a shot, and Kaiana followed, pushing the cart with Delmin. She went through the alley, right behind Mila, as she cleared a path—sometimes fatally, sometimes not, but always efficiently.

"This way," she said as they reached Vinny, and led them to the west, toward Waterpath and Aventil. Her prediction was correct—here there were no constabulary, no obvious Fenmere goons, and most of the people they saw scattered when they emerged onto the street. "Let's not waste time, anyone who spotted us will call sticks or Fenmere's men here. Stay with me and don't let up until we get to the shoemaker."

They kept going, across Waterpath, away from the smoke and the whistles and the sounds of chaos. Soon they were just on dark streets, the street lamps either already burned out, or never lit. Kaiana didn't even know her way around in this part of the neighborhood. Which gang ruled here? Waterpath Orphans? Were they going to be trouble?

"Here," Mila said as they approached the shoemaker. She brought them around the back, to an iron backstair. She helped Kaiana get Delmin out of the pushcart and carry him up the stairs, through the window, and into the apartment. Kaiana got Delmin laid out on the ground as Mila lit a lamp.

"I've got some ham and cheese here," Mila said, going through the cupboards. "And a bottle of wine, if that'll help."

"All," Delmin muttered. Mila came over with the food and started to get what she could into Delmin's mouth.

"I'm guessing he burned himself out out there," she said. "Did you see what happened?"

"He got really big," Kaiana said quietly. "I didn't know he could do that."

"I didn't either," Delmin said hoarsely.

"I understand," Mila said. Kaiana noticed her hands trembling as she fed Delmin. "I'm sorry, I should have realized . . . I shouldn't have planned to put you two in danger."

"Are you all right?" Kaiana asked.

"I messed up, it all went to blazes," Mila said. "Let's take a moment to get our bearings, and once Delmin is able to stand up, we wash up and change into other clothes."

"You have other clothes here?" Kaiana asked. "What is this?"

"I rented a couple apartments in Aventil and Dentonhill, stocked them with weapons and supplies, just in case."

"How?" Kaiana asked.

Mila shrugged. "I've got a fair amount of money. Should do something with it."

"I . . ." Kaiana shook her head. "I thought you were a street girl from the west side, no family or anything."

"Yeah," Mila said. "But I figured that, whatever Veranix was doing, if I'm going to be a part of it, going to help him, then I needed to use whatever I had to help. I know how to set up a safehouse apartment, and this gives us a place to lie low, rest and clean up, and walk out of here in a bit not looking like people who were a part of that whole fracas. We need to be able to get to campus without further trouble."

"It's after nine bells," Delmin said. "We blew curfew."

"Yeah," Mila said. "Which doesn't apply to staff."

"That's only me," Kaiana said.

Mila stood up, pointing to a desk in the corner. "I've got some papers there for all of us." She went to the spigot, stripping down to her chemise.

"How do you even think of this stuff?" Kaiana asked. "This apartment, the papers, the uniforms, the . . . all of it?"

"Taught by one of the best," Mila said as she washed the blood off her arms and face. Kaiana realized she must look a fright.

"How are you?" she asked Delmin.

"Clearer," he said. Lowering his voice. "I made the boom powder kegs big, too. I lost control, I . . . I think I killed people, Kai."

Kaiana didn't know how to respond to that, or even if she could.

"Do you have a drycloth or something so I can clean him up?" she asked Mila.

"Of course, under there," Mila said. "Delmin, if you can walk, let's try and be walking home in fifteen minutes. Good?"

"Good," Delmin said quietly.

Kaiana got up and wet a cloth, and got to work getting him cleaned off. The three of them were here, they were safe, and they could have been hurt so much worse.

Wherever Veranix was, she hoped he could say the same.

Lieutenant Benvin hadn't gone home when he signed out. He was constantly telling his squad they needed to go home, have a life, talk to people who weren't constables. He hoped they would listen, he hoped they would find someone to spend time with that could ease the burden on their soul. Benvin wasn't hopeful to find such a person in his life.

Instead of going to his apartment—he hadn't even been there for three days—he went to the flop above the Broken Spindle, the place he and the other members of the squad had rented out of their own pocket, a second headquarters away from the Aventil stationhouse, away from the watchful eye of negligence of Captain Holcomb, and the naked corruption of the rest of the Aventil constables. Here, hopefully, they could get real work done. Benvin had taken the files of the six escaped prisoners, and planned to read over them, copy critical information, and see what revelations he could glean.

He was not expecting to find Yessa, the Waterpath Orphan street captain who fed him information of what was going on in the gangs, naked in the bunk.

"Saints almighty!" she shouted as he came in, scrambling under the blanket. "The blazes are you doing here?"

"The blazes are you?" he asked, not letting any surprise or excitement show in his voice. "I don't even know how you got in here."

"Aint a room in this neighborhood I can't get into. Can you give me my slacks?"

They were discarded on the floor. He scooped them up and handed them to her. "Why are you here, naked, and clearly not expecting me?"

"I was expecting someone else," she said quietly. "I don't have a private place of my own."

"Is this a thing you do often?" he asked, putting down his papers on the table.

"Not very," she said in a tone that made him immediately think she was lying. Not that she had built up much trust between them, but he knew she had far more too lose in cooperating with him. She had given him intelligence that had panned out. A good portion of the work in dismantling most of the Kemper Street Kickers had stemmed from information she had given him.

"Important work is done here," he said. "That is the point."

"Life isn't all work, Lieutenant," she said. "I have tried to show you that."

"Never quite this directly," he told her.

"If I let you take a tumble, could that smooth this over?"

"Not necessary," he scoffed. "You don't have your own flop?"

"How am I gonna afford that?"

"I presume you have money from things I shouldn't know about."

"Bah," Yessa said. She had been holding her slacks all this time but didn't seem to be in any hurry to put them on. She had sat up on the bunk, wrapping the blanket around her body enough for the demands of modesty. "Very little finds my pocket. We're all scraping by."

He didn't have much response to that. He felt that himself, though he made a point to live frugal, so he could put more of his earnings into the work, into maintaining this place. For a moment, there was an uneasy quiet in the flop as she shifted under the blanket and he continued to lay out the papers he had brought on the table.

"Listen," she finally said after a bit, but whatever she was about to say was forgotten when the door opened and someone dashed in, shutting the door behind her.

"Sorry, it took me forever to get out of the Turnabout, I had to deal with a situ—oh!"

The young woman was clearly a Rose Street Prince—her sleeve had been rolled down when she came in, but she had stripped down to her chemise in the time it took her to say that and notice Benvin was in the room. Her arm had the tattoo, including the captain stars.

"Well, this is interesting," Benvin said.

"What is he doing here?" the Prince said as she got her blouse back on.

"It is his flop," Yessa said.

"If I had known—"

"I didn't know he'd be here," Yessa urged, getting off the bed and clinging to the blanket. "Please don't go."

"You know what a risk it is for me even walking through here?"

"I know," Yessa said, caressing her face. "All the more reason not to run off once you are already here."

"Deena Traskin, Rose Street Prince captain," Benvin said. "I've got files on every street captain in every gang in the neighborhood. I know who you are."

"And you're that lieutenant who's trying to clean up the neighborhood. Yessa, girl, why are you even messing with this? Why are you here naked with him?"

"That was for you," Yessa said sheepishly.

"He knows," Deena said in a low whisper. "And now . . . are you snitching?"

"I'm working out my own," Yessa said. "And with the winds blowing the way they are, you should too."

Deena frowned. "We gotta be smart, girl."

"I'm trying to be."

"By snitching on your own?"

"It was that or the Quarry," Yessa said. "He's been all right."

Benvin had heard enough. "I'm going to leave you ladies to yourselves."

"And come back with a dozen sticks to crackdown the freak girls?" Deena asked.

Benvin sighed. "There's nothing going on here that breaks any law that I'm concerned about enforcing. Just two people who want to enjoy each other's company."

He went for the door, and Yessa reached out and touched his shoulder.

"Hey," she said quietly. "Thank you. Really."

"Of course," he said. "You have a safe night."

"Listen," Deena said as he was almost out the door. "It's not a very safe night out there. Something big is going down in the south triangle of Dentonhill, and the word is already in the air about reprisal. Add in that, some folks are out of Quarry—"

"I know about those folks."

"They are coming for the Thorn," Deena said sharply. "They said as much."

That got his attention. "You heard from one of them? Did Juteron come home?"

"Stories were told," she said. "That's all I can say."

"That's something. Thank you, Miss Traskin." With that, he left them to their own evening, grateful that someone would have a nice night.

Because if what she told him was true, it was likely that by tomorrow night, the streets of Aventil would be washed with blood.

CHAPTER ELEVEN

VERANIX HADN'T PASSED OUT AT all, but his world did go gray for a bit. Lying on the ground helped, letting the pain stay with him, and keep him alert. He pulled up his shirt to get a better look at the wound. He wasn't sure how bad it really was, but, saints, it certainly looked bad. He needed to get it under control, get back on his feet, get himself back to campus. Once there, he could—

He started to get up and then slipped back down.

"Blazes, no, I'm not going to be stopped here and now," he muttered. "Get on your blasted feet, Calbert."

The door of the empty tenement opened, and Veranix's hand went to the empty quiver on instinct.

It was young officer Welling and a woman in a Yellowshield uniform at the door.

"Oh my saints and stars, it is him," she said.

"Who is this?" Veranix asked, trying to force himself up.

"You asked for a Yellowshield I can trust," Jace said.

"I was making a joke."

"And I got my cousin Ferah. You're welcome."

"Oh, good," Veranix said. "I'm getting to know the whole Welling family."

"My name is Serrick, thank you," Ferah said, kneeling down next to him. "Now stay rutting still so I can get a look at you before you bleed to death." She put two hands on his chest and forced him back to the floor, and he had no strength to stop her.

"Well, I can't pass up that offer," he said.

"This is decidedly nasty," Ferah said, her fingers touching at his side. "But the blade didn't seem to reach any organs. How'd you manage this?"

"He kept the knife from killing me," Jace said.

"Right, then let's make sure it doesn't kill him, either," she said. She dug into her bag. "Let's give you a slug of *doph* for the pain."

"No," Veranix said. "Pain will keep me here, keep me going."

"I need to sew into you," she said. "It'll hurt like blazes."

"Won't be the first time. Head clear."

"All right," she said, pulling out a few more vials. She handed one of them to him. "Then drink this one when I tell you to."

"What'll these—"

"That'll keep you alert, like a pot of tea horse-kicked into your face." She opened another vial and poured its contents over his wound, which burned like a hot poker. She ignored his cry of pain and kept going. "But it's going to turn your heart into a jackrabbit, which will send a lot more blood out the wound, which we don't need."

"I would think," Veranix said, as his hands barely cooperated getting the first vial open.

"Jace, get next to him," she said, taking out a syringe and glass barrel. She poured half the contents of another vial into the barrel, muttering something about going through her supplies. "Push the plunger when I tell you."

"I shouldn't—" Jace stuttered.

"When I tell you!" she said sharply. "That will thicken his blood, and I need to start stitching." She pulled out her needle and thread. "Are you ready, Thorn?"

"Ma'am, yes, ma'am," Veranix said, holding up the vial. "To your health."

"Yours is the issue," she said, as she readied the needle. "Drink."

Veranix did as ordered, and she wasn't kidding about the horse kick. He suddenly felt as if he had been running for an hour, yet also like he could keep running for the rest of his life. He could barely even breathe. Then there was a jab in his side.

"Push it!"

A cold flush washed over him in his side, and then there was the familiar sharp pain of a needle sewing up his skin. He had been under Kaiana's needle several times, this was an old friend.

Was Kaiana all right? Did she get out safe? Did Delmin? Or Mila? Of course Mila did, she always would. But they were all saints even knew where, and he was on the floor in some abandoned Dentonhill flop, only not dying thanks to members of the Welling family.

A few whistles blew outside. "This way," someone called from outside.

"Backup is here," Jace said, getting to his feet.

That was troubling.

"Backup as in Lieutenant Benvin?" Veranix asked.

"No, it would be—"

"Oh, *Jace*," Ferah said, her voice dripping with disappointment. "You can't let Dentonhill officers find him."

"But they're—"

"They will bring me to Fenmere," Veranix said. "You know they will." His heart had already been running like a fox in an Itasiana chase, and the fear of what might happen, what he would have to do, what they would do to him if he couldn't fight back . . .

"Give me a few minutes to finish," she said. "Hold them off."

"How?"

"Tell them who you are," she said. "They all know Eddie. He might even be with them."

"Eddie?" Veranix asked.

"Our cousin who works this neighborhood," Jace said.

How many Welling cousins were there?

"I'll just get out of here—"

"You stay put," Ferah said, putting a hand on Veranix's chest to stop him from getting up. "Jace, you go out there and tell whoever is out there that I'm in here treating a patient—use my name, hear?"

"Say that Ferah Serrick—"

"Say that YS Field Officer Serrick has a patient, and she's claiming triage priority. You're my officer of accountability."

"Your what?"

"Saints, I thought you passed your exams. Just go, tell them." Jace left, and she prodded Veranix's arm, and then her fingers probed along his head. "Anywhere else you get hit?"

"About everywhere," Veranix said. "What are you doing?"

"He's telling them that I've claimed that your condition is dire enough that my treatment of you takes priority over their necessity to arrest you. You know how a church can give sanctuary and the constables aren't allowed to go in?"

"Is that how it's supposed to work?"

"Well, I made this room a church of medicine," she said. "As long as you are my patient, they can't take you. And naming Jace as the officer of accountability, means he's already taken responsibility for my safety in your presence. So if you hurt me, he's going to get in trouble, hear?"

"Yeah," he said. "Presuming those Dentonhill officers respect that. Most of them are in Fenmere's pocket."

"Yeah," she said quietly as she dabbed an ointment on his wound.

"I'm guessing he doesn't bother to also put Yellowshields in his pocket."

She shrugged. "Maybe it hasn't trickled over to me yet. I do know that I've patched up a few park doxies and shop owners here in town that have nothing but kind words for you. But even if I didn't, as long as you are my patient, that comes first."

"Thank you."

"The job is the oath," she said. "Sit up so I can wrap that."

Jace came back in, shutting the door behind him. "There's seven Dentonhill constables, and they definitely think the Thorn is in here, and they definitely want him."

"Do they know Eddie?"

"Only in passing. He's apparently working the northern triangle right now."

"And what did you tell them?" Veranix asked.

"That they got the wrong end of the handstick on this one. That she's treating a civilian who was hurt when everything went wild out there.

And once you can walk that I'm going to take you in for a witness statement." Outside the door, several folks were coming into the hallway.

Veranix didn't waste another second, drawing *numina* through the
cloak to craft an illusion around him. The door flew open, and a half-
dozen constables stood shoulder to shoulder.

All they saw was Ferah working on a man old enough to be her
father, dressed in the simple brown trousers and vest of a shopkeep.
Veranix even gave himself the appearance of spectacles, which might
have been a little more showmanship than this subterfuge required.

"Saints!" he exclaimed, hoping he wasn't overplaying his voice with
either affect or accent. "Normally you can't get a constable when you
need one, now I've got a whole eight pins."

"Who is this?" the constable in the lead asked.

"This is my witness," Jace said after a moment of confusion. "He
saw—"

"Damn, kid," the constable said. "If he's a witness, I don't need you
telling me what he saw. He needs to tell his story."

"Without you feeding it to him," another one of them said.

"He needs you all to clear out," Ferah said.

"He's a witness, we want to know what he saw."

"I will walk him in and take his statement," Jace said. "Surely the lot
of you have something more you can do out there."

"It's madness out there, it is," Veranix said, playing up the character
he was portraying. "Just trying to walk home, and hooded fools in
cloaks causing trouble."

"You ain't our house," the constable said to Jace. "He should come
to our house."

"I ain't even supposed to be here," Veranix said. "Stupid kid
couldn't even deliver a package right, so I had to walk up through
Dentonhill, and I'm walking home and this happens!" He pointed to the
wound, which he had kept the same in the illusion.

"The Thorn do that to you?"

"Nah, nah. There's craziness in the street, the guy in the cloak—is
that this Thorn character—he's fighting these bruisers, some other girl in
a mask is in on it, there's blades and slash, and I'm in the mix of it, and
this kid pulls me out."

"Hrm," one of the constables said. "You see where the Thorn went?"

"I saw a knife in my face, mister. This town isn't safe, and you people should be out there doing something about it! I've got some things to say to your captain, and—"

"Fan out the blocks," the lead constable told the others. He leaned in to Jace and whispered something, gave a salute and left. Jace shut the door.

"Well, that was fun," Ferah said once they heard the constables had left.

Jace burst out laughing. "I don't know what that was, but—"

"Some old carny skills," Veranix said. He kept the illusion up. "I think I can walk now."

"You know how to change those dressings?" Ferah asked. "Twice a day until it stops seeping."

"Yes, ma'am," Veranix said as he got to his feet. "You have my thanks."

"It's the job and the oath," she said, packing up her kit. She offered her hand to him. "But it was a pleasure."

"Likewise," Veranix said as he took it.

"I'll see you out," Jace said. "Just in case they're watching."

Veranix walked out with Jace. "So what did he whisper to you?"

"Take him to your own damn house and lose his statement," Jace said.

"You're a credit to your name, Jace Welling," Veranix said after they crossed Waterpath. The constables had set up a barricade and checkpoints, but Jace had no difficulty getting them waved through. "Give Minox my best."

"Try to be careful," Jace said. "You really knocked open the hornet nest this time, you know."

"I know," Veranix said. "But someone in this neighborhood has to."

He dropped the illusion, shrouded himself in the darkness of the night, and leaped off toward home, hoping that his friends had made it there already.

COLIN REACHED THE BACK ALLEY BEHIND THE OLD CANAL, HE AND Cober carrying Terker, who had taken a blade to the gut back on Shade Street. Cober's left eye was swollen over, he had his own gut wound, and that was only the worst that Colin could see. Colin himself was a mess of bruises and slashes, none of them so bad he couldn't move—he was hurting, but he'd get his boys home. No boss could do less.

"We're almost there, Terker, just a bit farther," Cober was saying. "Stay with us, buddy."

Terker had been talking to them when they first got over Waterpath —just before the Dentonhill sticks cracked down a barricade along the whole street. Anyone who hadn't gotten back to Aventil yet wasn't going to anytime soon, unless they went around the whole campus. Colin could only manage to get a few people back out, sent them back to the Old Canal, and went back for Cober and Terker.

He had seen more than a few of his folks in irons. The last he saw Cainey was lying in the middle of the street, his head cracked open and covered in blood. He was a good kid, damnit, killed by some Fenmere goon, and over what?

You knew this was the price.

"Come on, Terker, keep talking," Cober said. "Open your eyes, man."

Colin looked down at Terker. His chest wasn't moving at all. "Put him down, Cober."

"But—"

"Put him down."

Cober helped put Terker down on the cobblestone, and Colin knelt down next to him. Eyes closed, not breathing. Colin put his hand on the kid's chest. Nothing.

Cober kept shaking Terker. "Come on, Terker, we're almost in the Canal. Sew-up will fix you right up."

"Let it be," Colin said. "He's gone."

"Nah, nah," Cober said. "Come on, man, we got you home."

"We got him home," Colin said. "Now he's gonna rest."

"Nah, he can't. He can't, boss." Cober grabbed Colin by the front of his shirt. "The blazes did we do, boss?"

"We fought like blazes out there," Colin said, pulling Cober's hands off him. He took off the Uni coat and shirt, now stained with blood. "There's a well pump right there, let's get you cleaned up."

"What about Terker?"

"We'll lay him out right, we will," Colin said, leading him to the well pump. "Let's get washed up ourselves first. We're the ones breathing. But this night won't end without a glass up for who we lost."

Colin pumped while Cober got the blood off his hands and face, and then Colin washed himself off as best he could. He got Cober's uniform coat off, and then did the same to Terker. He threw the bloody clothes into the refuse bin, and told Cober to wait as he slipped back out to the street. He found one of the lamps that was still burning and knocked its base open. He took the oil well out, singeing his fingers a bit until he could hold it from the cool part on the bottom, and brought it back into the alley, tossing it into the bin. The whole thing lit up.

"How'd we lose so hard?" Cober asked.

"You get beat sometimes, buddy," Colin said. "You either make it through that beating and get better, or you don't." He nodded over to Terker's body.

"We weren't together out there," Cober muttered. "We were a mess."

Cober was right about that. They went out there with a plan, and once things turned left, they weren't Sons of Tyson any more, but clusters of former Princes, Orphans, Kickers, Dogs, Knights, and Rabbits.

"I'll tell you what went wrong," Colin said, thinking about what he saw out there. "We were out there so we could help the Thorn. But our people went into that fight thinking the Thorn was coming to help them." He saw more than a few of his folks looking up to the rooftop, waiting for arrows to rain down and save them.

"Where was he?" Cober asked. "I thought he was with us."

"On this run, he had a job, and I hope he did it. I hope he's all right. We were there for him this time."

"Is he supposed to be leading us, boss? Is he a Son of Tyson, for real?"

Colin moved in close, getting into Cober's face. "He's my blood, am I clear? He is one of us, but he can't be here with us all the time. But he asked for us, and we came."

"We got killed!" Cober said. "Terker, Cainey!"

"And we're going to go in this and put glasses up for them, hear?" Colin said. "And we all knew the risks. You don't like that, then walk back to the Princes. Sure they'll welcome you with open arms and a pair of knives."

Cober's good eye burned in anger, but he nodded. "Let's have a beer. See who else made it."

They came in through the back, Colin signaling to the cook to start bringing out crisp and strikers for whoever was out in the main hall. There were nine people there, all of them still in those Uni uniforms, all of them looking like they had been put in the grinder and made into sausage.

"Get those things off, you fools," Cober said. "Saints, it's like you want the sticks to find us."

"Boss?" one of the boys asked.

"Go out back and strip down, throw those uniforms in the burn bin, and come back in here to put a glass up for the folks who fell. We'll say our words in our skivs if we gotta."

They all did that, and slowly they stumbled back in, cleaner if not any higher in spirit. Colin made sure they all got a glass and waited for them to come back in.

"Folks, we took a hit tonight. There's no lying about that. But we did it together, as a family. These folks around you, stripped to their skivs, who fought by your side, they are your brothers and sisters. We are here *together*. We are Sons of Tyson. Every one of us. As are the ones who were killed or pinched out there. Brothers and sisters. Hold up your glass and say the name of one of them you know isn't coming back here tonight."

He held his beer high above his head. "To Terker, who fought hard and was given harder. To Cainey, who will always be one of us."

"He made sure Sella got through," someone said. "That's how he got killed."

"And what happened to Sella?" Cober asked. "Anyone see her? She get hurt? She get caught?"

"Ain't nobody saw me, ain't nobody catch me!"

Sella strode in from the back, in just her bloodstained chemise, but carrying two sacks over her shoulder. She had a wicked slice on her arm that she didn't seem to care two whiffs about.

Colin whooped out loud on seeing her. "Look at her! That is your sister!" he shouted.

"Sister with the prize," she said. "I had a job and I rutting did it."

She dropped the sacks on the floor, and they spilled open, full of goldsmith notes. There must be a few thousand crowns in there.

Everyone cheered, even Cober.

"Blazes," Colin said. "That is some good work. More beers all around."

Everyone drank, and continued in melancholy celebration. Sella came over to Colin, taking the beer out of his hand and drinking it down to the bottom.

"All right, boss," she said. "We had a real bad night out there, I saw some real sewage happening. So I made damn sure we got something out of it."

"You did," he said. "Done real good, Captain."

That was the first time he actually called her that. She smiled and said, "We're gonna give each of these folks a few notes. You and I are gonna take the rest of the score up to the flop and lock it down."

"Lock it down how?"

"There's a hiding spot only I know about," she said. "Then we'll have a roll, you and I, because I think we deserve that."

Colin was more than a little surprised, but didn't object. "You want the sew-up to look at that arm first?"

"Nah," she said. "It's just a scratch. He works it, he'll give me the *doph*, and for once I don't want it."

After everything that had gone bad—and it was a bad night, one of the worst—that, at least, made him happy. He would take whatever joy he could grasp onto for now.

Tomorrow, he knew, would be when the real trouble came.

CHAPTER TWELVE

DESPITE THE PAIN—AND EVERYTHING hurt—Veranix made it back to campus, using the cloak to shroud himself as he crossed the lawn. Not that he needed to sneak his way to the bunker. The campus cadets were not patrolling with much vigilance tonight; it struck Veranix how different a world they lived in here, isolated from the violence just on the other side of the campus wall.

Entering the bunker, he immediately felt relief on hearing three voices: Mila, Kaiana, and Delmin. They had all made it, they were all right. That was a blessing. He needed to check in with Colin, but that would have to wait for tomorrow. He was far too spent to do anything else.

"Hey," he said, coming into the main room. "Glad you're all here."

Mila came up and grabbed him in an embrace right away, making him wince. "You're all right."

"Mostly," he said, pulling away from her enough so she wasn't pressing on his wound. "It got dicey out there, though."

"Oh, did it?" Kaiana asked sharply. She was sitting with Delmin on the bunk, cider bottle in her hand. Veranix noticed the three empty bottles by her feet. Delmin was sitting slouched over a book, barely looking up at Veranix.

"Frankly, I'm only standing thanks to a good-hearted Yellowshield,"

Veranix said, taking off the cloak. He hung it up, and immediately felt the potent drop in magical power as he let it go. It was strong enough that his knees started to buckle, and he barely kept himself on his feet. "I'm glad you got out."

"We barely got out of that," Kaiana said. "Only because she killed the folks coming at us."

"Only because Kai came for me," Delmin muttered.

"So what happened with you all?" Veranix asked. "Things didn't go great at the office, and I had to chase the carriages as they fled. And I wasn't able to get any of the records."

"It went sour," Mila said. "Far as I can tell, all four points of the plan went cock up."

"No," Delmin said. "May have gone badly, but the storehouse of drugs blew up completely." He didn't look up from his book when he said that.

"That's something," Veranix said. Delmin didn't react. He looked to Mila. "You didn't get yours?"

"Couldn't even get in," she said. "I didn't do the scout right, I didn't think of all the angles. I screwed up."

"No, no," Veranix said. "It was a good plan—"

Kaiana laughed at that.

"What is your problem?" he asked.

"A good plan, really?" Kaiana asked, getting up from the bunk. "Based on what? How well everything worked? How many people got hurt or killed? Did we really accomplish anything? And at what cost?"

"Delmin destroyed the stash in his place, apparently."

"And more," Delmin said, still in his book.

"More?"

"He blew up the whole damn building," Kaiana said. "You didn't see that. I saw it. I saw you scrapping in the middle of the street and being distracted. I saw constables clubbing Colin's people, I saw constables getting killed, I saw . . ." She glanced around vaguely, her eyes looking anywhere except at Veranix as she took another pull out of her cider bottle. "I saw too damn much."

"Are you hurt?" Veranix asked. "Either of you?"

"Nothing that needs sewing," Delmin said. "But I might have already killed myself."

"What?"

"He didn't just shrink down," Mila said quietly. "Something went wrong, and he grew twice his size. Maybe more."

"And did the same to the boom powder," Kaiana added. "So the boom was . . . more."

"That's amazing," Veranix said. If he could figure out how to do something like that, it would make his boom powder arrows even more effective. "How did you do it?"

"I don't care," Delmin said, throwing the book on the ground. "What matters is that I did. And now who knows what I did to myself."

"I don't understand."

"Of course you don't," Delmin snapped. "You do whatever pops into your stupid head, without regard. Without study. Without knowing a damned thing. Where I've been reading all about shrinking and growing. The strain it puts on your heart and other organs. The damage done to your body if you switch from being very small to very big too quickly. Which is what I did, you idiot! I was lucky I didn't drop dead right away. I still might not live more than a few months now."

"Are you serious?" Veranix asked, moving closer. "I'm so sorry, I had no idea—"

"You never have any idea," Delmin said. "And I don't know why I've let you drag me into this madness to, what, stop drug dealers from selling *effitte* to the people stupid enough to buy it? Why? What's the point?"

That stung. "You know that Fenmere—"

"Fenmere is your problem!" Delmin shouted. "I didn't ask to be a part of this and I certainly didn't want to be recruited to be on the ground for your war. To have killed people in the street." He started wiping the tears off his face.

"I didn't mean for that to happen to you," Veranix said.

"You don't mean for anything," Kaiana said. "I thought maybe listening to your new girl here might have put some sense in your skull, what with her 'plans' and having learned how to, I don't know, pull 'runs' or 'gigs' or whatever she calls them, like she's a rutting expert.

But she, at least, got Delmin and me out of the trouble. More than I can say for you right now."

"Hey!" Veranix snapped. "You said you saw me, so you saw what I was in. I nearly got killed myself."

"You decide to go out there every damn night, that's your risk," Kaiana said. "I didn't ask for that. I didn't ask to . . ." She dropped to her knees and started crying. "I just . . . I just want to go see my father. I just want to see him."

Delmin moved closer to her, and glared at Veranix when he moved in as well. Veranix stepped back as Delmin helped Kaiana back to her feet.

"Look," Veranix said. "I am really very sorry for how it went out there, and I am sorry I wasn't there to help either of you when things went bad. I shouldn't have put either of you in that position."

"But you did," Kaiana said.

"We're all hurting, tired, and we've got a bit too much fire in our chests," Mila said. "We should stop talking right now and all just go to sleep, and . . . go over this when our hearts are cooler."

"Fine," Delmin said. "Good plan."

"At least this one is," Kaiana muttered. She pulled herself away from Delmin, stomped off.

"Are you going to have trouble getting back into your dormitory?" Veranix asked Mila.

"Getting in, no," she said. "And I can handle Livvie and Jadonne if they give me grief for not being in bed by curfew." She came over to Veranix, moving in close enough to kiss, but then seemed to change her mind. Stepping away, she clapped his shoulder and said, "Get some rest, and we'll see what the real damage is in the morning. Good night."

She left, and Veranix watched as Delmin picked the book up from the floor and brought it over to his small collection on the back table.

"Should I sleep here?" Veranix asked, taking off the last pieces of his Thorn outfit.

"What?" Delmin shot back "Why would you do that?"

"I imagine that you don't want to see me in our room right now."

"It's our room," Delmin said. "I wouldn't kick you out. It's fine." His tone did not indicate he thought things were fine, though.

"Then let's get back to Almers and get to sleep," Veranix said. "Face tomorrow with clear heads."

"Sure," Delmin said. He stalked off. Veranix quickly put on his school uniform and hurried after him.

It had gone badly, but they had done some damage to Fenmere's operation. Hopefully, if nothing else, Fenmere would feel some pain from that. The rest would be sorted tomorrow.

"Tell me again what happened," Fenmere said.

Jullick and Jads had the decency to look ashamed as they sat in Fenmere's study. Jullick had two nasty bruises on his face, and Jads had a scratch down her face and her sleeve was caked with dried blood.

"So we were moving out of the offices and storehouses, and the Thorn crashes in on the office. Same time, a whole mess of Uni students, as well as another bloke and some bird dressed like the Thorn, and they all hit at the same time in all our places. And the Thorn is whooping us hard, my boys get all on him, and Jads and I barely get out of there with our papers."

"And . . ." Fenmere said, even though he knew the answer to the question he was going to ask. "And the product you had stored? The money in your countinghouse? What is the situation with those?"

"One of the storehouses was completely destroyed. Lost five men in there, as well as all the product. The other one, they didn't manage to hit."

"And the money, Jullick," Gerrick said firmly. He and Corman both had been pacing around the back of the study, and no one was happy to even be awake at this hour. At least the news of the disaster, as well as Jullick and Jads showing up at his door, happened well after the dinner party had concluded to reasonable satisfaction and the guests had gone home.

"The money is gone," Jullick said. "One of those Uni kids got it."

"How astoundingly stupid are you, Jullick?" he asked. "I am in awe, frankly, of the immense quality of idiocy, you absolute toad, that you possess."

"What?" Jullick asked.

"Who wants to explain it to him in small words?" Fenmere asked.

"Those weren't University students," Jads said. "Likely one of the Aventil factions wearing the uniforms."

"Corman," Fenmere said. "I presume the constables intervened and made some arrests in this debacle?"

"From what we understand, yes," Corman said.

"Talk to our people in the stationhouse about who they really are, not that it matters."

"Why doesn't it matter?" Gerrick asked.

Fenmere went over to his side table and poured himself a whiskey. "Because, once I finish this drink, I'm going to want you to mobilize every single rutting soul we have under our command, any one of them who can hold a knife or a knucklestuffer. Get every single one of them and then we are going to march across Waterpath and roll like a full moons tide over all seven of those godforsaken gangs and make them all pay for this insolence!"

"Sir, but—"

"It is *long* overdue!" Fenmere shouted. "I should have done it twenty years ago!"

"I don't think that's wise, sir," Corman said.

"I don't give a good rutting damn about wise! I want blood to flow through the garden streets. I want to have the guts of every member of every gang strewn like laundry lines from building to building. I want the head of every Prince, Boy, Orphan, Dog, Kicker, Knight, and Rabbit—"

"The Rabbits are gone, sir," Gerrick said. "And the Kickers are mostly at this point as well."

"And now there's the Sons of Tyson," said someone who walked into the study. Two men, actually, both looking like the low-class rousters they used to sell the *effitte* on the street. The sort of men he was never even supposed to see. They just walked into his home, into his study. The sheer impudence made him sick.

"Sons of . . ." he started. A new gang had sprouted up, and they were branding themselves with the names of rutting Cal and Den Tyson? Even dead those two remained a rutting canker, flies in his soup. Hadn't they done enough, hadn't they taken enough from him already?

"Tyson, yeah," the other man who came in said. "Which is why they were working with the Thorn."

"Who the blazes are you?" he shouted. His head was spinning, rage flooding his heart to the point where he couldn't even think straight.

"Me, sir?" one of them said. "I'm Lemt, this here's Jendle, and we're here to tell you what you needs to know."

"You're here to . . ." he stammered. "Has the whole world gone mad? Why are people continually walking into my home with the delusion that I can be spoken to in this manner? Where is the respect I am due?"

"You are due it," Jendle said. "But we all know, it's the Thorn what took it from you. Took it from us. Took it from these two as well. Really took it from her, I hear, back in the summer when he left her tied up in her own piss."

"Hey!" Jads snapped.

"Who are these fools?"

"They were part of Nevin's crew," Corman said. "And then Bell's. Since Bell slipped off they had been . . . forgotten about."

"Yeah, but we didn't forget," Lemt said. "We've been on the ground, doing the work, getting smart."

"Someone kill these two, please—"

"We know who the Thorn is!" Jendle said quickly.

"This seems to be everyone's claim tonight," Fenmere said. "The Thorn has been more careless than I thought."

"Someone else knows?" Lemt said, looking a bit deflated.

"Well, there are a handful of fools in the basement whose fate I'm still deciding, just like you," Fenmere said. "I'm still waiting to hear why we shouldn't tear Aventil apart."

"We don't own the Aventil Constabulary in the same way," Gerrick said. "They've got a few folks who will be hardliners, can't be bought or bargained or otherwise cajoled."

"That doesn't matter—"

"It does, sir," Corman said.

"You don't need to tear Aventil apart," Lemt said.

"Right, because you know who the Thorn is, and I can just knock on his door," Fenmere said. "Yes, I'm sure he'll be sitting with the Sons of Tyson."

"He will, because he is a Tyson," Jendle said.

That was news.

"Are you saying that gnat Colin Tyson is the Thorn? No, impossible."

"Nah, he's the son of the other Tyson brother," Lemt said. "We've been keeping our ear to the ground, asking questions, paying attention, and—"

"The Thorn is Cal Tyson's son?" Fenmere asked. His hands were trembling with rage. "It makes sense, who else would plague me so? But if he's a mage then—of course."

It all made perfect sense. Why, after years of being gone, did Cal Tyson come back to Maradaine? With a wife? Fenmere had always suspected that there was more family, someone who would come looking for that wife, which is why he kept tabs on her at the Lower Trenn Ward. He had let those reports slide.

"Have we gotten reports from our eyes at Lower Trenn?" he asked Gerrick. "Has anyone interacted with Tyson's wife?"

Gerrick reached into his briefcase and thumbed through it. "Nothing of significance, I thought. There was an incident today, apparently, where some college boys visited another one who had been in *effitte* trance. The parents and some charlatan who claimed he could heal someone in the trance were there as well. He then . . . well, that's interesting."

"What?"

"Well, the charlatan decided to test his method on one of the other patients, and briefly considered Missus Tyson. Our nurse there noticed one of the students looked particularly distraught when he suggested that. Name of Veranix Calbert."

"His last name is Calbert?" Fenmere asked. "Are you telling me to go into hiding, Cal made his given name into his family name?" The absurdity of it, the gall.

"Veranix," Lemt said, his tone questioning. "Yeah, that's what we knew. Veranix Calbert, University student."

"But—" Jendle started, and Lemt smacked his arm.

"Well then," Fenmere said. "This changes things. Changes them a lot, and I think we shouldn't just kill Mister Calbert. No, we need to hurt him first."

"How do we do that?" Jads asked.

"How much money and product was lost, Jullick? A rough value?"

"Maybe fifty thousand crowns, I'd say."

"A good round figure. Everyone, put the word on the street, that the price on the Thorn's head, for anyone who brings him in to me, is fifty thousand crowns. And make sure all the Aventil gangs know."

"As you say, sir," Corman said.

"And give our new friends in the basement whatever they need. I've decided to take them up on their offer. And send word of that around to some of the Circles we've been dealing with, see if they want a piece of it. Misters Lemt and Jendle, you can join in on that fun."

"Oh, really?" Lemt asked. "We'd love a crack at him."

"Then you shall have it." A plan was forming, a delicious plan that wouldn't just kill the Thorn, but pay him back pain for pain. "So will all the Aventil gangs, and every enemy Veranix Calbert has made. I hope he rests well tonight, because by tomorrow there won't be any place in all of Maradaine where he'll find safe harbor. Everyone in the city will be coming for him."

The Thorn wouldn't just be killed. He'd be outed. Hunted. Everything in his life taken from him. And once that happened, by this time tomorrow, the son of Cal Tyson would be dragged in front of Willem Fenmere, and he would finally have his last revenges on the man who had killed his brother Charlen.

CHAPTER THIRTEEN

DELMIN WAS GONE FROM THE room when Veranix woke up. This wasn't actually particularly remarkable, Delmin often woke up before him and went off to perform duties as floor prefect before everyone walked to breakfast. Delmin, as prefect, took his duties seriously, even if he hadn't been anywhere near the stickler Rellings was last year, especially about things like the walk to breakfast. There was no more queueing up together and being counted, nor were there bed checks or other power games like Rellings had played.

Veranix slowly pulled himself out of bed, feeling every scrape and bruise on his body. And those were plentiful. Checking the mirror, his face had not escaped those either. He'd had worse, but the yellowing bruise on his eye was particularly bad. He had grown adept at hiding his injuries with a bit of magic, masking an illusion over his face, but he'd have to keep it up all day throughout classes. That was not something he was looking forward to.

The bandage on his stomach had seeped through, and he unwrapped it to check the wound. The stitching was quite well done, and while it hurt like blazes, he felt it was going to heal nicely in due time. Though he had to take it easy for the next week, if not more.

Not an idea he was too happy about, but he needed to be reasonable. Last night had been a disaster, but hopefully it was also enough of a disaster for Fenmere as well that it stung. The Thorn needed to lie low, but he had given Fenmere a bloody nose, and that should be enough to last a few days.

Especially since Delmin and Kaiana both needed to cool down, and a few days with no Thorn business would help with that. They were right, too. Mila had convinced him to rush with her plan, that the moment was ripe—and she had been right about that—but he shouldn't have gone with any plan that put Del and Kai in the streets, in danger. It was a miracle that they got out unscathed.

Colin and his Sons of Tyson definitely didn't.

That was something he was going to have to reckon with. One thing in a long list.

But the first thing was breakfast, so he'd have the strength to face the day. He hurried up and got dressed and glamoured his face. Ready to deal with the world, he crossed over to Holtman behind a group of second-years, most of the residents having already made their trek to the meal hall.

"Pretty incredible, right?" Eittle said, coming up to him as he got his tray.

"Seems like the usual breakfast," Veranix said. Itasa rolls, stick buns, and hot oats, which had been the main fair for breakfast most of the semester. Fine, as far as Veranix was concerned, though it was oddly repetitive in ways it wasn't in previous years.

"Oh, no," Eittle said. "I'm talking about that Rassin fellow, bringing that tranced soldier back."

"Right," Veranix said. That seemed like a lifetime ago, instead of yesterday. "Sorry, my head was on the food. You know how it is."

"Sure," Eittle said, loading his plate with rolls and buns. The boy wasn't a mage, but he could eat like one. "You all right?"

"Didn't sleep well," Veranix said. He had slept quite heavily, but had been plagued with nightmares. A side effect of pushing himself too hard with the napranium cloak. He wasn't clear if it was due to overextending his natural magical ability, or if it was connected to long exposure to napranium. Delmin had been trying to research it, but he hadn't had much luck. The information just wasn't out there. Druth mystical scholars really didn't have much experience with napranium.

And Veranix knew damned well he wouldn't understand it without Delmin's help.

Delmin was sitting alone with his breakfast, head down, poking his rolls with his fork with tired disinterest. Veranix wasn't sure if he should sit down with him, but Eittle went right over and took a seat. Veranix stopped for a moment, wondering if it would be worse to not sit with Eittle now, or to sit with Delmin when he clearly wanted to be alone.

Saints, he could dive into fights with a dozen goons or jump on a winged lizard, but an awkward moment in a dining hall froze him up.

Eittle looked back up at Veranix, confused, and that was enough to get him to sit down. Delmin glanced up at them both as Veranix sat, but otherwise didn't acknowledge them.

"So I talked a bit more with Parsons's parents last night," Eittle went on. "They're happy to pay for Rassin to make a few more attempts on other patients first, get his technique right."

"I have to tell you, I have a bad instinct about that guy," Veranix said

"But I just . . . if he can help Parsons, and it looks like he can, well . . ." He shook his head. "I just miss him, man. And I get that you're mad about what he did, getting messed up with that *effitte* junk, but there ain't no one more mad than me about that."

"Hardly," Delmin muttered.

Eittle didn't seem to notice that, and he went on. "But you get that he deserves a chance, don't you?"

"Yeah," Veranix said. "Every person in that ward deserves it."

"Is that what this Rassin fool is doing?" Delmin asked. "Giving them a chance? Or using them for his twisted experiments?"

"What?" Eittle asked.

"We don't know what he did to Kai—to that old soldier. We have no idea if he really cured the guy, or if . . . blazes, I don't even know. We know nothing."

"The guy seemed recovered," Eittle said.

"Seemed, yes," Delmin said. "Maybe today he won't be. Who knows what Rassin did. Or what he gets out of it. Or anything."

"Yeah, but—"

"We're all so stupid," Delmin snapped. "We don't know anything about what we're doing. We certainly don't know why we're doing it.

Or what we hope to accomplish. We just fumble about like fools. Don't we, Vee?"

"Del—" Veranix said, not sure what to say right now.

"And maybe Parsons had the right damn idea. Might as well burn your brain out, and just get to sit up in the ward all day, not a worry in your head. Sounds a lot rutting easier."

Delmin got up from the table and stalked off.

"The blazes was that?" Eittle asked.

"Nothing about you or Parsons, I think," Veranix said. "Or Rassin. I think he's got something else on his mind."

"Should one of us follow him, find out what's going on?"

Veranix thought about that for a moment. He knew damn well what was going on, and nothing he could say would help, and certainly Eittle couldn't help Delmin either.

"Give him a bit to cool off," Veranix said. "I'll . . . I'll see if he's ready to talk after theory class."

It was not an actual violation of constabulary protocol for a lieutenant to sleep in the footpatrol bunks, but it certainly wasn't normal, and it was clear to Benvin from the stares he got when he woke up that the regular patrol folk were quite confused.

"You doing all right, Left?" one of them asked. "Your lady latch you out or something?"

"No lady at my house," Benvin said as he found his shirt and coat. "I was just working late and needed to close my eyes for a bit."

"Cap kept you here late?" another asked. "That happen a lot when you make left?"

"Man, that's what Benvin and his freaks do," a third said. "Extra hours, making us all look bad."

"Maybe you need to look better, son," Benvin said to him. "So why don't you run to the clerk and get all the reports from Waterpath from last night, and get them to my desk by the time I've hit the closet, gotten a fresh tea, and gotten back there?"

The patrolman stammered a bit, and then nodded. "Yes, sir."

To that officer's credit, he had managed to accomplish the assigned task in the time Benvin had given him, and quite a few files were waiting on his desk. He set his tea down and got to work going through them, to get a sense of what exactly happened last night.

There had been a whole lot of chaos, and while it was on the Dentonhill side of Waterpath, at least some of the scrum had bled over into Aventil, and there had been so many whistles calls that Aventil officers crossed the street to help out.

A whole lot of the arrests had been folks in Mary uniforms. Students. That didn't make much sense. He flipped through the pages, and saw that some of them had been taken here for filing. Scooping up the files, he went down to the floor clerks.

"Hey," he said. "We brought in a bunch of folks in that donny in Dentonhill, they in lockup?"

"That what it says?" the clerk asked without looking up.

"Yeah, but there's no names, just descriptions of what they wore."

"Then that's what it says," she offered.

"We brought them in and didn't turn paper on them?"

"Most didn't have paper," she said.

That didn't make any rutting sense. "No, come on, get up."

"What are you telling me to get up for?"

"Because we're going to walk down to the cell and see for ourselves. Come on, you and me."

She sighed and rolled her eyes, but got up, taking the lead as they walked down to the cells. "I don't know why you're all worked out on this."

"Because you get people's names when you lock them up, miss. You follow process, and honor their rights. Are there even Justice Advocate's people here for them?"

"It's still early, they won't come until nine bells at least," she said, opening the door leading to the lockup cells. "But here, you can ask everyone their name if it makes you feel better."

"I will, because surely—" he said as he walked in.

He saw about five folks in University of Maradaine uniforms, and he immediately understood what had happened.

"Surely," he said through his teeth. The fact that neither this clerk nor the arresting officers noticed what was screamingly obvious to him was appalling. "Surely, miss, if a group of university students were arrested and brought here, they would have identifying papers on them, yes?"

"You'd think, but no," she said.

"Or that they would call for a factor from the school to come down on their behalf, yes? Almost any student would know to call on that, or at least a Justice Advocate. Educated kids wouldn't just sit here."

"I don't know about that."

He sighed. "Then you would think that *just maybe* you could recognize that these supposed university students are *obviously* Aventil gangers? He's got a Prince tattoo on his arm, by the saint's sake. And that one has Orphan scars, and . . . saints, that one is Docker Pins."

"Heya, Left," Docker said. He had been one of the minor players in the Kickers, and Benvin and his folks had brought him in a few times.

"What the blazes is this sewage, hmm?" Benvin asked.

"What, you can't believe I cleaned myself up, got on the path of the decent life, like you say we should do? Started up as a Uni kid?"

"Where did you get these uniforms?" Benvin asked. "And what the blazes were you all doing in Dentonhill starting a fight in them? And why are you together with a Prince and an Orphan and . . . whoever the rest of these are?"

"I ain't no Prince no more."

"Not a Orphan, neither."

Benvin turned to the clerk. "Get their real names, get proper files going, and do your damned job right." He stormed off and went up to the captain's office, barging right in without even knocking.

"Saints above, Lieutenant," Holcomb said when he came in. "It's far too early in the morning for your usual foolery."

"Captain, do you have any idea what went on last night?"

"Bit of noise at the 'path, I hear," Holcomb said. "Some of ours and some of Dentonhill brought in a few of the troublemakers."

"Aventil gangs crossed into Dentonhill, wearing university uniforms," Benvin said. "We're going to get fallout over this, sir, mark it."

"Fallout?" Holcomb asked. "We might get more sewage and trash killing each other than normal for a day or two, but nothing so different from the usual mess, hmm?"

"Sir, we're going to want to put more boots on the street out there," Benvin said. "Hold the line down now before the dam breaks."

"The blazes are you talking about?"

"We need to call in everyone we can to work a double, work through the night the next few days. Call support from city central or the GIU. We have a duty—"

"Did you come into my office, *Lieutenant*, to lecture me about my duty?"

"As a matter of fact I did."

"I give you quite a bit of latitude, Benvin. Too damn much. And I only do that because you and your band of loons run good numbers. If you didn't get the job done I wouldn't put up with the sewage you say."

"Then let me get the job done, sir."

"You've got your team, use them," Holcomb said. "Now get out of here."

Benvin left, knowing full well that Holcomb could and would fire him if he pushed too hard. So he had to do what he could with what he had. So be it. His team of Loyals were the best in the stationhouse, and hopefully that would be good enough.

He walked into his squad room, where the team was already gathered.

"Tell me you have something on the business last night. Who knows something?"

Jace perked up. "I was in the thick of that while walking home."

That was good. "All right, what do you know?"

"Folks in Uni clothes—probably one of the gangs, I'm thinking Sons of Tyson—"

That made sense. The gang was formed from the castoffs and outcasts of the neighborhood. That was why the folks in the holding cells had markers from different gangs.

"We gotta clamp down on them hard," Tripper said.

"They hit a few spots at once in south Denton," Jace said. "All Fenmere spots."

"How'd they know Fenmere spots?" Pollit asked.

"Probably because they were working with the Thorn," Jace said.

"The Thorn was part of this?"

"Yeah," Jace said.

"He's a menace," Tripper said.

"No he ain't," Jace said, almost in a snap of instinct. Everyone was staring at him, glaring really.

"The blazes you say?" Saitle asked.

"What, did you talk to him?" Benvin asked.

"Matter of fact," Jace said.

"And you didn't try to bring him in?"

"Like I'm going to bring in the Thorn," Jace said. "You got him wrong, though. One of Fenmere's goons was about to decorate his knife with my insides and the Thorn saved me, taking the hit for me. And that's the second time he has saved me."

"Don't be a fool, Jace."

"I ain't no fool," Jace said. "The Thorn isn't like those other gangers."

"That is true," Wheth said. "He's more dangerous."

"He got stabbed?" Benvin asked, that part of Jace's story hitting his brain.

"Saving me."

"So he was hurt, and you were there."

"Yeah."

"And is he in custody now?"

Jace frowned. "That wasn't an option. And I don't think it's a good idea."

"You don't think, Welling?" Tripper asked. "Don't you remember he killed Mal, nearly killed the Left?"

"That wasn't him," Jace said. "You know damn well we got the guy who did that. That was Erno Don. And he's out in the streets right now. So who's gonna get him?"

Benvin was getting a headache over this. "What are you even on about, boy?"

"The Thorn isn't our enemy," Jace said firmly. "He's helping people out there, doing the same good work we are."

The room went quiet, all the rest of the squad looking back and forth between Jace and Benvin.

"Jace," Benvin said in as low, as calm a voice as he could muster in this moment, even though his hand trembled. Where did this kid, just got his brass on his chest, get these ideas in his head? What fool things was he thinking? "You should go home now."

"What, Left?" he asked.

"You heard me," Benvin said. "If this is where your head is at, I don't need you today."

"Boss, you know it's gonna be a lot of trouble out there today."

"I do," Benvin said. "Which means I need to be able to count on each person at my arm. Right now, that ain't you."

"Boss—"

"Go home, Jace."

Jace stepped back. He probably didn't even realize he had come up, nearly chin to chin with Benvin.

"Your call, Left. You know where to get me."

"I know," Benvin said.

"You call, I'm here," Jace said. "Never doubt."

Benvin didn't know what to say to that, so he just nodded. Jace left the squad room.

After a long silence, Tripper cleared his throat and said, "So what's the plan, boss?"

"The plan," Benvin said. "Is we get boots in the street, all up and down the east side of the neighborhood. Press those patrol to walk Waterpath, and we're going to make a full show of color, best we can without the captain calling for it. It will get bad today, no doubt."

"None," Pollit said.

"So let's be about it."

Veranix Calbert.

Fenmere had spent all night letting that name roll around in his head. Relishing in it. Savoring the knowledge of it.

I have you, you miserable nit. He would extract the Thorn from his side, finally, and with it, finally be finished with all matters of Cal Tyson.

A knock on his bedroom door, and then Corman opened it and stuck his head in. "Sir? I think we're ready downstairs."

"Very exciting," Fenmere said. "Are you excited, Corman?"

"I'm finding myself . . ." Corman stopped to think for a moment. "Yes, exhilarated."

"Tell me, Corman," Fenmere said. "You have made it very clear to the guests downstairs what our rules are, yes?"

"Very," Corman said. "If I may ask a favor?"

Corman had always been one of the most loyal of his men, and this was the first time he had ever asked anything. "Name it."

"The incidents in Seleth were . . . particularly humiliating. The Thorn relished debasing me and Miss Jads, as if he considered us . . . unworthy."

This was a first. Corman had never spoke in detail of his encounter with the Thorn. "Unworthy how?"

"That he let me alive so I could deliver a message. As if I wasn't an enemy he needed to take seriously."

"He's going to take things very seriously soon."

"Yes, and . . ." Corman looked down to the floor. "He threatened my teeth and tenders at the time. When you have him, I would very much appreciate the honor of depriving him of those things before he is killed."

"Oh, Corman," Fenmere said, chuckling. "If all goes well, that boy will spend quite some time in the bleed room, and the whole Bone Crew will drag the proceedings out for days. Weeks. And I can't see why you and I can't enjoy getting our hands dirty as well. We deserve that, my old friend. You can deprive him of whatever organ you wish."

"Thank you, sir." Corman gestured for him to head down the stairs to the parlor.

At the bottom of the steps, a rough young boy, no more than ten years old, stood at attention, which looked especially odd given his ragged, mismatched coat, pants, and boots.

"Mister Fenmere, sir," the boy said. "Pleasure to make yours."

"This is?" Fenmere asked.

"This is Mister Yont," Corman said. "He runs a cadre of boys who profess to be the best deliverers of the *South Maradaine Gazette* in four neighborhoods."

"Well then," Fenmere said, extending a hand to the boy. "Always glad to meet the captains of enterprise of tomorrow."

The boy shook his hand. "You've got a special edition of your own, sir?"

"I do," Fenmere said. He nodded to Corman, who produced a packet of pamphlets, printed over the night.

THE THORN IS A SON OF TYSON!
THE TRUCE OF WATERPATH WAS BROKEN!
THE SONS MUST PAY, OR AVENTIL WILL BLEED!
DELIVER THE THORN TO DENTONHILL!
FIFTY THOUSAND CROWNS UPON DELIVERY!

Yont looked at the sheets and whistled. "Where these need to go, sir?"

"Fill Aventil with them. Every nook and corner. Every bar and flop. Before the midday bells."

"My boys can do that, sir," Yont said. "But that'll be two hundred crowns for us all."

"Two hundred?" Fenmere asked. He glanced over to Corman. They had already set a price at fifty.

"You're showing me what you're willing to spend, here, sir," Yont said, tapping on the top of the pamphlets. "And I've got the crew that can get it done. So that's the price, which I mark as fair for what you want."

Fenmere chuckled. There was something in the way the boy spoke, the brash confidence, let alone the Dentonhill street accent, that dug out old memories. "I like this young man. Pay his two hundred, and then another twenty for his pocket."

"As you say, sir," Corman said.

"Pleasure of business, sir," Yont said. "Consider the job good as done." He took the packet and with a nod, went out the door.

"That was quite generous," Corman said.

"We're spending all sorts of money today, so I don't see why not," Fenmere said. "Plus he . . . is not unlike Charlen at that age." His brother had already been running a gang of boys by then. And if Cal Tyson hadn't have killed him, he'd still be here to run things at Fenmere's side.

"Of course, sir. Our special guests are in the parlor."

"And they have all been attended to properly?" Fenmere asked. "Equipped and fed and feted as best we can?"

"Yes, sir," Corman said. "I dare say, they are all quite excited."

"Let's not keep them waiting."

The sight of the people in the parlor was thrilling. Fenmere felt his heart race just a little faster seeing them.

First, there were the five people who had come here after escaping from Quarrygate. In light of the new information, Fenmere was excited about arming them and setting them loose. Cuse Jensett was now dandied up in a smart orange vest suit, with a belt covered in pouches. Erno Don and Enzin Hence were both in cloaks and hoods, the first in blue and the latter in crimson, with expensive bows and full quivers. They both did look quite like every description Fenmere been given of the Thorn, which was probably why both of them had been mistaken for him. Fenmere also realized he must have been mistaken about Enzin's body—he had looked all misshapen in the basement yesterday, but now he seemed just powerful and muscular.

Magpie was decked out in leather vest and tight slacks, with belt and bandoliers covered with throwing blades. And Jackdaw, the Ch'omik woman, was quite an impressive sight, her well-muscled arms, covered in tattoos, on full display, with her *n'disro*, a Ch'omik weapon that resembled a barbed rowing oar, mounted on her back.

Then his men, Lemt and Jendle. They had earned the chance to prove themselves here, and once he got them cleaned up and equipped, he admitted they looked quite impressive. Lean bodied, hair and beards trimmed, wearing clean quilted coats, they both looked like formidable opponents. Especially with the pairs of hatchets and short blades, respectively, they had at their belts.

Next came an associate from the Firewings—a fight with the Thorn would need some mages, after all. Pria Mandicall, who threw fire and flew with flaming wings, and had suffered humiliation from the Thorn in that incident in Seleth. He had brought a mercenary associate, by name of Rory Scanlin, who was clearly proud of his incredibly muscled body, since he wasn't wearing a shirt and had oiled his torso to a glistening shine. Fenmere didn't care, since the man had a pair of whips in his hand and seemed to be more than proficient in their use.

Finally, a man who was an associate of Gerrick's, and easily the most well-dressed person in the room, a Mister Endoriff. Fenmere did admire his style, with a dark blue suit fitted to his thin body, vest of Turjin silk, painted in swirls of blue, green, and violet, and gold and ivory hasps and buttons on his coat, vest, and cuffs. The boots were gold tipped, the high hat with a silk ribbon matching the vest, and smoked-lensed spectacles. Fenmere did admire a man of style.

"Mister Endoriff, Gentleman Mage," he said as he produced a card in a flash of fire, his accent indicating excellent schooling. "I understand you're looking to hunt sport on the campus."

Mandicall raised an eyebrow at him. "Didn't you get expelled from there?"

"I was wronged, deeply," Endoriff said. "Weren't we all, in some way? Which is why we're part of this?"

"I wasn't," Scanlin said. "But my man Pria was, so I've got his back."

"All of you have skills and motivation," Fenmere said. "Which is what I'm looking for. I've already put the call out to the Aventil gangs that I'm wanting the Thorn delivered to me, and will pay handsomely for him. And that applies to you as well."

"So what makes us special?" Erno asked.

"I only expect the gangs to tear each other apart over this. But you all, I expect to succeed. So each of you is being paid five thousand up front, and fifty thousand for delivering the Thorn to me, broken but alive. And you will know something that the Aventil gangs do not.

"The Thorn is a young magic student at the University of Maradaine, named Veranix Calbert. He lives in Almers Hall."

Corman produced a handful of charcoal drawings and passed them around. "We had someone scout the college already this morning, spot him, and draw these likenesses for you. He's currently in class right now."

As the assembled assassins looked over the drawing, Jensett chuckled. "That is him, all right. This is our man."

"I remember this prat," Enzin said. "He made some trouble for a few of my fellows from Kyst, he did."

"So," Fenmere said to the ten people assembled in front of him. "You know who the Thorn is. You know where he is, and you know what he looks like. Therefore I have nothing more I need to say, except: happy hunting."

CHAPTER FOURTEEN

JUTIE HAD BARELY SLEPT IN two days, and over the course of the night the bosses had kept coming in and out, asking him questions, making him tell his whole story again to someone else. Before he had gone to Quarrygate, he had probably never had more than five words said directly to him by any of the bosses. He doubted any of them had even known his name.

Not that he had been able to tell any of them apart, aside from Old Casey. They were all a bunch of has-beens, the ones who had survived the brawls in the Aventil Rows back in '94. You live long enough, too old to still fight, you end up sitting in the basement pretending to be in charge. That's how it felt as they came in and out of the room. Bunch of old bastards pretending like they mattered.

Jutie had been with all of them over the course of the night, down in the basement backroom. No windows, no sense of what was going on outside, and these old men coming in and out, asking questions and making him start over again and again. Giles, Nints, Bottin, Old Casey, and whoever else the others were. He was so damned tired he couldn't keep them straight.

"So tell me," one of them was saying to him. "What got you pinched again?"

"What was I arrested for, or what got me caught?" Jutie asked. He had already told the whole story five times.

"Start with the first."

"I was in here with Colin, when that stick left came in with his boys to make trouble. Things were said, he tried to grab Colin, and one of his sticks grabbed me, and I had my knife out. Happened so quick I didn't even realize."

"And then you ran," the boss said.

"Made sense."

"Don't make a lot of sense to kill a stick in the Turnabout, you know. Quite the mess up, you know."

"I know," Jutie said.

"Quite the mess we had to clean up."

"I'm aware, I've been told several times today already."

"Ease down the mouth, Juteron. You came in here, you came looking for help from the Princes when you screwed up like that. And after breaking out of the Quarry."

"You all have kept saying this," Jutie said. "I don't know what the point is."

"This is the point, son," the boss said. "Some of the other bosses, and especially Old Casey, they're real mad. They know that the sticks will like it if we throw you to them. They've got half a mind to do that."

"But not you?"

"I'm still making up my mind. But I respect you put up a fight, son. A stick tussled with you, you gave back. You got sent to Quarry, and you kept your lip tight. Lots of boys wouldn't. Lots of boys didn't. But I know you did."

"I'm still a Prince."

"And then you saw a moment, and you took it. And you're breathing free air now."

"Air's a little stale down here," Jutie said.

"We're keeping you safe, son. Don't forget. Don't forget who's here for you. You're still a Prince, right?"

"Still on my arm." All Jutie wanted to do was sleep right now. Why were they still talking to him? Why didn't they just let him rest?

"Good. *Good.* I'm glad you're with us, Jutie."

He got up and went to the door, opening it up. Tooser and Deena came in, bringing tea and biscuits.

"How are you, man?" Tooser asked, sitting down with Jutie.

"Tired. Is it morning already?"

"It is," Deena said quietly. "Eat something."

Jutie picked up a biscuit and started spreading some fruit preserves on it. "Look, I know me being here can bring down trouble, but—"

"We're gonna take you to a safehouse flop soon," Deena said. "It's just last night there was . . ." She paused and looked down at the floor.

"There was a lot of trouble out there," the boss said.

"Because of me?" Jutie asked. "Because of the breakout?"

"Not you," Tooser said. "I couldn't rightly say if the breakout was a reason. But there was a huge brawl over Waterpath last night. Truce really broken."

"The Dentons came to roll over us?" he asked. He picked up the cup of tea and drank it as fast as he could manage. "If a fight is coming, you can count on me."

"This kid," the boss said, grinning as he shook his head. "You got to love him. Full of vinegar."

"Yeah," Tooser said, frowning at the boss. "He's a good Prince, always has been. Haven't you, Jutes?"

"You know me, man."

"I do," Tooser said. "Colin always liked you, didn't he?"

"Sure, yeah," Jutie said. "All of us in his crew."

"I don't know about the rest of us, but you, you he might listen to."

"The Dentons didn't come across the 'path," Deena said. "Colin and his Sons crossed into theirs. And Fenmere has already run paper, declaring that the trouble is coming. We've got to be ready, we've got to stand together."

"Sure," Jutie said. It made sense.

She slid some paper and ink across the table to Jutie. "He won't listen to us, but he might listen to you. He might come if you called out."

"Me? Really?"

"Write to him," Tooser said. "Let him know you're out and you're here, and that the Princes need to talk with him. We need him to meet us here, talk about a new truce for the neighborhood."

Jutie nodded. If he could help bring things back together, sure. He'd do what he needed to. "Yeah, I can write that," he said, picking up the pen and dipping it in the ink. "But after that, I need to sleep."

"Sure, kid," the boss said. "You write that for Colin, you can do whatever you want. Sleep, drink, we'll send a bird down to you, whatever you need."

"Sleep," Jutie said as he wrote. "That's all I want right now."

KAIANA STOOD IN FRONT OF THE MAIN DOORS OF THE LOWER TRENN Ward for nearly a half an hour, smoothing the front of her yellow dress and pacing back and forth so much she thought she must have worn a groove in the cobblestones. She even took a few minutes to pull out the weeds that had grown through the cracks, telling herself that it was an important task that someone needed to attend to, lest the weeds continue to damage the already crumbling walkway in this part of town.

She had gone in before. In the early days, she'd go once a week just to sit with her father, prattle on about whatever was going on with her life then. Then it became once a month, and then once a season, and she'd usually just sit quietly near him.

But now he was awake, and she had no idea wat she'd say.

"'Scuse, miss?" A young constable had come up to her. "You can't just be standing in the street like this."

"I can't?" she asked. "What's the problem?"

He shrugged awkwardly. "I . . . I don't rightly know, miss, but a few women who live in those tenements made a fuss for me to come remove you. I'd rather not have to, you know, actually have to do that?"

"Remove me?" Kai asked. "Whatever for? I'm just . . . I'm here to visit the ward. I just hadn't gone in yet, is all."

"Then you best do that, miss," he said. "I don't want to make this into more than it has to be, just those ladies called me over and cried up

rooms. There, in one of the beds, looking frail and withered, lay her father, propped up with a few coarse pillows. But for the first time in years, when she walked in, his eyes found her. And then his face lit up with joy.

"Sweet saints bless me!" he said. "Look at you, my sweet girl!"

"Papa?" she asked, daring to come closer.

"You look—no, you're too grown," he said. "They won't tell me how long I've . . . I don't really know or remember . . ."

"Seven years," she said, sitting next to him. "Seven years ago I found you on the floor."

Despite wanting to show only love and joy in this moment, the hurt and anger bled through her words. She couldn't hide it.

"I don't . . . I don't . . ." he said, looking about. "So much of my mind is still in a fog, I think. I can't quite . . ."

"It's all right," she said, taking his hand. She sat down on the bed next to him.

"You're terribly upset with me," he said. "And I think . . . I think you are quite right to be."

"Not right now."

"It's all like a dream—a nightmare, rather—but even before I . . . even before I did this to myself, I know, Kaiana, I know that I was already gone. I wasn't the father you deserved then. I don't expect you to forgive me."

Kaiana wanted to say that of course she did, but her voice didn't let her. She couldn't put the lie to words right now.

"You're so grown," he said. "And look at how you're dressed. You can afford something this nice?"

"I work at the University," she said. "I'm in charge of the grounds there."

He gasped. "Did Jontlen take you in?"

She shrugged. "In a fashion."

"Oh, saints, that must have been—I know he was a cruel fellow."

"He . . ." She almost told her father that Jontlen had been killed, but that would have been too much to put on him. "He passed to his judgment a few months ago."

"I only hope he lightened his scales with how he treated you, though . . ." Papa looked at her face. "No, that was not his way."

"I made do," she said.

"And you should not forgive me," he said. "I was selfish and . . . lost. Don't forgive me, child." He squeezed her hand a little tighter, probably as much as his bony hands could manage. "But please, do not abandon me, not yet."

"Never, Papa," she said. "I have to go back to work soon, but . . . I will keep coming to you here, and when the doctors say you're ready to leave . . ."

"If I ever am," he said morosely.

"When they say," she said firmly. "I have home enough for us both on campus."

Tears welled at his eyes. "I do not deserve such a daughter," he said.

"But I'm the one you've got," she said. She picked up one of the newssheets that was lying on a table near the bed. "I have a little time, though. Would you like me to read something to you?"

He smiled. "You learned how to read. I missed too much. I failed too much."

"But we have now and this time," she said, quoting one of the lines from *The Promises of Summer*. She looked at the newssheet and picked something that would interest him. "The Bricklayers met the White Ashers on the field yesterday, in a spirited match that was joyful sport for the athletes and the observers. Bricklayers batted at the tetch first . . ."

"Boss? Hey boss?"

Colin didn't know what time it was, but there was a lot of sunlight coming through the curtains around his bunk. It was probably already midmorning. He had no clue what time it had been when he and Sella had finally passed out from their exertions, but it had been well into the night, so he wasn't surprised that he had slept this long. Sella was still quiet in the bunk next to him.

"Hold up," he called out. He really didn't need whoever was calling him—saints, he needed to get everyone's name down—to throw open the curtain right now. He pulled on his slacks and slipped out from behind the curtains.

A handful of the Sons were in the flop, standing guard around someone they'd really have no chance of stopping if she decided to start something.

"Good to see you, Bassa," Colin said to the old woman. She was the Princes' butcher, the one the basement bosses called upon to really hurt people if they thought it was needed. One of the few folks in the Princes who had been in it since the beginning, who had been around with Colin's dad back in the day. "I don't supposed you're coming to join with the Sons."

"I can't do that, Colin," she said with a mirthless smile. "I'm sure you understand."

Colin scratched at the stubble on his chin. "So why are you here? Wait, let me guess. The Princes have a message for me, yes?"

"That's right," she said.

"They sent you because they expect me to trust you?" He chuckled. "Or at least were confident you could walk back out without any trouble."

"We give her some trouble, boss?" one of his Sons asked.

"Ease down," he told them. "This woman could carve your arm clean off at the joint without even breathing hard."

"Could," she said calmly.

"So am I to trust you?"

"Trust that I'll tell you true and plain," she said. She unfolded a few sheets of paper and handed him one. "There's a bounty out there on the Thorn."

He looked at the print. "Quite a good one." He kept his face calm, but nowhere in Maradaine was going to be safe for Veranix with a fifty thousand crown price on his head. Every single person in Aventil would step on their own mother to get that.

"That right there is a declaration," she said. "Fenmere is pressing in, because your folks wrecked the truce. So we got to bring it together."

"As in, the Princes and the Sons? We need a new truce?"

"To start. They want you to come to the Turnabout."

"Me and all my Sons, we'll sit and talk? Nothing doing. I'll send Sella and Cober to a church meet, but that's all."

"No, they want you, just you."

"That is stupid, and I would never."

"I know, you shouldn't," she said. She handed him the next paper. "That's why they gave me this to give you."

Colin looked it over, and immediately recognized the scratch writing that had been left on so many notes in the flop under Kesser's back in the day.

Colin—

I'm out of Quarry, and at the Turnabout. Don't know all of what they're telling me, but it sounds like trouble, and they want you to come talk. I think it could be good, but I don't know. Still, I want to hear what you're saying. Come if you can.

Jutie

"This is real?" he asked. "Jutie is out of Quarrygate?"

"There was a breakout of some players, and he managed to slip out as well," she said. "Trust me when I say, he's really there."

"All right, so he is."

"And if you don't come, they're going to put me to work. I'd rather not have to."

Blazes. Rutting bastards. But she told it true and plain, like she said. He did respect that.

"So I come alone or Jutie dies?"

"And they'll want it to be bad," she said.

"All right, one tick," he said, and went back to his bunk.

"What's going on?" Sella asked, rubbing her eyes. Colin put the rest of his clothes on and belted his knives.

"A lot of trouble, but I got to take care of it."

She sat up. "What can I do?"

"Take charge once I'm gone. If you don't hear back from me by two bells, take that money, get some to all our folks, and get them the blazes out of Aventil. Out of the city if you can."

"Blazes," she said. "That bad?"

"It could be," he said. Saints, there was probably no way he would walk into the Turnabout and walk out again, but he wasn't going to let that happen to Jutie. And with that price on Veranix's head, with Fenmere willing to offer that, everything was going to catch fire here. Probably before the day was out.

Sella grabbed the front of his shirt and pulled him in. "At least you had a good night?"

"If it was my last night ever," he said, realizing how likely that it would be. "Then it was the best it could have been."

She kissed him hard. "I'm not done with you, so try to stay alive. I'll keep the Sons together until you're back."

"Keep them alive," he stressed.

"I'll see you here or in the blazes," she said.

He left the alcove with his bunk and walked past Bassa. "All right, let's do this. No need to waste the day."

Delmin wasn't in Methodology class.

In all the time Veranix had known Delmin, he had never skipped a class, and yet today he didn't come to Methodology.

On top of that, today, for once, Professor Alimen was actually giving the theory lecture. He had been absent this whole semester, and whenever Veranix had seen him, the man had been very withdrawn. Quiet.

Nothing like the vibrant man who had come to the circus four years ago, joyful and excited, eager to talk to Veranix and his parents about the incredible magical talent he had inside him, how imperative it was he come to the University of Maradaine.

That was the day that had changed everything.

That day, Mom and Dad pledged to make it work, no matter what. They'd bring him to Maradaine. Regardless of what risk it might bring.

That day his brother lost his temper, worse than ever before. He had already been sore about being taken off the show after screwing up a catch a few weeks before, assigned to working the rigging. He had always been hard on Veranix, and now that they knew he was a mage, Soranix blew up. He went on, screaming that of course Veranix did better in the shows because he had been cheating with magic, and of course they were going to sacrifice everything for Veranix, because they always gave everything to Veranix, and he was always left with nothing.

That day, Soranix ran off in the night. As far as Veranix knew, he never came back.

But also that day, Professor Gollic Alimen was excited, thrilled, alive to talk to Veranix about magic and how that was going to provide him with opportunities

Today, though, Alimen was going on monotonously about using lunar cycles and the effect it had on ambient *numinic* energy, and while theory lectures often drove Veranix to despair of boredom, this was the first time he had ever thought that Professor Alimen was bored with the subject.

"You should all read chapters seven and eight in Tandelin," Alimen said. "That information will be on the exam." Veranix made a point of writing that down, if for nothing else than so Delmin would know. Of course, surely Delmin had already read *Tandelin's Numinic Studies* front to back and back again. "But for now, dismissed."

That was even more unusual. The eleven bells hadn't rung yet.

Veranix closed up his notebook—he had barely written anything, which was typical—and made his way down from the upper gallery to leave the lecture hall. He was barely off the stairs when someone grabbed him and pulled him into an alcove.

"What is going on today?" Anduette asked him. She looked at him with an odd regard, scrutinizing his face.

"It's strange, right?" Veranix asked. "Not just that Alimen gave the lecture, but ended it early."

"Yes, but, not what I meant," she said. "First off, Del not coming to class. Is he sick?"

"No."

"I can't imagine him not coming to class even because of that," she said. "Blazes, three weeks ago he was there despite sneezing up a storm the whole time. So where is he?"

"I don't know."

"You didn't talk to him this morning? You share a room, you must have seen him."

"He left breakfast early, a bit upset. I was as surprised as anyone he wasn't here."

"Right. Upset about?"

"I couldn't rightly say."

"Hmmm. And what's with your face?"

"What about my face?"

"First off, you're giving off this hum. Almost like a bee. Just a *mmmmmmm* from your face, which tells me that you're, like, *numini*cally charging it for some reason. But . . ." She squinted and moved in closer to him. "It's also just kind of . . . wrong."

"Wrong?"

She touched his face, poking his cheek. "You're glamouring your face!"

"I am not!"

"Please, my finger vanished when I poked you."

"Do not poke my face."

"Are you hiding a blemish or something?" she asked. "Is it bad? Is that why Del isn't here? Did you two do something to your faces and you're glamouring yours and he's just hiding?"

"No, don't—"

"Oh my saints!" she exclaimed. "Did you two, like, go off to the pubs or something and get in an actual fight, and you've got a bruise? Does he?" She gasped. "Wait, you two weren't fighting each other, were you?"

"No, of course . . ." he started to say, but the weight of what had happened last night suddenly landed on his chest. What he went through. What Delmin must have gone through, how terrifying it must have been. What Veranix had put him through in his stupid insistence on dragging everyone into his fight. "Of course not, we . . . we . . . everything is fine."

The lie of that was evident, as he was already crying when he said it, and forcing the words out opened up a floodgate of tears.

"Hey, hey, whoa," Anduette said, pulling him further into the alcove, though there was no one left in lecture hall. "No need for that, or . . . no, you do what you need to right now, but . . ." She waved her hand and there was a pulse of *numina*. "No one else needs to hear it."

"Thank you," he managed to say. She must have magically caught the sounds of his crying, kept them from echoing out into the lecture hall or the corridor.

"You did get in a fight," she said. "Oh, my saints watching me above, your face is a mess."

He must have dropped the glamour.

"It's fine, I've had . . . it's nothing."

"Delmin didn't do this to you, did he?"

"Saints, no," Veranix said. "I really . . . please don't make me explain, but no, Delmin did not do this."

"All right," she said. "You tell me what you want to when you want to. But you really don't know where Delmin is?"

"He left breakfast, and . . . I really don't. But he is upset at me, and rightly so."

"Whatever it is, you two can work it out."

"I don't know."

"Listen, I've been on it with the two of you all semester. I have barely been able to keep up, frankly, because the two of you are always on the same note."

"We are not," Veranix said.

"You are, trust me," she said. "You're like brothers."

That made Veranix laugh, and then that laughter devolved into tears. "That's about right, because my own . . . saints, I was just . . . my own brother, I haven't seen in years. But the last thing he said to me was that he hated me."

"Oh, 'nix," she said, wiping his face with a kerchief. "You need . . . do you want me to go find Del? Or hunt Mila down for you? I know the two of you are . . . whatever you are."

"No, I just . . . I should get out of here, and . . ."

"No," she said, putting her hand on his chest to stop him from leaving the alcove. "You're a mess, you need some time to settle down, out of sight of people. I have just the thing."

That was not what he expected her to say at all. "What is that?"

"I'm going to show you my favorite place on campus."

CHAPTER FIFTEEN

C OLIN WALKED INTO THE TURNABOUT with Bassa right at
his back, and as soon as he was inside, he could feel every eye on
him, hear every knife pulled an inch out of their sheaths.

He ignored that and walked up to the bar front.

"Hit me with a striker, friend," he said. "I'm really dying for it."

"What?" the barman—not someone Colin recognized—asked.

"Listen," Colin said. "These fellows probably want to kill me, so if I
am going to die, I want one last Turnabout striker first, hmm?" He
leaned in closer. "I shouldn't say this, but the ones at the Old Canal do
not measure up."

"Give him one," Old Casey said as he came up from the back. "The
least we can do."

The barman snapped to the stove, and while the striker was slapped
together, the rest of the Princes placed themselves around him, blocking
the exits. How Colin expected it to go. He wasn't sure what was going
to happen exactly, but there was clearly something more they wanted
from him than just a price of blood and flesh.

The barman dropped the newsprint-wrapped sandwich on the
counter, steaming and bubbling with cheese.

"Obliged," he said, picking it up. Old Casey was about to speak,
when Colin held up a finger to silence him. Then he took a glorious bite

from the striker. Cheese and lamb and beer-cooked onion and potato, all in a perfectly toasted Aventil-style roll. Bliss.

Worth dying for, almost.

"Amazing," he said. "Now, Casey, what is the story?"

"I won't insult you with a dance," Casey said. "We know you and yours joined the Thorn in attacking a chunk of Fenmere's operations last night, and that's had consequences."

"Consequences was kind of the idea," Colin said, taking another bite.

"Fenmere wants war with Aventil—specifically the Sons—and he wants the Thorn. So you're going to help me clean up this mess."

"I doubt that," Colin said. "Bring Jutie up."

"Pardon?"

"You used Jutie as a lure to get me here," Colin said. "Bassa told me plain, so I came. So get him out."

"Go get him," Casey told someone, and they ran out the back. "While we wait, let me tell you how it's going to go."

"How it's going to go," Colin said. "This is rich."

"I will tell you," Casey said. "You know who the Thorn is. So you give him to us. You turn him over, you and your Sons are all welcome back in the Princes. With that, we can make Fenmere whole, make Aventil whole, and get the truce back on."

"I don't see how."

"We give him the Thorn, and the Sons are gone. Fenmere no longer has a beef to press."

"Sorry," Colin said. "I mean that as, 'I don't see how I could ever do anything that rutting stupid.'"

"Foolish," Casey said.

Jutie came out from the back, flanked by Tooser and Deena. Saints, that hurt. The fact that Tooser, of anyone, had stuck with the Princes, and was now being their lackey, that hurt most of all.

"Cap!" Jutie shouted. "You all right?"

"Are you all right, Jutes?" Colin asked. "They treating you decent?"

"I could stand to sleep," Jutie said.

"You should," Colin said. "Now let him walk."

"He's a Prince, he's not captive," Casey said.

"All the more reason he's free to walk out. Right? If he's a Prince, you trust him as your brother. Is he your brother, Tooser? Deena?"

"Shut your rutting hole," Tooser said.

"Let me make something clear," Casey said. "You are going to give us the Thorn, and you are going to do that now."

"Nothing on," Colin said. "No chance at all."

"Bassa," Casey said.

Something hard and heavy hit Colin in his back. Bassa's hammer. Colin tried to turn toward her, and got another hammer to his ribs. Then a kick to his knee dropped him down.

His hand went to his knife, and Bassa caught him by the wrist.

"Don't make me take the fingers," she told him. "Please don't try it."

"I would like you to take the fingers," Casey said. "That sounds interesting."

"I could," Bassa said, taking Colin's chin and turning his head to look at her. "But I will tell you, sir, I don't care to. And I don't think it will do anything you want."

"He'd have less fingers," Casey said.

"But he won't talk," she said, appraising his face. "Nothing we do will make him betray the Thorn, I can see that."

"The doing might be fun."

Bassa shook her head. "You want him to talk, you need better motivation. You two, hold him."

Tooser and Deena grabbed Jutie.

"Hey, what gives?" Jutie asked.

"Colin, do you know how many teeth Jutie has?" Bassa asked, walking over to him. "And how hard it truly is to pull a perfectly good tooth out? It requires strength, determination, and most of all, the right tool."

"Let him go!" Colin said.

"Look at this spanner," she said, taking the tool out of her belt. "You have some good leverage on this. A lot of real power there. But it doesn't grip the tooth well." She threw the spanner at Colin, hard metal hitting him in the chest.

"Now, these pliers, oh they can get a good hold of a tooth, but no leverage. No way to get your strength behind it. So what a dilemma. I have to choose between grip and leverage."

"Stop it!" Colin said.

She threw the pliers at him. "But look what I have," she said as she pulled another tool out of her belt. "Lock grips. Look at that. You've got the grip of the pliers, the leverage of the spanner. I don't have to give up either one. Hold his mouth open."

Deena and Tooser complied.

"So what's it gonna be?" she said, walking over to Jutie. "What are you gonna make me do?"

"Leave him alone!" Colin shouted. "Saints, he's a Prince, ink on his arm, you do that to him? To get me? Is that what you are? Is that what you do to your brother, Tooser?"

If Tooser faltered at all, it didn't show as Bassa closed the distance and put her tool in Jutie's mouth.

"It won't surprise you to know that I know exactly which tooth will hurt the most," she said. "Last chance."

"Wait!" Jutie shouted.

"You know something, kid?" Casey asked.

"Don't kill Colin," Jutie said. "Swear on your arm and Rose Street, and I'll tell you."

Casey scowled. "I swear, on my arm and Rose Street, if what you tell us gets us the Thorn, no Prince will kill Colin."

"All right," Jutie said. "The Thorn has two friends. A skinny magic student, stringy hair, and a Napa girl who works on campus. You find them, you get the Thorn."

"I know that Napa girl!" someone called out. "Saw her leave the south gate an hour ago, went west."

"Then take some folks and go get her," Casey said. A group of Princes were out the door in a trice. "And take Colin downstairs and . . . don't kill him."

Jutie pulled free of Tooser and Deena and ran to Colin, grabbing him in an embrace. "I'm sorry."

"It's all right," Colin whispered. "I'm just glad you're safe."

A few meaty fellows ripped Colin away from Jutie and dragged him toward the back rooms. The last thing he saw, though, was Jutie giving him a nod and making a point of taking a seat near the back door.

Colin hoped it would be enough. There was nothing else he could do to protect Veranix, not now.

JACE HAD NOT GONE HOME.

That was the last place he wanted to go right now. Going home would mean questions from Mother and Aunt Zura and whoever else was there, and that was not something he needed right now.

So he went to a tea shop on Kemper and Bush, one of the places that had been Kickers territory, but was now a corner untroubled by any gang. Though sitting at the tea shop, it wasn't clear that had made things here any better. There were still broken windows, graffiti painted on the walls, and a cluster of shoeless children up to mischief across the street.

Shutting down the Kemper Street Kickers hadn't really changed anything on this corner.

At least the tea and cresh rolls were fine. Nothing extraordinary, but fine.

"If you asked me to come out here, I hope you ordered some for me." Minox sat down at the table.

"Here," Jace said, pushing the plate of cresh rolls over.

"It's not appropriate to use a Constabulary page for a personal message," Minox said. "Which I know you know, thus I presumed you did it for a significant reason."

"Can't I have lunch with my brother?" Jace asked.

"Of course," Minox said, taking a bite of a cresh roll. "But that's not something you have ever done, which leads me back to significant reason. Add in, you are not wearing your uniform jacket, which tells me you are not currently on shift. So I think something has gone quite wrong."

"I got into a row with the lieutenant over the Thorn."

Minox nodded. "My experience with the lieutenant has been that he is a decent man who believes in doing the right thing, even when the right thing is in conflict with the law or social norms."

"What do you mean? He upholds the law."

"Yet he gathers around him people who would be rejected, some by the social rules, some by the law. Pollit, for example."

"Pollit is a good officer, we all know it," Jace said hotly. So many people in the station called Pollit a freak, and Jace wouldn't hear otherwise from anyone.

"I agree, I'm proud to have worked with him."

Minox just calling Pollit "him" was enough to calm Jace down. Plenty of the jerks in the stationhouse didn't have the same decency.

"But my point is, while Lieutenant Benvin does uphold the law, his morality is aligned differently. As is yours, as is mine."

"Yours?"

"More so in the last few months than before, but still. You and I have both observed, in different ways, that the Thorn is a force that does good, if outside the law. Else you would have arrested him last night."

"I couldn't do that and feel right."

"And I wouldn't either, knowing what I know about him."

Jace looked at his brother's face. He had never quite had the gift that Minox had for unraveling people's truths and secrets just by looking at them, but he did know Minox well enough to read him. "You do know who he is, don't you?"

"I do, but that confidence is not mine to share. And it's borne with a certain . . . higher duty to each other."

"So you're with me that the Thorn shouldn't be arrested, obviously. How do I get Benvin to see that?"

"The question is, how much do you need to?" Minox asked. "Are you saying you can't do your job, at least working with Benvin in his squad, here in Aventil in these circumstances? That your desire to respect the Thorn is too much in conflict?"

"How do you resolve it?" Jace asked. "Blazes, you're the most . . . the *most* 'constabulary' person I know."

"That's quite the statement," Minox said. "Especially give how unorthodox I am in the organization."

"Listen, I love you, you know that," Jace said.

"You have not, actually, articulated that before," Minox said, stiffening a little.

"But you're the one who knows the rules, knows the regulations, knows the book back and forth. Oren is a hard-ass about all sorts of things, but that's because he likes to pretend he's in charge of things."

"He is far more enamored of authority than justice," Minox said.

"That's what I'm saying," Jace said. "Justice is . . ." He couldn't quite find the word for what he wanted.

"It is beyond the letter of the law, the enforcement of regulation, or even the social rules of orthodox. Justice is beyond what is written by mankind."

"That sounds almost religious."

"I've been listening at church more and more, since . . ." Minox faltered. He had been going with Mother to Saint Veran's on the outskirts regularly since Corrie vanished. "Well, I don't know how much stories of saints and miracles are meaningful to me, but the underlying message has . . . I have experienced things recently that have given me a kind of faith. At least in the idea of justice."

"I can get behind that," Jace said. "And that's why you are all right with the Thorn? Because he's about justice?" Jace wasn't even sure what his own answer to the question was, just that he knew it wasn't right to arrest someone he saw trying to do good. Whose instinct was to put himself between a blade and a constable.

"I think he is . . ." Minox trailed off. "I think he is my friend, and I'll leave it at that."

"Then I guess he's mine as well," Jace said. "But maybe that means I can't do my job anymore."

"I'd say you need to do your job, because you're someone who understands that. I've been seeing more and more problems in the Constabulary. Right now, most of my time is spent in the archives, reading through files, and there are too many . . . too much . . ." Minox shook his head. "We need more people who can see where the law casts a shadow over the light of justice, and do what's right. And I've always seen that in you. I think that's why Benvin put you on his squad." His attention had shifted to something else.

"Maybe," Jace said. "Do you want some more cresh rolls, I think—"

Minox had stood up and grabbed a piece of newsprint up from the ground, bringing it back to the table. "There's a price on the head of the Thorn, as well as a call to attack the Sons of Tyson."

"New gang in the northeast corner," Jace said.

"This price is very high, but this . . ." Minox's head tilted. "This is a distraction, to keep him out of Aventil. Perhaps to create chaos in the neighborhood while . . ."

Minox turned to Jace in a snap.

"We need to get to campus."

KAIANA WAS HALFWAY BACK TO CAMPUS WHEN THEY GRABBED HER.

She didn't even see it coming, didn't get a chance to shout or fight back meaningfully. Just all of a sudden there was a sack over her head, strong arms wrapped around her body, and then she was boxed in a crate before she could take two breaths.

She pounded on the wooden slats of the crate, screaming all sorts of invectives, as she felt herself being loaded onto a wagon and driven off. Clearly none of her screaming and banging made anything resembling a difference.

After a few minutes she felt her crate being carried out of the wagon, brought in somewhere. She kept shouting and pounding, and could hear plenty of voices around her. Then the crate was flipped over and she was unceremoniously dropped onto a wooden floor.

"Damn and blazes," she muttered as she tried to get up, her eyes adjusting to the change in light.

She was in the middle of a pub floor, surrounded by people on all sides. Rose Street Princes judging by the tattoos on their arms. Knives and knucklestuffers all around.

"Is this Napa slan the one?" an old man standing over her asked.

She answered that with a well-planted foot in his tenders. He doubled over and all the ones with knives moved in closer.

"If you wanted me dead I would be," she said quickly. "And I will not be disrespected by the likes of you."

The old man waved back the rest of the Princes. "She's got a good foot. Is she the one we want?"

"How many Napa sl—Napolic girls are there in town?" someone else asked.

"Jutie!" the old man called out. "Is this the girl?"

All the attention went to a young man in the back of the pub. "I'm not sure, maybe."

Kaiana had seen that young man before, she remembered him. When Veranix had been caught by Jensett, she and Delmin were looking for him, that boy—Jutie—helped them. He was one of Colin's people. What was going on here?

"He says maybe," the old man said, shaking his head. "Pull Colin up here."

Colin was here. That couldn't be good.

"What do you want with me?" Kaiana asked.

"If you're the girl, you know the Thorn," the old man said. "So we would be inclined to have you tell us how to find him."

"The who?" Kaiana asked, hoping she sounded convincing.

"The Thorn," the old man said firmly.

"Is that some sort of nickname for someone?" she asked.

"You know who I'm talking about!" he shouted, and he snapped his fingers. One of the Princes jumped forward and pressed a knife against her throat.

"I'm just a gardener who works for the University, I don't know any of the things that happen out here!"

"She's got to be lying," the old man said. "Bassa, make her talk."

A beefy woman strode over. "I do not like doing this sort of thing to uninvolved girls. Are we sure she is the one?"

"Jutie?" the old man shouted.

"I don't know! Maybe?"

"Colin will know, he'll rutting know."

"Look," Kaiana said. "I won't say anything, but I can just go."

"Rutting blazes, no. If you aren't the Thorn's Napa, we'll hold on to you until we find her."

Three guys came up from the back, dragging Colin who was bound, with a gag over his mouth.

"So, Colin," the old man said. "You see we have the Thorn's favorite bird. Now, you tell us where to find him or she's going to get what's coming to him."

One of them pulled down his gag, and he spat on the floor. "You just made a stupid mistake," Colin said. "You hurt her and there is *nothing* that will keep him from hunting down every last one of you."

The old man's face brightened. "So she *is* the Thorn's Napa slan."

Colin winced.

"He is right," Bassa said. "If we have her, we should not hurt her, not yet."

"She's not going to tell us where to find him unless we do," the old man said.

"Very dumb," Colin said. "If the Thorn finds out she's here, if someone was able to send him word, oh . . . you'd rather have every sinner in the canon chasing you down than face what he would bring upon you."

"He's not going to, though, because we've got you both, and you're going to tell us—"

There was a crashing sound from behind Kaiana, and when she turned to see where it came from, the table Jutie had been sitting at was empty.

"Where did he go?" the old man shouted. "Did he just run out of here?"

"You bet he did," Kaiana said, holding up her chin. Even though her heart was hammering, she kept her fear off her face. She had to. "And he'll let the Thorn know I'm here. That we're both here."

"Now, Bassa. Make her scream!"

"Ah, ah . . ." Kaiana said as Bassa took a step forward. The sight of this powerful woman advancing on her almost frightened the words out of her mouth. "When he comes, I don't think you want him finding a single hair out of place on my head, do you?"

"You saw what he did to the Trusted Friend, didn't you?" Colin asked. "He wasn't even mad that day."

The old man growled. "All right, tie them both up, right here in the middle of the room. Deena, take three and go after Jutie! The rest of you, secure every damn door, get on the roof, in the alleys, line along

Rose Street. Get ready to put everything we've got into taking down the Thorn!"

Hands dragged her to a chair and tied her to it, and Colin next to her.

"I'm serious," he whispered to her. "They just made the worst mistake they ever could."

Kaiana nodded, but didn't say anything. She knew too damn well he was right. And that was the last thing Veranix needed right now.

VERANIX WASN'T ENTIRELY SURE OF ANDUETTE'S INTENTIONS, BUT HE was glad when he realized that her "favorite place" on campus was in Bolingwood Tower, rather than up at the dormitories for the Ladies' College. The last thing he needed was further complications in his life, and any romantic intentions from Anduette toward him would be an absolute broomstick in the wagon spokes of a complication.

"What are you going to show me?"

"Just wait," she said. "It's a surprise."

"Surprises are not exactly a thing that I need right now."

She looked back and chuckled. "I promise that it's a safe surprise."

"I'll hold you to that."

She took him up four flights to one of the magic practice rooms, not the one he usually met Minox in, right below Alimen's offices.

"Really?" he asked her. "This is your favorite place on campus?"

"This tower, and especially this room, was built with steel reinforcement, with the hope that it would hold together in case of magical accident. You don't want a young mage experimenting and knocking down the tower."

"Right," Veranix said. "Almers Hall is the same."

"Now, you were a recruit, right? You didn't have to come here and demonstrate your ability to get accepted, did you?"

"No."

"I did," she said. "My audition was right here in this room, for Professor Echram and Mistress Inarda." Veranix hadn't had a class with Echram since first year.

"So this is about your magical audition, that's why it's your favorite?"

"I realized why this room was special that day," she said. She led him to the middle of the room. "Whatever they did when they built this room, they made right here, where we're standing, a perfect spot."

"For?"

She smiled, and snapped her fingers. Then the sound of the snap echoed around him, and that echo intensified reflecting back on itself, creating a drumbeat that lived on all around him. From the *numinic* surge coming off Anduette, she was clearly maintaining that.

"That's really—" he said, but she put her finger over his mouth, and then gave a trilling whistle. That tune joined in with the beat, underscoring it. Then she sang in a low voice, adding to the sound. All of it, echoing and repeating around him. She sang again, a different tune in a higher voice, mixing that with it, the harmonies blending together.

Her magical song bounced back and forth, themes repeating and blending together in new ways. Veranix didn't have words to describe it, but he closed his eyes and let it fill him with joy and peace.

And then the music died off, piece by piece, as the final echoes faded into silence.

Veranix opened his eyes, tears streaming from them.

Anduette smiled. "I thought you could use a moment of . . . beauty."

"I really did," he said, wiping his eyes. "That was incredible. I had . . . I had no idea you could do something like that."

"My parents wanted a musician," she said with a shrug. "They got the sports-loving, magical me instead."

"Which is an incredible gift, indeed, Miss Nessick."

Veranix turned to see Professor Alimen standing in the doorway, his eyes as full of tears as Veranix's.

"Sir," Veranix said, wiping his face. "I'm sorry, we didn't mean . . ."

"And yet you did, and it was beautiful," Alimen said. "Please, children, I have some tea, come up."

He went out, and Veranix and Anduette followed him.

"How are you, sir?" Veranix said as they came up into his apartments. "We've not really talked this semester at all."

"This semester has been quite the trial. As you two are surely aware.

I do not like what you've been put through. I fought against it, but I was stopped. And I don't know what else I can do."

"It hasn't been that bad," Veranix said.

"Maybe a little too focused on the martial," Anduette said. "Though I do like the points and competition of it."

"That indeed," Alimen said, bringing them to a table by the window. He poured out three cups of tea. "And these . . . Altarn Initiatives. It gives me pause, Veranix. So much pause."

Veranix sat down. "Is there more to it than just the change in curriculum?"

"I had thought it was all it was," Alimen said. "But then I've seen more memos. Things with higher level magical theory than even I am versed in. Equations for the mathematics department. There was a file meant for the department at RCM that was delivered to me, which I can't . . ."

He trailed off into silence. Veranix reached out and took the old man's hand. He remembered things Delmin had said, especially with the magical machine that had turned Crenaxin into the dragon. That involved magic and science and steam and metals and Veranix didn't even know what else. "Higher theory. Like, how magic interacts with other forms of mysticism?"

"Indeed. Altarn is obsessed with it. I wish Mister Golmin and Miss Kay had stayed here to help me unravel it, but I'm glad they aren't here to be forced into work that . . ."

"That what?" Veranix asked when Alimen was silent for a long time.

"That . . . I fear . . . Altarn is dabbling in forces beyond any of our understanding, that would—"

Anduette's hand grabbed Veranix's shoulder and squeezed. "Nix, the blazes is that?"

"Is what?" he asked, following her terrified gaze out the window.

On the lawn below, letters burned in the grass in bright blue. Magical burning so intense Veranix could feel the heat and *numina*. Most people—except the purposeful few standing near the fire—were shouting and running off in every direction, away from the burning words that were meant for him.

WE'RE HERE FOR YOU, VERANIX

CHAPTER SIXTEEN

JUTIE RAN, KNOWING DAMN WELL that he probably only had a few steps of lead time over the other Princes. There were surely a few hot on his heels.

He was running from Princes now. How had it gotten this bad? But the folks in the Turnabout were not the same brothers and sisters he had had when he had gotten arrested. He couldn't believe that it had come to this.

He still knew how to run, and how to hide in this neighborhood, and all he had to do was get to campus and let the Thorn know what was going on.

Stopping for a breath at the mouth of an alley by Lilac and Hedge, he glanced back. No one was right behind him, not yet. Just run across the street, and past the gate, the pair of sleepy cadets on guard, and he'd be on campus.

And then . . .

He had no rutting idea what then. He needed to find the Thorn, but had no clue how he was supposed to do that.

This was a completely stupid plan. But he didn't have a better one.

"Spread out!" he heard Deena shout. A few of the beefy Princes were with her. "He can't have gotten far!"

Deena as a captain. And Tooser was with her. The two of them betrayed him more than anyone. Holding him down so Bassa could tear out his teeth. Blazes to them.

Deena was in front of the gate, her boys moving in every direction. One shot.

Jutie tore out of the alley, bringing up his fist like a hammer as he came up on Deena. She spotted him just as he had closed the distance, and didn't have a chance to dodge his blow on top of her head. He knocked her down, and kept going, running past her, through the gate as the cadets shouted ineptly after him.

He would have loved to have stayed there, giving Deena the beating she deserved for her treachery. But he didn't have the time.

He ran through the campus grounds, looking wildly in each direction, seeing who he could see, maybe he would spot the Thorn, maybe it would be obvious where or who he was. But he had no idea. A glance back toward the gate showed that the cadets were busy keeping Deena and the rest from following him. That should buy him some time, but to do what?

He was about to start shouting for the Thorn—which would surely bring more cadets on his head—when he spotted two familiar faces, two people who definitely should not be walking on campus.

Magpie and Jackdaw.

They were walking with purpose. They knew where they were going.

Jutie ran after them as they approached what must have been one of the dorms. Was this where the Thorn lived?

Magpie and Jackdaw approached one of the doors, and a trio of fellows came out telling them they weren't permitted entry. Jackdaw whipped out her weapon knocked each of them with ferocity. Two of them, the blows practically took their heads off, no chance they survived. The third managed to duck enough that he only took a glancing hit, still enough to drop him to the ground in a stream of blood.

Blazes, Jutie knew had to do something. Didn't even have a knife on him.

Only one option left.

"Thorn!" he shouted. "Thorn! You got some Deadly Birds coming for you! Hey, Thorn!"

The Birds both turned to him.

He was in the mix of it now.

DELMIN NEVER SKIPPED A LECTURE IN FOUR YEARS, WHICH MADE HIM feel like he had earned the right to do so at least once. And if there was a day he deserved it, it was today.

It wasn't like he had skipped class to hang out in pubs or playing card games. He had gone to the library to dig through more books, to figure out if he had done himself permanent damage by growing to twenty feet tall.

That wasn't Veranix's fault, he had screwed up, he knew it, but it was easier to blame Veranix.

And it was Veranix's fault that he had been in that situation. He should not have even been messing with size-changing magic. That was some advanced work, almost no one had even dabbled in it. All the literature about it boiled down to "Shrinking is very bad, growing is extremely bad."

He never should have let himself be talked into it. He stumbled onto figuring out how to do one thing—saints, he actually had a knack for something besides sensing *numinic* energy—and it was a discipline that almost every reputable theorist wrote in large letters, DO NOT DO THIS.

Stupid, foolish stuff.

The most thorough information he found was a journal from a medical student who had been friends with a mage who had done growing experiments, where he detailed the damage that he discovered to his friend's organs after dying at the age of seventeen.

The very thought of it made Delmin's heart flutter like a humming-bird. And from what he had read, he couldn't risk pushing his heart too hard. He may have already destroyed it.

Though he needed more information. He was going to go back to his room, and write to Phadre and Jiarna. They might have some further insight for him, something that would put his mind at ease. Of course, it was at least two weeks for a letter to get to Trenn College, and presuming a timely response, another two weeks to receive it. He might be dead in a month.

"Thorn! Thorn! We need you out here!" That voice rang out over other cries and shouts.

Delmin ran toward the shouting before he even realized how stupid such a thing was. What had happened to him that he now, on instinct, ran toward trouble? Was this what Veranix had done to him?

There was a brawl in the courtyard between Almers and Holtman halls, and two women were trying to kill some street rat, who kept shouting for the Thorn.

Not some street rat—Delmin remembered him. Jutie. One of the Princes under Colin. What was he doing here?

One of the women—the Ch'omik woman—came in swinging at him with what looked like a rowing oar with spikes on it. Jutie kept moving, staying clear, as the other woman flung darts and blades at him. One of the blades hit Jutie in the arm, while the rest flew across the common toward the doors of Holtman, where several people were gawking at the fight.

Delmin reached out with magic—messy and hard, it was always hard whenever he did anything that reached out of him—and swatted those blades to the ground before they hit anyone.

"Get out of here!" he shouted at them. "Run!"

"Thorn!" Jutie shouted. "You need to get out here!"

Veranix wasn't in hearing, that was certain. As angry as Delmin was at him, he knew Veranix would not ignore something like this if he knew it was going on. But the fact that something like this was happening, happening here right outside their dormitory, that was Veranix's fault. They had come—somehow, they all knew to find him here, and they had come for him. The seeds Veranix had planted finally yielded their poisonous fruit.

Delmin dashed past the fight as best he could to the doors of Holtman. "Get in, get in," he told people. If nothing else, he'd make sure the other students were safe until the cadets came. From there, he could see bodies on the steps to enter Almers. Two clearly dead—Delmin held his stomach down—one still moving. Trandy, the second-floor prefect, bleeding from a large gash in his head. Delmin ran to him, taking off his scarf to wrap the wound.

"Go find him," the blond woman told the Ch'omik. "I'll handle this one."

The Ch'omik woman pivoted and came for the doors, and Delmin realized he was the only thing between her and Almers Hall. She stared him down, a wicked grin crossing her face.

Delmin's heart stopped in his chest. No choice but to draw the *numina* into himself, and pray to his saints that she didn't kill him, or that he killed himself in the process.

Whistles blew all around, cadets rushing in from all sides.

The Ch'omik woman glanced around, gave him a wink, and then ran off into the quad. The blond killer followed after.

The cadets swarmed over Jutie, grabbing hold of him. As they dragged him to the ground, he looked up and saw Delmin.

"Hey, you! I remember you! You gotta tell the Thorn!"

"Shut up!" a cadet said, pushing Jutie's face into the ground.

"The Princes grabbed the dark girl! They've got her!"

A boot met Jutie's face, and the cadets hauled him off.

Delmin stood stunned for some time, not sure what to say, not moving until a cadet touched his arm.

"You hurt?"

"No," Delmin said, softly releasing the *numina* he had built into himself. Pointing to Trandy, he added, "But he needs help."

"Best get inside, man," the cadet said. "There's trouble all over chaos, south lawn is a madhouse."

"South lawn?" Delmin asked. And then he realized he could feel *numina* swirling and raging in that direction. The power there built and grew, some of it with a flavor he knew all too well.

Veranix.

Whatever fight was happening there, he was in the heart of it. And what had Jutie said? The Princes have . . . Kai? Was she in trouble too?

"Really, get inside," the cadet said, pushing Delmin toward the door. "There's nothing you can do. You should just stay safe."

He should. He knew he should.

"VERANIX, WHAT IS THIS?"

They knew his name. They knew who he was. And if they knew, they surely weren't the only ones. If they were doing this, here and now, blazing his name in great letters across the lawn, it was to tell the world.

"Nix, who are those people?"

Veranix knew who some of them were. Cuse Jensett, the Alchemist. Enzin Hence, and the other bowman was probably Erno Don. The Hunter and the Jester. Then Pria Mandicall, controlling the flames, and his own burning wings sprouting from his back. He didn't know who the shirtless man or the well-dressed one were.

They had been sent.

Fenmere knew. Fenmere knew and sent these six men to get him.

"Veranix, answer me!" Alimen said, snapping Veranix out of his reverie.

"It's my sins coming back on me, sir," Veranix said. "They found me, they know me."

"Who do?" Anduette asked.

"Old enemies," Veranix said. Down on the lawn, they were all looking around, waiting for him to respond. But not looking up. They didn't know where he was. This was an attempt to draw him out. A trap.

"How old?" Alimen asked him. "When have you ever made an enemy out of these people?"

"Professor," Veranix said. "I'm so sorry, I know . . . I know how much you did to bring me here, to give me a chance to be a proper mage, and I . . . I . . ." It was so hard to say it, but he had to. In a minute, he would have to run, have to fight, have to do something, but there was no way he would be able to stand here with Professor Alimen as a student again. That part of his life was over when these bastards lit their flames.

They had already destroyed him.

"You what?"

"I'm sorry," Veranix said. "I did what I thought I had to. I tried to stop the people who had destroyed my family, who killed my father, ruined my mother, and I—"

"Who did what?" Alimen asked. "I thought your family was on the road with the circus . . ."

"The circus?" Anduette asked.

"Not now, Miss Nessick!" Alimen said. "My boy, whatever you've done, whatever choices you've made that has brought . . . whatever this is to us, you need to understand—"

"Veranix Calbert!" a shout came echoing through the room. Magically amplified voice. "Come out and play, or we'll have to find other folks to play with."

Veranix looked back out the window. Enzin and Erno had grabbed a couple of students, holding them in armlocks. The shirtless man had two more people entrapped in his whips, choking them both.

"I can't let them hurt anyone else," Veranix said. "No one else gets hurt because of me."

"Veranix!" Alimen said. "I know . . . I've always suspected you have been involved in something dark, but we can find a way to resolve this. We can . . ."

Veranix glanced around the room, spotting one of Alimen's walking canes. It would do.

"I need to answer for this, sir," Veranix said as he grabbed it. "But thank you for your faith in me, I didn't deserve it. But I've always been grateful to you, sir."

"You always deserved it," Alimen said. "And you still do."

"Still," Veranix said. If only Alimen knew how much Veranix did not deserve any grace. He took a deep breath, centering his focus. Drawing in the *numina*.

"Veranix, what are you doing?" Anduette asked as Veranix jumped up on the windowsill.

"Do me a favor, Andi?" he asked. "Boost my voice."

"Don't do anything foolish, Veranix," Alimen pleaded.

"That's all I can do, sir," Veranix said. "That's all I have left." He gave Anduette a nod, and she nodded back, spinning her finger. Veranix turned back out to the lawn, where they were grabbing more students.

"Gentlemen!" he called out, Anduette's magic making it reverberate throughout the south lawn. "You've made the dreadful mistake of courting my attention!"

All six of them looked up to the tower. Enzin and Erno let go of their hostages, as did the man with the whips.

"Is that really him?" the well-dressed man asked. "He seems so . . . slight."

"It is," Pria said. He launched into the air, rocketing at Veranix on his flaming wings.

Perfect.

Veranix leapt from the window, hearing Anduette and the professor cry out as he went. He knew how to fall, knew how to aim himself, and spun his body to collide directly into Pria midair as the fool conjured a flaming ball in his hand.

Pria Mandicall was a formidable mage—he had given Veranix a blazes of a fight in North Seleth a month or so back, and that was when Veranix was fully armed with all his tools, including the rope and the cloak. Right now, nothing to amplify his magic. No arrows, no tricks. Just his body, muscle, and bone, and a wooden walking cane.

Veranix slammed the cane against Pria's face when he made impact. His flames sputtered and crackled, and they both dropped together toward the ground. Veranix cracked the man's face two more times, making blood gush from his nose and mouth, while the man tried to reignite his fiery wings. He finally got them lit again, just enough to slow them down before they hit the earth. Veranix dove clear right before Pria crashed, rolling and leaping onto his feet, cane at the ready.

"That was impressive," Erno said, drawing an arrow and training it on Veranix. "But so are all of us."

"And we're so glad you came," Cuse said. He pulled a vial out of his belt. One of his alchemical tricks.

"Only six of you," Veranix said. "Hardly seems sporting."

Enzin snapped an arrow and fired, and Erno fired his as well. Veranix dodged to one side, leaped up to bring the cane down on Enzin, planning to club him, grab his bow out of his hand, and use it to take down Cuse next.

That was the plan, but he only made it half the distance before something grabbed his ankle and yanked him backward.

"Not so easy, little Thorn," the absurdly muscled man with the whips said. Veranix was ensnared with one whip, and then the other was being drawn back to snap it on him.

Veranix rolled back up on his feet, closing the gap between him and the shirtless fellow, forcing the whip to go slack, while quickly throwing up a wall of magic between him and the archers. Just in time, as two more arrows bounced against that wall, as well as Cuse's vial, which created a sizzling smoke on impact.

"Get him, Scanlin!" Pria shouted as he pulled himself back on his feet.

"Scanlin?" Veranix asked, shaking his foot free. "You shouldn't have made this your fight, man."

Veranix had gotten too close to him while getting free of the whip, and Scanlin's meaty fist slammed into his chest. He tumbled backward, where the well-dressed man caught him.

"Don't tell me," he said with an accent that sounded like it came from the best schools of North Maradaine. "You're one of those pitiful Lord Preston charity cases."

A magical surge came through the man's hands, a painful bolt that somehow felt burning and freezing at once. Veranix screamed, lashing back with the cane, only succeeding in knocking the man's smoke-lensed spectacles off his face.

Veranix heard the twang of Erno firing another arrow. Forcing through the pain of the magical attack, Veranix pulled up his legs and let himself drop down, grabbing the well-dressed mage and flipping him into Scanlin as the arrow narrowly missed.

Then a flaming ball also narrowly missed him, and then another vial came right for his head. With an almost wild swing, he batted it away.

Another arrow grazed his face.

He spun toward Enzin again, drawing another arrow. He risked a snap of magic, then another and another. Straps and buckles snapped, and Enzin's quiver of arrows fell to the ground. He pulled back the arrow he still had on hand and fired the shot, slicing through Veranix's coat. Enzin roared in frustration, swinging his fist at the empty air so hard, his shirt tore.

Then Veranix's whole body came crashing to the ground, as whips went around both his legs and pulled them out from under him, and a magical force grabbed his chest and slammed him down.

"Oh, poor Thorn," Cuse said. "Quite a tumble you took."

"So falls the Thorn, a sorry sight," Erno sang. "Didn't even give us a proper fight."

Veranix tried to get to his feet, but the pressure of the magic force— the well dressed mage—was too much.

"Don't even try to get up," the mage said. "Disappointing. This school really turns out a low quality of mage."

"All the more reason to teach him a lesson," Pria said.

All six of them stood over him, circled around and looking down.

"We should get just a little more fun, lads," Erno said with a smile. "Before we turn him over to the boss."

CHAPTER SEVENTEEN

I N HIS MONTHS WORKING AVENTIL, Benvin had seen plenty
of bad days, but this one was the worst. Brawls up and down
Waterpath, and all around Cantarell Square, and he only had his few
people to try to get a handle on it. Most of the rest of the footpatrol for
the neighborhood had stayed near the stationhouse, working territories
in the neighborhood far from the trouble.

Pollit and Saitle were both wrestling some perpetrators to the
ground, Orphans and Sons, it seemed, whose fight had spilled through
several shops. Benvin had chased two more fellows—who didn't seem
to be Aventil gang at all—but lost them around Waterpath, and had to
make his way back to the place of this latest fight empty-handed, while
trying not to look winded.

"We got them?" he asked Pollit.

"Got these two," Pollit said. "But I've called for a wagon and
haven't even gotten a Return Call yet."

"Damn it," Benvin said. "And we've got—"

"Hey, help! Constabulary! Help!"

That sounded like it was a block to the east.

"Get them to a way station," Benvin ordered Pollit, and he ran off
east, drawing out his crossbow as he went.

Corner of Waterpath and Carnation, he found a small crowd around a woman sitting on the walkway, her head bleeding.

"Ma'am, what happened?" he asked as he pushed through the crowd. "Are you all right?"

"Do I look all right, you utter radish?" she snapped.

"No, ma'am," he said. He took out his whistle and called for a Yellowshield, even if that call was in vain. "Can you tell me what happened, who did this?"

"Some heavy bunker just smashed into me, clobbered my head, and ran back that way with my purse!" she said, pointing across Waterpath. "The rutting blazes is wrong with this town? We're just knocking ladies to the ground now?"

"I'm so sorry," he said, squatting down. Her head was bleeding a lot, but Benvin had seen more than his share of head wounds that looked worse than they were. She would probably be all right, once the shield got here. "Is there someplace we can move her, get her off the street?" he asked the crowd.

Someone offered a seat in the tea shop, and he helped her to her feet and let her sit. He took a kerchief out of his pocket and pressed it to her bleeding head.

"Sorry it's taking a bit for the Yellowshield," he said. Again, there had been no Return Call. "I'll call again."

"Not worth it," she said, holding the cloth to her wound. "It'll probably stop bleeding by the time they're here."

"Can I get you somewhere safe? Back home?"

"Home hasn't been safe since the Orphans took half the apartments in the tenement," she said.

"Maybe we can do something about that."

She raised an eyebrow. "Like anyone could. Or would. You sure you're a stick?"

"Trying to be," he said with a small laugh.

Wheth came running over. "Hey, Left! We've got some real trouble."

"I've noticed," Benvin said. "We need Yellowshields and lock-wagons and—"

"Boss!" Wheth interrupted. "There're whole rutting brawls happening on campus right now."

"Campus isn't our beat."

"Magic brawls, sir. And archers, and who even knows what else," he said. "I think it's our prison escapees, sir."

Blazes.

"You!" Benvin said, pointing at a server. "I'm deputizing you to get this woman to the Yellowshield way station on Violet Street."

"But I—"

"Wheth, get over to Pollit and Saitle, and then put out a rutting Riot Call."

"But, sir . . ."

"I know it's probably too much," Benvin said. "But we need to cool this whole damn town down before it burns to ash. So do whatever you have to so we can get a show of color to campus right damn now."

"And you, Left?" Wheth asked, already running backward toward Cantarell Square.

"I'm going to campus straight away." Breaking into his own run, Benvin hoped he wasn't about to end up alone in the middle of a whole damn war.

TODAY HAD BEEN A TERRIBLE DAY FOR MILA TO TRY TO GET HER HEAD together. She had gone to breakfast, gone to her morning classes, but her thoughts were entirely on last night, and the mistakes she made. She had gotten people killed. She had killed people.

She sat in a common room of the ladies' dormitory, forcing herself to be in public, to be seen, because she wanted to hide and disappear. It'd be so easy to wallow alone about how much she had failed. In the months she was living at Kimber's Pub, she had seen so many folks drowning themselves in whatever could be poured for them.

It'd be so easy.

She didn't let herself do that.

Force herself to be present, to be better, to keep learning. Do it right next time.

On that, she wouldn't delude herself. There would be a next time. Maybe not with Veranix, not as the Rose, but there would be another time where she would have to make a plan, bring the fight.

The Rynax boys had thought they were going straight before the fire.

Mila chuckled to herself at the thought of finishing school, living a clean and honest life for years, and then as an old woman being pulled into some wild scheme.

"What's so funny?" a girl sitting near her asked. Yenira Mast, second-year studying literature, third child, daughter of a captain of industry who owned three canneries in Wheaton, but lived flush in East Maradaine. Parents were both disappointed in her marks, that she had to go to University of Maradaine instead of RCM like her sisters. Had a secret paramour in Shadow Star Social House who she was desperate to keep from her family.

Mila knew too much about every girl in her dorm building. She should break the habit, but she felt it was too useful a skill to abandon.

"Nothing, just something in this book," Mila said, though in truth she hadn't been able to focus on her reading at all.

"Parliamentary Declarations of the 1150s?" Yenira asked, raising an eyebrow. "Was the start of the Island War quite amusing?"

"No, but there was a whole thing on fruit tariffs that a Chair of Scaloi got absurdly worked up over."

Two girls ran into the common room, both out of breath. "There is madness down on the south lawn!"

"Like what?" someone else called out.

"As in, this group of thugs—"

"Mages, Kaela."

"I don't think they were mages, Laurie."

"They were *definitely* mages. The whole thing with the fire?"

"Maybe some of them, but that absolute *drink* with the whips, no."

"What did they do?" Yenira asked.

"So these guys—six of them, they stroll onto the lawn, and then one of them magics magics magics, fire all over the lawn. And these guys with bows are stalking about, grabbing people, looking at their faces."

Bows, whips, and mages. Mila's attention was now fully engaged. "Then what?" she asked.

"Then they start grabbing people and are shouting, like, 'Come face us Vendamir Caskill!'"

"That wasn't the name, Kaela."

"The name doesn't matter. Vexamin Carlbern. Something like that."

Mila jumped out of her seat. "Veranix Calbert?"

"Was that it?" Kaela asked Laurie.

"I think that was it," Laurie said. "You know him? Anyway, then whoever they were yelling for was, like, in that mage class tower, and he literally *jumped from the top of it* to, like, fight these guys, and that's when the cadets—"

Mila didn't listen further, as she was dashing out of the common room, down the hall, and bursting into her room.

Livvie and Jadonne, her roommates, both scrambled with bedding and blankets to cover themselves and ineptly hide the Whisper Fox House boy they had been sneaking into the dorm on a regular basis.

"Mila!" Livvie cried. "You . . . how dare you . . . you can't . . ."

"Just carry on," Mila said, grabbing her knapsack off her peg on the wall.

"You can't tell," Jadonne said. "Please don't tell."

"Fine," Mila said, pulling out the crate from under her bed, opening up the false bottom and taking out the knives, ropes, and a few useful vials, throwing them all in the knapsack. "Then you never saw this either."

"Are those knives?" their boy asked, his eyes wide.

"Mutual silence, girls," Mila said as she closed the crate and pushed it back under. "It serves us all beautifully. Now get back to it."

She tore out of her room, out of the dorm, and into the quad. She had to get to Veranix. She had to help him. She had to make things right.

Veranix tried to grab the cane, get at least one good hit in, but Enzin stepped on his wrist.

"None of that, Thorn," he said, craning his neck to one side. His nostrils were flaring, breath heavy.

"I was expecting a better show," Erno said.

"How much can we hurt him before turning him over?" Pria asked.

Cuse smiled. "I think we can—"

Whatever he was about to say was drowned out by a deafening screech, like the worst note played on a thousand fiddles at once. All six of them covered their ears and stumbled back, and the magic and muscle holding Veranix to the ground fell away.

Covering his own ears, Veranix forced himself up to see Anduette screaming, her whole body glowing with *numina*. She stopped and ran over to him, helping him back to his feet.

"You need to get out of here," he told her. "I—"

"Violet Squad together," she said plainly. "We didn't do those drills for nothing."

Further argument was impossible, as Scanlin was recovered and snapping his whips at the both of them. Veranix pushed Anduette out of the way and jumped back before either of them got lashed. His foot knocked something on his landing—Erno's bow. He must have dropped it when Anduette blasted her scream. He kicked it up into his hands as Erno came in swinging a punch.

"Nope," he said dodging the punch, stepping to one side enough that Erno's back was to him. He clocked the man in the back of the head and drew two arrows from his quiver as he dropped. He nocked one arrow, flew it at Enzin, and then the next at Cuse. The first was dodged, but the second hit the Alchemist square in the arm.

"How long can you keep this up, Thorn?" Pria asked. "I imagine you're pretty worn down already."

"Barely warmed up," Veranix snapped back as he swerved away from a poorly thrown fireball. "But you're down to embers."

Scanlin was focused on Anduette, and he had gotten one of his whips around her neck. She was holding on to it, trying to keep him from choking her by pulling it tight.

"You know what this will do to your pretty flesh, girl?" he asked her as he drew back the other whip.

"I know what sound it makes," she wheezed out as he snapped the whip at her, but the snap hit with a deafening boom that knocked him to the ground. She held up her arms in triumph. "Nessick with the double-jack!"

"Oh, a mage with a gimmick, how very quaint," the gentleman said. He whipped off a lightning bolt that struck her in the chest. "But thunder is just noise."

Anduette fell down with a muffled scream.

Veranix tried to get to her, but was too busy batting away more vials from Cuse, which burst in the sky into clouds of acrid smoke of various colors. It was getting impossible to even see through the haze of it, and he couldn't keep track of the six men he was fighting. He hadn't been able to put any of them down, just pushing them away long enough to be able to handle the next one. They were wearing him down.

He had to get out of here, get Anduette out of here. Maybe draw them from here, get to his proper gear—

Suddenly a gust blasted across the lawn, and all the smoke blew off, leaving a clear field as Professor Alimen soared down from the tower, bristling with *numina* like Veranix had never seen before.

"Enough!" he shouted. "This foolishness will no longer abide!"

"You gonna stop us, old man?" Pria asked, refreshing the flames over his body.

"You weren't on my list before," Cuse said. "But I remember you well enough."

"You were expelled for your reckless behavior, Mister Jensett," Alimen said. "And you, Mister Endoriff, were merely an abysmal pupil."

The gentleman threw out a lash of bright purple light that wrapped around Alimen. "I just couldn't learn at such a pedestrian institution. You had nothing to teach me." His accent dropped slightly as his voice turned to an angry snarl.

Alimen waved, and the purple light from Endoriff shattered. "I think I still have quite a few lessons left to impart. Mister Calbert, get Miss Nessick to safety, I'll handle these miscreants. We'll discuss your role later."

"But, Professor—"

Alimen turned to Veranix and gave him a small, weary nod. "Go, Veranix. I've invested too much in your education for you to die today."

With that, he summoned a vast array of light and thunder and smoke that flew out at the six assassins, which didn't seem to swallow them entirely only because Pria and Endoriff threw up countering shields to keep the power Alimen was wielding at bay.

Enzin got between Veranix and Anduette, teeth bared. Veranix flashed a bit of magic at him, just sparks in his eyes, but the man howled and pulled away, tearing at his shirt as he dropped to the ground.

Veranix scooped up Anduette and carried her off, away from the fight, away from the lawn, as magic echoed and boomed behind him. Most all the other students, and even some of the cadets, were running away from the raw chaos. Only one person was running toward it.

"Vee!" Delmin shouted as he got closer. "What did you do this time?"

"They came for me," Veranix said, trying to keep his voice steady. He wanted it to break, wanted to fall down and weep. "I'm so sorry, Del, I'm so—"

"Save it," Delmin said.

Veranix dropped Anduette's limp body into Delmin's arms. "Get her out of here, get her safe."

"Her too?" Delmin asked. "When does it end?"

"Today, obviously. I'm sorry. I need to get back there, the professor—"

"Wait, you need to know—" Delmin started, and then his face blanched. "Oh no."

"What?"

"The professor, he's . . . he doesn't have much power left."

Veranix spun around and ran back, drawing in what ambient *numina* he could, but the whole lawn was a dry sponge, everything had already been pulled into the swirling maelstrom of power around Professor Alimen, churning and roiling with Pria's fire and Endoriff's lightning.

"Bind him in!" Cuse shouted, and Scanlin whipped both his whips around Alimen's arms.

Cuse tossed vials to Enzin and Erno. "On my mark, all throw!"

Veranix had a bow, but no arrows. And no magic to pull right now.

But Enzin's quiver was still on the ground. He dove for it, scooping it up and securing it over his shoulder in one fluid motion.

"Now!" Cuse shouted. The vials flew in at Alimen as Scanlin released the whips, and Pria and Endoriff boxed him in with their magic.

The vials broke over Alimen's body, and the professor screamed as green smoke ate through his flesh, a white fluid engulfed his body, and violet flames consumed him. His face was twisted in agony and horror until he was nothing but a statue of ash.

"Bastards!" Veranix shouted, shooting arrows at all of them. True shots sent Cuse and Pria to the ground, painful but unfortunately not fatal. Veranix drew another arrow as Constabulary whistles pierced the air.

"A tactical withdrawal is warranted, fellows," Endoriff said.

"Undoubtedly," Erno said, throwing down a few smoke powder bombs. Veranix couldn't see anything through the smoke, only hearing the shouts and cries of the people all around, the whistles of the constables approaching, and the raging beat of his heart as blood raced through his brain.

They had killed the professor. They needed to pay.

In his trembling fury, he didn't even notice the owner of the pair of hands that grabbed him and pulled him out of the smoke.

CHAPTER EIGHTEEN

VERANIX BROUGHT UP THE CANE and was about to smash it against the face of the person who had pulled him out of the smoke, but at the last moment he saw it wasn't anyone trying to kill him.

"You," he said, looking at the young man who had been part of Colin's Prince crew. Jutie? That was it. "Sorry, I . . ."

"Hey, man, it's fine. It's fine, let's get you clear of this before the sticks roll in."

"How did you get—" Veranix asked.

"Been trying to find you, had to slip the cadets, and . . . come on . . ." Jutie had brought him behind a hedge, out of sight of the rest of the lawn. "You've got to—"

"No, I . . ." Veranix was still reeling from what had just happened, the horror he had just seen. It had been the most terrible thing he had ever seen. No one should ever die the way Professor Alimen just had.

That was his fault. Another one was his fault. That man had been . . . for the past three years, with his father dead, his mother destroyed, Professor Alimen had been the closest thing to a parent he had had.

He had been lying to the man for all this time, sneaking behind his back, fighting this stupid war against Fenmere. Those sins were now visited in full upon him, upon his life, and Professor Alimen had paid the price.

"Oh, Saint Senea," Veranix said, sinking to the ground. "There is no atonement for this. No prayers, no penance that can bring absolution."

"What are you doing?" Jutie asked him. "Thorn, you've got to move, there's—"

"There's no Thorn," Veranix said to him. "All there is now is me. A foolish, stupid boy who picked a fight he couldn't win, and this is what happened."

"That old man meant something to you, huh?"

"Yes, you chowder," Veranix snapped. "That was my teacher, my friend, my—"

"Yeah, well Colin means something to you too, right?" Jutie snapped back. "Same with that Napa girl?"

"Kaiana?" Veranix asked. "What about her?"

"The Princes wanted to get you. So they grabbed her, and Colin, and have them both tied up in the Turnabout."

Veranix's heart slowed back down. He checked the bow, Erno's bow. The draw was a little heavy for his taste, but fine. Checked the quiver, Enzin's. Over a dozen arrows remaining. The cane was serving well as a staff. *Numina* was starting to bleed back in, and there would be plenty at the Turnabout.

"Where are they in there?" he asked Jutie.

"Last I saw before I ran out, they were tying them up in the main bar. But they might have brought them to the back rooms in the basement."

"How do you get down there?"

"Door's in the alley, and there's stairs down from the storeroom in the back of the bar, I think, I've never—"

"Fine," Veranix said. "Are you with me on this? You came to warn me, so are you with me if I'm fighting the Princes?"

"Those aren't my Princes, not anymore," Jutie said. "I don't even know them."

"Good." Veranix said, leading Jutie to the south wall. "Because I'm going to get Kaiana and Colin, and if they're hurt . . ."

"Yeah," Jutie said. "We jump over the wall here, that's about where?

Lilac and Bush? A few blocks away from the Turnabout. Can you fly us over there?"

"I don't fly," Veranix said.

"Well, jump really far, whatever," Jutie said.

"That takes magic, and I need to be smart with it right now. Save it for the fight."

"Makes sense," Jutie said. "I know an alley we can take, and then cut through a tenement, cross Hedge, into another tenement that we can get to a window right over the alley behind the Turnabout as well as the roof."

"That's a plan," Veranix said. As much of any plan that he ever had. And the last plan got people hurt, got everyone in this mess. "Get me to that window, you don't need to be a part of anything else."

"They got Colin, and Colin was there for me, even right now," Jutie said. "He's the only one who ever was, it seems, so I need to do right by him. He's the only family I've got."

"He is my family," Veranix told him. "And so is she."

Jutie nodded, drawing out a knife. "Then stay on my shadow, Thorn. Let's show them what Sons of Tyson can do."

THINGS WERE BAD ENOUGH ON CAMPUS BY THE TIME JACE AND MINOX made it to the south gates, that the mere sight of Minox in his Constabulary coat was enough for the lone cadet on guard to just wave them through. It was clear immediately why they were understaffed at the gate and eager for any formal help.

Dozens of campus cadets were on the lawn, helping cordon off a section of the lawn that was scorched. More were helping get people onto wagons, with what looked like a variety of injuries.

"The blazes happened here?" Jace asked.

"I have a theory that it's exactly what we came here hoping to circumvent."

Minox was being himself, talking smart and not saying a lot. "I'm still five lengths behind you, Minox, catch me up."

"The escaped fellows from the prison, the strike on Fenmere's operation last night, the bounty for the Thorn's head. Those old enemies likely deduced his identity and came here to directly confront him."

Jace knew the Thorn was a Uni student, so that tracked. "And it looks like they got the fight they wanted."

"Cadet!" Minox called out to one who had more chevrons on his collar than the rest. "Do we have a report of what occurred? Any witnesses? Any casualties?"

"Oh, um . . . Inspector?" he asked. "I think we've only started with getting the scene cleared, checking on the injured, and . . . I'm sorry, we're just not there yet."

"Understood," Minox said. "In moments like this, it can take some time before you can even start the process of figuring out what happened."

"Someone was killed, though," the cadet said. "I could get—"

"No need to get anyone, cadet!" someone else called out. "Carry on, I'll deal with the inspector and his . . . boy."

A man in a gray military-style coat approached them, scowling at Minox.

"Can you tell us what happened, Major Dresser?" Minox asked.

"What authority do you have to even ask, Welling? Why are you even here? And who is this child with you?"

"My brother, Jace Welling, officer in the Aventil Constabulary."

"Brother, hmm?" This Dresser fellow stepped in closer and prodded Jace's face, peering directly into his eye. "You ever exhibit magic power, son?"

"Off," Jace said, brushing him away. "And no."

"Good," Dresser said. "Though your first manifestation was at a late age, no?"

"That's not why I'm here," Minox said. "Someone was killed?"

"I'm certain you aren't here under any official capacity," Dresser said. "You remain on restricted duty, and your brother here isn't even in uniform."

"We were in the area and reacted to the chaos," Minox said. "And we want to be of use."

"And I have no use for you. I have enough trouble to sort through."

"Major," Minox stressed, "it's clear a large magical altercation occurred here. People were hurt, reportedly killed. If nothing else, I have a vested interest in . . . the student who has been helping my training."

"Oh, that one," Dresser said. "I cannot account for him at this time. And I need to handle several matters, as I'm currently ranking faculty of the magic department, and—"

Minox's face changed. "So the chair of the department is who was killed?"

Dresser closed the distance on Minox. "You insist in acting like you are smarter than everyone, don't you, Welling?"

"I'm not acting, Major," Minox said.

"Cadet sergeant!" Dresser shouted. "Take these two to your holding room."

The cadet looked confused. "Are you sure, sir? He's an Constabulary inspector."

"He is out of the authority of his office and has no jurisdiction, and he's interfering with our own investigation. Take them to holding and contact Aventil Constabulary to come collect them."

"It's fine," Minox told the cadet. "Do as you're ordered. We'll follow quietly."

"Really?" Jace asked as the cadet led them away from the scene.

"We learned enough from that exchange."

"Like what?" Jace asked.

"Major Dresser said he's now the ranking member in the department, so this fight, right near Bolingwood Tower, either killed or incapacitated Professor Alimen, the chair of the department. Given what I overheard in the whispers from the folks being questioned and taken away, I'm surmising he was killed in a gruesome magical manner."

"I didn't overhear—"

"Also these attackers escaped in the chaos, but their primary fight wasn't with the professor, but a student whose name they called out. The witnesses I could hear got the name wrong in a variety of consistent ways that makes it clear the student is exactly who I feared it would be."

"How did you hear all that?" Jace asked. "And put all that together? I was right next to you."

"And you were attentive to my conversation with Major Dresser, which was the least valuable part to hear. You need to learn to take in the whole scene, Jace."

Jace reeled at the way Minox's mind worked. He didn't know if he could ever piece together information like that, listen to several muttered conversations at once, or understand half of what his brother did.

"So now?"

"Now, we know the Thorn was in a fight with several others, some of them magical, and that fight ended with Alimen dead, the attackers fleeing, and the Thorn not here."

"Meaning?"

"He is either in pursuit of them, or going after a target of higher value. He did not stay here. Which means, for the moment, he isn't dead. But there's nothing we can do without causing more disruption than necessary, for him or our careers. Thus complying with the request to be detained keeps us in the right."

"But we're going to be in trouble with the Constabulary?"

"For? Neither of us claimed authority or jurisdiction, nor did anything that violated the law for any concerned citizen. Neither Dresser nor the cadets can claim otherwise. In short order Aventil officers will get us released, and we will be in a position to get further information for our next steps, if any."

"And the Thorn?" Jace asked.

"He has his people," Minox said. "Trust that I know this, and that he has confidence in them, and for good cause. He is in dire trouble, but he is not alone. If there's anyone in this city in whom I have faith in their capacity to rise above such trouble, it is Ver . . . It's him."

"All right," Jace said. "I hope you're right."

"I'm worried for him, of course," Minox said as they were led into a building. "But I've seen the impossible, and I've seen him holding the rein to ride it through."

Jace nodded. "You're not wrong about that. But still—"

"But still," Minox said. "If you feel inclined toward prayer, it wouldn't be amiss."

There was no sign of Veranix on the lawn, even with all the chaos, so Mila went where she presumed he would go—back to the bunker. Either he'd need to be patched together, or he'd need his gear, or . . .

She shut the other ors out of her mind. He'd be at the bunker.

Mila went to the closest entrance and made her way down, and was relieved to hear voices as she approached the main chamber.

Not voices. Just one voice.

"All right, now, where is it, I know . . . yes! *Untrind's Compendium.* I knew I had read it somewhere here. If I can just . . ."

She came in to find only Delmin flipping through his books. A glance about made it clear that Veranix's entire costume, his weapons, the rope and cloak, they were all still here.

As was Anduette Nessick, Veranix's squad partner, lying on a table.

"What is she doing here?" Mila asked.

Delmin looked up. "I brought her here, because I . . . I knew I had the book down here, and I think I'm going to need an anchor, and I mean, of course, napranium, that would do it, and . . ."

Mila came closer, and realized that Anduette was out cold.

"What happened?"

"She got hurt on the lawn."

"You were there," Mila said. "Where's Veranix? Where's Kaiana?"

"Not here," Delmin said. "And I don't have time to . . . Anduette is hurt, and . . ."

"And you brought her here, not the hospital ward?"

"Hospital ward wouldn't have helped, her problem's magic-based. At least, there's nothing they could do unless we first solve this." He sighed and went over to her. "Probably no one but me can even see it. But Anduette's body is here." He gestured over her. "And her magical energy is . . . just a little bit over here." He gestured a few inches to the right.

"And you can do something about that?"

"I've read about this sort of thing, and we need to snap her back into alignment." He pointed over to the rope. "Grab that and bring it here. I probably shouldn't touch it."

"Why shouldn't you touch it?"

"Because I can't control it."

Mila brought the rope over to him. "But what happened? Where is Vee?"

"Let's try to solve one problem at a time," Delmin said.

"Fine, but tell me what happened on the lawn? Where is Vee?"

"He went running back in, but it was too late for Professor Alimen," Delmin said. "Then in the smoke, I lost sight of him."

"You what?" Mila couldn't believe what she heard. "We need to find him, we need to help him . . ."

"First, Anduette," Delmin stressed. He started examining Veranix's specialized arrowheads. "Veranix built his own wagon to ride. She's hurt because of that."

"What do I do?"

"Get the rope on the left side of her body," Delmin said. "And then I'm going to—are these copper?"

"I don't know."

"I think they're copper." He placed the arrowheads on Anduette's right side. "If what I've read is correct, once I run a *numinic* charge through the copper, it'll pull her magical energy further out of sync—"

"Isn't that bad?"

"But then when I release, it'll be pulled back all the way with the rope helping it. And it should fall into place."

That made a bit of sense to Mila. "So she's like a puzzle box with a gear out of place, and if we nudge it right, it snaps back into groove?"

"Right. Yes. I think."

"And if we nudge it wrong?"

"I'm going to try really hard not to," Delmin said. "Like I said, I don't think anyone else can see this like I can."

Mila grabbed Anduette's limp hand. "Anything else?"

"I don't think so."

"So stop wasting time and do it."

Delmin screwed up his face, which suddenly turned beet red. Then the arrowheads all glowed briefly, and then the glow burst. Mila felt a vibration through her hand as Anduette gasped for breath and sat up in a shot.

Delmin collapsed to the ground.

"Veranix!" Anduette said. "Where is . . . what is . . . where . . ."

"Hey, hey," Mila said. "You all right?"

"I . . ." Anduette touched her chest. "My heart is knocking like a bee's wings, but . . . I think so."

"Good," Delmin said from the floor. "I was only pretty sure that would work."

"Why are you both here?" Anduette asked. "And where exactly is here? Is this an abandoned dungeon from the Inquest?"

"I told you!" Delmin said as he pulled himself up. "I always thought that."

"That doesn't matter," Mila said. "We need to find Vee and get his gear to him. He's probably—"

"He's probably in some stupid fight," Delmin said. "Feel free to join him if you want. I've had enough of the pain."

"Enough of the what?" Anduette asked. "What are you even talking about?"

"I'm talking about Veranix, who had a whole fight in the middle of the lawn with a bunch of, what, nemeses? Got you hurt, got the professor killed . . ."

Anduette gasped and covered her mouth. "They killed the professor?"

"I know," Delmin said, putting a hand on her shoulder. "This is Veranix's mess, and the best thing we can do is stay clear of it. Before anything more happens to us."

Anduette looked up. "Yeah, but what about him?"

"He caused this, Andi!" Delmin said. "His stupid crusade against Fenmere's drug empire, he's cost more lives than he saved. You were nearly killed today, I was nearly killed last night."

"Wait, last night, you were with him?" Anduette asked. She looked around the room, taking it in. "Wait a blazing moment, is Veranix that Thorn character?" She stared at Delmin, who turned away. She looked to Mila. "Is he?"

"He is," Mila said. "That secret seems to be fully down the river at this point."

"I knew he had been through something. And you all . . . you've been helping him with that?"

"I'm done with that," Delmin said. "The price is too damn high."

"It is, especially for him, Delmin. I saw his face, he had been through I don't even know what. You seem fine."

"I'm definitely not," Delmin said. "You don't know what I've already been through being a part of this."

"Fine. But I do know that, when those bastards were on the lawn, calling out for him, grabbing hostages, he didn't hesitate. He launched himself off the tower to save those people."

"Is that why you got into the fight?" Mila asked.

"I couldn't let him be in it alone, not after seeing that," Anduette said. "We're being trained to be, I don't even know, military mages, so I knew I couldn't just stand there."

"If that's what you want," Delmin said. "I'm tired of this."

Mila had heard enough. She gathered up the rope, and then went for the rest of Veranix's gear. "He's out there, and he probably needs our help."

"Where is he?" Anduette said, getting to her feet. "Saints, is there anything to eat in this place?"

"Here," Mila said, handing her some dried meat. She put more in the pack. Veranix would surely need something. "And where is Kaiana? We should find her."

Something fell to the floor, the apple that Delmin had picked up. He looked stricken.

"Kai," he said quietly.

"What is it?"

"One of those street kids, he had helped us back during the thing with the Alchemist, he . . . he said the Princes had grabbed Colin and Kaiana, and . . ."

Mila slapped him before she even realized she had done it. Even Anduette yelped. "You forgot to mention that?"

"In all the—"

"Get over yourself, Delmin. Right now, it's job skunked, but we still drive forward, so let's go."

"What does that mean?" Anduette asked. "And why did you suddenly turn all westtown?"

"Plan," Mila said, ignoring that. "Do we know where Colin and Kai are?"

"At the Turnabout, I think?"

"Got it," Mila said, trying to figure out the best course of action. "We need to get there, but also find Veranix, and . . ." There was a way to find Veranix, she realized, she just had to put the two parts of it together. She pulled the cloak out of the knapsack and threw it over Delmin's shoulders.

"What are you d—" he said before he screamed like he was on fire.

"We need to find Veranix, and you can sense him. The cloak amplifies his magic, so let it amplify your senses."

"I . . . can . . . feel . . . all . . . *numina* . . . in the . . . city . . ." he gasped out.

"What is that?" Anduette asked, getting cautiously closer to him.

"It's woven with some metal that amplifies magic," Mila told her.

"Holy blasted saints, napranium? How did you—you know, I'm not even going to question. Delmin?"

"I . . . I . . . I . . ."

Anduette took his hand, and a low rumbling sound filled the chamber. "I got you," she said. "Violet Squad together."

"R-R-Right," he said, locking eyes with her. "Yeah, do that. Send out a quiet pulse of *numina*, and I can feel it as it rides out, and see if I . . ."

Mila didn't understand what was happening, but it didn't matter. "Can you feel him?"

"The lawn is like an ashpit," he said. "And the other students on campus, mages of all sorts and . . . wow."

"What?"

"There's a massive source of *numinic* power on campus, but . . . it's not Vee, I'm . . . looking past campus. In Aventil. There's something that tastes wrong. Oh."

"What?"

"The Alchemist's things. I can feel his work, it feels wrong. And then the other mages from that fight. The ones that killed the professor."

"Doing great," Anduette said.

"Got him!" Delmin said. "Take it . . . take it off."

Anduette knocked off the cloak, yelping for a moment when she touched it. Mila put it back in the pack of Veranix's gear.

"So?"

"He's in Aventil, on Rose Street. Near the Turnabout, I think?"

"I'm going," Mila said. "Come if you want."

"Absolutely," Anduette said.

Delmin winced, and nodded. "For Kaiana, at least."

"Then let's stop wasting time," Mila said. "We've got a job to finish."

COLIN WAS IMPRESSED BY AT LEAST ONE THING—WHOEVER TIED HIM TO this chair knew what the blazes they were doing. When he was a kid, one of Pop's "games" was tying Colin up so he could learn how to get out of anything. Once Colin was able to get out of any rope job his father concocted, then he graduated on to a pair of constabulary shackles. That had proven much harder, but he had developed the knack for twisting his thumb in a way to slip out of anything with a minimal amount of pain or fuss.

His early days in the Princes, he was famous for his ability to do that, and the bosses remembered well enough to make sure he was bound particularly well. Not only had they isolated his thumbs so he couldn't bend them in, they had strung the ropes binding him around his neck in a way that almost any shift or pull resulted in him choking himself.

Colin still had faith he could get himself out of it, but it would take him a little longer.

Kaiana, tied up next to him in nowhere near as intricate a fashion, but clearly enough that she wasn't able to escape anytime soon.

Not that, at the moment, getting out of their chairs would be advantageous for either of them. They were in the center of the pub floor of the Turnabout, with a dozen armed Princes between them and any door or window. The best he could hope for would be to free himself from his binds in a way that he could use to his advantage if the right moment arrived.

That right moment would have to involve Veranix crashing through the doors like an absolute fool, which was both the last thing Colin wanted him to do and the one thing he desperately needed him to do.

Saints, he had made a promise to keep Veranix safe, to get him to finish school, and now he was counting on Veranix being as stupid as possible to save him. He really had screwed up.

But he knew, if Jutie had gotten the word out, if Veranix knew that he and Kaiana were here, that would be it. That was no bluff. The Princes were going to get more fight than they had bargained for.

And they were getting ready for it. Knives and handsticks and crossbows all around.

"That's not going to help you all," Colin said. "You think the Thorn is just some guy? Just a fellow who is going to stroll in here and let you kill him?"

"He's still just a man," Giles said. He was looking like he was eager for a fight, checking his knives over. He probably hadn't been in a scrap in a good ten years, if not more, but he looked anxious. "Mages bleed just like anyone else."

"And he is your blood, yes, Colin?" The weary, croaking voice of Vessrin came from behind Colin. One of the ropes around his neck was yanked, choking him hard for a moment. "Isn't that right? The Thorn is your kin?"

Colin couldn't force any words out, but tried anyway.

"Stop it!" Kaiana snapped. "You'll kill him."

The rope was let go, and Vessrin walked around into Colin's view. "Well, we don't want that, not yet." Half his face was now scar tissue, red and angry from the hot iron Colin had dropped on it.

"Love the new look," Colin wheezed out.

"Oh, we don't want you to die, not yet, Colin," Vessrin said. "Not until you feel the pain like this, ten times over. We're going to do this to you, and do this to this girl, and you better believe we'll do this to your cousin when we catch him."

"You really think you're going to catch him?" Colin asked.

"He's coming for his girl, no?"

"He'll be coming angry," Kai said. "I actually feel pity for you." Good, she was matching bravado with Colin.

"Right, because I'm sure he's got a temper, no? Just like his father did, back in the day. Oh, you didn't want to get Cal Tyson mad back in the day, did you? Giles, you ever see Cal when he got mad?"

"Oh, yeah," Giles said. "He was a damn storm when he wanted to be."

"Now, of course, Cal put his head between his legs and ran away when the trouble here started, didn't he? Ran off, left your pop holding the bag? So I wonder, I really wonder, when the cards are on the table, is that what the Thorn will do?"

"You have no idea," Kaiana said. "He'd never run, even when he should."

"Good," Vessrin said, almost purring the word out as he knelt closer to Colin and Kaiana. He lowered his voice to a hoarse whisper. "Let me tell you, I don't even care about the reward. I just want him, so I can kill him myself. Finally have the revenge I was denied."

Colin didn't need to hear this sewage a moment longer, and spat on Vessrin's face. "Your revenge? Your revenge, you worthless pile of fetid rot? What in the name of every saint do you think you deserve revenge for?"

"How dare—"

Colin raised his voice. If nothing else, every Prince here would finally hear this, the secret he never dared tell the rest. "You are the one who betrayed Cal and Den Tyson! You're the one who killed Fenmere's brother and framed it on them! You did that to get rid of them so you could be the King of Rose Street! And I've been expected to swallow that all these years, which I did for my father's sake, for the Princes' sake, and—"

That was as far as he got before a hard cross from Vessrin knocked Colin and his chair over. Hurt like blazes, but it did screw up the knots and ropes just a little, gave him more slack around his neck, let him get one thumb free.

"The Thorn will get what his father should have gotten twenty years ago," Vessrin said.

"The Thorn is coming, traitor," Colin said. "And believe me, he is going to come for you."

Shouts and cries came from the street outside, and then a echoing boom.

"That's him!" Vessrin cried out. "Get ready! You boys, get out front and take him down!"

"If you had any sense, you'd run instead!" Kaiana said. She drew in a deep breath and screamed, "Thorn! I'm here!"

"Shut her mou—" was all Vessrin was able to say before half the roof was torn off.

CHAPTER NINETEEN

"THORN? YOU ALL RIGHT?"

Veranix had been taking a moment, just to breathe, just to get his head clear, before jumping from the window to the roof of the Turnabout. Jutie's path had been perfect, leading him here with minimal fuss or notice, which was especially good since the streets of Aventil seemed to be filled with constables and various gang members and the whole place had an air of a place about to ignite.

"Yeah, yeah, I'm—"

"Did they get more of a piece of you than you thought, mate?" Jutie asked. "Your shirt is seeped with blood."

Veranix looked down. He hadn't even noticed. "No, that's from last night's fight. I must have torn a stitch and not even realized."

"How can you not realize something like that?"

"It's been that kind of day," Veranix said. "How easily can you get down there, in the back door without too much notice?"

Jutie gave a glance out the window down to the alley.

"Right now, not very."

Veranix glanced himself. Several bruisers out there. Plus three on the roof, who luckily hadn't spotted them yet.

"All right, here's the plan, such as it is. I'm going to make enough commotion to draw attention—"

"How much?"

"Real loud. When I do, you get in the back and try to get Colin and Kaiana out. I'll do my best to keep them off you."

"There's a few dozen of them, man."

"All the more reason I need to keep their attention. Good luck."

Veranix took a deep breath, took out three arrows, drew just enough *numina* to sweeten his jump, and leaped across the alley to the roof.

While in the air, he drew and shot, snap, snap, snap. No time to waste or fool around, and the three guards went down quick.

He landed a bit harder and more awkwardly than he had intended. A landing like that would have gotten his grandfather and mother snapping at him to practice more, and mockery from Soranix. His leg was hurting for some reason. He must have taken a hit in that last fight and not realized it.

Stay focused. Kaiana is counting on you.

As much as he wanted to just storm in like a damned hurricane, he had to be a little smarter. Give Jutie that distraction. A couple of boom powder arrows would do the trick.

He reached for the arrows and remembered—he didn't have his quiver, but Enzin's. No trick arrows from Verci Rynax, no boom powder from Mila's apothecary friend. Just regular sharp, killing arrows.

Not that he wouldn't need those. He retrieved the three arrows from the bodies. Couldn't waste one. No time to go back to the bunker and get his gear. It had to be now. Kaiana couldn't wait.

The main thing you need is noise.

A bit of simple chaos, easy enough. He drew in *numina*—slowly, carefully, in full control. Not a chance of draining himself or burning out. He didn't have the cloak, just his power, so he had to use it smartly.

He looked out at the street outside the Turnabout. More Princes on watch, and a usual crowd of shopkeepers, merchants, wagons, carts, and folks going about their day.

"Forgive me, Saint Senea, for what I'm about to do."

This wouldn't be good for the regular folks of Aventil, but nothing happening today was good for them. If he was still alive tomorrow, he'd do what he could to make it right.

Carefully crafting the magical energy, he grabbed three carts off the streets. Ones with no one sitting on them, ones where the merchandise didn't look too breakable or irreplaceable. He pulled those three carts up into the air, above the buildings well above the now gawking crowd.

Then with one hard throw, he hurled the carts back down to the ground, causing enough of a commotion, which was amplified by the screams and shouts in the streets.

A trio of Princes took position in the street. "He's here, he's got to be!" one shouted.

Veranix fired those same three arrows in rapid succession, this time aiming to disable. He wanted them to shout this time. Leg, shoulder, leg, all three went down, crying in pain.

More Princes came out of the Turnabout, which was just what he was hoping for.

Then one more scream. A voice he knew all too well.

"Thorn! I'm here!"

He drew in more *numina*, and now he had to use it faster and harder than before, because he couldn't waste any time. Not with Kaiana down there, not with her in danger. With that magic, he reached through the roof and tore it open, revealing at least a dozen Princes down there, all looking up through the hole and glaring.

"Get him!" someone shouted. A few crossbow bolts were fired through the hole, and when Veranix heard them reloading, he jumping down, nocking arrows while magicking his fall to land like a cat.

Princes on all sides, including two older fellows, one of whom had half his face burned off.

This was Vessrin. The "King" of Rose Street. The one who had betrayed Veranix's father to make the Princes his own.

And Kai and Colin tied up in chairs behind them all.

Veranix drew down on Vessrin.

"Set them loose."

Vessrin laughed. "You think you can drop in and give me orders, boy?" He snapped at a group of Princes to Veranix's left. "Tear him up."

Veranix didn't blink. No gestures, no showmanship, not even a muscle moved from his draw on Vessrin. He just summoned *numina* and let it fly as raw force at the Princes on his left, bowling them over.

That took more out of him than he wanted right now, more than he should have expended. He hoped the display of magical power would at least give the rest of the Princes pause, and he couldn't dare show an ounce of weakness. Not now.

"I said set them loose," he said. "Or your quarrel with me will get much uglier."

He drew in more *numina*, as best he could, as cautiously as he could. These bastards would in all likelihood take another run at him, undeterred by his magic without at least one more blatant display of power. He wasn't sure how much he still had in him for another one.

"Ugly?" Vessrin asked. "Oh, little Tyson boy, you have no idea."

"Do it, Thorn!" Colin shouted. "He's the one who forced your pop to run! He's why Fenmere killed him!"

"And I'm only sorry I didn't get to do it myself," Vessrin said. "If I hadn't killed Charlton Fenmere, you know what this town would be? This street? It'd be the rutting smallest block of the Fenmere empire, and the Tyson boys would have been his simpering lieutenants! I built a line here! I made Aventil what it is!"

The other old man took a start at Veranix, and he pivoted and put the arrow in him in the space of a breath. Other Princes took the moment, but Veranix had another arrow nocked and drawn before they could close.

"This one goes in your throat!" Veranix roared, and he had the whole room's attention. Which was good, because Jutie was slipping in through the back. No one marked him, not yet.

"Why?" Vessrin asked. "Because I did what needed to be done? I kept their paws out of this neighborhood? If it wasn't for me, Aventil would have as much *effitte* as Dentonhill does! And if it wasn't for me, your father would be the one getting fat off the sales."

That made Veranix's hand quiver, but he didn't drop his aim, or the *numinic* charge in his body. "No, he—"

"Who do you think brought it from the Islands with Charlton?" Vessrin shouted. "Colin, your boy here seems to think that his father was some kind of saint, and he really should be disabused of that notion."

"My father," Veranix said, trying to keep his voice together, keep his breath even, so there wouldn't be the slightest quaver in his aim. "My father didn't deserve what you did to him. And my mother did not deserve what Fenmere did to her."

"There's always . . . collateral." He looked to the old man, wheezing on the floor. "How many of my Princes are you going to kill today?"

"How many are you going to make me?" Veranix asked. "He could live, if you let them go, we all walk away."

Jutie had gotten behind Kai, and seemed to have cut her free. She gave Veranix a little nod. Now just Colin.

"I think our odds are better here," Vessrin said. "Just like they've always been with you vermin. I wrecked your father, and kept Den under my boot, and that meant Colin was mine. Until you showed up and stirred the rutting pot up. Gave that boy ideas. So, yeah, we're gonna have a war, and I'm gonna win."

"I've had enough of wars in this city," Veranix said. "You all don't want to see your king killed, you want to get his man here to a sew-up, you step back."

"You think you're gonna—"

"I am giving you a chance," Veranix said, turning his head to the others while keeping his eye and his aim on Vessrin. "All of you. Take it."

"He's not taking the shot," Vessrin said. "Just bring him—"

Jutie cut Colin's ropes.

"Floor!" Veranix shouted to Kai. She dropped to the ground, grabbing Colin and pulling him with her.

He pushed out with the magic in every direction—hard, sharp, and high. Everyone except for Kai, Colin, and Jutie—and the old man he shot—were struck and knocked down to the ground.

"Come on!" he said to them, and Kaiana jumped to her feet and dashed to the door. Veranix sent his arrow to the Prince he spotted right outside when the door opened, and followed right behind.

"Are you—" he started as he caught up.

"Not now," she said. "We need to get—"

Back to campus, she surely was about to say. But back to campus, at least from here, was going to be impossible.

Princes were in a full brawl with a Constabulary blockade, preventing anyone from going north of Rose Street.

Campus was a disaster, and Benvin quickly tasked his people to get every officer they could whistle up to support the cadets and get the gates secured. "Blockade the whole damn street if you have to."

"Excuse me, Lieutenant," one of the cadet captains said as Benvin came straight to their offices near the southern dorms. "I'm sorry to keep having to say this, but city Constabulary doesn't have jurisdiction here."

"You've got to be kidding, kid," Benvin said, checking the young man's badge. Wermont. While whatever brawl had happened here was already over, the place was still a mess of aftermath. Fires burning, injured people still being triaged. "I can see you need Brigade, you need Yellowshields. Let alone ironing up whoever did this."

"We're working on things," Wermont said. "And there is no one to iron up, frankly."

"Well, who did this? Give me what reports you have."

"I'm not authorized, and the campus faculty—"

"I thought it was Druth Intelligence," one of the other cadets interrupted.

"Druth Intelligence is here?" Benvin asked.

"No, that man is a professor in the magic department, Ethan," Wermont said.

"That's an Intelligence uniform, man. Didn't you pay attention in heraldry class?"

"He is a professor and an Intelligence officer, and it is unclear with which authority he is acting," a voice called from around the corner. A voice that was oddly familiar.

"Who was that?" Benvin asked.

"Left!" That was Jace's voice. "They put us in holding!"

Benvin pushed past Wermont and around the corner, to see Jace and his brother, Inspector Minox Welling, in the holding cell. Jace was holding on to the bars with a tight grip, while his brother sat calmly.

"What are they doing here?"

"We were ordered to put them there by Major Dresser," Wermont offered.

"That would be the magic professor who is also an Intelligence officer," Minox said.

"Get them out right damn now," Benvin said. He snapped at Ethan, who scurried over and opened up the cell. "Is this what you do to Constabulary officers?"

"They weren't technically—"

"I will send reports," Benvin said. "You do understand that the autonomy of the campus to police yourselves is a *courtesy*? You are still part of this city and the Maradaine Constabulary has every right to step in when actual crimes have occurred? And you had assaults, destruction—"

"Death," Jace said as he came out. "We think a professor was killed."

"You will give me everything—"

"They don't have anything I haven't already surmised," Minox said as he passed Benvin. "Thank you, Lieutenant, but there is little value in any of us staying here. There is far more trouble afoot."

Benvin watched as Minox left the offices.

"Where is he going?" Benvin asked Jace. "And what are you two doing here?" He waved for Jace to follow him going after Minox.

"Minox, he—I mean, you've seen him, he gets these insights," Jace said. "He realized that there was going to be trouble on campus, people coming after the Thorn, and he was right. But it was done when we got here, and then he argued with the major—"

"The magic professor from Intelligence?"

"And the major had us sequestered since we weren't here on proper authority."

Benvin shook his head. "So the Thorn is someone on campus, and you knew."

"I didn't strictly know," Jace said. "Though I had a suspicion."

"None of this 'didn't strictly' sewage, Jace," Benvin said. "I need my people to be fully honest, no games. We're all that stands between this neighborhood and chaos."

"We're not, though," Jace said. They came out of the cadet offices, near the southern dorms, and no sign of Minox.

"Where did your brother go? And why was he even in Aventil?"

"He and I met for lunch," Jace said. "We had no intention of getting involved in any trouble, we were just—"

"Fine," Benvin said.

"And I'm sorry we . . . quarreled," Jace said.

"You were insubordinate," Benvin said.

"I was fully honest, no games," Jace said. "I told you what I think, I'm sorry you don't like it."

Benvin wanted to be mad at that, but honestly he couldn't. Despite his foolish notions about the Thorn, Jace was too good a kid, too good a constable, and the sort of decent man the force needed.

"So Minox said he's already surmised everything."

"He did. I can't keep up with how his head works, sir."

They glanced around and saw Minox coming out of one of the dormitories.

"What the blazes were you doing in there?" Benvin asked.

"Confirming that the Thorn is not currently present on campus," Minox said.

"You know who he is? Where he lives? In that building?"

Minox held up his gloved hand. "For a variety of reasons, I cannot disclose information that could compromise separate investigations I am involved with."

Benvin raised an eyebrow at that. "Something with the GIU?"

"I cannot fully disclose, especially given my own status on restricted duty. Let's walk out. I fear our talents will be needed in Aventil."

"What is going on?" Benvin asked.

"Listening to everything I overheard on the lawn earlier, and in our holding later, I have worked out the following," Minox said as he led them toward the gates. "Six men came onto campus with the intention of confronting the Thorn. Three of them were your recent escapees: Cuse Jensett, Erno Don, and Enzin Hence. Then there were two mages, one a well-dressed, high-spoken fellow, and the other with flaming wings."

The second one rang a bell from Benvin's own files. "Pria Mandicall. Mage for hire, he's been involved in spots of trouble all over the city. Was the last man a shirtless, muscular man with whips?"

"He was indeed," Minox said. "Capital, Lieutenant. What do you know of him?"

"Rory Scanlin, a mercenary. He and Mandicall like to work together. There was an assault on a manor house party in North Maradaine a few months back, and—"

"Yes, good, good," Minox said, interrupting him. "You are aware that Willem Fenmere has put a bounty on the Thorn's head."

"Yes."

"I surmise these six—and there are probably more—have been explicitly hired to, if not kill the Thorn, wear him down enough to bring to Fenmere. Which is part of what they did here, and they also killed Professor Gollic Alimen in the process."

"And now? The Thorn isn't here, you say?"

"No," Minox said. He held up his hand, which was now glowing a sickly green. "As you likely recall, I do have some magical ability, and while my capacity for tracking with it is extremely limited, to the south of here I can feel quite a bit of energy being expelled. I believe the Thorn is in Aventil, still fighting, and we must assist him."

"Arrest him," Benvin said.

"Our first duty must be to stop these mercenaries, given the destruction they've caused."

"Our first duty is to protect the people, Inspector," Benvin said. "And the Thorn is just as much a part of that destruction. Furthermore, you are on restricted duty. I cannot—and I'm sorry, Minox—I cannot have you acting in any sort of official capacity here. Not with my squad, not in Aventil."

They reached the gates, and Minox nodded. "Of course, that is only proper."

Out in the streets, the whistles were blowing like mad. Constables had lined up between campus and Rose Street, trying to erect barricades as they held back a full riot of Aventil gangs trying to smash through.

"Jace, you're back on duty," Benvin said quietly. "And Minox . . ."

"I will get to the GIU with all due haste and have our Special Tactics Squad dispatched to this neighborhood. You will clearly need them," Minox said. He took that pledge seriously, and ran off east like a crossbow shot.

"Come on," Benvin told Jace. "Let's get this place sorted."

COLIN COULDN'T FOLLOW VERANIX AND KAIANA OUT THE FRONT DOOR of the Turnabout, scrambling out the back with Jutie as the rest of the Princes got on their feet.

"What's the plan, boss?" Jutie asked him as they burst out into the alley. At least three of the bigger bruisers in the Princes—the ones who stayed around Vessrin most of the time—were right there, and they shouted at Colin as soon as they spotted him.

"Where do you think you're going?" one asked. He swung a lumbering punch, which Colin ducked under, following that with a flurry of jabs into the big man's side. They seemed to do absolutely nothing to this bruiser, and the other two moved in to grab Colin.

"Boss!" Jutie shouted, tossing him a knife. Colin caught it in the air and delivered the blade into the wrist attached to the beefy hand grabbing his throat. That guy screamed in pain, and Colin drove his foot into the man's knee, and then hammered the hilt of the knife against his nose when he dropped down.

Another bruiser moved in on Colin, while the third made for Jutie. Colin took a few steps back as the big fists came at him, and when a wild haymaker was thrown, Colin ducked it and threw the fellow over, letting his own overpowered punch take him down. Then he jumped in on Jutie's fight, and together the two of them delivered several slices with their knives, dissuading the bruiser from further fighting.

"Come on!" Colin said, grabbing Jutie's wrist and pulling him out.

"I can't believe this, Colin," Jutie said. "That the Princes would be like this."

"It's all Vessrin," Colin said as they got out of the alley. "He was always a bastard, but he's even worse now."

"He's not my street king, I'll tell you that."

Colin clapped Jutie on the shoulder. "I don't know if we'll still be breathing by the time the sun sets, but you got a place at the right hand of wherever I am, if you want it."

"Damn right," Jutie said.

Out of the alley, Rose Street was an absolute mess. Half the Princes, as well as several folks who just lived here, were brawling with the sticks who had formed a street barricade. The other half of the Princes were trying to get Veranix.

Trying being the word.

There were easily a dozen folks between Colin and Veranix, but from there he could see his cousin fighting with ferocity, like a hungry dog. He had put up his bow and was just fighting with a cane, but he was an absolute whirlwind. He whipped that cane about, brutally delivering blow after blow, back and forth, putting down every Prince in his path as he carved his way through the crowd.

"Come on," he told Jutie. "We need to get through this and—"

"Push!" someone yelled from the constables. They had formed a wall of bodies, and starting walking forward across Rose Street, clubbing everything in their path. Everyone in the street surged back, and Colin was pressed against a wall by the throng. Nowhere to move, unless he started just stabbing indiscriminately.

"Got you," Jutie said, pulling Colin into a shop doorway so the two of them weren't smashed.

"Did you see the Thorn and the girl?" Colin asked him. He had lost sight of Veranix in the press.

"No, but—blazes." He pointed to the opposite building. Two women —a blonde and a Ch'omik—were up on the rooftop, running south and leaping across the alleyway with ease. "They're hunting him."

"Who are they?"

"Magpie and Jackdaw. Deadly Birds. They escaped from Quarrygate when I did."

"We need to get out of here," Colin said. Catch up with Veranix and Kai before they hit Orphan territory. But there was no way out of this crowd, not yet.

"Rooftop it?" Jutie asked.

"Never was my strong suit, but let's go for it," Colin said. With a strike of his elbow, he smashed the window in the shop door. Normally this place would have pulled down its iron gate when locking up, but they must not have had a chance. Through the shop to the roof, and hopefully from there, he could get to Veranix. Or at least be able to see what was happening while Aventil tore itself apart.

CHAPTER TWENTY

KAIANA HAD BARELY CAUGHT A breath as Veranix pulled her past Orchid into Cantarell Square. The Rose Street Princes he had smashed his way through to get here, at least, hadn't chased them any further. They had their own troubles, it looked like.

"Wait," Kaiana said. "Give me a moment. What are we doing?"

"We'll cut through Cantarell, and get to the Sons of Tyson," Veranix said, looking around. "From there, get up to one of the east gates onto campus, and . . . that's as far as I've thought it through."

"What is going on?" she asked him. She couldn't believe what had just happened. She had expected—or at least hoped—that he would have come into the Turnabout like a vengeful Sinner to get her, but she was still wrapping her head around what she was seeing. Veranix hadn't come as the Thorn, but in his school uniform, armed only with a cane and someone else's bow.

"Too damn much," he said. "If I'm lucky, I'll end the day only expelled."

"Why aren't you disguised?" she asked.

"No point," he said. "They all know who I am. Bastards were on the south lawn, calling my name, and . . ." His lips went tight, and he looked away. "We need to keep moving before—"

"Hey! The Thorn is here!"

"Before that," he said, nocking an arrow and spinning to the voice. One of the Princes had managed to follow them. "I don't think you want this, friend."

The Prince first puffed up his chest, but then seemed to realize that he was alone in the square, and Veranix had him in his aim.

"Fine," the Prince said, and dashed off.

"There's going to be more of that," Veranix said. "So we need to—"

"Yeah, we're not alone," another voice said, this time from the other side of the square. And the owner of that voice wasn't lying—there were a dozen tough-looking folks standing shoulder to shoulder, walking closer.

"Who are they?" Kai asked.

"Waterpath Orphans," Veranix said. "I've got no feud with you and yours, Orphans."

"This is the Thorn?" the lead Orphan asked. He had the scars on his cheeks, and stars branded on his neck. That must be how they marked their captains. "He looks like a wet cat."

"It's been a busy day," Veranix said. "I didn't get a chance to get dressed."

"Shame." The Orphans had moved in position to block their way east. "You know that they're calling for your head, kid. Offering some numbers."

"And believe me, friend, you will not be collecting those numbers."

"Dozen of us, one of you."

"Two," Kaiana said. "Don't think he's alone."

Veranix gave her a small look from the corner of his eye, keeping his aim on them, and she could have sworn she saw a tear forming there.

"Still like the odds," the Orphan captain said.

"Thorn isn't your quarry, he's ours."

Two women strode into the square. One blonde, Kaiana had seen her before. She had tried to kill Veranix and Kaiana during the incident with the Alchemist. She was fingering a handful of throwing blades in each hand, flipping them around with an intimidating air that was terrifying enough to make Kaiana's heart race. The other woman, a tall, black-skinned Ch'omik with the most powerful arms Kaiana had ever seen, was carrying a weapon like a bladed rowing oar. It looked like she could cut a person in half with a single stroke.

"Well, Magpie and Jackdaw, now it's a real party," Veranix said. "How about you all fight each other for the right to catch me, and we'll slip off?"

The blonde hurled her blades at Veranix, and at the same time the Orphans charged. Light and sound erupted from Veranix, and when Kaiana's eyes cleared he was grabbing her arm. "Run, come on!"

She started to run, instinct taking her away from Cantarell Square, toward the south, away from the fight. Veranix was right with her, even though he was limping as he ran.

"Are you—"

"Just keep moving," he said.

One of the Orphans came at them, swinging a chain, wrapping it around Veranix's leg and pulling him off his feet.

"Vee!" Kaiana shouted. She tackled the Orphan dragging Veranix, pummeling his face and chest. Veranix managed to get the chain off his leg and get back on his feet just as a few other Orphans caught up, a few of them occupied trying to fight Magpie and Jackdaw. While Veranix slapped the Orphans about with the cane, dodging and rolling to keep ahead of their attacks, Kaiana pulled up the chain and kicked that Orphan in the face.

Veranix's fight wasn't going well. He had managed to knock those Orphans about just enough so each punch or crack of the cane he landed bought him only enough time to handle another Orphan. None of them were staying down. Kaiana whipped the chain at one of them, knocking him off balance.

"We need to get off the streets," he said. "This is—"

"Our patch!" a young woman, also marked as a captain with scars and stars, came with another dozen Orphans. "Looks like the Thorn is going to be ours."

"Saints," Veranix muttered. "Do you all really want a piece of this?"

Those Orphans charged, answering the question, including the woman punching Kaiana right in the jaw. Kaiana resisted the urge to just crumple to the ground, and instead hit back, letting the chain hammer the Orphan. She kept in the fight as best she could, though Veranix was taking the brunt of it. She glanced at him, noticing his leg was bleeding, one of Magpie's blades still in it.

Magpie. She was closing in fast, about to throw more of her darts. Kaiana whipped out the chain, largely ineffectively, attempting to protect Veranix. All she manage to do was clip Magpie on the chin as she threw.

Magpie's blades didn't strike true, and she looked at Kaiana with murder in her eyes as she wiped the blood from her chin.

Jackdaw was right on her heels, walloping Orphans with her terrifying oar weapon, damn near cleaving bodies in half. Veranix managed to get out from the Orphan fight and bring up the bow, firing two arrows at Magpie and Jackdaw, and get himself farther away from the fight. Kaiana moved to keep with him, but the Orphan woman knocked her in the knee, sending her down.

"Kai!" Veranix shouted.

She tried to get up, as Veranix pummeled his way through the group of Orphans, and the lady Orphan kept kicking and knocking her. Veranix shouted, and a blast of light came from him, knocking the Orphan down. He got to her and hauled her to her feet, but Jackdaw was right on them.

She raised up that mighty bladed oar and started to swing it right at Veranix's head. Kaiana tried to scream at him to duck, but she couldn't.

She couldn't speak, she couldn't move.

Her whole body had frozen, refusing to obey.

VERANIX BLINKED, UNSURE OF WHAT HE WAS SEEING.

All the madness was completely still. Everyone—the Orphans, Magpie, Jackdaw—weren't moving a muscle. Same with the people on the street, in the shops.

And Kaiana. Her hand outstretched to him, her face in terror, as Jackdaw's weapon was bearing down on both of them.

Except it wasn't. Jackdaw was like a statue. They all were.

"Kai?" Veranix asked.

"She can't answer," someone called out. "I would say she can't hear you, but I'm doing a *lot* right now, so I don't think I can accurately claim that." Veranix spun to the source of the voice. Tor Rassin sat at an outdoor table in front of a sandwich shop, a pair of strikers and beers in front of him.

"The blazes are you doing?"

"Thought you might want a moment to catch your breath, have a bite?" Rassin said with a chuckle. "I mean, maybe this is all fun and games for you, but it certainly looks exhausting." He gestured to the empty chair.

Veranix walked toward him, his steps slow out of caution as much as from the pain in his leg. Magpie's dart still stuck in it. He couldn't pull it out, not yet, not without bleeding out in the middle of the street. "But what are you doing to them?"

"Holding them at bay, of course."

"You're controlling their minds?"

Rassin sighed, took a sip of beer. "Actually controlling minds is much harder. You've got to fight upstream, making a person do a thing when they don't want to. I'm just holding them in place so they are simply . . . not doing. Much less exhausting. Speaking of, sit, you look absolutely wretched."

Veranix was highly skeptical, but he still dropped into the chair. He did not drop his guard or loosen his grip on the cane. If he needed to crack Rassin across his stupid skull, his body was ready to do that on instinct. "More to the point of my question, why are you here at all?"

"So," Rassin said, picking up a striker and taking a bite, while gesturing that Veranix should do the same. "There I was at the Lower Trenn Ward, wanting to give another test before working on my client's son. And while I'm wandering about, there's this dark girl. And her thoughts are just shining. You know why?"

"Because you had healed her father?" Veranix said. Despite himself, he grabbed the striker and took a bite. He hated even the idea of taking this reprehensible man's hospitality, but he had been going full on since . . .

Since the fight on the lawn. Since Alimen was killed.

He swallowed that down with the bite of striker. It helped, but he was in so much pain, so tired.

"Exactly. Such a bright mix of thoughts, and from such a delight-fully lovely girl, of course I had to dip my toes in that pool."

"You are depraved."

"I am!" Rassin said with a laugh. "Most people are, I just embrace that. Remember that few people's thoughts are hidden from me. Except mages like you, which I always find delicious. But this girl, so many of her thoughts are singing of you. Your face is so strong in her head."

"You shouldn't—"

"Including you in a charming scarlet ensemble, nothing like this ragged uniform look you're working right now. And here I have a revelation—that boy is this Thorn I keep hearing about. So when she left I followed her out of idle curiosity—"

"Don't you have something better to do?"

"I really don't!" Rassin said, still with his hollow laugh. "Especially since I started to pick up other thoughts along the way. People are looking for the Thorn. People are hunting the Thorn."

"You think I don't know that?"

"For a bounty of fifty thousand crowns!"

That was news.

"How much?"

"Fifty thousand. I mean, I won't lie to you, Vee. I could use money like that."

Veranix stood up, holding up his cane to strike.

"Easy, Vee. I'm holding a few dozen minds in place right now. Like a basket of eggs. Who knows what could happen to the eggs were I to be suddenly . . . jostled."

"I will not be a bounty so easily collected."

"Of course you wouldn't be. And, frankly, it's more work than I'm interested in investing. Fight you? Like I haven't already seen you tear up these street folks. I mean, look at that, what you did here, and earlier up on Rose Street. Very entertaining."

"So what do you want, Rassin?"

"Veranix," he said, sounding wounded. "Here I am, trying to be hospitable. Trying to be a friend."

"A friend?"

"And you should be friendly to me," Rassin said. A sly smile grew across his face. "Isn't that what your mother would want?"

"You mention my mother—" Vee said, grabbing Rassin by the front of his shirt and hauling him to his feet. Someone behind them screamed —Veranix turned to see one of the Orphans convulsing on the ground, blood streaming from her eyes, nose, and ears.

"Temper, Veranix. There goes one egg. Who knows who could be next."

"My mother—"

"Is perfectly safe for the moment," Rassin said. "But I know who she is. And I tested . . . well, I tested the idea of fixing her, if you will."

"If you hurt her—"

"On the contrary, I found her real, true self hidden within that mess. The horror of her last lucid moments at the hands of Fenmere. And he's the one who's put this bounty on your head, no?"

"Surely."

"I want you to consider an idea, Veranix. I do not want a physical altercation with you, even when you're run ragged like this. Yes, like a cornered cat in an alley, you are. Very dangerous."

"So don't try me, Mister Rassin."

"Veranix, you should call me Tor. Mister Rassin was my father, a right bastard who got what was coming to him." Rassin peered closer at Veranix. "But you know something about troubles with fathers, yes?"

"Stay out of my head," Veranix said. "My father was a good man."

"Yes, you think that. But you were just told something to make doubt drip through the cracks. If it's true . . ."

"It's not true."

"Lying to me is pointless, Veranix," Rassin said. "I can see your father loved you very much, and I'm happy for you. But now you wonder who he really was, don't you."

Veranix pushed the anger down. He couldn't let what Vessrin had said rattle him. Or Rassin, for that matter. "Don't test me, Tor."

"I won't. I have no urge to fight a dangerous man, especially one whose mind gives me such challenges to touch. So, instead, I propose: you let me bring you, alive, to Fenmere. I collect the bounty, and walk my way to the Lower Trenn and fix your mother up. Good as the last time you talked with her."

"What . . . you can—"

"And, because I like you, Veranix, I'll give you one more thing. When we deliver you to Fenmere, I will touch their perception so they see you as beaten and broken. But you will actually be as hale as . . . well, as you are now. And more importantly, fully armed. But they won't see you that way. It's the best of all worlds. I get money, you get your mother, and you get to have an honest-to-the-saints fighting chance in that bear's den."

Was that true? Could that even be possible? Could his mother be fixed, like Kai's pop had? And was it worth the price? If he was delivered to Fenmere, with his bow, his arrows, his staff . . . could he—

No. All of that relied on Tor Rassin being trustworthy. Being believable.

"Not a chance," he said. "Now get out of here before you find out what a physical altercation with me is like."

He chuckled and got to his feet, taking a sip of his beer. "I do like you, Veranix Calbert. You've got a fire in you, and you're also enough of a mystery that you're worth talking to. I'd love to collect your bounty, but I don't—at least right now—want to see you die. I enjoy this show far too much. In fact, grab your lady and start running. I'll give you a few seconds before I let go of the rest."

"What—"

"Only a few seconds," Rassin said, waving as he walked away. "So run, my friend. Run!"

Kaiana cried out, "Duck!" as she dropped to the ground, and then scrambled away as if expecting to get clobbered. Which, judging from the position of Jackdaw and her oar, she was about to be.

"Kai, let's go," Veranix said, grabbing her hand.

"But what—"

"Come on!" He enveloped them in magic, and with that, they bolted down the block like a blast of lightning. They came to a stop as he released the magic, breathing hard, and he glanced back. The chaos of the fight between Magpie, Jackdaw, and the Orphans was going full out, until one of the Orphans shouted.

"He's getting away!"

"Vee!" Kaiana said.

He drew out an arrow, pivoting on his heel. "Kai, you need to run, get out of here, and I'll draw them off. Just get out."

"Don't be an idiot," she said, grabbing his arm before he could nock the arrow. "You'll be dead in seconds."

"But you won't. Run."

She pulled him into the mouth of an alley, "We're staying together."

"This is my fault," he said, keeping his guard up toward the street, ready for Magpie and Jackdaw to come at him. "Nearly got you killed, and I got . . . I got . . ."

"This way," she said. "We'll—"

She stopped short, and Veranix turned his head to see what stopped her.

Seven more fellows, Aventil gang types, with tall hats and buttoned vests. Knights of Saint Julian.

Veranix turned to them. "Ready to make your try at me?"

The Knight in the lead held up his hands. No weapons. "I take it you're the Thorn?"

"And I still have fight left in me."

"Good," the Knight said, "because those Orphans won't back down. But the reverend has tasked us with giving you a safe walk to the church, so that's what we're here to do."

His fellows dashed out past Veranix and Kaiana into the street, immediately getting into it with the approaching Orphans.

"This way," the Knight said. "While we've still time."

CHAPTER TWENTY-ONE

"WHY ARE WE HEADING THIS way?" Jutie asked. "We just saw them fighting in Cantarell . . ."

"And we couldn't get to them without getting killed," Colin said as they scrambled onto the next roof. Colin was nowhere near as good at this as he had been when he was younger. The times he had fearlessly jumped over an alley or pulled himself up a ledge, those were gone. Not that he had fear about it, but his arms and legs were nowhere near as obedient about it.

Or at least having spent a few hours tied within an inch of his life had taken a toll.

"Come on," Jutie said, pulling him up. "You're right about that." He jerked his head toward the street below. It was now even worse, as right below them Orphans and Princes were in a full brawl with each other, and both of them with the constables attempting to hold some kind of barricade. It was near impossible to even tell who was fighting who, and no one had any goals beyond "punch the closest person."

"And where are your folks?" Jutie asked. "Sons of Tyson?"

"Last thing I told them was to clear out, take the money we took from Fenmere and get out of Aventil completely. And look."

To the east, club-wielding goons were coming across Waterpath, in groups of a dozen each, beating down just about anyone they came across. When they didn't have a person in front of them, they broke windows, smashed in doors, any damage they could.

"They're crossing Waterpath now?" Jutie asked.

"To be fair, we did it first," Colin said. "The Sons joined the Thorn in cracking up part of Fenmere's empire."

"Then we better hope the Sons are still around," Jutie said. "Because that line needs to be held. Ain't that the point?"

"Yeah, it is," Colin said. Those shopkeeps, hard-working folks of Aventil, they didn't ask for this, they certainly didn't deserve it. The whole point of any of the gangs of Aventil was to look after their patch, keep their neighbors safe. "But that's an Orphan patch."

"And I only see Orphans down here," Jutie said. "What do you want to do?"

Colin didn't have an answer. He needed to find a way to get to Veranix, keep him safe. He had made a promise to his uncle.

But he had also made a promise to Rose Street, and even if he wasn't a Prince anymore, the street still mattered to him. All these streets still mattered to him.

"Well, pray to whichever saint still listens to you that the Sons haven't run yet," he said. Jutie was already on the move toward the next roof.

"Over there, there's a backstair we can—"

A flash of metal blurred through the air, slicing right past Jutie, and he went flying over the edge.

"Jutie!"

Colin ran toward him, but something snared his leg and pulled him off his feet.

"What?" was all he could say as he was yanked, a rope coiled around his foot, over the lip of the roof. He dropped his knife and tried to grab the edge, but it all happened too fast. He only fell a few feet, though, finding himself hung upside down, staring at a woman standing on the wrought iron backstair. Dark leather, painted eyes, veiled face, holding the other end of the rope in one hand and a round blade in the other.

"Who are you?" he asked, looking around for some way out of this.

Jutie was a few yards away, clinging onto the side of the building, no good way up or down from his position.

"I'm looking for the Thorn," she said. "You know where I can find him."

"Everyone is singing the same song today," he said. "You missed him by only a few minutes. Your loss."

"Yes, I lost him in the crowd, seems everyone wants a piece of him."

"You'll have to move fast to collect that bounty, then," Colin said. If he had a knife, he could pull it quick and throw it right in her throat. But it was still on the rooftop.

"Bounty?" she asked. "Has he angered someone else enough there's a price on his head?"

"What hole have you been sleeping in?" he asked. "That's why the neighborhood's gone crazy for him."

"Jox and Javer," she muttered. "Can't let any of them get him before I've killed him."

"You aren't looking for the reward?" Jutie asked from his precarious perch.

"I just want to make him bleed, make him fall," she said. "But you, I hear, you are kin to him."

"That is the word," Colin said. "But I don't know where he's going now, or, frankly, if he'll survive."

"But if he does," she said, her voice a husky whisper. "If he slips through my fingers, I still want him to be devastated. I want him to know what I felt, to have someone he loves be callously dropped onto the street below."

"What?"

She threw the circular blade, and it sliced the rope above his foot as it flew past him. The threads of the rope started to strain and snap as the blade bounced off one wall, then another to ricochet back, slicing the rope again on its return to her hand.

"Goodbye."

She whipped the rope in her hand as she jumped off the backstair to the ground below, and that was the last straw to make it finally snap. Colin was about to drop headfirst onto the cobblestones below when something crashed into him, knocking him into the backstair and grabbing hold of his leg.

Jutie, hanging on to him and the iron railing with everything he had.

"Not losing you today, man."

Colin pulled himself up and the two of them fell over onto the stair. He hadn't had the chance to be afraid, but now the reality of what had almost happened hit him as hard as his face would have hit the ground were it not for Jutie. "I really thought that was it."

"Where did she go?" Jutie asked.

"After the Thorn," Colin said. "And she's going to try to kill him."

"Do we go after her?"

Colin hated to answer that, he had made that oath, but he knew what he had to do. One a promise, the other a responsibility.

"No," he said. "We need to get to the Sons, and with whoever we find, we hold that line. The Thorn will have to handle her on his own."

And whatever other enemies were coming his way.

Enzin's arms were pulsing. Surges of power in one muscle, withering in the other, the pain increasing every minute.

"Your fix didn't last!" he snapped at Cuse, who was mixing up a powder to put on the arrow wound the Thorn had given him. Cuse was too damned calm, given the situation.

"Easy, champ, easy," Erno said with a nauseating smile. This fool had one on his face far too often, took nothing seriously. All Enzin had wanted was to cure himself from this cursed damage done to his body, after taking that magically spiked overdose of the Soldier's Fist, and then the Thorn and that constable ruining him. His body hadn't been the same since. Constant pulses, fits of strength, spasms of weakness, and the pain. Always the pain.

He had only even approached Cuse in the prison because he had heard the man was a genius with chemicals. Cuse had understood entirely, since Enzin's malady was both apothecarial and magical. "No one else is remotely suited to help you, Enzin. No one."

Which was the only reason why Enzin had tolerated Cuse bringing the others in for his escape plan. Erno was bad enough, but bringing those two Deadly Birds, the filthy assassins who had killed Enzin's family, that was near intolerable. Still Enzin kept his mouth shut, went along, for Cuse's sake. Cuse had the plan, and he said he needed them all. All of them had been wronged by the Thorn.

"Is all this really necessary?" Endoriff asked. "Surely there are better places to regroup than this moldering pit of decay?"

As much as Enzin despised the dandy mage, he had a point. This building was half collapsed, and smelled like stale death.

"We're all very lucky that one of my laboratories still exists," Cuse said. "If we're going to go another round with the Thorn—"

"Are we?" Scanlin asked. Rory Scanlin leaned against one wall, massaging oil into his arms. "I mean, we had our bout, and we did some damage. That's the job, yeah?"

"We want to make him hurt, Rory," Pria said, putting pressure on his own arrow wound.

"I've got no beef," Scanlin said.

"He humiliated me, killed my Circle mates, and tore down my house," Pria said. "He's got more pain coming to him."

"I mean, fine, but I don't need to get killed for this," Scanlin said. "We're not getting paid that well."

"Does it look like we're at risk of getting killed?" Cuse asked.

"You got shot," Erno said.

"Nothing to worry about," Cuse said, and applied the yellow powder to the wound. There was a flash of fire, and when it passed, the wound was closed. He started to do the same to Pria.

"That professor was quite the fight," Erno said. "I should come up with a ballad for that one."

"Hush," Enzin said, very tired of all of their voices, especially Erno's. "This was never the deal. Go to Fenmere with what we knew, use him to get back on our feet. Go after the Thorn, yes. But I didn't join in on this to just kill anyone. Especially old men."

"That old man had it coming, trust," Endoriff said.

"I really don't," Enzin said. "In any of you!"

"Hey, hey," Cuse said, coming over with a vial of orange liquid. "I told you, I told you before, what I gave you this morning was a patch, just a patch. Proper curing you will take time, expensive ingredients, which is why we need to do all this."

"Patch didn't last, look at me!" Enzin said, showing him his arms. Another surge made the muscles in his forearm swell, and then drop.

"I know, I didn't account for the amount of *numina* we would encounter. The Thorn, the professor, these two mages."

"You have a problem with me?" Pria asked.

"It's not a problem, it's not you," Cuse said calmly. "I just didn't take it into account in my calculations. This is a new patch, should be more stable, like being back on the Fist at the best of times."

"Give it to me," Enzin said. "Give it now!"

"Hold on," Cuse said. He held up a small ingot of metal to Endoriff. "If you could be so kind as to apply a *numinic* charge to this piece of copper?"

"I fail to see why," Endoriff said, but still held up his hand, and the metal started to glow.

"Because it's a faster activation, and will make this more stable," Cuse said. He dropped the piece of copper into the vial, and with a flash, the liquid went from orange to green. He gave it to Enzin, who drank it down greedily. Almost immediately, the pain in all his muscles subsided. His arms swelled, evenly, powerfully.

"Better?" Erno asked him.

"It's fine," Enzin said.

"Good," Erno said. He handed over a quiver. "New arrows for you, new bow for me. And we'll add those debts to the Thorn's tally."

"Shouldn't we be hunting him again now?" Endoriff asked. "If we are quite done recovering?"

"You know where the Thorn is?" Scanlin asked, putting the cap back on his oil. "If so, we can go. Or do you mean you want Pria to fly up and scout again?"

"He could be anywhere," Cuse said.

"Now, that's absurd."

A little girl, no more than seven, came out of the shadows of the door. Enzin drew an arrow and bore down his aim.

"Easy, mate, it's a child," Erno said.

"I mean," the little girl said. "He really couldn't be anywhere, could he? It's highly unlikely he went to, say, Poasia or Tsoulja."

"Who the blazes are you?" Cuse asked.

"I mean, of course, when you said 'anywhere,' you really were talking about the neighborhood."

"I weary of this," Endoriff said, his hands charging with magic.

"Ah, ah," the little girl said, waving her finger. "You can kill this little girl, but that really won't affect the person you're talking to. All you would be doing is killing a little girl."

Enzin stepped closer. "So who are we talking to?"

"An interested party. The lot of you want the Thorn, don't you? You're working for someone who is paying handsomely for his head on a platter, only, like you said, he could be anywhere. Well, not anywhere, but still."

"I kind of still want to kill the little girl," Endoriff said.

"Wouldn't that be a hoot?" the girl said. "Then I'd have to find a different emissary, and that . . . well, it wouldn't be hard at all, actually, but I think it would make this whole thing very tedious. The point is, you work for Willem Fenmere."

"Not true," Erno said.

"You are doing a job for him, fine," the girl said, rolling her eyes. "Let us not quibble about semantics. You are doing a job in which you hunt that delightful boy called the Thorn. Fenmere, I can tell, wants him alive, yes?" The girl looked at Scanlin. "Ooh, his mind is delightfully uncomplicated, so, yes, I can see that is what Fenmere wants. Delightful."

"And what do you want?"

"Comfortable compensation for my efforts," the little girl said. "I . . . that is, the person you are speaking to, well, I have no interest in any sort of physical grapple with the Thorn, but I would like to get paid."

"For what?" Enzin asked.

"His current location, of course," the girl said. "I know where he is, and as he keeps moving, I know where he goes. So, you want to find him, I can help. But only if I get paid."

Pria went to the girl and picked her up by the front of the blouse. "Or we can rip your teeth out until you tell us."

"Oh, savage!" the girl said with a wide smile. "I mean, that is delightful, but again, nothing you do to the body you have in your hands will have any effect on me, safely ensconced a block away from you all. It certainly won't compel me to talk. So, let us not bother with the tedious waste of time, and instead, you bring Mister Fenmere so we can settle my finder's fee."

"Bring Fenmere?" Cuse asked.

"Well, none of you have the money. He's the one paying, he's the one to talk to."

"Pria," Enzin said. "Put the girl down and go tell Fenmere."

"Why are you ordering me?" Pria asked.

"I'm not ordering you, I'm saying she's right, this is tedious. And you are the fastest. So let's stop wasting time, let's stop killing people who we didn't agree to kill, and move along."

Pria scowled, put the girl down on the work counter, and his flaming wings sprouted from his back. He launched into the air, smashing through the roof in the process.

"That was just excessive," Cuse said, looking at the hole just made.

"I do hope he hurries," the girl said, swinging her legs about as they dangled over the edge of the counter. "I would hate for you all to miss the fun the Thorn is about to have."

CHAPTER TWENTY-TWO

K AIANA WASN'T SURE IF THEY could trust these "Knights of Saint Julian," part of her was certain they were being led into a trap. But at least, for the moment, as they surrounded her and Veranix in a protective circle as they made their way across Tulip Street to the church, she wasn't being tied up or attacked.

For the moment, she could breathe.

"They probably are right behind us, though," Veranix said. "So if we could . . . I didn't catch your name, Captain?"

"They call me Four-Toe," the Knight captain said.

"You missing a toe or something?"

"Got them all," he said.

"His parents named him Fortill," one of the other Knights said. "But as a kid, he couldn't say it right. So here we are."

"Hush it, Scants," Four-Toe said.

"Those Orphans and the two other killers are right behind us, so maybe a little faster, Four-Toe?" Veranix said.

"I'd agree, but we've got Hallaran's Boys pushing in, and we spotted wagons of Fenmere's men coming up from the south. So the streets are rutting full of trouble."

"All the reason to go faster, no?"

"Go smarter, Thorn," Four-Toe said. His Knights signaled, and Four-

Toe pulled Veranix into a shop, and one of the other goons pulled Kaiana.

This is the trap, she thought. Though an old clothing shop didn't seem like much of a trap.

"Just cool here a moment," Four-Toe said. "Hey, Nonders?"

An older woman came out from the back room. "What now?" she asked, not even taking the pipe out of her mouth to speak.

"My friends need some new coats to look less conspicuous."

She looked Kaiana up and down, then Veranix. "She's a Napa and he's bleeding. Ain't nothing gonna make that less conspicuous."

"Watch your mouth," Veranix said.

"Don't bother," Kaiana told him. "She's not worth thinking about. How far are we from the church? A block and a half?"

Four-Toe looked out the door. "Yeah, but we've got a group of Orphans walking through here. Let's let them pass, Thorn."

"Fine by me," Veranix said. "But let's make one thing clear."

Four-Toe turned back to Veranix, raising an eyebrow. "The only thing clear is the Rev asked me to do something, so I'm doing it."

"That's fine," Veranix said. "But if something happens out there, you get her out, get her safe."

"I'm supposed to protect you," Four-Toe said. "I'm letting the girl tag along out of respect."

"And I'm saying, she never should have been dragged into this. So her safety comes first, above all else."

"Safest thing for her is to stay out of it, then. She should stay here with Nonders." He looked to the back of the store. The shopwoman was gone. "Where did she go?"

Kaiana went to the back room, and saw the door to the alley was still swinging open. "Looks like she ran."

"That ain't good," Four-Toe said. "Blazes, I called you Thorn, she heard, so she must have—"

"Oh, Thorn!" a voice called from the street. "We know you're inside."

"We've got a score to settle with you," another man said.

Veranix furrowed his brow. "Who is that?"

"Let's not stay and find out," Four-Toe said, brushing past Kaiana to the back. "Come on, we'll—"

Five goons charged in from the back of the store, all fists and clubs. Four-Toe launched himself right at them, and Veranix grabbed Kaiana's hand and pulled her with him back out the front.

At least a dozen more goons were there, led by two fellows in heavy coats, armed with pairs of short swords and hatchets. A few of the Knights were dead on the ground at their feet.

"There he is," the one with the hatchet said.

"Well, my very stars," Veranix said, and Kaiana could see his whole demeanor had shifted, like he had just put on the persona of the Thorn with a shift in the tilt of his head. "If it isn't Lemt and Jendle, two of the most useless wastes of skin I've ever met."

"Finally seeing the real Thorn," the one with the hatchets said. "I'm going to enjoy this."

"I wouldn't think you'd enjoy humiliation, Lemt," Veranix said. "But I don't judge people for that sort of thing."

"Make him bleed!" Jendle—who held the short swords—jumped in at Veranix with both blades swinging. Veranix moved like a rabbit, faster than Kaiana could see, and in a fluid motion he had blocked both blades with the cane, flipped over Jendle, and yanked the man by the hair, pulling him to the ground with a hard crash. Veranix popped up and pressed his boot onto the man's face.

"Anyone want to be the next?" Veranix asked, pulling up the bow with a nocked arrow. "You'll all get a turn if you think it's worth it."

"He's only got four arrows!" Lemt shouted. "We can overpower him!"

One of the goons stepped toward Kaiana, and Veranix sent that arrow right into his neck. The man dropped, and Veranix had two more arrows ready.

"That's a great deal for whoever goes fifth," Veranix said. "But the next three fellows might not like their odds."

"You've got your back against that store, which also has our boys in it, and we've still got the numbers," Lemt said.

Jendle tried to grab at Veranix's leg, but Veranix stomped hard on him, and then kicked one of the swords away, near Kaiana's foot. She scooped it up, holding it out in a fighting stance.

"Blood will cost you blood," she said. "Think of what it will cost you."

"I should have hit you harder."

Jackdaw strolled into view, her bladed oar over her shoulder. Magpie, with an obnoxious smile on her face, was right behind her.

"Didn't think we'd let you fellas have all the fun," Magpie said.

"You two had your dance, get to the back of the line," Veranix said. "Everyone should just stay right where you are for the moment."

"Someone shut him up!" Jendle shouted.

"I'm more than ready to wipe that grin off his face," Lemt said, twirling his hatchet.

"Oh no, oh no," Veranix said. "If we're gonna have a real fight here, we need to have some ground rules."

"What is he on about?" Magpie asked.

"I mean, I think we should all agree that punching the tenders is just off limits. That's not a fair fight."

"What are you doing?" Kaiana asked.

"I'm buying us time," Veranix said. "For them."

"Them" was the dozen Knights of Saint Julian who charged in on the goons. Veranix fired an arrow at Lemt, then another at Magpie, just as Four-Toe—who was covered in blood—came roaring out of the clothing shop.

"Knights stand tall!" he shouted as he leaped into the fray.

Neither of Veranix's arrows found their target, but he was already moving to spar with Lemt, making a space for Kaiana to have a clear run toward the church.

"Go," he shouted, drawing the last arrow. "I've got you covered!"

Kaiana ran, using the sword to parry and shove off the goon who came at her. Three more surrounded her, and Four-Toe was right at her side, an absolute animal with his knives.

"Safe walk her!" he shouted to the other Knights, pointing to her.

Darts flew past her ear, and she heard Four-Toe cry out as one hit him.

"You aren't getting out of here, girl!" Magpie shouted. "Not this time!"

Two Knights flanked her just as Magpie jumped in, driving her darts into one of their throats while bringing her boot down on the other's knee. Kaiana swiped with the sword, a wild swing, but enough to make Magpie stumble back a few steps. Just in the distance, Jackdaw carved through Knights like they were blades of grass.

"Pathetic form, girl, but—" Magpie said before an arrow struck her in the shoulder, knocking her to the ground.

She looked to Veranix, his hand outstretched, his face pale and clammy. He had magicked the arrow to hit her, and that had clearly pushed him too far. How much more could he handle?

"Behind you!" she shouted to him, as Lemt and Jendle were both coming on him with swords and hatchets. He brought up the bow and cane to block, and both cracked under the barrage of blows.

Kaiana wanted to shout, wanted to cry to him, wanted to run in there and beat off all of them, but her feet were frozen.

A thundering sound of hooves bore down on them. Kaiana glanced in their direction, saw a pair of horses galloping at them, pulling a cart that was careening wildly, nearly out of control. And in the driver's seat: Delmin, looking completely terrified as he tried vainly to hold on to the reins.

"What are you—" she muttered in disbelief.

He lost all control, and the horses whipped around the corner while the cart disengaged completely. Delmin launched into the air, as did the young woman clutching on to him from behind. Someone else launched into the air from the crashing wagon, though she looked like she had jumped clear with intention.

Mila, in her full Rose regalia, with a bundle under one arm and a rope in the other hand. She whipped that rope out as she landed, coiling it around Veranix's waist. With a yank, she pulled him back toward her, away from Lemt and Jendle, away from Jackdaw's oar, and into her arms.

"Sorry I'm late," she said as she caught him, kissing him as he melted into her embrace.

Then his hand tightened its grip on the rope—Kaiana realized it was his rope, the napranium-laced one—and his pale face flushed. He drew away from Mila and stood straight. He clutched the rope as it wound into a tight coil around his fist. Mila, meanwhile, shoved something else into his other hand—the cloak.

The intersection of Tulip and Tree crackled with energy that even Kaiana could feel, the hairs on her arm standing up. That crackling built up to a flash that forced Kaiana to shut her eyes.

A hand grabbed her throat, and Kaiana opened her eyes to find Magpie on her, one hand choking her while the other brought up a blade.

Before Magpie could bring it down, she was yanked away, pulled up in the air. The rope around her, and Veranix—no, the Thorn. The boy in the shredded school uniform was gone, and now there was just the crimson-clad, shadowy force of nature, pure and powerful like she had never seen. The Thorn held her up high with the rope as magic crackled off him.

"As I said, ground rules," he said, his voice awesome and terrible. "And the first one is, you do not touch her."

WITH THE ROPE IN HAND, THE CLOAK ON HIS SHOULDERS, VERANIX felt a surge of magic course through his exhausted body. That and anger fueled him, kept him on his feet, but it couldn't be for much longer.

So it was high time to end this.

With Magpie coiled up in the rope, he pulled her away from Kaiana and hurled her into Jackdaw, sending them both flying into an alley.

"Thorn!" Delmin called out. He had Veranix's staff, tossing it over. Veranix caught it just as a pair of Fenmere's goons tried to jump on him. He whipped it around in a wide arc, clocking the first and blocking the second's attack before he got stabbed.

"Not today," Mila said, wrapping her own rope around the goon's neck. She pulled him back, kicking out his knee as she dragged him down. "Not ever."

"You think that makes a difference?" Lemt taunted. "We've got fellows all around. More are coming."

"Then let's dissuade you," Veranix said. He charged at Lemt and Jendle, with Mila right at his side. Saints, it felt good to have her there. Especially since these boys were tougher fighters than he had expected. He remembered them as sad sacks at the Dogs' Teeth, a pair he had slapped around with ease. Now they were lean and grizzled, formidable opponents. Veranix had to focus on Lemt and his hatchets, blocking blow after blow and barely able to get a jab in, while Mila danced with Jendle. She held her own, though.

"Thorn's got a girl, now?" Jendle asked.

"Thorn has a Rose," Mila said. "But she still cuts." She took a swipe at Jendle, getting a piece of his coat. "No, I didn't like that one."

"Needs work, yes," Veranix said, hoping that keeping his tone light would hide how hard he was fighting, how tired he was, and throw Lemt off his game.

"Maybe stings?" she asked.

"See, that doesn't work for a flower at all. And I think it's too late to call you Honeybee."

"Shut it!" Lemt said, swinging too hard with the hatchet, putting him off balance. Veranix spun the staff around and clocked him hard enough to send him flying onto his back.

"I'd prefer Hornet to that, thank you," Mila said, parrying Jendle's blade enough out of the way to give Veranix the clear shot to knock him on the ground as well. "But Rose is more me. Next?"

"Get running," Veranix said. Despite the magical boost of the napranium, he was still nearly spent. He couldn't keep this up much longer. "Four-Toe, we need to move!"

"That's a problem, boss!" Four-Toe said, pointing down Tulip toward the church. At least a dozen green-capped Halloran's Boys were coming, and Princes from the north up Tree Lane, and Orphans coming from the east. The Knights were moving in to intercept, but the numbers were not on their side here.

"Plan?" Mila asked as they backed to the intersection, where Delmin and Anduette had moved in close to Kaiana, the three of them with their backs to each other.

"You know me and plans," Veranix said. "Hit hard, move fast, get to the church."

"So punch through those green caps," Anduette said. "Just like our exercises, right?"

"A little more serious," Delmin said.

"Knights!" Four-Toe shouted, jumping up on the wrecked wagon. "Knock through those Halloran's Boys! Show all these bastards whose patch this is! For the saint! For the reverend! Knights sta—"

Then his throat erupted with blood.

A whirling blade flew past Veranix's head, barely missing him, bouncing off a lamppost and into the waiting hand of a leather-clad woman in Kellirac veils, standing in front of the Princes. The Revanche again.

"Who is that?" Kaiana asked.

"Vengeance," the woman said, bringing out three more *dektha*s.

"Tell me you have my bow," Veranix said to Mila.

"It and your quiver are still on the wagon."

"Perfect," Veranix said. "Buy me some time."

Veranix jumped at the wagon as the *dektha*s flew past him. Who was this woman? She had come at him last night. Was she part of this price on his head, this collection of old enemies? He had never fought her before, not that he remembered.

Not the moment to worry about it. He got to the wreckage of the wagon and threw a few planks aside. There, under the wheel—his bow and quiver of arrows. The full lot of them. He scooped them up and turned back to his friends.

Anduette was doing something that made Lady Revanche and the Princes all cover their ears. Kaiana and Mila were doing their best to hold off Orphans, while Delmin struggled to hold up a magic shield to protect them from Halloran's Boys' crossbow shots. Lemt and Jendle were getting back on their feet, Magpie was stumbling out of the alley, and Jackdaw—

Jackdaw was charging full speed at Kaiana, oar raised.

Veranix drew up an arrow, but Mila was already moving. She knocked Kaiana out of the way while whipping out her rope, ensnaring Jackdaw's powerful legs. The Ch'omik woman fell forward, but she was still swinging her terrible weapon as she went down, striking Mila across the chest.

Mila crumpled, and only didn't hit the ground because Kaiana was there to catch her.

Veranix ran over to them, firing two boom powder arrows at the Halloran's Boys, blowing them all back, clearing a path.

Mila was seizing in Kaiana's arms. As Veranix closed the distance, Magpie threw a trio of darts, one of which hit Delmin in the back, sending him down. Veranix managed to catch him with one arm before he dropped.

They had to get out of here. No more time.

"Everyone get ready to run," he said, hauling Delmin up. "Andi, bring the thunder."

She gave him a glance that told him she understood. She brought her hands together and clapped as he pulled out two smoke powder arrows and hurled them to the ground. Smoke surrounded them immediately as a deafening boom echoed around them from Anduette. Veranix drew in all the magic he had, pushing it into the rest of them, forcing it into speed, and pulled them all with him as he ran.

In the blink of an eye, all five of them were in the next intersection, at Tulip and Vine, in front of Saint Julian's, while a block behind them it was still smoke and chaos.

"Inside, hurry," Veranix said, though he stumbled as he tried to carry Delmin. Anduette got on the other side and helped him take his friend up the church steps, while Kaiana carried Mila. Mila's eyes were closed, her shirt stained in blood. Veranix didn't want to think what that meant, how bad it might be. He couldn't even think, his head was a spinning fog.

A few more steps, into the church. He got Delmin and Anduette into the narthex, and let Kaiana bring Mila in before he put as much magic as he could still muster into slamming the door shut and dropping the bar.

He turned around, facing the statue of Saint Julian, standing tall with his shield.

"Hey," he said weakly. "I know I'm in no place to ask of you, but watch over them."

Then he dropped to the floor; everything went dark.

REVEREND PEMMICK HAD SEEN HIS SHARE OF BLOOD AND HORROR IN HIS days, so when the racket at the front door came from a group of people who looked like they had just faced off with a host of sinners, he wasn't shocked.

"Children, what is ever—"

"We're with the Thorn," the young man said weakly. He had a blade in his back, blood dripping on the floor. "We need sanctuary, the streets are full of people trying to kill him."

"Where is he?" Pemmick asked. "I asked the Knights to get him here safely if they could find him."

"He was right behind us," the dark Napolic girl said. She was carrying another girl, dressed much like Veranix did as the Thorn, who was clearly quite hurt.

"Sisters!" he called out to the cloistresses, hoping they could hear him from their cells in the upper floor.

"Upstairs?" the girl in the university uniform asked. "I'll go."

"Thank you, child," he said, helping the Napolic girl get the injured one to the ground. "I'm not as versed in the healing arts as I would like."

"I've got her," the Napolic girl said as she worked her friend's vest off. "Look to . . . the Thorn. He was right behind us."

Pemmick went to the narthex, to find the doors already barred, and Veranix—poor, impossibly young Veranix—lying on the ground. He was awash with injuries, bruises, and cuts. It was a miracle he made it this far. He picked the poor boy up and carried him into the nave. The Sisters of Saint Julian had already come down, and two were tending to the injured girl, while another was helping the young man.

"Sisters," Pemmick said, holding up Veranix's battered body.

"We have him," Sister Inietta said, and two more of them took him from Pemmick and carried him off upstairs.

"And the girl?" he asked.

"I believe we can help her," Sister Inietta said. "But we must get to work." More of them took the girl up and took her away.

"Well," he said to Veranix's compatriots. "Now if you could explain—"

"Sanctuary," the young man insisted. "And I mean, like, the full on, Reverend Ott protecting Oberon from the Inquest, lock all the doors kind."

"You ask a lot," Pemmick said.

"You saw him," the young man said. "Several people are trying to kill him. They already killed our professor, and saints only know who else. It won't take long before they find us here, and I doubt these damned people set much stock in the sanctity of ground."

Pemmick regarded this young man for a moment. Sincerity and conviction, plus a fair amount of cheek to blaspheme in front of a man of faith in a church nave. Yes, this boy was right.

"Sister," he told one of the remaining cloistresses. "Bar all the doors, and set your prayers to put us all under the saint's shield tonight."

"As you say, Reverend," she said, leaving to enact his orders.

He turned back to them "So, my children, let us start from the beginning. I am Reverend Aurien Pemmick. I gather you are associates of our friend The Thorn. He's told me quite a bit, so I'm gathering . . . Kaiana, Delmin, and Mila."

"Mila is the one you had carried away," Kaiana said.

"Anduette Nessick," the other girl said, extending her hand. "I'm . . . not really a part of all this. At least, not until today. But people came to kill my friend, and did kill my teacher, so . . ." She took a moment, her face showing her effort to swallow her grief. "That's what today was, so here I am."

"I've seen the paper, offering a price on his head," Pemmick said. He was glad that for once, the Knights had actually listened to him and followed the loyalty they often claimed to his office. "Did one of the Knights help you get here? Was it Fortill?"

Kaiana's face blanched. "He was killed by one of the assassins out there."

Pemmick closed his eyes and said a small prayer for Fortill's wayward soul. He was, in many ways, a callous, petty boy who was far too eager to dispatch violence, but there was a spark of decency within him that Pemmick had kept trying to reach. He wished he had had the time, and hoped, if nothing else, his prayer could intercede, grant some measure of mercy, on Fortill's final judgment.

"They're still out there," Kaiana said. "And I imagine we can't hide here forever."

"No," Pemmick said, opening his eyes again. "I don't think that's practical."

Delmin winced as the cloistress tended to his wound. "How bad is it?" he asked her.

"You were fortunate that it did not go very deep," she said. "You were smart to not pull it out, or you would have bled to death."

"I couldn't reach it," he said.

"So what now?" Kaiana asked.

"Sister, when you are done tending to that wound, take them to the kitchens, get them fed, and let them rest. I'll be about in a bit to check on them."

He went up into his own study, found some paper and ink to write a note. Then to the upper levels of the church, to the private quarters, to find Sister Inietta. "How are the patients?"

"The boy is battered, but none of the injuries are life threatening," she said. "Am I correct to assume he is magically talented?"

"Yes, that's right," Pemmick said.

"Hmm," she said. "He's not waking up yet, so I've been having one of our girls pour broth down his throat. Crude, but it should help him."

"And the girl?"

"The injury looks bad, but it's shallow, thank her saints. I have faith she'll recover. I think the shock of pain did more to her than the injury itself. But we are making her comfortable."

"Good. And the doors are locked?"

"We are closed up tightly, at least for the moment," she said, in a tone that told him how little she approved of the idea.

"Pick one of the sisters," he said. "One who is comfortable moving through the streets alone."

"Them being comfortable and me being comfortable are two very different things," Inietta said. She ground her teeth for a moment. "Sister Ramella is quite capable."

"Have her go out and find a constable, Lieutenant Benvin. Only Benvin, and deliver this note to him."

She took the note. "You are sheltering these children but plan to call the constable on them? How can you—"

"I'm not calling the constables on them, nor would I ever turn them over. But I fear we will require the institutions of law to resolve things in a safe manner. When the Thorn awakens, I will counsel him and let him decide his next action. But I want to give him options."

She shook the note at him. "As you say, Reverend. I will have Sister Ramella deliver this, and then I will pray for all the souls under this roof on this dark night."

"For that I am grateful."

She stalked off. Pemmick looked into the sleeping chamber where they were tending to Veranix. He looked like such a boy right now, so broken, so vulnerable. Pemmick had pledged to him whatever help he needed, and he would give it, gladly. But at this point, he feared the only thing that could save Veranix Calbert from a dark fate tonight would be intercession from the divine.

CHAPTER TWENTY-THREE

D ARKNESS.
Church steps.

Battle-torn plaza.

Not Saint Julian's. Saint Bridget's, in North Seleth.

Veranix glanced about the square, just as it was last month, except empty. No deformed creatures, no Crenaxin turned into a giant lizard, no Minox and the others. Just him, alone in the square.

"I've missed you so much."

He turned around. Not alone. Sister Myriem, but not as she had been here. No shield, no mace, no hardened, weary look in her eyes. Instead she seemed scared, even small. And far too young, just like he was. Too young to have already lived the life he had.

"I don't understand," he said. "How can you miss me when we only met then?"

She looked at him. "I don't know. I still don't know the why of so many things. I don't think I even know who I was then. But I think . . . who I was then, who I was to become . . . she was very familiar with who you're going to be."

"And who is that?" Veranix asked. "Is this a dream? Am I dreaming about you?"

"I think so," she said. "And I'm dreaming about you. Right now . . . dreaming is all I can do."

"This doesn't make any sense."

"I won't pretend it does," she said. She sat down on the church steps, and gestured for him to do the same. Lacking a reason not to, he joined her. "I just know that I see you, Veranix Calbert, and even though I don't know you, I know—know down to the center of my soul—that you are my friend, and you need a friend right now."

"All my friends hate me right now, I think. And with good reason."

"I think the only real hate is what you are doing to yourself. You've gotten this far, done what you've done, because your friends believe in you. They're there for you."

"What have I really done, Sister?" he asked. "I've been a damned fool, thinking I could stop *effitte* in this town, that I could stop Fenmere, and—"

"That you could save at least one person from the pain you felt when you lost your parents. You are no fool, Veranix."

"My current circumstances say otherwise."

"It's dire," she said, nodding. "Yes, many of your failures have now compounded and are being visited upon you."

"I'm glad you aren't trying to comfort me," he said.

She laughed, just a little, ever so lightly. "I don't think there's much comfort for either of us, not in the coming days."

"Do you know the coming days?" he asked her.

She looked out at the empty courtyard. "Imagine you saw a target in the distance there. You could draw your bow and hit it plainly. But if a fog rolled in, you wouldn't see it anymore, but you might still remember what you saw. You could still hit the target."

"I suppose."

"The days to come are a fog, but I know one thing, my dear, old friend whom I've never met. I know I need you to be there for them, or it's all catastrophe."

He chuckled. "How are you on the past?"

"I can't answer your questions about your father," she said, cutting through to what he was thinking. "You have to ask yourself, whoever he may have been, whatever he might have done . . ."

"This fight was about him," Veranix said. "If it's true, that he was planning on selling *effitte* himself, what does that say about you—"

"What you believe, who you are, that hasn't changed." She chuckled ruefully. "At least, that's what I can see in that fog. There are beacons guiding me, lighting the path, and you're one of them."

That was heavier than Veranix could handle, even in this strange dream. "So what are you telling me?"

"I'm telling you, you have to survive, Veranix. I need you to."

"That's a lovely plan, I hope it works out for both of us."

She shook her head, getting agitated. "No, Veranix. You *have* to survive. No matter what."

"And how am I supposed to do that? Presuming I'm out cold in Saint Julian's, beaten all to blazes . . ."

She put her hand on his chest. "I'll do what I little I can to ease that."

Her touch did fill him with warmth and light. "I appreciate that. Even still, all those killers are surely coming, and I don't think a little bit of fear of holy wrath will keep them at bay."

"Then you need to do it," she said. "What you do best. A little fear, a little power, and a lot of theatrics. Your enemies think they're going to win? Let them remember *who you are*." She touched his face, and with that touch, a calm, quiet came over him. He understood. "I'm looking forward to when we properly meet, my old friend. Until then, stay alive. And always, faith."

Then darkness.

Then sound, and shadow, someone over him, hand over his heart.

He grabbed that hand. "Don't even—"

"Easy, Nix," Anduette said. "Just checking your bandaging."

"Andi," he said, his eyes adjusting to the light to see her. "You're all right?"

"Nothing an hour in the bathhouse won't cure," she said. "You're the one who took the worst of it out there."

"Well, I'm the one they want dead, after all."

"Still," she said, looking at his chest. "You aren't glamouring over your injuries again, are you?"

"Not at all," he said.

"It's just . . . you seemed more banged up before. Even your face. Are you in pain?"

"Not as much as I ought to be," he said, looking at the injuries on his body. None of the bruises and cuts were anywhere near as bad as they ought to be. Even the slice from last night was looking more like a scar than a recent wound. Was it possible that Sister Myriem had . . . even in a dream? No, impossible. He laughed uncomfortably. "Those sisters must have given me something pretty good."

"I don't know anything that good," Anduette said. "But you should—"

"Stop wasting time." He sat up, realizing he was in a cot in one of the upper floor rooms of the church. He barely remembered even getting inside. "Everyone else?"

Andi shrugged. "The grounds girl, Kai? She's all right. Delmin needed some patching up but he was sitting up and talking last I saw."

"And Mila?"

"The reverend here says she'll make it, but she's not in great shape."

"And you would probably like an explanation, I suppose."

"That you've been this Thorn character all this time?" She sighed. "Honestly, it makes a bit of sense, but it does make me think you've been holding out in squad runs."

"I got Professor Alimen killed."

She looked at him, her eyes piercing. "No. Those bastards killed him, but you . . . no, you were clear as glass when that started. As soon as they were hurting other students on the lawn, as soon as you saw that, your mind was made up. You jumped down there and took them all on, like something out of the *Testaments*."

"I'm no saint."

"I don't imagine any of them thought they were, either."

The dream of Sister Myriem was starting to fade, but the clarity, the sense of what he needed to do, that was still with him. "Can you help me with something, Andi?"

"If I can," she said as he got up from the cot. He was anticipating his leg screaming at him, but, no, no pain at all. The only word he could think of was miraculous. He would need more of that if he hoped to make it through the night. "Your clothes and other things are right there."

"You can," he said, getting dressed. His school uniform was in complete tatters—not that he would need it again, not after tonight—but Mila had brought his Thorn outfit with his weapons and other gear. He got dressed quickly and put the rest of his things on.

He was probably going to die tonight, but he would do it with every bit of fight he had. His bow, his staff, his power. Putting the cloak on, putting the rope on his belt, he could feel that surge of the extra *numina* they were drawing in.

"Come with me up to the tower," he said as he finished getting ready.

"What's in the tower, besides the bells?" she asked as they went up the stairs.

"Clarity," he said. From up here, one of the highest spots in the neighborhood, he could see the campus to the north, Trenn Street Ward to the southwest, and all the patches of the neighborhood, run by the Rose Street Princes, Knights of Saint Julian, Waterpath Orphans, Hallaran's Boys, Toothless Dogs, and Sons of Tyson. Down there were constables, Fenmere's goons, and all those old and new enemies who wanted his blood.

"What do you need?"

"Hold on to the cloak and the rope," he said. She came closer and took hold.

"Whoa," she said with a shuddering breath. "That's quite the feeling."

"Boost my voice," he said. "I want them to hear me."

"Who exactly?" she asked.

"All of Aventil."

She took a deep breath, and he could feel the mighty surge of magic around her. She looked at him and nodded.

He took his own deep breath. Time to give the show.

"Hello, Aventil!" he shouted, and as he did, his voice echoed all around. Anduette grinned wildly, joy radiating off her with her magic.

"You tried to take me today, you tried to kill me, but guess what? The Thorn is still alive, despite your best efforts!

"Oh, and your efforts, they were good, but they were not anywhere near good enough. And let me tell you, I was not ready for you at all, friends. I had no weapons, none of my tricks, and certainly no plan, and *still* your best efforts were *not good enough.* And so you have made a terrible, horrible mistake. You have caused pain, you have hurt me, you have hurt the people I love, and that means I am done playing games.

"Listen to me, all of Aventil. Listen to me, gangs and assassins. Listen to me now, Willem Fenmere. *Beware.* Right now, I am ready for you. I have all the fight in the world in me, and I am far too stupid and stubborn to quit. So if you're the next one to come try to collect the price on my head, let me tell you this.

"The cost will be too high."

He gave Anduette a nod, and she let go of the cloak and rope.

"Well, that was something," she said, shaking out her hands. "Though I'm not sure it was a good idea."

"Probably wasn't, like most things I do," he said. "But hopefully bought us a little time. Now let's go talk to our friends, figure out what's next."

"The cost will be too high."

Benvin had no idea where the Thorn's voice had come from. It seemed to come from everywhere and nowhere.

"That's the truth."

One of the older bosses in the Princes had muttered that. Benvin had been surveying the damage in the Turnabout, where almost half of the Rose Street Princes were broken, bruised, and busted up. Not to mention the condition the pub itself was in.

"Sounds like the Thorn is really mad," Saitle said as he directed the Yellowshields to haul out the more injured Princes. "Hate to be the next one he's up against."

"So who is going to tell me what the Thorn did in here?" Benvin called out. He looked to the older man who had muttered, who had a few of the bigger fellows flanking around him. "You one of the bosses here?"

"We don't talk to the sticks," the old man said. "You're lucky we don't chase you out with a knife in your gut."

"You might recall that happened to one of yours last time you were in here, Left," Deena said. She was one of the few who hadn't been cracked up. "Do you need further reminder?"

"None of us wants that," Benvin said. If this place had been razed to the ground by the Thorn, that would have been justice. This place, all the damned Princes, if he had arrived to find them all dead, he wouldn't shed one tear. But right now, he had no direct call to arrest any of the ones in the pub. Plenty of the Princes in the street had brawled with Constabulary, and those were ironed up and going in to the stationhouse.

They had only just gotten this particular block calmed down. Reports from other parts of Aventil were crazy, especially along Waterpath, and down by Saint Julian's. He needed to be in nine different places right now, but he was here, trying in vain to get someone to talk about the Thorn, because it was clear this is where he came after the fight on the school lawn.

"So why don't you boys walk along?" the old man said. "Let me go home."

"Why do you want to go home, sir?" Benvin asked. "Isn't this your place, your people?"

"Because my home is secure, and the Thorn wants me dead. Colin and those Sons of Tyson want me dead! I need to get out of here."

"You hear that, stick?" Deena said, moving closer. She gave Benvin a shove, but one where her body made it look harder than she actual gave. "Get out of here, you're not wanted. The man wants to go home."

Benvin grabbed Deena by the wrist and turned her around. "Let's see if there's a lockwagon for you, hmm? The rest of you, clear out. This club is a crime scene."

He pulled her outside and took her over to one of the wagons.

"So what did you want to tell me?" he asked her once they were at the wagon.

"Glad you picked up on it. The big boss there is scared out of his mind over the Thorn now."

"The big boss?" Benvin asked. "That's Vessrin? Huh. I always pictured him, I don't know, taller."

"He's out of his mind over this stuff with the Thorn and the Sons, and that's just more trouble here," Deena said. "But you don't want to hassle us, you want the Thorn."

"You have something to tell me?"

"He and Colin Tyson are kin. Cousins."

"I've heard that before," Benvin said.

"So here's the thing you haven't. I only know this because my boy Tooser used to run with Colin, but Colin has an aunt who's up on the ward on Trenn. That ward. Says he can't look in on her."

"All right, and?"

"Saints, Left," she said. "Colin only had his pop and his uncle Cal Tyson. Cal is dead, killed by Fenmere a couple years back when he came back to town. Most folks in the Princes know that. But they don't know about the aunt."

It clicked. "The Thorn is Cal's son, and that aunt is the Thorn's mother."

"Hit all eight pins, Left."

"All right," Benvin said. "If anyone asks, I got pulled away by a whistle call and you slipped off before I got you in the wagon."

"Obliged." She turned to do just that.

"Oh, and, if it matters, no one is at that flop tonight. And no one is going to be."

She glanced back to him and nodded, a glint of sincere appreciation in her eyes. "You're not all bad, Left."

"Neither are you."

He went back to the front of the Turnabout, where Saitle, Pollit, and Wheth were all gathered. "What's the word, boss?" Wheth asked.

"We need to make our way to the Lower Trenn Ward," Benvin said.

"Really?" Pollit asked. "Word is that part of the neighborhood is the quietest patch."

"It may be, but apparently the Thorn's mother is a patient there. So let's get down there. From all we hear, he's a wounded animal, so he'll go back to the den if he can."

"Hey, boss!" Tripper came over, escorting a young Cloistress of the White. "This lady says she needs to talk to you, and only you."

"Sister," Benvin said. "What can I do for you?"

She handed him a note. "The reverend says you're needed at the church of Saint Julian, Lieutenant," she said. "We've locked down completely, so come to the side door of the chapel, and knock in the manner prescribed there, so he knows it's you."

Benvin glanced at the note, which told only a little more than the sister had conveyed, but that little more was critical.

"Change of plans?" Pollit asked.

"Indeed. I want you staying here to coordinate things. We're expecting a special trained squad from Inemar, and work with them to quell down Waterpath best you can."

"Absolutely, Left," Pollit said.

"The rest of us, we're heading to Saint Julian. It seems the Thorn might be willing to parlay."

Veranix came down to the chapel, where Reverend Pemmick was praying before the altar.

"I hope I still have a place in those prayers, Reverend," Veranix said.

"You always will," Pemmick said, getting up. "I heard you were doing something bold and possibly ill-advised."

"That is my usual story, no?"

Pemmick smirked and took Veranix in an embrace. "I'm very glad you are alive, my friend. Now let's keep you that way."

"That is my plan," Veranix said.

"And yet, you taunted the entire neighborhood just now, and you are dressed for battle."

"Hide not from your enemies and gird yourself for their coming."

Pemmick smiled. "You have been reading your *Testaments*. Very good."

"There's some good lines in there," Veranix said.

"Come here," Pemmick said, taking one of Veranix's hands and pulling him in close, touching his forehead to Veranix's. "Saint Julian, as your appointed servant, I am aware of this fellow's sins and mortal failings, and I have found his heart to be true, and having opened it, beseech that you intercede and grant him absolution for all his wrongs. Guide his soul as it goes to judgment."

"Reverend," Veranix said quietly. His knees trembled at hearing those words, and fresh tears were flowing. "I don't think I deserve that."

"Of course you do," Pemmick said.

"But I got my professor killed."

"Sewage," Anduette called from the doorway to the chapel.

"Miss Nessick, this is—"

"No, I want it clear, he's still talking sewage about getting Professor Alimen killed. I was there."

"You were already out cold when he was killed."

"I'm talking about in his tower, when you jumped into the fight. I was with him up there. He was torn up over the idea of you facing that alone. He thought it was his fault."

"How was it his fault?" Veranix asked. "I'm the one who picked a fight with Fenmere. I'm the one whose carelessness brought that fight to campus."

"That's true."

Delmin came in, Kaiana right behind him. Delmin looked pale as the white moon, somehow even skinnier than usual. Both of them had cleaned up, changed into fresh clothes, but still looked like they had been dragged through the streets.

Which is exactly what Veranix had done to them.

Veranix went straight to Delmin. "I am so sorry, Delmin. Sorry for bringing you into this, sorry for everything that led to you hurting your-self, to getting hurt out there. Sorry for bringing my own sewage to campus, getting so many other people hurt, and . . ." Veranix broke down in tears. "I got Professor Alimen killed. There is no reason for you to forgive me. No reason for you to grant me absolution, Reverend."

"I'm telling you, that isn't true," Anduette said. "First off, those bastards, they killed him. The professor didn't 'get killed,' and you certainly didn't get him killed. They killed him."

"Still—" Veranix said.

"No still about it," Mila said, coming in through one of the doors from upstairs. One of the cloistresses was fussing behind her, and Mila slapped her hand away. She was loosely covered by a cloistress robe, her entire torso wrapped in bandages stained with seeping blood. She limped over to Veranix, holding his shoulders. "You can't blame yourself for this."

Veranix looked to Delmin and Kaiana, and saw something different in their eyes. "You both know, don't you?"

"We're all barely alive," Kaiana said. "But you can't take all the blame for this. It's been our fight all this time."

"It was probably a lot smarter when it was just you and me in the carriage house."

Delmin moved closer, his face still unreadable. Then his expression broke, and he started weeping. He grabbed Veranix and pulled him in a tight embrace. "I'm just glad you're still alive, you rutting idiot."

"I never wanted you to get hurt. I never should have brought you in this deep."

"Hey," Delmin said, pulling out and cupping Veranix's face with his hands. "I did plenty of my own stupid things. And the . . ." His tears flowed heavier, and he couldn't speak for a moment. Wiping his own face. "The professor, he'll . . . he's going to be avenged. One way or another. This life or the next."

Veranix nodded, and looked to Mila. Saints, she looked so fragile. "You need to be in bed or something."

"I'm not lying down while you're still in this." She had abandoned any attempt to hide her westside accent.

"She's incredibly stubborn," the cloistress said.

"You should meet the guy she gets it from," Delmin said.

"I knew all the damn risks before I even met you, Vee," Mila said. "Remember, you did not pull me into anything." She kissed him again, which Veranix liked very much, but felt wrong to do in the middle of the chapel.

Pemmick cleared his throat. "There is the matter of what now."

"Yes, absolutely," Veranix said, pulling away from Mila.

"You're suited up," Kaiana said. "And based on that announcement you made, it sounds like you plan to fight."

"I intend to be ready if it comes. When it comes."

"Get me my knives and clothes," Mila said to the cloistress. "Get them right now."

The cloistress looked concerned, but Pemmick gave her a wave to do that.

"I would prefer none of you engaged in further violence, as the consequences of that have already had incredible gravity," Pemmick said. "But I also recognize that one doesn't always have a choice not to engage in violence when it is visited upon them. Which is why I want to counsel you to consider other options."

"We're not going to be safe without protection," Delmin said. "Or at least, Veranix isn't. I don't think they're explicitly looking for the rest of us."

"The Princes knew who I was," Kaiana said. "Or at least that I was connected to him."

"And they know about Colin," Veranix said. "I can't leave him out in the world alone."

"Of course," Pemmick said. "And I presume that your enemies cannot be negotiated with in any good faith."

"No, definitely not."

"Then I would suggest thinking about who you can negotiate with. Namely, the City Constabulary."

Veranix felt that suggestion like a weight on his chest. "That's presuming that any of them aren't in just as deep with Fenmere, and wouldn't be just as happy to collect the price on my head."

"I have confidence that Lieutenant Benvin and his people are not."

That was probably true. "He's a good man, isn't he?"

"He is a man trying to do good, as he understands it," Pemmick said. "I have taken the liberty of sending word to him to come here, that the Thorn would be willing to talk to him. But if that isn't what you want, I will maintain your sanctuary and not give him access to you."

"No, I think that you're right," Veranix said.

"What, you're going to surrender to the sticks?" Mila asked.

"I don't like it," Anduette said. "They can't be trusted. Not for mages, and certainly not ones doing what you are."

"The lieutenant is an unusual man," Pemmick said. "I've gathered he's not subject to senseless prejudices, and I think that would include mages."

"If I can negotiate protection and safety for the rest of you?" Veranix offered. "Do you think he would help keep them all safe, without charges or arrest, if I do surrender?"

"I cannot speak to his mind," Pemmick said. "But I will be the best possible advocate for you all along those lines. And the protection of this church is extended as long as all of you need it."

"And can we negotiate for Colin as well?" Veranix asked.

"Again, I will do what I can. Though I would imagine the lieutenant would want to do whatever is possible to return this neighborhood to the tenuous peace between the local factions."

The cloistress returned with Mila's clothing, which she quickly put on with little concern for modesty. Delmin briefly fled, and Pemmick turned around. Delmin retuned once Mila was dressed, bringing a handful of cold lamb sandwiches.

"I apologize if I'm taking liberties with the kitchen, Reverend," he said as he gave one to Veranix and passed the rest around. "But three of us are mages, after all."

"Of course," Pemmick said, taking one himself. "There is probably some edict about eating within the chapel, but I think circumstances are mitigating."

Veranix happily dug into the sandwich, and turned to Anduette. "Why did Alimen think it was his fault?"

She swallowed a bite of her own and said, "He was a bit rambling, but something about how he knew your family had a history, knew there were enemies, and that he had promised your father he would protect you."

Veranix tried to think back to those first days in the city. He had been so overwhelmed by everything—the streets, the campus, all the people—that he had barely noticed what his parents were going through. There had been quiet conversations between his father and Alimen, but he hadn't paid attention.

Saints, if he had known those days were going to be the last days he saw his father, talked to his mother, he would have savored them more, paid more attention.

"Hey," he said, turning toward the rest. "I want you to know, I am sorry for bringing you in on my fight here—"

"Our fight," Kaiana said, moving closer to him.

"But all of you—I mean, blessed saints, Andi, you just fell into this . . ."

"Our fight," she said, echoing Kai. "Bastards came onto my campus and killed my professor, I'm invested."

"Our fight," Mila said. "You were there for mine when I needed it, I will stay here for yours to the end."

Delmin chuckled ruefully and shook his head. "I certainly haven't been part of all this because I didn't care, Vee. I saw Parsons. I saw everyone in the Lower Trenn Ward. I knew damn well what this was about. Our fight."

"Our fight," Veranix said. "And, I wanted to tell you all, while I still can, how much I appreciate you being here with me all this time. Back at the circus—"

"Again the circus," Anduette said. "That explains so much."

"Back at the circus, my grandfather would say, you're only as good as the one on the wire with you. I . . . I have only gotten this far because I've had you on the wire with me." He looked at Kaiana on that, and she took his arm and squeezed it. "So thank you."

Knocks came on the side door of the chapel in an unusual pattern.

"That would be the lieutenant," Pemmick said. "So let's not keep him waiting."

Veranix finished the last bites, brushed himself off, and put on the magical shading over his face. Perhaps for the last time. Mila, Delmin, Anduette, and Kaiana all stood behind him, chins high. "Let him in, Reverend."

Pemmick went to the door and unlatched it, but as he started to open it, it flew open, knocking Pemmick to the ground.

It was not Lieutenant Benvin and his loyal squad who came in the door, but an older man in an expensive suit, followed by the nearly dozen killers who Veranix had been fighting all day. The man whose face was burned into Veranix's heart, who was responsible for years of pain, including all that had been dealt out today.

Willem Fenmere.

CHAPTER TWENTY-FOUR

"WELL, WOULDN'T YOU KNOW, YOU pay for good information, and it actually comes through," Fenmere said, an infuriating smile on his horrible face.

The man was here. The man was rutting here, in front of him. Every ounce of anger that had been festering in Veranix's gut for four years came bubbling up, wanting to explode.

Kaiana's hand on Veranix's shoulder was the only thing that kept him from leaping out at Fenmere the moment he walked in. He had no advantage in charging into a fight, not yet. If he tried to just kill Fenmere right now, the other folks would cut him to ribbons. Fenmere had come in with the people who had been plaguing Veranix all day: Cuse Jensett, Enzin Hence, Erno Don, Pria Mandicall, Scanlin, Mister Endoriff, Jackdaw, Magpie, Jendle, and Lemt. Only the Racquin Revanche was missing.

Anduette also put a hand on Veranix's shoulder. But not in comfort—she was touching the cloak, and then she took Delmin's hand. A field of violet magical energy dropped down between all of them and Fenmere and his killers. Only Reverend Pemmick, dazed on the floor, was on the other side. Lemt and Jendle wandered over to him and picked him up.

"And look at that," Endoriff said, eyeing the shield wall. "The sound mage does have a few more tricks."

"So, this is the Thorn himself," Fenmere said. "I finally get to see you in the flesh before you die."

Veranix tamped down his rage, as much as he wanted to fire every arrow, unleash every drop of magic, burn everything to ashes. This was still Saint Julian's, this was still a holy place. *The shield is over you,* he thought. Both the one Anduette made, and, hopefully, that of the saint himself. But he had to keep calm, take control, not let his anger show now.

Wear 'the Thorn' like armor.

"Will," he said, putting on the circus performer voice, "if you just wanted to meet me, you could have sent a calling card. All of this extravagance is just gaudy."

"You think this is extravagant?" Fenmere asked.

"I mean, honestly, ten assassins *and* fifty thousand crowns for the gangs? I would have popped by the house if you just asked."

Fenmere glanced at his hired help. "Is this always what he's like? The yapping like a scared dog?"

"Always," Lemt said.

"It's incessant," Jendle added.

Veranix scoffed. "From the boys who were weeping, please, no Mister Thorn, we'll tell you anything."

"Can we just kill him?" Enzin asked.

"Patience, Mister Hence," Fenmere said.

"Yeah, he's not good at that," Veranix said. "This collection of sewer rats you've brought is just pathetic."

"Says the boy, standing up there with children," Fenmere said.

"My friends are the best people in this town," Veranix said. "Don't test yourself against them."

"That little girl is barely standing."

Mila spoke up, her voice a growl. "This little girl's the one who choked the last gleam of life out of Mendel Tyne."

That raised Fenmere's eyebrow. "Really? I should probably thank you for that. Friends, when the killing starts, make her death an easy one."

Veranix drew an arrow and aimed it at Fenmere, and in that moment a barrage hit the violet shields: arrows from Erno and Enzin, fireballs from Pria, darts from Magpie, a vial of something from Cuse, a magic blast from Endoriff. The shield rippled but didn't buckle, though Veranix felt Anduette shudder briefly. She and Delmin had been whispering to each other this whole time, too quiet for Veranix to hear.

"Let's make something clear," Veranix said. "None of us are going to go easy. And if you think you're going to walk out of here alive, Willy, you are deeply mistaken."

"Oh, why?" Fenmere asked. "Because you have that cloak, that rope? Those things that were made with my connections. Brought here at my expense. You owe everything you are to me, Mister Calbert."

"I owe you, all right," Veranix said. "I owe you for every life your poison ruined. I owe you for the torture you put my mother through. And I owe you so much for what you did to my father."

"Your father?" Fenmere's reserve cracked. "Your father betrayed my brother! They brought *effitte* to Maradaine together from the islands, and then he double-crossed us!"

So Vessrin had been telling the truth.

"You think I don't know that?" Veranix asked, masking his anger. If he let it, it would consume him, and he couldn't afford that. Not now. And it didn't matter, because whoever Cal Tyson had been died when he fled Maradaine and became Annin Calbert. He had changed his life, given all of this one up. And he had been the best father he could be, and when Veranix needed to come here, sacrificed everything for him. "I know who my father was, and I know what you did to him."

"And how proud Cal would be, his son a petty killer, hiding in a church in his last moments," Fenmere said. "So take your shot, Veranix Calbert, Veranix Tyson, whoever you imagine yourself to be. Because all I see is a scared little boy who's about to die."

Anduette snorted with laughter.

"Does something amuse, young lady?"

"Oh, does it," she said. "So I'm clear, you're Fenmere, right? The big crime boss? And let me make sure I've got it right." She then pointed to the rest. "And Cuse, Enzin, Erno, Magpie, Jackdaw, Lemt, Jendle, Pria, Scanlin, and the ever so cocksure Mister Endoriff."

"What the blazes are you doing?"

With casual lightness, she said, "Sorry, I'm new, I don't usually do this. I usually just call tetchball games. I just want to make sure, when I'm announcing to the whole city how much my boy here is kicking all of your sorry asses up and down Tulip Street, that I get each one of your names right."

"Impudence," Fenmere said, walking over to Lemt and Jendle, who were still holding Pemmick up, covering his mouth. He brushed off Pemmick's cassock. "You'll find forgiveness in your heart, Reverend, for what's about to happen. But if you don't, I hardly care."

"Veranix," Anduette's voice came right in his ear. "Get ready to move. Delmin and I have a plan, if you trust us."

Keeping his aim still at Fenmere, he looked back to her. "Violet Squad together."

"Good," she said, and more particulars of the plan came to his ear. He wasn't crazy about it, but it was probably the best choice in this moment. As per their plan, he drew *numina* into himself, slow and easy.

"Now," Fenmere said. "I have what I need, Veranix. I've seen who you are, who you really are, and I'm almost mad at myself that I let a petty boy like you cause me so much trouble. I almost feel pity on you, boy. Almost."

"Save your pity," Veranix said. The *numina* kept building, filling him more and more.

"Oh, I will," Fenmere said, lightly slapping Pemmick with a chuckle. He wandered through his group of killers, keeping Veranix from getting a clean shot. "They're going to kill you now, and while they do that, I'm going to drive down to the Lower Trenn Ward and . . . how did your charming little friend put it? Right."

Standing behind Pria, who he patted on the shoulders, he smiled an empty, hollow smile. Veranix could barely concentrate on Fenmere, the *numina* within him was about to burst. He couldn't hold it much longer.

"I'm going to choke the last gleam of life out of your mother."

"Now!" Anduette roared, and the violet shield dropped.

Veranix let the arrow fly and, fueled with the magic he had built up, he launched himself into the middle of the assassins.

CHAPTER TWENTY-FIVE

"**N**OW!"

Mila was following the lead. Delmin had a plan, and she was willing to go with what he and Anduette had cooked up. Veranix had jumped into the group of assassins, one arrow rocketing at that Firewing mage, and he whipped out the rope as he flew past them all.

Past being the key—he had to get the fight outside, so part of the plan was just him going through the chapel door and getting them all to follow.

The other part was coiling the rope around the reverend and pulling him out with him, tearing the man out of the hands of Lemt and Jendle.

Mila was given three jobs, in rapid succession. The first was throwing down two of her smoke powder bombs as she charged after Veranix. He was already out the door when the chapel started to fill with smoke, and the assassins all shouted in confusion and anger as they started after him.

Then Anduette did her part to flush them out—a piercing whistle flooded the room, so loud and hard Mila couldn't see straight, and she had been prepared for it. The last of the assassins stumbled out after Veranix. Namely Cuse, Scanlin, and Jackdaw.

Jackdaw was Mila's second job.

"Don't try to fight her, you're in no shape for that," Anduette had magic-whispered to her. "Just get that weapon away from her."

As much as Mila wanted some payback, she stuck to it. Despite the swirling dizziness in her ears, she threw out her rope and snared that oar. Before Jackdaw even had gotten her bearings from Anduette's noise, her weapon had been ripped out of her hand and went skittering across the cobblestones.

Then Kaiana was there, wailing on Jackdaw with the short sword she had taken earlier.

In the street, the rest of the assassins were focusing on Veranix, who was launching himself in the air, after Fenmere, who was running to his carriage. And on the ground right where Veranix had just jumped, the third part of Mila's task: the reverend.

Veranix got the reverend away from them, but as he was about to be embroiled in the fight of his life, it was on her to get the reverend to safety. She hated that, she hated that she wasn't going to fight at his side right now, but against these bastards, she wouldn't last. Not in the condition she was in. She was already barely able to keep on her feet as she ran to the reverend, lying on the side of the street.

"Got you," she said, pulling him up.

"Child, I . . . may the saints preserve me . . ." He stared in horror as Veranix engaged in the fight with the assassins, jumping one step ahead of the arrows, darts, and flames coming his way.

"Let's get you back inside—"

"But all this . . ." he said.

"Is outside the church, if nothing else," she said. "And you need to be in it."

"As should he," Pemmick argued.

Lemt and Jendle were trying to get back in the church, as Kaiana held the door, but she wasn't able to keep them both off. Mila hurled one knife at them—throwing knives was never a skill she had mastered—and the hilt knocked Jendle in the skull. He turned around, scowling, and that gave Kaiana enough opening to hammer him with his own sword, and then shove Lemt far enough away that Mila could carry Pemmick over the threshold.

Kaiana pulled the door shut, getting a piece of Lemt's hand as he tried to reach in, and then threw down the bar.

"That should do that," she said.

"But Veranix is outside, we can't—" Pemmick said.

"None of us are any good to him out there," Kaiana said.

"He'd focus on protecting us," Delmin said, up on the altar, holding Anduette's hand. The two of them were both faintly glowing with magic, and something was taking shape in front of them.

"This is the part you were a little vague on," Kaiana said. "I agree that Veranix needed to focus on the fight, not protecting us, but how does this help him?"

"A little applied theory," Anduette said. "Delmin and I have different magical knacks. When I did that whistle, I marked Fenmere and Veranix and all the assassins, like a *numinic* paint job, which Del can sense."

"And Anduette is guiding me through sharing what I'm seeing," Delmin said. "Focus together, and . . . there."

The image in front of them came into focus—twelve human figures in wild action. It was amazing, magic nothing like Mila had seen before. Not only could she see everything the folks outside were doing, but it was clear who each of them was.

The whole fight, played out right in front of them.

"How does this help?" Pemmick asked. "Why is this the plan?"

"Because we can see what Veranix can't," Anduette said.

"We can watch his back, see the big picture for him," Delmin said. "But he doesn't have to worry about our safety."

Anduette chuckled wickedly, "And I did promise them, I would call it out."

"How are you going to do that?"

"You got a hold of it, Delmin?" Anduette asked.

"I think so."

"Then let's play some ball," she said. She touched her throat, and when she spoke next, her voice echoed throughout.

"Hello, Aventil! I hope you're looking forward to a spirited match tonight, because we have the rumble to end all rumbles, the fight of the year going on as our man, our hero, the defender of Aventil himself, the

Thorn, faces off against ten lowlife scum, hired thugs of the worst quality, and he is here to give them the drubbing they so desperately deserve. And they deserve it, don't you know, because they were hired by one Willem Fenmere, the sad, horrific man who lines his pockets by selling poison. Yes, the *effitte* lord himself, who has dared to come down here to see this show, but it looks like he is already trying to run away."

"Who can hear this?" Pemmick asked.

Mila shrugged. "I think . . . everyone?"

"How much everyone is everyone?"

Anduette went on, "The Thorn—he's in fabulous form tonight folks, he's trying to chase after Fenmere, but the Alchemist—the despicable Cuse Jensett—he's throwing bottles of his homemade gunk at our boy. The Thorn is batting them away and—"

The church shook from an explosion outside.

"Looks like the Alchemist is not getting any luck, and the Thorn has closed in and *crack*, hit like a double jack and the Alchemist slams to the stone like a sack of potatoes. Now that Firewing, Pria Mandicall, he thinks he can fly down and surprise our boy from above. Up and behind, Thorn!"

The image of Veranix spun around and fired two arrows, striking Pria, who went spiraling down to the ground.

"Fenmere is getting away!" Mila shouted.

"The Thorn is now giving everything he's got, knocking those imposters, Erno Don and Enzin Hence, back and forth, and he's not staying still for a click, folks. It's just strike, jump, hit, flip, and those boys can't even get a shot in. The Thorn could be in trouble if he doesn't notice Magpie, that Deadly Bird, getting into position on his left side. Take her down, Thorn!"

The fight was astounding, Veranix was unbelievable. Mila had seen brutal fights, she had seen Asti Rynax when he let the beast take over and he became an unstoppable killer. But here, Veranix was beyond what she thought was possible. His body moved like a cat, never a misstep, and with each jump, block or flip, he was delivering as hard as he was given, with everything in his arsenal. Grabbing one of his attackers with the rope and bowling them into someone else. Arrows flying to their mark, and every one of Verci's trick arrows was being deployed.

But still.

"Tell him about Fenmere!"

"And that weasel, Willem Fenmere, he's gotten in his carriage and he's running away, folks. Fenmere has fled from this fight! You have to see it to believe it!"

FENMERE HAS FLED FROM THIS FIGHT, YOU HAVE TO SEE IT TO BELIEVE IT!

"Go, go! To Lower Trenn Ward!" Fenmere shouted at his carriage driver as he piled in. His own guards—Kenny and the rest of the Bone Crew—were still waiting inside, and they looked shocked as anything when Fenmere clambered inside and started shouting. That infernal voice was still coming from everywhere.

NOW, SOME OF THESE FOLKS, I'M TOLD, THEY'VE GOT THEIR OWN GRIEVANCE WITH THE THORN, SINCE HE HAD ALREADY MOPPED THEIR HAIR UP AND DOWN THE STREET THE FIRST TIME THEY TANGLED WITH HIM. BUT SOME MUST BE ASKING THEMSELVES, IS THE MONEY WORTH IT, BECAUSE —OH! RORY SCANLIN, THE SHIRTLESS WHIPMASTER, JUST ATE THE COBBLESTONE, FOLKS! I DON'T THINK HE'S GETTING BACK UP!

WAS IT WORTH THE MONEY, RORY? WAS IT?

The carriage surged forward.

Fenmere had heard the stories, he'd excoriated his men for what they had let the Thorn get away with, but seeing the boy—the rutting boy—out there in the street, that was something else entirely.

Cal's son was a savage, a sinner, an unholy force.

THE THORN SHOULD KNOW HE'S HEADING WEST ON TULIP. I KNOW THE THORN HAS HIS HANDS FULL TAKING ON THIS CREW OF BASTARDS—PARDON MY COARSE LANGUAGE,

GENTLES OF AVENTIL, BUT THEY TRULY ARE—BUT FENMERE IS HEADING WEST ON TULIP.

"Go faster!" he yelled at the driver. They had to get to the Lower Trenn Ward. Fenmere would make good on that promise.

"Boss?" Kenny asked. "Should me and the boys get out there and help take him down?"

THE MAGIC IS CRACKLING, THOUGH, FOLKS. MISTER ENDORIFF, THE SELF-STYLED GENTLEMAN MAGE, HE'S THROWING DOWN SOME POWER! BUT DID YOU KNOW HE FAILED OUT OF SCHOOL? HE'S UNCIRCLED BECAUSE HE JUST. COULD. NOT. HACK. IT. DOES HE THINK HE'S GOT WHAT IT TAKES AGAINST THE MAGIC OF THE THORN?

"Did you see what went on out there?" Fenmere asked. "No, you are staying with me, at my arm as we get down there."

"Why are we going to Lower Trenn, though?"

"Long unfinished business."

OH, SWEET SAINTS ABOVE, I DON'T SEE HOW JENDLE IS WALKING AWAY FROM THAT ONE. WHEN THE THORN HAS YOU IN HIS ROPE, IT IS OVER FOR YOU. IF YOU'RE NEAR SAINT JULIAN'S CHURCH, FRIENDS, YOU KNOW YOU ARE SEEING ONE BLAZES OF A FIGHT—FORGIVE MY COARSENESS—AND YOU ARE SEEING THE PRICE YOU PAY FOR TUSSLING WITH THE THORN! FENMERE KNOWS, THAT'S WHY HE'S RUNNING.

"Who is this bird that won't shut up?" Kenny asked. "And where am I hearing it from?"

"A young mage whose impudence we'll deal with," Fenmere said. He had seen all their faces, he would find them again, all students on campus. They couldn't hide. He would have glorious punishments for each of them. "When we have her, Kenny, you can carve her just how you've been wanting to."

BUT IF YOU'RE NOT THERE, IF YOU ARE, SAY, AT TULIP AND TRENN, AND YOU SEE A CARRIAGE TURNING SOUTH, THAT CARRIAGE BELONGS TO THAT COWARD, WILLEM FENMERE! HE'S TRYING TO GET TO THE LOWER TRENN, CAN YOU BELIEVE IT, TO KILL AN INFIRM OLD WOMAN. THAT'S THE SORT OF MAN HE IS.

"That true, boss?"

Fenmere had no intention of gracing that with an answer, but he didn't have a chance to, as a rock cracked against the carriage. Then another. Then a third, and there were dozens of Constabulary whistle calls in the far distance.

"The blazes is this?" the driver asked as the carriage stopped.

"Just go!"

"Can't!"

Fenmere grabbed a crossbow from one of the Bone Crew and stormed out of the carriage. A small crowd of rabble had formed in the street. Fenmere raised the crossbow and put the bolt in the chest of the closest person. The rest screamed, some ran away, some charged. Kenny and his boys piled out and started delivering beatings on anyone who got too close.

A FEW OF THE ASSASSINS ARE STILL ON THEIR FEET, BUT IT DOESN'T MATTER, THE THORN IS ON THE MOVE! HE FLYING DOWN TULIP, LOOKS LIKE HE COULD CATCH UP WITH FENMERE!

Fenmere ran ahead, smashing the crossbow into the face of the first person who got in his way. "Follow me!"

The Lower Trenn was just a few blocks away. If he had to crack every skull of every petty fool who got in his way, so be it.

AND THE THORN IS MOVING AND . . . HE'S STOPPED. WHY'D HE STOP? NO, I CAN'T SEE ANYONE ELSE, IF THEY'RE NOT— THORN YOU NEED TO MOVE! HE'S GETTING AWAY!

THORN YOU NEED TO MOVE! HE'S GETTING AWAY!

Whoever was advising the Thorn, or calling out his fight like a tetchball match, didn't seem to know that Benvin and his squad had him surrounded, crossbows raised.

"Consider yourself bound by law!" Benvin shouted. The Special Tactics Squad from the GIU were in the church square, grabbing and ironing up the various folks the Thorn had left in his wake, and it looked like they could handle it. They had most of them ironed up, though it looked like a few of them were still putting up a bit of a fight.

But taking in the Thorn, that was all for Benvin and his people.

The Thorn had the sense to have his hands out, not giving Benvin a reason to fire.

"We got you, bastard," Tripper said. "Give us a reason."

"He's not gonna," Jace said. "Ain't that right, Thorn, you won't give them a reason to have to hurt you?"

"I've got reason," Tripper said. "I haven't forgotten what he did to Mal."

"Wasn't him," Jace said.

"Cool heads, Tripper," Benvin said. "Wheth, Jace, take his weapons."

Wheth came up to the Thorn, taking hold of the quarterstaff, while Jace took the rope from his hands. The Thorn didn't make a move to stop them, nor did he when Wheth took the bow.

HE'S ALMOST AT THE WARD.

"Lieutenant," the Thorn said quietly, "please, he's going to kill my mother."

"Shut it!" Tripper said.

"If you need to take me in, fine, but send someone, or go yourself, to the Lower Trenn, before Fenmere can get there."

Even though the Thorn's face was still in shadow, there was a strange sincerity in his voice. That was what Deena told him, the Thorn's mother was a patient in the ward. Was this all some elaborate trick?

Benvin nodded to Saitle, who put the mage shackles on him. The Thorn winced but still didn't fight back. Instead he just looked to Jace.

"Please."

"Left, we should at least send someone—"

Benvin snapped a finger at Jace, which silenced him. He didn't need to hear this, not right now. Especially since he needed to say the words.

"Consider yourself bound, your charges will be named, including and not limited to—"

"Hey, hey!" someone shouted in the distance, followed by a great booming sound. Smoke filled the church square. More shouts, then screams.

Benvin signaled to the squad. "Go, help them. I'll get him to the wagon." Tripper gave a wave, and the squad all ran into the smoke.

Benvin looked back to the Thorn. "Once this is cleared up, I'll send a few patrol to the ward, but you . . . your chaos is over, son. After seeing what you've done to this neighborhood, I'm more than happy to—"

An arrow struck Benvin's arm. He stumbled back, dropping his crossbow, going down on one knee as a cloaked figure, bow raised, came out of the smoke.

Erno Don.

"Oh, dear lieutenant, I think you'll find this job you're doing is solely mine," he sang, bringing up two arrows and nocking them together. "But I do like getting to clean up loose ends, so it's an absolute joy to kill the both of you properly this time."

He shot both arrows, one of them coming straight at Benvin's heart. He always knew he'd die serving these streets, but didn't think it would be tonight.

The Thorn moved in front of him, screaming with effort and surrounded by a red nimbus of light. The arrows stopped midair, also glowing red, and then whipped around lightning fast, striking Erno in both shoulders so hard he fell to the ground with a resounding thud.

The Thorn turned to Benvin, kneeling next to him. That shadow was gone from his face, and Benvin could see he was just a kid. A scared, desperate kid, same age as Jace at most. His hands went to Benvin's coat pocket.

"What do you think you're—"

The Thorn pulled out Benvin's whistle and blew a Yellowshield call. "How bad is it?" he asked looking at the arrow still in Benvin's arm.

"I'm going to live," Benvin said, really looking in this boy's eyes.

THORN, FENMERE'S IN THE WARD. The mysterious woman's voice echoed all around.

This boy, whose mother was about to die. Die at the hands of a man that neither Constabulary nor the law would touch.

What the blazes am I doing?

Benvin fumbled with his good arm and brought out the key to the mage shackles, unlatching them. "Go, son. Go get that bastard."

The Thorn nodded, "Thank you, sir." His face went into shadow again, and he scooped up Erno's bow, and then with two steps, launched himself into the air.

"He could have done that anytime," Benvin muttered. That boy was willing to let himself get arrested, when he could have easily laid the whole squad out without blinking.

Tripper emerged from the smoke. "Boss, where'd he go?"

"I made a call," Benvin said, forcing himself up on his feet. "But your man Erno is right here."

"Oh, Erno," Tripper said, a horrifying smile crossing his face. "It looks like you're in a right spot of trouble now."

"I do like the sad songs the best, I suppose it's fitting," Erno wheezed.

"What happened?"

"The Special Tactics boys had a bit of trouble, there was a tussle, and Erno, Enzin, and Cuse got away. Looks like we've nailed down one of those three."

"Thanks to the Thorn," Benvin said. "Iron him up and find me a Yellowshield, I'm in a lot of pain."

"But what about the other two, boss?"

LADIES AND GENTELMEN, FAST AS LIGHTNING, THE THORN IS ON THE MOVE! IF YOU'RE LISTENING, WILLEM, I'D CONSIDER A PRAYER TO BALANCE YOUR OWN SCALES RIGHT NOW.

"Boss?"

"Spread a wide search," Benvin said. "And for their sake, I hope we find them before they find the Thorn. I pity anyone who gets in his way tonight."

CHAPTER TWENTY-SIX

LADIES AND GENTELMEN, FAST AS LIGHTNING, THE THORN IS ON THE MOVE! IF YOU'RE LISTENING, WILLEM, I'D CONSIDER A PRAYER TO BALANCE YOUR OWN SCALES RIGHT NOW.*

Veranix wished he was fast as lightning, wished he could pour magic into speed, make himself jump all the way to the Lower Trenn in one bound. But even with the cloak, he was flagging. Only so much magic left to tap right now, only so much he could spare. He had no idea what fight was still ahead of him at the ward, who Fenmere had there. Plus Erno had gotten away from the constables, who knew who else had.

Had to focus. Get to the ward. Save his mother.

The first time he had come down here, racing with just as much fury, desperate to get to the Lower Trenn and see her . . . he never made it that time. Within sight of the door, a stranger grabbed him and pulled him into an alley. He had tried to blast light in the stranger's face, and that just earned his hand being swatted away.

"You can't go in there, Veranix," the street rat told him.

"The blazes are you?" Veranix asked. *"How did you know my name?"*

"Because your father told me it." He was pulled deeper in the alley.

"I'm Colin, I'm your cousin, and you cannot go into the Lower Trenn Ward."

"My mother—"

"I know damn well what happened to your mother. There's nothing you can do for her. She's all but gone."

"But I need to see her."

He got slapped.

"You know why she's alive? As a trap. To see who comes looking, and then kill them too. You cannot get killed."

"Why do you blazing care?"

"Because we're blood, and I made a promise to your pop, and I'm going to keep it, even if I have to tan your hide and drag you back to campus."

No one to drag him back now. Nothing left to be dragged back to. Not that he could worry about his academic career right now, as shattered as it must be. Only one task ahead, and he couldn't fail.

He bounded one more time, up on top of a tenement on Horn and Drum, and then from there, jumped down and landed in front of the Lower Trenn Ward.

Five muscly bruisers, armed with cleavers and long, wicked knives, stood at the front door.

"You're all Fenmere has left?" Veranix asked.

"He's already inside," the one in front said. "But we'll take care of you."

He lunged at Veranix with his cleaver, but Veranix rolled out of his way, nocked an arrow and let it fly, hard shot, dead center. No wasting time, no dance with these five. He had to get in there. Draw, aim, fire. Again. Again. One was his last trick one, acid-filled. That fellow screamed something fierce as he fell.

Draw—nothing. No more arrows.

The last fellow—big lunk with a boning blade—came at him hard and fast. Veranix stepped back, wisps of remaining magic sent to his legs. Flip over the guy, to one of the fallen. He yanked the arrow out of the dying man, nocked and fired just as the lunk turned around.

Solid hit right in the eye. Which was terrible, Veranix shouldn't have even been trying for the head. Center mass, more reliable target. He was getting sloppy, getting tired. He couldn't waste—

A clatter of glass, a hiss of steam, and then a wall of ice crystals sprung up over the front door to the ward.

"Lovely show, Veranix," Cuse said, strolling across the street to him. Enzin was with him, now half a foot taller, his arms decidedly larger. He looked much like he had in the fight on the lawn, but now there was no irregularity to his body, no misshapen limbs. "But we can't have you just going in there."

"Not when we still want to tear you apart," Enzin said.

"Normally I would play with you gents," Veranix said. "But you have used up all my patience."

"You think you get to decide?"

"I think you're an idiot, Cuse," Veranix said, drawing in as much *numina* as he could manage in the moment, as much as the cloak would let him, hard and fast. "All your brilliant concoctions, your knack for making magically fueled chemicals, and what do you do with them?"

"Use them to get my revenge?"

"No, you fool, you keep them on your belt," Veranix said. "*While fighting a goddamned mage!*"

He unleashed most of that *numina*, pure raw power, not shaped into anything, aimed at Cuse's waist.

"No, no!" Cuse said, scrambling at the buckle, but it was too late. Ice and smoke and fire and stone and who even knew what else bubbled out of the pouches, and Cuse screamed—an agonizing scream—as all those things rose up over his body, burning and roiling as they interacted with each other, and then, with one horrible, final sound, became one twisted thing with Cuse inside.

Veranix didn't stand around to watch that, and shaped the last of the magic into power into his legs, and leaped up to a fifth-floor window with the last drop of magic he could manage. He was about to crash through the glass when his leg exploded with pain, and then he fell into the window, tumbling across the floor.

One of Enzin's arrows was in his leg. Veranix struggled to get off his belt so he could stem the bleeding enough to get it out. He wrapped the belt around his leg and pulled it as tight as he dared.

"You won't get far, Thorn!" Enzin hollered from outside.

"He's got that right."

Veranix looked up to the speaker, looming over him in dance veils and holding two shining blades.

The Revanche.

VERANIX HELD HIS HANDS UP AS THE REVANCHE CROUCHED IN FRONT OF him, bringing her razor-sharp *dektha* to his neck.

"Clearly, you think I've wronged you," he said. He didn't have any strength left to draw in *numina*, let alone hold her off. She could easily kill him with a flick of the wrist.

"Are you going to deny it, Thorn?" she asked.

"I've wronged many people, so I can't deny it out of hand," he said. "But you could at least tell me which wrong you intend to kill me for."

"I was told you had a smart mouth," she said. "It won't save you."

"If I really wronged you, fine," he said. "But I'll demand a boon for the dead."

"You dare claim that custom?" she asked.

"Kill me if you have to, but save my mother. Verona Aylixi. She doesn't deserve to pay for my crimes."

"Did you give my sister a boon when you killed her?"

"Who do you think I killed?" he asked. "Who the blazes are you?"

Keeping the blade at his throat, she pulled off the dance veils, revealing a face with Racquin complexion that looked eerily familiar.

"My name is Xiala Quope, and my sister—"

"Emilia," he said quietly.

"So you do know her."

"I didn't kill her," he said.

"They told me the Thorn killed her, do you deny that?"

"I believe you were told that, but I didn't. But the man who did is right outside."

"Do you think me a fool?"

"I swear by my dead and yours," he said, evoking an old Racquin oath. "She died while saving me. And I can prove it."

"How?"

"I'm going to call out, and if you don't like what you hear, slice away."

Her eyes narrowed, but she nodded.

"Hey, Enzin!" he shouted to the window. "I thought you were supposed to be dangerous! Did you really kill those Deadly Birds?"

"I'm coming to kill you just like I killed them!" Enzin called back, and he definitely sounded closer than the ground. He must be climbing up the building.

That was enough for Xiala to pull away a little, her brow furrowing.

"I don't know, the rumor was I killed Blackbird. You sure you did it?"

"I killed that rotten slan right in front of you, and when I'm done with you, I'm going to finish off the rest of them!"

Veranix looked to Xiala. "Proof enough?"

She stepped back. "If she was saving your life, it would dishonor her to take it." She offered her hand to pull him up.

"Thank you," he said as he took it. He was barely able to put any weight on his leg.

Enzin pulled himself up through the window. "Well, well," he said. "Looks like you found another Bird for me."

"Bastard!" Xiala shouted, hurling one *dektha* at him. It sliced his side, but he barely flinched. "Blackbird was my sister!"

He came at her, swinging enormous fists. "And she killed mine!"

Xiala blocked one punch with another *dektha*, slicing his hand, but Enzin's other hand grabbed her throat and lifted her off the ground. She hammered on his arm with her blade, and despite the bloody cuts she was making, he didn't relent.

"Go," she said. "Take your boon."

Veranix pulled the arrow out of his leg. Just one arrow, all he had left. No rope, no staff, and no strength left for any magic. He could barely even walk. As he limped toward his mother's ward, nocked the arrow and hoped it would be enough.

TWO WARD NURSES WERE COWERING BEHIND THE FLOOR DESK AS Veranix came through. They seemed to be the only ones here, besides the patients. The poor women looked terrified, and with the raging battle between Xiala and Enzin behind him, and him surely looking like a deranged maniac, he couldn't blame them.

"Stay down," he told them. "Did he come through here? An older man?"

One of them nodded and pointed toward the wardroom where his mother was usually kept. So many times, he had watched her through the window. So many times, he wished to come in and see her, hold her. This was the first time he had ever gone in.

The room had several patients in beds and rollerchairs, all of them immobile. All of them victims of Fenmere and his poison.

And there was the man himself, standing right over Mother in her chair. Saints, they had so many patients now, she didn't even get a bed anymore.

Veranix drew back his bow. "Step away from her!"

Fenmere glanced back, and moved just enough for Veranix to see he had a knife, and it was right at his mother's throat.

"Well, well, Mister Calbert," Fenmere said. "Astounding you came all this way, but now you get to see this."

"Drop the knife!" Veranix didn't have a shot he could take, not one that would save his mother. Not unless he got Fenmere to move away somehow.

Fenmere laughed—the bastard laughed—as he slipped behind mother's chair. "You can barely stand, son."

Veranix still held the bow drawn. "You step away and drop the knife."

"You've got nothing left," Fenmere said as his fingers tightened around the knife. "I mean, as much as I loathe you, I am impressed you made it here. You fought so hard to stop me, to get here, through so much, and yet here I am, knife at your mother's throat, and nothing you can do to save her."

"You do anything to her and I will put you down."

"Suh . . ." Mother moaned.

"And yet you haven't, and you know why?" Fenmere asked. "Because you don't want the consequence of that. While I want nothing but consequence. I want the consequences of your father's choices to echo pain through you. I did this to your mother, and made him watch, and now I'll kill her and make you watch."

"She is literally the only thing keeping you alive right now," Veranix said. He wanted to move closer, but he couldn't even take a step without his aim faltering. "You think anything will hold me back if you hurt her?"

"What are you waiting for?" Fenmere asked. "You've got your shot, see what it gets you. Your father took his shot—"

"He didn't kill your brother!"

"He still betrayed him! He still tried to take what wasn't his! And it got him a life on the run. It got him his wife like this. And it got you, a sad, broken little boy who thinks he's a hero."

"Suh, suh, suh," Mother said. One of her hands tried, ineffectively, to push Fenmere away. Her once powerful arms had no strength in them.

"My father," Veranix said, his voice shaking. It was shattering to see her like this, to see this monster of a man over her. To have his father's memory torn down in front of her. "Was a better man than either of us. And he was an incredible shot. If he were here, bow in his hand, arrow drawn, with you in his sights, this would be over. He could shoot that knife out of your hand and not shave a hair off her head."

"I remember," Fenmere said. "He was amazing with a bow. An artist. But you? No, you're nowhere near that good."

"Shuh . . . shuh . . ."

"No," Veranix admitted. But he was still Annin Calbert's son, and he would do right by him. No matter what ills his father did, he would, by every damned said, do that now.

"Pathetic," Fenmere said.

Mother's eyes found Veranix, and with power and fire they locked onto him. For just a second, he saw her, knew that she was there inside the haze of whatever horror the *effitte* had done to her. And in that second, she was able to force a word to her lips.

"*Shoot.*"

CHAPTER TWENTY-SEVEN

VERANIX LET THE ARROW FLY, knowing all too well what doing so meant.

Fenmere's flicked his wrist, and the blade sliced open mother's throat.

The arrow struck true, dead center in Fenmere's chest.

He dropped to his knees, as mother coughed and choked, blood flowing from her neck.

Veranix rushed to her, as fast as he could manage, ignoring the pain in his leg. Nothing in his body mattered anymore, nothing it could feel was anything as shattering.

Fenmere was still twitching on the ground when Veranix got close, but seeing the monster dying meant nothing.

Veranix picked up his mother's body from the chair, and collapsed on the ground, touching her face. "I'm sorry, Mama. I'm sorry I wasn't fast enough. I wasn't good enough. I'm sorry."

Her eyes found his one last time, and what might have been a smile crossed her lips. Or it might have been that last, failed attempt to breathe.

And then her light was gone.

Veranix sat on the cold stone floor of the ward, cradling his mother's body for what felt like an eternity. He didn't know when he started crying. He didn't know if he could ever stop.

A hand touched his shoulder.

"If you're here to kill me, just do it," he said numbly.

The hand's owner knelt beside him, holding Veranix's head to his chest.

"I'm sorry," Colin said. "I'm sorry I didn't get here sooner."

"Not your fault," Veranix said. "This is all on me."

"Come on," Colin said. "You can't be here. Constabulary is coming, who even knows who else."

"Doesn't matter anymore," Veranix said.

That got him slapped.

"Like blazes it doesn't matter," Colin said. "I made . . . I made . . ." He started to get choked up. "I made a promise to keep you safe, damn it. And I failed that, but, no, it's what your father wanted. It's what she wanted."

"Don't say what she wanted."

"You know," Colin said firmly. "You know damn well she wanted you to be in school. It's what all of what they went through was for."

"That's ruined, like everything else."

"Either way, we're going," Colin said, lifting her body up out of Veranix's arms. He didn't have any strength to stop him. He gently put her back in the chair, and wiped the blood from her face. "Go to your judgment, blessed auntie. I'm sorry I didn't do better."

Veranix looked back at Fenmere. Just a dead man, nothing more.

Colin looked at him as well. "And you, you right bastard. The sinners will dance on you until the moons fall from the sky."

"I'll face the same," Veranix whispered.

"Come on," Colin said, hauling him up. "Let's get you out."

Veranix let Colin carry him out, he was in no position to stop him. The nurses were gone when they went into the hall, and as Colin took him to the stairs, they passed Enzin and Xiala, both in heaps on the ground. Both covered in blood. He definitely seemed to be dead, but she was still breathing, if nothing else. Odds were that wouldn't stay true for much longer.

"Look at that," Veranix said. "That's all vengeance is, in the end."

Colin didn't say anything to that, but dutifully carried Veranix down the stairs as Constabulary whistles came from all around. Veranix didn't even notice how Colin got them out of the building or away from there, the next thing he realized was Colin cleaning off his face with a wet rag from a back alley well spigot.

"How did you even get here?" Veranix asked.

"I started coming when I heard your voice, and followed that lady's announcement from there. Left Jutie in an abandoned Orphan flop and told him I needed to take care of this, take care of you."

"I really don't know if there's anything to take care of." He looked at Colin. "What Vessrin said in the Turnabout. That's true. You knew that, didn't you?"

"Not rightly," Colin said. "But my pop always danced around a few details, I knew he was hiding something about yours. Does it matter? He was still your pop."

Veranix wasn't sure what to say to that. "I'm not sure what matters now. Except, it's over, now. Everything."

"Maybe," Colin said. "But you're still breathing. Let's get you home."

"No," Veranix said, a little bit of sense cutting through the numb, hollow feeling in his chest. "Get me to the church. The others are still there."

"Church it is," Colin said.

THE MAGICAL SHADOW PLAY OF LIGHT AND SOUND SHATTERED WHEN Veranix flooded Cuse with magic, and no matter how much Kaiana screamed at Delmin and Anduette, nothing they could do could get it back. The wave of *numina* just washed over their tracking, Delmin had said. Nothing he could latch on to anymore, not without going down to the ward himself.

"I should have just stayed with him," Kaiana said. Delmin and Anduette were lying down on the pews, both exhausted. Mila was sitting on the floor, hand on her chest. Kaiana could only pace back and forth, no chance of sitting. "I could have stayed with him." She knew that wasn't what he wanted, but she should have ignored what he wanted and had his back out there.

"Same," Mila said.

"You were in no condition," Anduette said. "Veranix wanted us in here, because he didn't want to have to worry about our safety."

"Instead we just worried about his," Kaiana said. "At what point do we leave? Go to the ward to see what happened? Or back to campus?"

"Not for a bit," Reverend Pemmick said. He had stuck his head out of doors once the Constabulary whistles had slowed down, and had been told that the constables were calling for the streets to be cleared. A soft curfew to let everything calm down.

"And what's next?" Delmin asked.

Pemmick sat down with them. "For you all, I suppose that depends on Veranix's state."

"How can you be calm?" Kaiana asked him.

"Don't mistake my reserve for calm," Pemmick said. "I am nothing but worried prayers for him. But there's little else I can do. I did say Absolution over him, so if nothing else . . ." His voice choked. "If nothing else, I have done what I could to secure his judgment."

"Guide him home, Saint Senea," Delmin said.

"That's your saint?" Anduette asked.

"It was his," Mila said. "Can you give a little extra blessing to her, Rev, for his sake?"

"I will pray to every saint for him, if it would help," Pemmick said.

Kaiana closed her eyes, wishing she knew better how to pray to Druth saints, or more about the beliefs of her mother's people. Her father had never explained that very well, something about how everything is one spirit, and that spirit guides all beings with life. She had never understood, and she suspected he didn't either, as he hadn't given any mind to the Druth church either. Though maybe that would change now.

Maybe she should change now.

If any saint is still watching Veranix, she said in the center of her heart. *Please guide him home.*

There was a knock on the chapel door. First just a heavy pound, but then the same special knock as before. Pemmick went to answer it.

"You're just going to trust that again?" Mila asked, getting on her feet.

"Faith, child," he said as he opened it.

Veranix stumbled in, propped up by Colin.

Kaiana went to run to him, but Mila was already ahead of her, getting her arms around Veranix and holding him tightly.

"Thank god and every saint you're alive," Mila said.

"I am," he said. He gently pushed her back, indicating that he was in a lot of pain. There was a horrible wound in his leg, barely dressed.

"Can we get the sisters to look at that?" Kaiana asked.

"I will summon them," Pemmick said. He passed Veranix and gave him a solemn nod, and then patted Colin on the shoulder before he left.

"So what happened?" Anduette asked. "We lost our connection when you flooded magic on Cuse."

Veranix sighed as Colin got him to a seat. "Cuse is dead. Enzin is dead, as Xiala killed him."

"Who is Xiala, now?"

"She—the one in the Racquin veils, with the circular blades," Veranix said. "She was after me because she thought I killed her sister, but Enzin killed her sister, so . . . there you are. She killed him, he probably killed her, too."

"And Fenmere?" Kaiana asked.

"Fenmere is dead. And so is my mother."

"Oh, Veranix," Kaiana said, taking his hand. "I'm so sorry."

"No one more than me," Veranix said.

"What do you need, mate?" Delmin asked.

"This stitched up, I suppose," Veranix said, his voice filled with defeat. "Then we might as well find our way back to campus. Most likely be expelled and arrested in the morning."

"No, don't talk like that," Mila said.

"Just setting realistic expectations," Veranix said. "But I would like to get back, sleep in my bed one last time."

"I should make myself scarce," Colin said, standing up. "You all can get him home." He bent down and kissed Veranix on the top of his head. "Love you, cousin."

Veranix looked up, and an empty smile crossed his face. "Love you, too. We're the only family we've got left."

Colin glanced at the rest of the people in the room. "We'll see." He went to the door, but Kaiana caught up to him.

"You don't have to go," she said quietly.

"I've got other people also counting on me," he said. "I put him first, and I always will. But he's safe with you all. I got him to you, that's my job."

"Thank you," she said. "I don't know if he said that to you, but thank you."

"Thank you," he said firmly. "He's going to—he's going to need you a lot in the coming days, no matter what happens. So I'm glad you're here for him."

She grabbed his hand before he went out the door. "And you? Do you need anything?"

He smiled softly. "I've got my streets, and I kept my promise to his pop. That's all I need."

Kaiana went back to the rest of them, now all sitting on the floor near Veranix, him leaning on Mila.

"We should probably get you out of that outfit," Kaiana said. "There's some spare clothes in the back rooms, like the ones Del and I got."

"Sounds good," Veranix said. "But when I take my cloak off, I will probably pass clean out."

"We'll get you home safe," Kaiana said.

"Right to your bed," Delmin added.

"I really am grateful to you, all of you," Veranix said. "I'm sorry for what you went through, tonight and yesterday, and up until now. But you all stood by me in this stupid fight of mine."

"Our fight," Mila said quietly.

"But it's done," he stressed. "Even if I'm not expelled or arrested, it's over."

"What do you mean?" Kaiana asked.

"I mean," he said, taking the cloak off his shoulders. "This is the end. I'm done with being the Thorn."

He dropped the cloak, and collapsed.

CHAPTER TWENTY-EIGHT

V ERANIX WOKE TO FIRM, RESPECTFUL knocks on the door.
He opened his eyes—his bed. His room in Almers Hall. He
had no memory of getting here, and for a brief moment, he thought all
the horrors had been a dream.

But, no, the pain told the truth. Everything burned into his memory
of yesterday was real, and the bandages and stitches on his body were a
testament to that. Written in blood, at that.

The knocks came again. Veranix pulled himself out of the bed,
making everything hurt even more, and wrapping the blanket around his
nearly naked body, opened the door.

No fewer than eight cadets stood in the hallway.

"Veranix Calbert?" the one in the lead asked.

"That's me," Veranix said.

"You're being called to answer some questions about the events of
yesterday. Will you come without incident?"

"Absolutely," Veranix said. "If you'd give me the courtesy of going
to the water closet, getting properly dressed?"

"I've been told to bring you straight away, Mister Calbert. It is after
nine bells, you should be in proper dress already."

"Add it to my charges," Veranix mumbled.

"Hey, hey!" Delmin's voice cracked through the hallway. He pushed his way through the cadets. "Ease down, fellows. I'm the prefect of this floor, he's my responsibility."

"I've been told—" the cadet started.

"Back off, cadet," Delmin said sharply. "He is my responsibility, and I will get him washed up and dressed and delivered to—where?"

"Condolin Hall," the cadet offered. The offices of the dean and other university administrators.

"Just so. I will have him there at ten bells. Go off and report that to whoever told you. They have issue they can come to me."

Delmin closed the door instead of waiting for an answer.

"That's not going to stop the inevitable," Veranix said.

"It's not, but I'm not going to let them drag you there in a blanket," Delmin said. "Nor are you going to go to whatever that is without me at your side."

"Even still?" Veranix asked.

"Even still," Delmin confirmed. He held up a paper bag. "Five Itasa rolls. I figured you were ravenous."

"I am," Veranix said, even though he didn't feel like eating. His body demanded otherwise.

"I had seven," Delmin said. "I would have gotten you more but the women in the kitchens were glaring at me."

"This is perfect," Veranix said, already finishing one.

"Finish up, and then clean yourself up as best you can," Delmin said, laying out a clean version of Veranix's uniform on the bed. "No matter what happens when you walk out, you will walk into Condolin Hall the absolute embodiment of a University of Maradaine student."

"Thank you, Del," Veranix said. "I really don't deserve you."

"No, you don't," Delmin said. "But you've got me anyway."

As presentable as he could be without glamouring his face—which Delmin told him not to do—the two of them arrived at Condolin Hall, where they were promptly escorted to a meeting room, where they were seated before a panel of several faculty and administrators, with Major Dresser in the center.

"Mister Sarren, your presence is neither requested nor required," Dresser said.

"I'm the prefect for Veranix's floor," Delmin said. "Part of that role includes being liaison between student and administration in any matter of discipline. I'll stay by his side."

Dresser frowned. "If Mister Calbert doesn't object, so be it."

"I don't at all," Veranix said. "Let's just get through this, I'm in no mood to draw it out."

"Good," Dresser said. "Then let's start. Just to begin, some facts at hand. Yesterday afternoon, there was an incident on the south lawn where several gentlemen of delinquent nature explicitly called out your name, and threatened the student populace until you engaged in an altercation with them."

"I fought them, sir," Veranix said. "No need to mince words."

"Yes, well," Dresser said. "In said altercation, Professor Alimen also engaged with these gentlemen, and was subsequently killed."

"Murdered."

"I would appreciate you not continuing to interrupt me over semantics, Mister Calbert."

"You say semantics, I say crucial distinctions."

"Nonetheless, Mister Calbert, let me continue without further disruption. You'll have opportunity to have your say soon enough."

Delmin tapped Veranix's arm. He was right, this was surely going to go badly enough, no need to further antagonize this board.

"After this altercation came to a head, both you and the delinquents were gone from campus. We are given to understand there were further attacks on your person in the Aventil neighborhood. It's clear from looking at you that you have been through quite a bit of abuse since yesterday. Would you say that's accurate?"

"Probably an understatement, sir," Veranix said.

"All of this was deeply confusing for all of us here," Dresser said. "And we were in some degree of shock over the loss of Professor Alimen. I'm certain you were as well, which is why we understand you not being immediately forthcoming after the attack."

Veranix wasn't sure where this was going, so he just nodded.

"We were, of course, all perplexed why you had been attacked by these men, how such an incident could possibly occur here."

"I will take—" Veranix started, wanting to just accept whatever they were going to do without further ceremony, but Dresser held up a hand.

"Vice Provost?"

"Yes," said the older man sitting a few seats down. "Mister Calbert, if you are not aware, I'm Vice Provost Descalin, I'm in charge of all student records and transcripts. As part of my duties, I am entrusted with materials of a sensitive nature."

"A pleasure, sir, but—"

"Which is why I had this sealed file from Professor Alimen, with your name on it," Descalin said. "As is sometimes the case with students accepted into the Magic Program through trust from Lord Preston's Circle, there are sometimes extenuating circumstances of their life that must be matters of record for the University, but are kept sealed with only the recruiting professor aware of the contents. This is not uncommon in cases such as your own, where the student lacked the formal education that would normally precede acceptance into the University of Maradaine."

"It's considered more important for magic students to get the education they need here," Dresser said. "Even if they otherwise would not be eligible to attend."

"Of course, but what—"

Descalin opened the file. "So we are only now aware that your father had a previous identity, that he had open charges for his arrest, and he was involved with the criminal underworld of the city. Involvement which resulted in his death shortly after your enrollment. This is accurate?"

"It is, but—"

"It's also clear that Professor Alimen was aware of this, which is why he took steps to protect your identity. He writes extensively here that it was his belief this criminal element would also make an attempt on your life if they learned who you were."

Dresser held up a sheet of paper.

"Here is the last thing Gollic Alimen wrote," Dresser said. "We found this on his desk, and Miss Nessick has already testified she observed him write this minutes before his death."

"He what?"

"It reads, 'Clearly I have failed to protect Mister Calbert's identity from the enemies of his family, so now I must protect his life.

Whomever holds this chair, should I falter in this, I beg that you do not hold him culpable for these sins, which are not of his making.'"

Veranix stood up, almost out of reflex, as his heart threatened to leap from his chest. Delmin grabbed his arm and pulled him back into his chair.

Dresser put the note down. "We have also heard from several witnesses that you acted selflessly—if perhaps foolishly—to protect your fellow students from these miscreants. But the University acknowledges its own failures in security that allowed these circumstances to occur."

"It . . . does?" Veranix asked.

"The fact that these criminals were even able to come to campus to wage their battle against you is a great embarrassment," Dresser said. "The Dean of Cadets will be launching a full review and investigation."

"But on behalf of the University," Descalin said, bowing his head, "We offer our apologies for failing to protect you and the student body, on behalf of ourselves and Professor Alimen."

"No, it wasn't his fault, I—"

"You, young man, should never have been in that position," Dresser said. "As Gollic's own words testify."

Veranix was without words, but fortunately Delmin was there for him.

"So you're wanting to make a formal apology on behalf of the University?" he asked. "Is that why we're here?"

"We cannot and will not be doing that," Descalin said. "And the entire contents of this discussion must be considered under a seal of privacy, with expulsion or termination the penalty for breaking that seal."

"We are going to insist, Mister Calbert, for your own safety, as well as the reputation of the University, that you keep all elements of this incident a secret. The University will, in exchange, waive further tuition costs for you for the remainder of your education, and the parts of the trust that pays your tuition will now be apportioned to your living stipend. As a method of informal apology."

That shocked Veranix out of his silence. "So you want me to keep quiet about what happened, and you'll pay me to do that."

"I wouldn't put it quite so crudely," Dresser said. "But it's not an incorrect assessment. Mister Sarren, you are considered under the same bond, but you will be held by your honor as a prefect."

"Fine, sir," Delmin said.

"Yes, I agree," Veranix said.

"Then it is decided," Dresser said. "I expect to see you both in class tomorrow."

Delmin grabbed Veranix by the arm and pulled him out of the chamber, shushing every attempt Veranix made to speak until they were out of the building.

"What was that?" Veranix asked. "How am I not expelled? How am I not, I don't know, named in every newssheet in South Maradaine right now?"

"I don't know," Delmin said. "Professor Alimen saved you, one last time."

"Doesn't quite add up," Veranix said.

"But don't complain. You . . . you're still here. You get to finish your education, get circled. That's good."

"It is," Veranix said. But something still gnawed at his gut.

"You're still going to stop . . . you know . . ."

"I am," Veranix said. "But this only means I won't be expelled. I still have the law to contend with."

"And how are you going to do that?"

Veranix though on this for a moment. "I think I need to talk to my own student."

The paperwork had covered Benvin's desk, as well as Tripper's, while the rest of the squad dug through the reports.

But today, it seemed, there was a breath of calm in Aventil. But only a breath, and it was sure not to last.

"So, we've got arrests from every part of town, and bodies as well. A lot of Knights and Orphans dead, as many ironed. Same with Princes," Pollit said after tallying things up on his slate board.

"Looks like the Dogs and the Halloran's Boys are the big winners after this," Wheth said. "We have any report on the Sons?"

"We're still not sure who are Sons, besides Colin Tyson," Saitle said. "But we don't know if they made out well in this, or got caught in the squeeze. There's a lot of bodies we're presuming were Fenmere's folks, but we don't have them identified yet."

"And Dentonhill house?" Benvin asked.

"I've called for records," Jace said. "And called for favors where I could, but they're not pitching to our tetch right now."

"Figures," Benvin said.

On top of the gang situation, there were the arrests and deaths with the higher profiles.

Arrested: Erno Don, Magadina Kend, Kat'rick-Ra, Orthon Lemt, Carson Jendle, Rory Scanlin. All of them destined for a long stay at Quarrygate. Some of them may have earned a spot on the next caravan to Fort Olesson. Poor souls.

Arrested and immediately delivered to the Archduchy Sheriffs: Pria Mandicall and Trent Endoriff. Benvin was happy to send them, happy to have them out of his hair. From what he had heard, the Archduchy was going to show little mercy, and the Circle lawyers were not arguing for either of them with much zeal.

Arrested but escaped: Xiala Quope. A mystery, that one. Near dead when found on the ward, and the doctors there insisted on saving her life. Ethics of medicine, they said, treat everyone equal. Somehow she had slipped off when the guards presumed she was sleeping. Benvin wasn't entirely sure how she was involved in this, save she was the one who killed Enzin Hence.

Dead: Enzin Hence and Cuse Jensett. At least, it was presumed from what little remains were found that they were Cuse.

And also dead, Willem Fenmere.

And still at large: the Thorn.

There was no evidence that the Thorn had killed Fenmere. The arrow in his chest matched the others in Enzin's quiver, and Enzin was found dead only fifty feet away. The two nurses on the fifth-floor ward were useless as witnesses, and Benvin had no interest in pushing them. Willem Fenmere was dead, and that was all that mattered.

Benvin knew there would be consequences for that death. It was plain as a clear sky. The man controlled the *effitte* trade in Dentonhill, holding tight reins on a dozen block bosses, and on top of that, his fingers were tied to threads in every part of the city. Those reins were loose, those threads would snap, and Benvin couldn't even guess how things would fall out in the coming weeks. Half the lieutenants in the Aventil stationhouse, as well as all the inspectors, they all seemed in a blind panic.

Probably wondering who was going to line their pockets now.

But whatever trouble was coming, he and his would be ready.

"Am I disturbing you, Lieutenant?"

Benvin looked up from his desk to see Jace's brother Minox, in civilian clothes. "Never, Inspector. Though this doesn't seem to be an official visit, is it?"

"What's up, Minox?" Jace asked.

Minox frowned. "I'm here to deliver a message, and given its nature, it would be completely improper for me to be here in any official capacity, or even in uniform."

Benvin stood up, more than a little concerned. "What's the message?"

Minox moved closer, lowering his voice enough for this to only be for Benvin's ears.

"The Thorn wanted to express his gratitude for your compassion, even though he did not succeed in his goal."

The other body on the ward, only listed as "Miss Ayxa," a Racquin woman who had been there for four years, no family or kin listed. That must have been the Thorn's mother. Her throat slit by the blade still in Fenmere's hand.

"I'm not interested in his gratitude."

"Of course," Minox said. "He has also told me, and I believe his resolve in this, that he is done being the Thorn. He wanted me to assure you of his intentions."

"I'm even less interested in his intentions."

"Which is why there was one more part of his message. If you insist, if you want it, he is prepared to surrender himself to you."

That took Benvin by surprise. "You would deliver him to us?"

"He'll deliver himself, and confess whatever you need, if you feel that justice would best be served by such a thing."

"Would it be?" Benvin asked Minox, trying to get some read off the man's inscrutable expression.

"I can only tell you if it would serve my sense of justice, Lieutenant," Minox said. "I cannot speak for yours."

Benvin looked to the squad, who were all watching them with intent. They weren't even pretending they didn't hear.

"Thoughts, gentlemen?"

They all looked to each other for a moment, and their gazes settled on Tripper.

"Listen, Left," he said after a long pause. "Ain't we got enough paperwork for now?"

Benvin nodded. "Agreed. Insp—Mister Welling, please relay the message that we will, for the moment decline the offer."

"Happily," Minox said.

"But I expect him to keep that pledge."

"I will make that clear," Minox said, walking across the squad room to the crates destined for the evidence shelves. He glanced at the manifest briefly. "I see you confiscated the Thorn's bow, staff, and rope."

"He can't get them back," Benvin said.

"Of course," Minox said. "These things, especially the rope, should not even have the possibility of falling into the wrong hands."

"Especially the rope?" Wheth asked. "It's just a rope."

"I'm sure, as long as these things stay in a secure place, in *loyal* hands, it will be fine." Minox stressed. "Yes, you should definitely keep this somewhere safe." He picked up the manifest again with his gloved hand. Suddenly the paper caught fire and instantly became ash.

"What the—"

"My apologies," Minox said. "Deeply careless of me. I am, after all, an untrained, Uncircled mage, still learning how to master my abilities. That is why I'm on restricted duty, after all. Someone will have to rewrite that official manifest for the evidence logs."

"I'll do that," Jace volunteered.

"Excellent," Minox said. He went to the door, passing Benvin on the way, and placed his good hand on his shoulder. "Somewhere *very* safe, Lieutenant."

Benvin didn't understand, but he did trust. "As you say."

"Capital," Minox said. "Then I'll leave you to your business."

Benvin watched him leave, then turned to the squad, who were all gawking a bit too much. "All right, folks, back to it. We've got plenty of work to do, and these streets aren't going to keep themselves safe."

They certainly weren't, not anymore.

COLIN HAD STAYED OUT OF SIGHT MOST OF THE DAY, SQUATTING IN abandoned tenements down in old Kicker territory. He thought it best to let everything in the neighborhood cool down before slipping his way back to Orchid Street.

Jutie was not in the lockdown flop he had left him in. Colin went to the Old Canal, to find the staff happy to see him, but no sign of Jutie, or of any Sons there. The cook told him, no, things were all right despite the trouble last night. The Sons had kept the place safe.

Colin went up to the flop above the sew-up, and as he approached the door, there was a fair amount of sound and commotion inside. Then a scream. Jutie.

Colin kicked the door open, knife drawn, and charged in. "Don't you dare—"

All eyes on him, several folks gathered around, most of them the Sons he knew were still alive. But there were more faces he didn't know.

"The boss is here!" Sella shouted jubilantly. She was holding a smoking hot iron, and someone was kneeling in front of her, cradling his arm. "We weren't sure what happened to you, so we were initiating the new blood before we were going to come avenge you."

"Nothing to avenge," Colin said. "I told you to clear out of Aventil, though."

"I'm bad at following orders," Sella said. "And we got new recruits, so I didn't want to run."

The kneeling fellow got up and turned around: Jutie. Though now he had shaved his head, and let the faint wisps of stubble grow on his chin. With that, and the fresh burn scar over what was his Prince tattoo, he was barely recognizable.

"You did say there was a place for me in the Sons, boss," Jutie said.

Colin smiled. "I am . . . I'm real glad to see you here. See all of you. I got to tell you, I was worried there would be nothing much left to see."

"Princes tried to run us last night," Sella said. "Same with Fenmere's mooks. But we held. Didn't we, Sons?"

"Sons stand together!" they all shouted.

"What do we bleed?" she asked.

"The same blood!" they all shouted.

"Whose blood?"

"The Blood of Tyson!"

"Friends," Colin said. "Brothers and sisters, really. I . . . I'm honored by you. Especially since I wasn't with you."

"But you were with us, as far as matters," Sella said. "Jutie told us all, you went to go help the Thorn."

"Tried to," Colin said.

"And his blood is the Blood of Tyson. And we saw it paid back here."

That threw Colin a bit. "Paid back how?"

"We all heard him taunt the whole neighborhood," Cober said.

"And then we heard that girl run down his fight," Jutie said. "Wish I could have seen it."

"And then he ran down Fenmere goons up and down Waterpath," Sella said.

"He did what?" Colin asked. Veranix had been in no shape for that. "You all saw him?"

There were shrugs. "I didn't see him, or at least he didn't come talk to us," Sella said. "Not me, anyway."

"Someone rained arrows on Fenmere's bastards, though," Cober said. "We all saw that."

"You saw someone doing it?"

"I did," one kid said. His burn was fresh, like Jutie's. "Rooftop, cloak flowing, arrows like mad. Why do you think I'm here?"

That wasn't Veranix, not last night. If someone was killing Fenmere's folks out on Waterpath, Colin welcomed the help.

But who the blazes was it?

A mystery for another time.

"Well, then. We've got new brothers and sisters, and we have made ourselves felt in Aventil. So let's go get a beer together, Sons of Tyson, and then hold our streets. What do we bleed?"

"The same blood!"

"Whose blood?"

"The Blood of Tyson!"

Colin whooped out a holler and led them down to the Old Canal. *Whoever you are, cloaked stranger, you better also bleed that blood.*

CHAPTER TWENTY-NINE

KAIANA UNLOCKED THE DOOR OF her apartment and held it open, letting her father make his way in. He wasn't able to walk much at all, with two canes to hold himself up. At the ward they said he'd probably never walk normally again, but they also didn't want him to stay any longer. Beds were at a premium, so they were thrilled Kaiana was able to take him home.

"This whole place is yours?" he asked, looking around.

"It's the quarters for the head of grounds," she said, helping him to a chair. "I'm actually not even in here too much." So much of her time had been spent in helping Veranix, in the fight against Fenmere. Was it really over now?

"I'm not going to be a burden to you," he said.

"I've got a good position," she said. "And I told you, home enough for us both."

"It certainly is," he said. "But I imagine you do have a lot of work. I will be productive, I swear. And no more . . . no more of me . . ."

She took his hand. "I want one promise from you, Papa. When you feel yourself . . . drawn to do dark things to yourself. To seek out the *effitte*—"

"Never again."

"I know enough about it to know the hold it had over you. The hold it has. Don't just say never again."

"But—"

"When you feel the need again, and I am sure you will, then you come to me. No matter the time, no matter the place. We will get through together, but promise me you will come tell me, and I will be strong when you can't." Because while Fenmere was gone, there was still *effitte* in the city, surely. She wished Veranix would still work to destroy it all, but she understood. He had been through so much, he was at his limit. She couldn't ask more of him.

But as long as there was a drop in Maradaine, Papa would be able to be tempted. She needed to be there to stop that from happening again, and the only way she could think of was to be as open and honest as she could with her father. No room for secrets.

"When you want it again, when you feel the urge again, we will sit and talk about anything, everything. Any time at all, Papa. About anything—"

"You don't know the things I've seen, I've done. Why I had to get you off that island . . ."

"And I've seen and done a lot, too, Papa. I can handle any of it. Never doubt me."

"I failed you, Kai," Papa said, tears coming to his eyes. "Forced you to be strong when I should have been strong for you."

"It's a new chapter now," she said. "We're each other's strength."

A knock came on the door frame. Veranix, carrying a package wrapped in brown paper. "Sorry," he said. "I know I'm intruding, but—"

"It's fine," Kaiana said, coming over to him. She took his hand and brought him inside. "Papa, this is Veranix, he's . . . he's my very good friend. His . . ." She looked to Veranix for a bit of confirmation.

"My mother was also in the Lower Trenn Ward," Veranix said. "We've . . . we've been able to support each other through that."

"I'm so sorry, son," Papa said. "I'd stand and shake your hand, but . . ."

"No worries," Veranix said.

"Is your mother still there?"

"She . . . she passed, sir," Veranix said with a catch in his throat. "But she's able to rest now."

"I'm very sorry for you," Papa said.

"What do you have?" Kaiana asked, trying to bring a bit of light back.

"Pastries," Veranix said. "The Junk Avenue Bakery on the west side is a bit of a hike, but I think it's worth it, and . . ." He shook his head. Quietly he added, "Accounts to settle."

Kaiana took the package from him. "It's very thoughtful. Do you want to have some tea?"

"No, no," he said. "I've intruded on your life enough. You should . . . you should get to enjoy this, Kai. You deserve it."

She took his hand as he started to walk away. "You're never an intrusion, all right?"

"Thanks," he said quietly. "But I need to get some studying done. I've put it off long enough." A soft smile, and he walked off.

Kaiana put the package on the table. "Well, that will be nice. I'll make us some tea."

"That boy is your friend?" Papa said.

"He is," she said, going to her stove. "He's really done so much, you can't imagine."

"I can," Papa said. "I've seen men with eyes like that. Back in the islands, back in the war. Broken men who didn't last long when they came home."

"He's been through a lot," Kaiana said. "But—"

"I'm just saying, dear one," Papa said. "I am so grateful for your strength, your support. But if you care at all for that boy, save some of it for him. He will absolutely need it."

SOME SMALL MEASURE OF NORMAL CREPT BACK IN AS VERANIX WENT TO classes, read his assignments, and went for several days without even leaving campus. What remained of his life as the Thorn, including the napranium-laced cloak, was in a crate in the bunker, and the entrances to the bunker were latched up.

Even still, Veranix's guard stayed up, in every class, every meal. His name was still out there, and Fenmere's people surely knew it. Someone else might come, and every time there was an unexpected sound, a brush against his arm in a crowd, his body tensed, ready for a fight.

That was going to be normal for some time to come.

But still, he went to every class, every meal. Dinners at Holtman Hall, with Mila and Delmin and Anduette and the rest of Violet Squad became regular, and it was good to have them around him.

Especially when the trouble arrived.

Only a few days after the worst day, Eittle came into the dining hall at dinner with two others. Veranix didn't even notice him at first, didn't even see who he came with until they all sat down.

"Hello, all," Parsons said weakly, a nervous smile on his face. "I, um, I am back here. I gather it's been a busy few months since I've . . . I've been absent."

Delmin and many of the others focused on Parsons, but Veranix's attention was entirely on the companion who had sat down with him.

"Why are you here?" he asked Tor Rassin.

"This man is a marvel," Eittle said. "He brought Parsons back."

"I'm just a specialist, here to help my patient integrate back into his environment," Tor said. "Surely such a moment would spark, emotions, memories. I thought it best to monitor his reactions, just in case."

"I'm very glad to be here," Parsons said. "Honestly, I'm very glad to just . . . to just *be*, again."

"Glad to have you here," Eittle said.

"Not to ask an uncomfortable question, chap," Delmin said. "But aren't you expelled?"

"That never formally happened," Eittle said.

"My parents might be funding a new library wing or naturalist lab or such," Parsons said. "But I am welcome at the school." He looked away sheepishly. "I hope I'm still welcome here."

Eittle and Delmin both looked to Veranix.

"Of course," Veranix said. "You, Parsons, are very welcome here."

The sound in the dining hall stopped completely. Everyone around them froze in place. Anduette's soup spoon was held halfway to her mouth. Mila was mid-sentence in some argument with Jemica. Everyone was still, save Veranix and Tor.

"Now, Veranix, there's no need for you to be so rude," Tor said. "Your intentions and emotions are just falling off of you."

"Why the blazes are you here?"

"Honestly, why I said. But also to talk to you."

"We have nothing to say to each other."

"After everything I did for you, old boy? Hardly kind."

"What do you think you did for me?"

Tor chuckled. "Let's see. First, I got Fenmere to come to you. He would have stayed hidden away in his little fortress, but I coaxed him out with an offer, and then tweaked his pride so he would succumb to that desire to see you beaten with his own eyes. So you have me to thank."

"You expect me to thank you for that?"

"Well, I also got paid for it. Imagine, he paid me to do that, the fool. But cleaning up the rest of your mess, that was just a favor for a friend."

"What do you mean, cleaning up my mess?"

"Memory can be such a malleable thing," Tor said. "Especially when there aren't strong emotions attached, when it isn't formative. A nudge here, a push there, and folks who saw the Thorn's face, well, what face do they remember seeing? Those who heard the name Veranix Calbert being shouted, what name did they hear? It gets jumbled. And when a school official here or there remembers things just a little differently, well . . . then a student becomes a simple victim. No need for him to get expelled."

"Are you claiming you did that?"

"Honestly, it wasn't even that much. The scale was already going to fall either way, I just gave it a little extra push in your favor. I couldn't do something like that to, say, this girl's head." He gestured to Mila. "Her knowledge of who you are is so entangled in so many other memories and emotions, it would tear her brain apart."

"Leave her alone," Veranix said hotly.

"Of course," Tor said. "I wouldn't do that to her. You've been through enough. I mean, the amount you're still churning over your father. Do you want to talk about that?"

"Stop that."

"I mean, he did bad things and you thought he was such a good man. At least my father was a right bastard from the start, no illusions here, but, that . . . I mean, you can see I'm not a well fellow."

"On that we agree."

"But you get that, dressing up in a cloak and fighting drug dealers, over your father's now tarnished honor. I see why you're torn up, you did so much, hurt yourself, so many others, and for what?"

"I'm done with that."

"I see you think that," Tor said. "We'll see what the future holds together."

"We're not doing anything together," Veranix said with a hint of a growl. "Now let them all go and get out of here."

"Or you'll what? Remember, basket of eggs, dear boy, basket of eggs." Tor sighed and absently took the bread from Delmin's plate. "But don't worry, in a moment, everything will be back to normal. I just wanted a private moment with you for a bit, Veranix Calbert. You are so *very* interesting, and interesting is far more valuable to me than money."

He tore off a piece of the bread and put it in his mouth.

"So if I could do you a favor, and keep you around to be interesting, well, that suits me. Friends do favors for each other, after all. A point you'll do good to remember in days to come."

"What are you on about?"

"That you should think of me as a friend, Veranix," Tor said. "Because you wouldn't like me to be otherwise."

He winked, and the activity in the dining hall resumed, chatter and motion all at once. Eittle was going on about catching Parsons up. Anduette was explaining a bit of theory to Leon. Mila argued some point of civics with Jemica.

And Tor was gone, just the half-eaten bread on the table.

Mila's hand touched Veranix's leg. "Something's wrong, what is it?"

"How did you know?"

"Your body shifted, and . . . I don't know, almost like a hiccup. Like the world blinked for a moment."

"The telepath wanted a word," Veranix said. She was already aware of Tor and what he had done during the street fight.

"That was him?" She glanced around. "It makes my skin crawl to think of someone like that."

"He wanted to impress on me that I owed him a favor." In a low voice, whispered to her ear to not draw in Delmin or Anduette or any other attention, he told her the whole thing. Anyone watching would have presumed they were merely young lovers having an intimate conversation. Which was true, to some extent. She was probably the only one in his life right now, the only one who knew everything and had been through enough herself, to really understand what he was feeling.

She took it all in, and then kissed him on the cheek when he finished. "Anything you want to do, I'm with you," she said. "And if what you want to do is nothing at all, I'm still with you."

"I know you are," he said. "That's the main thing that keeps my head above the water right now."

She looked into his eyes, and got it. "It's going to be nothing, though."

He nodded. "I'm lucky to even still be breathing right now, still be able to be here, be with you." His hand brushed her chest for a moment, touching the stitches of her still-fresh injury. "I've caused enough hurt, and I don't want any part of it anymore."

"And that's fine," she stressed. "You've done enough. Really." She kissed him again to make it clear she meant it.

It had been enough. The Thorn had done the work that needed to be done, and he could let it go. He had already stopped Fenmere. He had saved the city, even. He could just be Veranix Calbert, fourth-year magic student at the University of Maradaine. That was a very good thing to be, and, in time, he hoped he could be happy being that again.

The next trouble that came to Maradaine, that could be someone else's job.

EPILOGUE

THE SOUND OF BROKEN GLASS woke Vessrin. He sat up quickly, which didn't rouse either of his bed companions, still blissed out of their skulls. After everything that happened a few nights ago, after everything still happening in Aventil, he had deserved a night of decadence with a few of his favorite playthings, and a dose of the *efhân* gave them both an impressive amount of stamina and energy, as well as dropping their inhibitions delightfully. It had been an absolutely debauched night, and a part of him wished he could have gone in as far as the two of them did.

But he knew better than to touch any of the *efhân* himself. There was no way he would risk getting himself hooked on the stuff. He had a fair supply now, and with Fenmere gone, who even knew if more would be coming into Maradaine, or when. That stash of the stuff had the potential to finally take his accounts to the next level, finally have real control over all of Aventil.

So he knew his head was on straight, and he wasn't imagining things. He had heard the glass breaking.

But there were no windows in his house. So what had broken?

"Neric?" he called out. "Everything all right?"

Neric was the night guard, and should have been right outside the door. Ready to respond to anything in a moment, sweep him out of the room and into his bunker if there had ever been trouble. Twenty years, there hadn't been trouble, but Vessrin was still alive after all these years because he had remained prepared. Ready for trouble to come.

Silence.

Vessrin got out of the bed, grabbing his robe. Neric damn well should have been right outside the door, and if anything had pulled him away, he should have made sure Vessrin had been secure first.

Vessrin went to the door. "Neric, what's the situation?" he called through it.

Silence.

What the blazes was this?

He went back to the bed and got his knife from under the mattress. If someone was here for him, he wasn't going to let them take him easy. Then back to the door, where he pulled the alarm cord. The bells would ring, and his boys from all over the house would come.

Silence.

No rutting bells.

Where were his rutting bells?

"Neric?" he called out. "Anyone?"

Silence.

Glass breaking again. This time from his water closet.

There wasn't a window there. What the blazes broke?

He crept slowly to the water closet, knife at the ready.

One candle was burning in there, which was normal. Not normal was the shattered mirror on the ground, or the words painted on the wall.

YOUR RECKONING HAS COME

Vessrin ran out of the water closet, back into his bedchamber. Before he could catch his breath, he saw the door was open now, with Neric's body holding it open. An arrow deep into Neric's throat.

"You think you've got a reckoning?" he called out. "You think you're scaring me? You don't know who you're messing with!"

"The King of Rose Street," a voice called out, mockingly. "I'm here to kill the king."

"You picked the wrong fight!" Vessrin shouted, coming out into the hall. "You don't know what's going to happen to you!"

"So feckless," the voice called. "The so-called king, hiding in his castle."

"You think I'm hiding!" Vessrin looked around his parlor. No sign of this fool. Just a voice, coming from a different direction every time. And more of his guards, scattered around the room. All dead, all riddled with arrows.

"You don't even live on Rose Street!" the voice called. "You hide down on Carnation, where you never thought I'd find you!"

"I am the king of the Princes, and if you think—"

"I think it's time for you to pay for your crimes," the voice said.

"Show yourself, coward!"

"Here, traitor!"

A twang of a bow, and in a moment an arrow went through Vessrin's hand. The knife clattered to the floor as he screamed.

"Who do you think you are?"

Another arrow, straight into Vessrin's leg. Sending him to the ground.

A figure came out of the shadows, bow raised, cloak flowing as he gracefully strode across the room. "You should know who I am."

"The Thorn," Vessrin said. "Here to take me down?"

"I'm here for what you did to my father," the Thorn said. "And to take back what was his." He shook back the hood to reveal his face. He looked so much like Colin, with the same face as that boy in the Turnabout, but harder, darker, wilder.

"You think that will change anything? Killing me will change things?" Vessrin asked. "Things are already a mess with Fenmere dead, this neighborhood will fall apart!"

"I hope so."

This idiot, he had no idea what he was playing with. "You are Cal's son, a fool just like him."

"You're right." A mad smirk crossed his face as he drew back on the bow. "My name is Soranix Tyson, and I am here to avenge my father, against everyone who betrayed him, especially you. Even if all of Maradaine has to burn for it."

TO BE CONCLUDED IN

THE NEW KING OF ROSE STREET

RECOMMENDED READING ORDER

It is the author's opinion that the best reading order for the Maradaine Saga is in-world chronological for Phase One, and the release order going into Phase Two. Therefore:

PHASE ONE

Thorn of Dentonhill
Murder of Mages
Holver Alley Crew
Way of the Shield
The Alchemy of Chaos
An Import of Intrigue
Lady Henterman's Wardrobe
Shield of the People
The Imposters of Aventil
A Parliament of Bodies
The Fenmere Job
People of the City

PHASE TWO

An Unintended Voyage
The Assassins of Consequence
The Mystical Murders of Yin Mara
The Quarrygate Gambit
Hultichia
The Withered Boy

That said, there is no "wrong" order. Read the books as you like, as much as you like, and enjoy it your way.

ACKNOWLEDGMENTS

And here we are, back to Maradaine, back to Veranix. Back, in many ways, to where we began. And this is its own beginning, in a way, as we get into the second phase of the Maradaine Saga.

Years ago, when I knew how I would be breaking up the phases of the saga, one phrase kept drumming in my head: ***Autumn in Maradaine, everything will fall.***

Writing this book, throughout the continued pandemic, was its own emotional journey, but I'm thrilled about being able to continue telling you about Veranix and the world around him, as Maradaine's story gets even more complex.

That complexity was fueled, of course, by the work I've been doing on my podcast *Worldbuilding for Masochists,* and I can't express how much my co-hosts, Rowenna Miller and Cass Morris, are just the best people to work with. Brilliant, creative minds, and incredible anchors of support. More support came from patrons and fans, like Nina Mulligan and Ember Randall.

Also instrumental were my usual sounding boards: Daniel Fawcett, forever my absolute rock when it comes to every element of this saga; and Miriam Robinson Gould, the best first reader I could ask for.

Of course, as usual, I relied heavily on my publishing team, including my agent Mike Kabongo (who was *all in* when I said I had a weird idea with motorcycles and psychic mushrooms), my editor Sheila Gilbert, and everyone at DAW and Penguin Random House: Betsy, Katie, Josh, Leah, Alexis, and Stephanie, plus countless others whose names I don't know.

On top of that, my family remains a source of strength and inspiration. This includes my parents Nancy and Lou, and my mother-in-law

Kateri. And, of course, my son Nicholas and wife Deidre, who have continued to put up with me during this incredible journey through Maradaine and beyond.

And thank you, dear reader, who hopefully just read the last words of this book, and are eagerly awaiting the promise that it holds. I am equally excited to deliver on that promise.

-April 2021

ABOUT THE AUTHOR

Marshall Ryan Maresca is a fantasy and science-fiction writer, author of the Maradaine Saga: Four braided series set amid the bustling streets and crime-ridden districts of the exotic city called Maradaine, which includes The *Thorn of Dentonhill, A Murder of Mages, The Holver Alley Crew* and *The Way of the Shield*, as well as the dieselpunk fantasy, *The Velocity of Revolution*. He is also the co-host of the Hugo-nominated, Stabby-winning podcast **Worldbuilding for Masochists**, and has been a playwright, an actor, a delivery driver and an amateur chef. He lives in Austin, Texas with his family.